Jigsaw Nation
Science Fiction Stories of Secession

Edited by

EDWARD J. MCFADDEN III
AND E. SEDIA

A Member of Wilder Publications, LLC

Wilder Publications, LLC
c/o Spyre Books
P.O. Box 3005
Radford, VA 24143

Spyre Books & logo are trademarks of
Wilder Publications, LLC

All contents © 2006 Edward J. McFadden III and E. Sedia,
except where otherwise noted

All stories © 2006 by each respective author. Table of contents serves as an extension of the copyright page.

Cover © 2006 by Lara Wells

All rights reserved. No part of this book may be reproduced or transmitted in any means electronic or mechanical, including recording, photocopying or by any information storage and retrieval system, without the written permission of the copyright holders. Unauthorized reproduction is prohibited by law and is probably a sin. This is a work of literary criticism. No similarity between any of the names, characters, persons, situations and/or institutions and those of any preexisting person or institution is not intended and any similarity which may exist is purely coincidental.

ISBN: 0-9773040-2-7

Printed in the USA

Other Books by Edward J. McFadden III:

Shadows & Dust (forthcoming)
The Best of Fantastic Stories: 2000-2005 (forthcoming in 2007)
Cosmic Speculative Fiction #1 (forthcoming in 2006)
Time Capsule
Epitaphs: 20 Tales of Dark Fantasy & Horror (w/ Tom Piccirilli)
Deconstructing Tolkien
The Second Coming: The Best of Pirate Writings Vol. 2
The Best of Pirate Writings Vol. 1
Thought's of Christmas

Other Books by E. Sedia

According to Crow

Table of Contents

INTRODUCTION → 7

ESCAPE FROM NEW AUSTIN • Paul Di Filippo → 9

THE IDAHO ZEPHYR • Douglas Lain → 23

WAKING WACO • Cody Goodfellow → 40

RETURN TO NOWHERE • Ruth Nestvold and Jay Lake → 53

THE MAN FROM MISSOURI • Patrick Thomas → 76

THE SWITCH • Darby Harn → 85

DOWN IN THE CORRIDOR • Robert Lopresti → 94

HOMECOMING IN THE BORDERLANDS CAFÉ • Carole McDonnell → 107

PLACES OF COLOR • David Bartell → 116

JUNETEENTH • K.M. Praschak → 130

THE PATRIOT • Erin Fitzgerald → 142

SECONDS • Seth Lindberg → 151

MISSION CONTROL • Tara Kolden → 167

THE STATE OF BLUES • Gene Stewart → 176

VICTORY WITHOUT HONOR • C.J. Henderson → 183

FIELDWORK • J. Stern → 193

THIS DIVIDED LAND • Michael Jasper → 202

ABRAHAM LINCOLN FOR HIGH EXULTED MYSTIC RULER OF THE GALAXY • Edward J. McFadden III → 210

RHYMES WITH JEW • Paul G. Tremblay → 216

Edward J. McFadden III & E. Sedia

Introduction

Soon after the Election of 2004, the talk of secession has begun. Maps of the United States of Canada (incorporating both coasts, as well as Northern Midwest) were plastered all over the internet. New Englanders spoke of starting a nation of their own. Anger overwhelmed good sense, and old school patriotism disappeared faster than the ballots of African Americans.

This led many people to vent their frustrations with friends and family, and on blogs and message boards. At SFReader.com, we participated in one such discussion that led to the idea for this book. We talked about how the red states provided all the food. Not so! How the blue states are self-involved. Maybe. How the red states seemed to feel that denying gays their right to marry was more important than stopping the war, and so on...

Surely, it was not the first time when a significant portion of the US population was dissatisfied with presidential election results. But never before had half of the country felt so disenfranchised. This is the testament to the failure of the two party system, where one is forced to pick the lesser of two evils.

The Republicans said that it was time for healing. They said not to be sore losers, and likened the election to 2004 World Series where the Red Sox had won, and life did not stop. They failed to realize that politics is not sports; that the World Series is the end of the season, while the election is just the beginning of four more years.

They said that it was time to end feuds and name-calling, they blamed 'liberal media' for presenting a skewed view. They urged us to be 'fair'. In this scary place where any criticism leads to the accusations of being unpatriotic or un-American, where any expression of frustration with the voting irregularities gets 'liberal whiner' thrown your way, where any promise of security in the old age or affordable healthcare is slipping through our fingers… Well, you get the picture. In this divided world, what is left to the writers but to pour their anger and frustration onto a page?

In this book, you will not find many thoughtful attempts to see every side to an issue. You will not find calm objectivity. Instead, you will find frustrations, fears and warnings, and an occasional ray of stubborn hope.

Please read on and enjoy!

Edward J. McFadden III
April 15th, 2006
Long Island, NY

E. Sedia
April 15th, 2006
Southern New Jersey

Edward J. McFadden III & E. Sedia

Escape From New Austin
By Paul Di Filippo

The song was a few years older than Amy Gertslin, but it still spoke to her and her plight.

"Redneck Woman," by Gretchen Wilson.

Amy sang along to the tune pumping through the wireless earbuds of her fifth-generation iPod, the model that held 50,000 songs in a unit the size of a Triscuit cracker, which Amy wore on a necklace of living synthetic seaweed.

"'Cause I'm a redneck woman, and I ain't no high-class broad. I'm just a product of my raisin', and I say 'hey y'all' and 'yee haw!'"

Amy's skinny fifteen-year-old arms and legs flailed about as she emulated the playing of various air-instruments. She indulged in high kicks and thunderous stomps, weird line-dancing shuffles and slides. Plainly, she had a lot of pent-up energy to release.

The door to Amy's bedroom opened just as she was bellowing out the line about knowing all the words to every Tanya Tucker song. In the doorway stood her father, Batch Gertslin.

Batch was short for Batchelder: a maternal family name used as a given name in this instance. The Gertslins descended in part from the famed Boston Batchelders, bioindustry pioneers. A branch of the family, verifying the legendary strength of the Boston-to-Austin cultural axis, had relocated to the former capital of Texas a couple of generations ago. So although Amy and the rest of her family were Texas natives, they also boasted a rich Agnostica pedigree.

Only fitting, since Austin was nowadays an integral if non-contiguous part of Agnostica, an azure island in the crimson sea of Faithland.

Batch Gertslin possessed a somewhat moony face, shadowed by a messy thatch of black hair and generally expressive of an amiable curiosity and frisky intellect. But now he was definitely irked.

JIGSAW NATION

"Amy! You're bringing the ceiling in my office down!"

Batch Gertslin was a freelance ringtone, screen-wallpaper, emoticon and dingbat designer, and worked from home.

Amy pretended not to hear. "What?!"

"Turn that music off!"

Batch's face was shading into purple—a nice bi-national mix of red and blue, actually—and so Amy dropped her pretense of non-comprehension. A flick of her tongue against her Bluetooth dental implant controller deactivated the iPod. Her earbuds resumed their default task of ambient sound enhancement and noise filtering.

Batch's face regained a measure of composure and normal coloration. "Thank you. Listen, Amy. Your mother and I don't ask very much of you. You're almost an adult, we realize, and deserving of being treated as such. For the most part. But this senseless caterwauling has got to stop. It's most annoying."

Amy felt her own face coloring now, heating up with anger. "'Senseless caterwauling!' You're talking about some of the greatest music ever made! The music I love!"

Batch advanced into the room, holding out his hands in a paternally placating gesture. "I know you don't like any of the music your mother and I enjoy, Amy. That's only natural between generations. After all, you weren't raised on classic acts such as Eminem and Linkin Park and Ol' Dirty Bastard the way your mother and I were. Those old-school performers and their modern heirs are just not for you."

"Damn straight! You know I hate all that emo-crunk-harsh-metal shit! Classic country-western is my zome!"

"Fine, fine. But why do you have to favor the, ah, more downmarket acts in that genre? Couldn't you at least try some of those other artists I've suggested. Lyle Lovett, k. d. lang, Alison Krauss—"

"Oh, *Dad*! You're making my neurons go all apoptosis! Those wimps, those feebs, those posers, those *zygotes*! Charlie Daniels would eat them all for breakfast and still be hungry enough to swallow Shania Twain whole."

Batch assumed a dreamy look. "Shania Twain. What a hottie. Now there was a singer...."

"Ugh! Dad, I promise not to rattle the plaster anymore. Just leave me alone now. Unless you had something else to say—"

"I do. Your mother wants you downstairs now to help with dinner."

"Why can't Hilary do it?"

"Your little brother is busy studying for his Virus Construction finals. And besides, he helped last night."

"Arrrrgh! Okay, I'm coming!"

Batch left, and Amy waited the maximum amount of time before she knew she would receive a second notice to show up in the kitchen. Only then did she grudgingly tromp downstairs.

Phillipa Gertslin stood by the methane-fueled gas range, stirring a pot of free-range-turkey chili. Phillipa's parents had been—still were—a famous team of young-adult writers, whose current serie—sinvolving a budding teenaged paleontologist trapped by accident of birth into an intolerant Faithland community—was a best-seller all across Agnostica. They had named their daughter in honor of Philip Pullman and his quintessential Agnostica fictions.

This evening Phillipa wore loose white cotton trousers and a plain black short-sleeved cotton top. For the nth time, Amy sized up her mother's slim figure, wondering if her mother's decidedly non-voluptuous shape was to be her lot too. Why couldn't Philippa Gertslin have had an endowment of Dolly Parton magnitude to pass on to her daughter, or at least one of Shelby Lynne proportions? Oh, well, Amy would just have to go in for an outpatient boob job when she came into her majority next year.

"Mom, you look like some kind of robot *sushi* chef! Don't you ever feel like glamming it up a little?"

Phillipa regarded Amy's own embroidered red synthetic shirt, rhinestone-studded denim pants, and hand-stitched cowboy boots with a barely concealed distaste.

"You know I don't believe in regional fashions, dear, however ironically worn. Clothes are critical signifiers. I don't want my outfits proclaiming some false allegiance to Faithland, of all places."

Phillipa Gertslin taught popular culture at Howard Zinn University -- what used to be known as UT Austin, before the Agnostica-Faithland split. Her last published book had been titled *The Hermeneutics of Hypocrisy* and concerned itself with the frequent preacher sex scandals that continued to plague Faithland at regular intervals without, inexplicably, managing to undermine in any way the basic beliefs of the heartland.

"Now, please," Phillipa continued, "if you could just set the table without offering any more fashion critiques...? I've got to nuke these duck tortillas."

Grumbling, Amy took down a stack of four clunky, hand-fired plates from the cupboard. Each plate weighed as much as brick.

"Why can't we get a set of those faunchy e-paper plates? The ones that let you eyeball content while you eat?"

"Paper? I'd rather eat off the backs of exploited migrant laborers. Who knows what horrid toxins might leach out of that e-paper? It's only been around for a couple of years. I know the government says it's safe, but I hope you realize just how far you can trust our elected officials—even our Agnostica politicians need to be kept on a short rein."

Amy set the weighty plates down on the table with enough force to have shattered a lesser vessel. "And that's another thing. How come you and Dad are always talking trash about our government? Whatever happened to, like, patriotism in this house? 'Agnostica Number One! My half of the USA right or wrong!'"

Phillipa dumped a bag of blue-corn chips into a handwoven Guatemalan basket and carried it to the table. She looked at her daughter as if Amy had suddenly sprouted bat wings. "Now you're just being ridiculous. You know that no one in Agnostica talks or thinks that way. It's only in Faithland that you'll hear people shouting those mindless chants. Our mode of government is based on rationalism and skepticism. It's only through constant questioning of the empirical that— "

Amy rattled a tray of silverware to cover the sound of her mother's voice. "La, la, la, la! Can't hear the semiotic discourse!"

Phillipa didn't pursue the argument, but just frowned and shook her head, then went back to her meal preparations.

A short time later, the Gertslin family assembled for their evening meal. From his seat across the table from Amy, her brother, Hilary, sneered and said, "Hey, shitkicker, pass the tortillas."

Hilary was a smart, wiry tweener who, unlike the others in his family, boasted a natural skin coloration the shade of a dusky plum. Hilary had been adopted by the Gertslins when he was just months old, an African child orphaned during the post-Mugabe chaos in Zimbabwe. He was as much a product of Agnostica as Batch or Phillipa, even down to his given name. Hilary had been named after the politician Hilary Clinton, who, during the year of little Hilary's birth, 2010, had been elected the first president of Agnostica.

Batch objected now to his son's language. "Hilary, I warned you about using that form of address."

"Aw, Dad, it's a compliment. Isn't that right, Amy? You're proud of being a country girl, aren't you? Barefoot and pregnant all the time? Double-wide trailer living? *Coon*-hunting? Am I right?"

Amy shoved her chair backwards and stood up, stiff as a vibrating board. "That did it! I don't have to sit here and be insulted! None of you understand me at all! This bleeding-heart family sucks! This tight-ass city sucks! This whole peachy, super-sensitive, liberal *country* sucks!"

Fleeing to hide her tears, Amy ran upstairs to her bedroom.

Several hours of sobbing and listening to Alan Jackson and Lee Ann Womack, a long interval during which no one came to console her, convinced Amy of one thing.

She had to run away to Faithland right now. Defect. She couldn't stand to wait a year till she was legally an adult.

But where would she go in that unknown land?

The answer dawned on her almost immediately.

Nashville. The home and source of the music she loved.

Gretchen Wilson was still alive, Amy knew, though the woman had retired from the music business some years ago. Maybe Amy could track her down in Nashville, become her protégé....

Amy began packing. She stuffed a few extra clothes into a backpack, along with her favorite plush toy, an alligator bearing a stitched tourist motto from the Everglades, which she had found discarded in a thrift store and named Mr. Taxes. From the closet she grabbed a black cowboy hat. The hat was still crisp and unworn, since too many local people made fun of Amy when she appeared in public wearing it. But where she was going, it would command respect.

While waiting until the rest of her family had gone to sleep, Amy studied road maps on her pocket ViewMaster. It looked like she could pick up Route 35 North to Oklahoma City, then catch Route 40 West and barrel straight on into Nashville.

That is, if she could get past the border.

Two AM, and everyone in the Gertslin home was asleep save Amy.

Out on the lawn, Amy looked back without regret at the only home she had ever known. Goodbye to its solar cells and rain-collecting system, its weedy lawn planted in a water-conserving mix of native plants, its faded political poster from the recent election: RE-ELECT STERLING FOR MAYOR.

Red River Street was quiet. Amy felt as if the neighborhood was already a ghostly figment of her past.

A few blocks to the west, she knew she could catch one of the hydrogen-fueled mass-transit buses heading north to the city limits, one step closer to the border; the bus-stop was adjacent to the former State House, in a safe neighborhood.

When Austin joined Agnostica in the 2010 division of the USA, renaming itself New Austin, the Texas state capital had perforce relocated to Houston. Nowadays, the former home of the governor served as the Waldrop Museum and Cultural Center.

Amy had to wait only a few minutes at the bus shelter. It was a little scary to be out alone this late at night, but luckily no one bothered her. The most frightening person she saw was a man with patches of armadillo skin grafted onto his bare arms, and he seemed more concerned with reading a manga on his ViewMaster than in bothering a skinny teenager.

Finally onboard her bus, Amy tried to imagine how she would get past the Customs and Immigration officials at the limits of New Austin.

When the partitioning of the country was first being adjudicated, New Austin had managed to claim an irregular circle of land some sixty miles in diameter around the urban core. This allowed the city to retain many natural attractions and resources, not the least of which was The Salt Lick BBQ Restaurant in Driftwood. Texas could afford to be magnanimous: the chunk was the only tiny bite that Agnostica had managed to take out of the mammoth, imperturbable Faithland corpus of the state.

Route 35 exited New Austin territory at the small burg named Georgetown. There, Amy would have to undergo scrutiny by two sets of inspectors, those of both Agnostica and Faithland. They would ask to see her ID and inquire about her reasons for leaving one country and entering another, demanding her destination and intentions. First, she'd be busted for being an unescorted minor. Even if she could get around that, she had no definite arrangements in Nashville or en route to offer as legitimate support for her trip.

Well, no point in worrying about that now. With the innate optimism of her years, convinced of the rightness of her quest, Amy assumed some option would present itself when she got to the border.

So she sat back, relaxed, and played some George Jones.

At the outskirts of New Austin proper, Amy had to change to the long-range bus for Georgetown, which she did without trouble. Luckily, she had her life savings—five hundred and ten euros—available via her personal chopcard. Amy wasn't sure what the exchange rate for Agnostica euros versus Faithland dollars was at the moment, but she hoped it was favorable.

She fell asleep for the last twenty miles of the bus ride, her head cradled on Mr. Taxes, awaking only when the driver called out via the onboard PA, "End of the line, folks."

Only half-awake, Amy stumbled out.

The Customs and Immigration plaza was a vast expanse of parking-slot-demarcated pavement hosting many restaurants, motels and duty-free shops, as well as some official government buildings. A hundred yards from where her bus had deposited her, near an Au Bon Pain, a single lane of traffic—fairly light at this hour—crawled toward the lone inspection checkpoint that remained open.

Amy went inside the restaurant, hoping to assemble her thoughts. She ordered a pain chocolat and a café au lait. Sitting at a table near the door, she nursed her refreshments and tried to come up with a scheme to circumvent the inspectors.

After half an hour of pointless cogitation, nothing had revealed itself to her. So she activated her earbuds and began quietly singing along to a Loretta Lynn tune.

A shadow fell across Amy's field of vision, and she looked up to see a man standing by her table.

The fellow was about six feet four, possessed of an enormous red beard matched in impressiveness only by his beer gut. He wore a one-piece outfit that looked like the inner lining of a taikonaut's suit, with various hookups and jacks.

For a moment, Amy was frightened. But then she noticed that there were tears in the man's eyes.

The stranger seemed to want to address her, so Amy deactivated her iPod to allow them to talk.

"Honey," said the man, "I ain't thought of that song in nigh on fifteen years, since my Mama died. She loved that song, and used to sing it pert near every day. 'Course, she could actually nurse a tune, not strangle it like you. Nonetheless, it done my heart good to hear you attempt it. Pertickly here, 'midst all these Chardonnay-swillers."

Amy chose to ignore the insult to her singing abilities, as well as the blanket categorization of her fellow New Austinites as foreign-wine imbibers — especially since the latter accusation was true. The man seemed friendly enough, and might know some way of getting her across the border.

"Thanks, mister. I'm purely sorry to hear you lost your mama, even iffen it were a hound dog's age ago."

Amy was surprised to find herself falling into the speech patterns and diction of the stranger, a mode of speech that resembled the vernacular of the songs she loved. She had never allowed herself to indulge in such an affectation before, for fear of ridicule by her peers. But now that she had cut loose from her old life, nothing seemed more natural than to talk this way.

"I appreciate the sentiment, little lady." The man extended his hand. "Bib Bogardus is the name, and I hail from Pine Mountain, Georgia. What's yourn?"

"Amy Gertslin."

"Pleased to meet you, Amy." Bib lowered his bulk precariously into a seat at her table. "Now, just call me a nosy nelly if I'm stepping on any toes with my curiosity, but what brings you out to this place all alone at this hour?"

Amy hesitated a minute, then decided to confide everything to this friendly ear.

JIGSAW NATION

Bib listened to her story attentively and without condemnation. When she had finished, he said, "Waal, I can't say I'd be totally happy iffen my own daughter upped and hit the road. She's just about your own age, you know. Name of Jerilee. But I can unnerstand how a young'un has to find her own destiny. Especially when you're trapped in such a hellhole as New Austin. Why, did you know that you can't even buy a Lone Star beer in this whole territory anymore?"

Emboldened by Bib Bogardus's sympathy, Amy leaned toward him. "Is there any way you could help me scoot past these revenooers, Bib? What do you do anyhow? How come you're here?"

"I drive a big rig, Amy. Carrying a load of tomacco from Mexico to Oklahoma City."

"Why, that's just where I'm going! I figure on hitching a ride from there straight to Nashville. I'm gonna try to get into the music biz."

Bib scratched his beard ruminatively. "Hmmm, best you concentrate on being a producer or songwriter, with them pipes. But hail, who'm I to say what you can do, once you put your mind to it. They got plenty of tricks to sweeten up anyone's voice these days. Just look at thet there little Simpson gal. If it weren't for her mother, Ashlee, pushing her, she'd probably be serving grits at a Waffle House. Or whatever similar place they got in Agnostica. Caviar at the French Embassy, I guess."

"So you'll help me?"

Bib got to his feet. "I sure will. C'mon with me, darling."

Amy, holding her pack by the straps, followed Bib outside to Bib's rig, an enormous, streamlined, diesel-powered tractor-trailer combo bearing the proud name *Dixie Belle* on its prow in cherry-red letters. Amy was awed.

"Does this actually run on *fossil fuels*?"

"You bet, honeychile. I know that's an illegal substance in Agnostica, but they give us truckers an exemption so long as we're just passing through. You won't catch me driving one of those water-farting hydrogen creepers, no sir! Take me twice as long just to break even on my routes."

Bib opened the passenger-side door and removed a crinkly silver suit identical to the one he wore.

"Here, darling, slip into this."

"Do I have to get naked?"

Bib laughed. "Well, you would if you were planning to drive 24/7 like yours truly. Then you'd want to be hooked into the *Dixie Belle's* waste-recycling system, epidermal scrubber, nutrient feeds and booster drips. But since we're only gonna use this suit to fool the federales, it just needs access to one of your veins. So roll up your right sleeve."

16

Amy did as requested, then snugged into the suit, which seamed invisibly at the rear and automatically shrunk to fit her. Then she and Bib got into the tractor cab.

"Wow! This looks like the inside of the *Long March* Mars ship!"

"Waal, we ain't going quite so far as Mars, but I do believe in comfort and technology. Jack yerself in at that port there— "

Once Amy's suit was plugged into the dash, she felt a deft pinprick on her arm. She worried for an instant that Bib was going to drug her and deliver her to the harem of some Yemeni prince. But when nothing happened to her as the big man started the mighty yet purring engine of the truck, she relaxed.

"Just let me do the talking at Customs, 'kay?"

"Sure."

The *Dixie Belle* ambled throatily up to the crossing.

On the New Austin side, the border was protected by a variety of biological barricades, many of them with Batchelder Bioengineering pedigrees: hedges of thorny plants, troops of fire ants, pods of minishoggoths. On the Georgetown, Faithland, side, the barriers were strictly inanimate: robot lenses and gun muzzles, monomolecular wire, gluball anti-personnel mines. This natural-artificial interface was as clear a political statement of the differences between Agnostica and Faithland as any tract.

Two New Austin inspectors came up to the stopped truck. The first, a short, stocky Latina, led a redacted dog, a Rhodesian Ridgeback with a hypertrophied snout. This mutant canine proceeded to sniff all around the tractor and trailer, while the women inspected the intelligent seals placed on the trailer at its point of origin. The second inspector, an African-Agnostican with a jaunty goatee, came around to Bib's door.

"Blood sample, please."

"Sure thing, officer." Bib extended his hand and pressed his thumb into the sampling pad on the inspector's ViewMaster. Then the guardian of the gates came around to Amy's side, and she did the same, stifling her reluctance to reveal her identity.

Surely the game was up now...?

In a few seconds, both inspectors seemed satisfied.

"You and your daughter go safe now, Mr. Bogardus."

"Will do, compadre!"

Once through the New Austin arch, the *Dixie Belle* sailed beyond the corresponding Georgetown gate and its comparable procedures just as easily.

JIGSAW NATION

Once they were a few miles down Route 35, Amy finally felt it was safe to speak.

"'Daughter?' How did you—?"

Bib patted the dashboard affectionately. "The ol' *Dixie Belle* has a handful of useful genomic codes on file. She just injected you with a batch of silicrobes that had a tropism for the cells of your thumb. Once they got there, they started scavagening up all your original blood cells and making replacement blood with different DNA in it. For a second or two, your thumb belonged to somebody else. Then they put everything right again and croaked. Otherwise, you woulda had one helluva immune reaction."

Now that Bib had explained things to her, Amy could sense a faint soreness in her thumb. "Oh. So I can't pull that trick again?"

"Nuh-huh. Not unless you're hooked up to the *Dixie Belle*. 'Fraid you're on your own otherwise."

"Well, I guess I'll just have to hope I don't have any more run-ins with the federales on my way to Nashville."

"Not too likely. Faithland's perty quiet these days on the homeland security front, ever since President O'Reilly unleashed that sweet little global virus."

Amy remembered learning about this Faithland anti-terrorist measure in school. Forgetting to employ her new accent and diction, she said, "You mean the Glowworm Patch? The one that spreads by touch and retroengineers into humans a luciferase gene that's activated by certain high-order brain chemistry patterns?"

"That's the one, honeychile. Mighty hard to commit terrorism when thinking about it make you glow bright blue in public."

Amy gave vent to a huge yawn at this point.

Bib regarded Amy tenderly. He paid no attention to the road, since the *Dixie Belle* was on cyber-control. "Maybe you should get some sleep now, honeychile."

"You wouldn't mind...?"

"No, I'll just punch up some Government Mule in my earbuds and do my road-warrior thing."

"'Kay. Thanks..."

Before she knew it, Amy was asleep.

When she awoke, daylight reigned outside, and they were approaching a major metropolitan area.

"Is that—?"

"Oklahoma City? Sure enough. Here's where you and me gotta part ways, I fear. I'm gonna drop you off at the Greyhound terminal. I figger you prolly got enough cash for a ticket to Nashville. Or do you need some bits on your chop?"

"No, no, I'm all set, Bib. Thank you so much for all you've done. You been—you been sweeter to me than mama's ice tea."

"Waal, Amy, you done reminded me of my own little princess, so warn't no way in God's creation I could let you be disappointed. You take care now, y'hear, on the rest of your trip. Faithland's a mighty safe place for the most part, but there's always folks out there looking to score."

Stripped of the truck's passenger suit, wearing her backpack, Amy stood on the sidewalk outside the bus terminal, waving goodbye to the *Dixie Belle*.

So much for all the horrible things the Agnosticans liked to say about the Faithlanders. Amy felt confirmed in her decision to leave the elite enclave into which she had been born.

She looked around now at the streets of the first Faithland city she had ever visited, expecting to see immense differences from home. Truth to tell, however, many of the same franchises occupied various storefronts, although a few names were new to her. She wondered if JENNA'S PEIGNOIRS was equivalent to VICTORIA'S SECRET.

It would've been nice to explore a little, but Nashville beckoned.

The ticket to Nashville took almost fifty of Amy's euros, which she exchanged for forty dollars at an ATM in the terminal. She even had a few dollars left over for breakfast at the terminal café.

A few hours later, Amy was on her bus, heading east. She had taken what appeared to be the seat with possibly the most congenial companion: an Asian woman not much older than Amy herself. Although conventionally pretty, the woman had chosen to downplay her looks with a lack of makeup, severe hairstyle and drab clothing.

After a dozen miles of mutual silence, the woman turned to Amy and introduced herself in a perky manner.

"Hi, there, my name's Cindy Lou Hu."

The woman's English was excellent, but accented. After Amy volunteered her own name, she asked, "Are you from, like, another country?"

"Yes, of course. Shanghai, China. I'm here to visit Brother Ray's Gospel Mission in Nashville."

"Huh?"

Cindy Lou explained that her family had been evangelical Christians for two generations, ever since adopting the creed from American missionaries. Now she was returning to the source of her faith for instruction in spreading the gospel even further.

JIGSAW NATION

"Faith is one of your country's last, best exports. No one sells religion abroad like Faithland. Brother Ray and his peers are everywhere around the world. They might assign me to Latin America or Africa or Mongolia even. It all depends. Wherever I can do the most good bringing the word of Jesus to unbelievers. Are you a believer, Amy?"

Amy began to squirm. This kind of conversation was never encountered in Agnostica. "Uh, well, I guess I'm kind of a, um, secular humanist."

Cindy Lou's smile did not waver, but definitely acquired a steely gleam. "Oh, you must read some of these tracts I happen to have with me. Right now. And then we'll talk about them. We've got *tons* of time."

Fifteen hours later, as the bus pulled into Nashville, Amy's brain felt as if it had been extracted, pureed and reinserted into her skull. She was convinced that the friendly "dialogue" on Jesus and all matters Biblical that Cindy Lou had subjected her to was a form of torture banned by the Geneva Convention.

Still, Amy had not crumbled. She managed to refuse Cindy Lou's repeated importunings to stay at Brother Ray's mission. And engaging in a mass baptism was definitely ruled out. So as the two women parted around midnight outside the Nashville terminal, Amy was finally left extensively on her own, for the first time since she had escaped from New Austin.

The first thing she did was find cheap lodgings with her ViewMaster. In the Ikea capsule hotel on Commerce, not far from the Cumberland River, Amy gratefully rested her head on her thin pillow the size of a handkerchief — a Snööli, according to its label — knowing that she was only a short distance away from all the famous musical sites she had come so far to see.

And perhaps close in time as well to a career in music.

The next morning Amy was up early, eager to see all the attractions that Nashville had to offer. Surely by nightfall she would have connected through some magical serendipity with the forces that would transform her life and allow her musical talent to blossom.

The first place she intended to visit after breakfast was Music Row, the district where all the famous recording studios thrived. Here had so many of her favorite songs been digitized. The sidewalks practically gleamed golden with glory in Amy's mind.

But when Amy arrived at Music Row, she quickly found the district to be a hollow recreation of what she had envisioned, a series of museums and shops without any professional musicians around at all. Only fatuous tour guides and sullen gift-shop cashiers afforded any connection to the fabulous heritage of Nashville.

A few simple inquiries soon revealed that Music Row had been obsoleted about ten years ago, by the ultimate perfection of home-recording software and the changed nature of music distribution. Music Row was now distributed unevenly across all of Faithland, in a thousand garages and bedrooms, of tract houses and mansions alike.

Saddened but still hopeful after touring the simulated remnants of the district, Amy decided to treat herself to some barbecue. She found a place called Hog Heaven on 27th Street and walked the long blocks there. But the meal disagreed with her. Tennessee barbecue, it turned out, wasn't anything like New Austin's. Weird sauces, weird coleslaw, weird beans, weird cornbread.

But even this disappointing repast failed to dim Amy's excitement at the thought of what awaited her tonight. The Grand Ole Opry was performing in the historic Ryman auditorium, and she had snagged a cheap ticket with her ViewMaster.

Amy spent the remainder of the afternoon strolling around the clean and pretty city. She listened to the locals talk, working on her own accent. Despite a few letdowns, Amy felt sure she would still settle here. There must be a club scene through which she could meet like-minded fans and aspiring artists.

A brief nap back in her hotel room refreshed her for the Opry.

At the theater, Amy debated buying some snacks to serve in lieu of supper. But her money was rapidly dwindling, and she held out despite the grumblings of her stomach.

Inside, Amy settled into her seat, full of anticipation. Even the snickers of some nearby girls her own age—who apparently had nothing better to do than make fun of Amy's outfit—failed to quash her fervor.

But with the very first act, her faith evaporated, and she knew she was in for heartache.

None of these performers were familiar to her. Favoring the old-time classic singers, Amy had not kept up with the latest voices and faces. Still, she could have become emotionally invested in their songs if they hadn't been all tarted up with synthetic sounds and pop arrangements. Where was the soul and heart of a Willie Nelson or Hank Williams III? Nowhere, it was obvious by intermission.

Amy didn't even stay for the rest of the show, but instead trudged downheartedly back to her hotel, where she deluged Mr. Taxes with a monsoon of tears.

In the morning, Amy realized she had one last place to go that would reaffirm her connection with this city, would justify her arduous trip here, would inspire her future course.

JIGSAW NATION

The Country Music Hall of Fame.

With a lighter step, Amy hurried down to the corner of Demonbreun and 5th, arriving just as the museum opened.

She went immediately to the Gretchen Wilson exhibit.

Gretchen, Amy knew, had retired five years ago, after a long and fruitful career. But perhaps the exhibit would contain updated information about her current whereabouts (surely Gretchen still called Nashville home). Or perhaps — hope sprang eternal — there would be notice of a comeback tour.

At the Gretchen Wilson display, Amy synced her ViewMaster with the kiosk there and brought up onto her screen all the information the Country Music Hall of Fame had to offer on her heroine. The digital guide's voice came through her earbuds.

"Since retiring from the road, Gretchen Wilson has invested much of her wealth in Batchelder Bioengineering and now resides in New Austin where she can more closely monitor her business affairs...."

Amy found herself out on the sidewalk without any memory of having exited the museum. For a long time she just stood rooted to the spot as foot traffic surged around her. Then she turned toward her hotel to reclaim her pack and check out.

As she walked, she punched up some Johnny Cash.

"Lead me gently home, father, lead me gently home..."

Edward J. McFadden III & E. Sedia

The Idaho Zephyr
By Douglas Lain

"You're one of those people who think that solutions emerge from your judicious study of discernible reality. But that isn't how it works anymore. We're an empire now, and when we act, we create our own reality."
-Bush Aid to Journalist Ron Suskind

I'm not really interested in the election but I'm watching the results on television anyway. Other people care about it and since the anchors are repeating the same information over and over again—Bush wins, Red States, Bush wins, Blue States—it's easy to just half listen while I keep working on my train photos.

I'm piecing together a panorama for photography class. The final project is due in two weeks and I'm trying to get the train to look right. I took over a hundred snapshots, black and white, 35mm, and I tried to keep track of the edges of the frame from one shot to the next, but now I'm finding I'll have to cut the prints if I want to fit these images together.

My father will be happy tomorrow, at least outwardly. And his students will be pissed.

Dad teaches political science at Colorado College and that's why I'm enrolled there. The tuition is waived and the professors are nice to me, at least most of them are. I'm worried about the photography project. Ms. White doesn't seem to get what I'm doing. She keeps talking about social realism and subtexts.

"You should consider how artists approached industrialization at the turn of the last century," she said. "Seurat put factories in his paintings. Why did he do it? And why are you aiming your lens at trains and technology now? You need to be conscious of your subjectivity."

But I'm not interested in Seurat or subjectivity. Everything that is good about this country arrived by train. I just need to fit the pictures together.

JIGSAW NATION

Everything that matters or is good about America arrived by train. The laying of rail from one coast to the other prefigured the rest of it: airplanes, automobiles, satellites, moon missions, recorded music, electricity, comfort, leisure, magazines, television, and so on... It couldn't have happened if the Chinese hadn't laid down track and simultaneously their lives; it couldn't have happened if the Unions had won, if the rails hadn't fought back.

America emerged in a puff of steam.

The two permanent staff members for campus security resent the work-study program. They talk about full time wages and benefits and are dismayed by the term "permanent temp." They say the work-study kids are undermining them and there is something going on involving an outside union, but I try not to be too interested. I don't usually talk to the permanent staff, just to the other students. Mostly I hang out with Margaret; I try to flirt with her a little bit. I wait for Barry and Leslie to leave and then try to strike up a conversation. Maybe I'll ask her out.

"What are you reading?" I ask. Margaret gazes up from under the bill of her cap and I can just see enough of her face to recognize that her cheeks are red. Is she blushing or is she wearing too much rouge? Either way she looks all wrong in the security guard outfit that gives the impression that she's pretending. Her blonde hair and green eyes and the security guard cap, the whole thing is a game.

"What was that?" she asks.

I ask what she's reading a second time and she holds up her text, a book entitled "The Empiricists", and shrugs.

"Science book?"

"No, it's for philosophy class," she says. "Actually I was writing a letter to my parents, but I don't have enough cash to send it. I keep thinking that what I really need is a stamp."

I check that my flashlight is properly secured to my belt and then lean across the table to get a closer look at her book. "Locke, Berkeley, and Hume? Interesting stuff?"

"Impenetrable. Everything in it is counter-intuitive," she says, and hands the book to me. "Have you noticed that there isn't any mail delivery anymore?"

I pretend to be interested in the table of contents, and read the back cover aloud. "'The rise and fall of British Empiricism is probably philosophy's most dramatic example of pushing premises to their logical and fatal conclusions.'"

"You know, letters? Stamps? PO Boxes."

"You don't get any letters? I tell you what, I'll Fed-Ex you a letter tomorrow," I say.

"That's what I mean. There used to be public mail service. Didn't there?" Margaret takes off her cap and starts to play with her hair, pulling a few strands in front her eyes. I study her face, figure out that she's not blushing, not wearing any rouge or make-up. Her cheeks are chapped. Her security route is outside in the dry cold.

"How's your semester going?" I ask. "Ready for finals?"

Margaret doesn't answer, but seems distracted by her hair. She holding strands over one eye, staring through them.

"Do you want to go out with me?" I ask this as quickly as possible, blurt it out.

"What?"

"I mean, as friends. I've got to take some more pictures of trains, for my photography class, for the final project. You want to go train spotting with me? This Friday?" –

Margaret nods. "What time?"

"Four?"

"Okay."

"You got the time off?" I ask.

"Yeah."

"I'll pick you up at your dorm?"

"Yeah. You don't remember it?" she asks.

"I remember. I'll remember."

"No, I mean the mail. You don't remember mail?"

I shrug. The two of us check the time clock; we've talked past starting time and have to clock in at three minutes after, but it was worth it.

I check my flashlight again and set off to secure my section of campus. I'm happy to get started.

I spend most of my time in the University library. After making the rounds, after checking a few of the smaller buildings, just the front door and perimeters, I check each floor of the library and then sit behind the circulation desk with a book, usually a history book or a sociology book, or something about mass transit and trains. It's this chance to read that makes guarding a pleasant job. A quiet building full of books and I can read or just think. Or I can just stare out the front of the library, through the panes of glass and across at Lincoln Hall, and not think at all.

I look at the copy of "The Empiricists", the book that Margaret was reading. I found on the fourth floor, I had to use the catalog to find it. I open it at random, and find it difficult. I have to read each sentence over and over before I understand anything.

Phil: This point then is agreed between us, that sensible things are those only, which are immediately perceived by sense?

JIGSAW NATION

I read this three times and then stop. At the top of the page is the name George Berkeley. If I can understand this it will give me something to talk about with Margaret, but I'd hate to get it all wrong and spend the whole time listening to her correcting me.

I reread the sentence again; what is Phil getting at? Is it something more than the cliché that "what you see is what you get?"

Phil: It seems therefore that if you take away all sensible qualities, there remains nothing else.

Hyl: I grant it.

Phil: Sensible things are nothing else but so many sensible qualities or combinations of qualities.

My legs are falling asleep, going numb, and it's time to check the floors again, and then walk outside by Lincoln Hall. I get up and stretch and find the right keys on my giant ring. I take the stairs. I have to make sure nobody is hiding out in the stairwells. We've had homeless people try to sleep there, there and in the stacks on the fifth floor, up where the shelves are close together, and my job is to make sure it doesn't happen again. I've got to walk each row.

On the fourth floor I stop at the computer again, just for a minute. I want to find something else about George Berkeley, something that will go ahead and explain it straight out. I'll get back to doing the rounds in a minute.

Common sense dictates that there are only two crucial elements involved in perception: the perceiver and what is perceived. All we need to do, Berkeley argued, is eliminate the absurd, philosophically-conceived third element in the picture: that is, we must acknowledge that there are no material objects. For Berkeley, only the ideas we directly perceive are real.

This seems more straightforward, but it still doesn't make any sense. If there is nothing outside of perception did he mean that everything is just in my head?

There's nobody on the fifth floor, at least nobody I can see when I get to the top of the stairs. I head for the stacks on the West Side, but stop when I get to the study tables and open the book again.

I want to make sure I understand this. Berkeley is difficult stuff and if I can figure it out in one night, if I can explain it to her instead of making her explain it to me, if she doesn't have to correct me, maybe that will impress her a little.

When I get off work I head home, back to Dad's, for breakfast and to do laundry. It's all perfectly normal.

Dad is getting older. He always represented something strong and orderly and wise, but now he's too weathered and bleary-eyed to stand in for anything. He's just himself in his bathrobe and pajamas. He's my dad, but that isn't so impressive anymore.

But, this new outlook does not trouble me. I figure his diminishment is actually a good sign. I'm in college, out of the house; it's only natural that Dad should wither in the face of all that. There's nothing sad there. Nothing to worry about.

"Have you read Berkeley?" I ask him. We're sitting under birthday streamers at the kitchen table. The streamers have been up for a long time and their color is fading, the blue is growing pale in the sunlight. The streamers have been decorating our table for nearly a year now, since my 20th birthday. She put them up for a party that was just another meal really, just the three of us because I would never invite friends to such an event. She'd bought a cake at Safeway and it said happy birthday on it, and dad gave me the keys to a new car, and it was all fine. But she never took down the decorations and Dad doesn't seem to notice that they're still there.

Dad butters his toaster waffle, spreads on the margarine, and then pauses to think about my question. The name George Berkeley is ringing bells in his head but he can't quite match up the signifier to the thing signified.

I explain Berkeley's immaterialism but Dad's just curious to know which one of my classes requires Berkeley.

"Actually, I know this girl. It's something she's reading for one of her classes, and I read a little because of her."

"You going to run the train today?" Dad asks. It's an HO gauge Amtrak train and I've been putting it together, laying down track, building and rebuilding the communities around it, perfecting it, since I was ten years old. I've spent most of the last decade in this attic, in these two rooms that hold my father's O gauge rail and my own, larger, HO line.

■■

It takes a little while to get the line running. First I have to remove the dust cloths from the engines, make sure that none of the cars are derailed, and then I have to plug in the set and wait for it to warm up. Then I can slowly turn the switches. Slowly because when I try to jump them to full speed the engines always derail. You've got to build up to it, but once it's really moving smoothly I can keep the train going at full throttle for hours.

The train circles a world that I created and my likes and dislikes—the ideas, celebrities, music, and movies that have made the biggest impression—are part of the design. The town's tiny movie theater is always running "Witness", and I imagine the car radios are all tuned to KRDO Classic Rock. The houses are all orange or green.

I've spent the last decade fitting this world together, and while Dad is worried about being historically accurate, he spent hundreds on his courthouse, my set isn't tied to any particular period. I can rearrange history, drive circles around it.

But, I've always got to start slow.

I'm looking at my photography project in the dark, by the light from the TV. Even in the dim light from the television, even as I listen to triumphal administration officials, the uneasy awe from the announcers, the endless babble about the Red and the Blue, the casualties, the stock index, employment figures, Christmas shopping before Thanksgiving, I can see that I won't be able to fit these pictures together. I'll have to cut more out, exclude more of the image.

Winston O. Link perfected the railroads. He made the steam engine new, but I can't do it. My vision is fractured. All I have is a series of static images, disconnected parts, without synergy.

I drive my father's station wagon to campus. It's about five minutes to four and I'm on time. The back of the station wagon is full of equipment—a boom mike, video camera, notebooks, 35mm camera, tripod, and a reel to reel tape recorder. The tape recorder is old, of course. It's my Dad's, but it's perfect for this sort of project. It's easy to change speed on a reel to reel recorder, easy to synch everything up.

I'm on time but Margaret isn't. She's still in her pajamas, which is a bad sign even if she does work nights. After all it's nearly four and there are places to go, but she's sitting on her cot in the dorm room and apparently on the phone. She gestures that I should come in and tells me to sit down, but I'm impatient so I just stand in her doorway.

She picks up the phone again and, to my irritation, starts dialing. She hangs up and then dials again, the same number, and then she does it again.

"It's disconnected," she says.
"Yeah?"
"Anyhow the voice says the line is disconnected, but that can't be right."
"Who you calling?"
"Parents."

She doesn't want to leave, doesn't want to quit dialing, but I eventually convince her that it's time to go. I let her get dressed and wait for her in the parking lot, but once she's in the car she's useless. She sighs a lot and fiddles with the lock and window buttons, and when I pull off the road to get to the train tracks, when I stop and start to set up for our first shoot, she acts surprised.

"This is nowhere," she says. "Not to seem paranoid, but what exactly are we doing out here?"

I unfold the tripod and set the camera on top of it, screw it into place. "Train is coming," I explain. I put the video camera on the roof of the station wagon, and then wander through the tumble weeds and gravel, set the boom mike closer to the tracks, and then unwind the mike's cord and plug it into the station wagon's lighter.

Margaret just stands there in her leather jacket and trendy knit cap and doesn't understand.

"I don't like this," she says.

"What?"

"I think I'm going to ask you to take me back."

"Take you back?" This is going all wrong. "The California Zephyr is due in ten minutes. I've got to set up."

"I'm sorry."

I've spoiled it with the train stuff. She doesn't get it. This is all fucked up.

"I read that book about Berkeley last week. What a strange person he was," I say. "I guess he thought everything was in our heads, or in God's head."

Margaret stares out the passenger window and counts cars on the highway. She counts the cars that don't have passengers, the drivers who are traveling alone. "This can't last," she says, then she turns to me and seems to have heard. "If everything is just a matter of perception then I guess it really matters what we think about."

"No, it matters what God thinks," I say.

"Oh yeah, God. Him again."

I turn on the radio, tune in the oldies station. KRDO, 96.5 on the dial, plays pop songs from the '70s and '80s. We catch the tail end of Devo's "Whip it" and listen to the beginning of the Romantics one hit.

"I'm sorry you didn't want to do the train thing. It's just that my final project is a panorama of a passenger train," I say. "I really wanted to take pictures of the train."

"No. I'm sorry. It's my fault. You're not mad at me, are you?" she asks.

"I'll just have to come back out here tomorrow."

"'You tell me that you need me! You tell me that you love me!'" the

JIGSAW NATION

Romantics sing. My father's stereo system sounds good, and I turn it up, modulate the bass.

When we arrive back at the University Prince's "When Doves Cry" is on the radio and we just sit there in the parking lot and listen to his erotic and romantic vocals. I reach over and squeeze Margaret's hand, not really thinking, and she looks me in the eye and smiles. The problem between us, whatever it is, has been solved. I turn off the engine, switch off the music in the middle of the guitar solo, and then sit silently.

"You don't have to go," Margaret says.

"What do you mean?" I ask.

"I just didn't want to be out there, on the road," she said.

"You want to go somewhere else now?" I ask.

"Whatever you want to do is fine with me," she says.

"You want to see a movie?" I ask.

"Not really." She smiles.

"What then?" I ask.

"Are you hungry?"

There is nothing going on. I tell Margaret this fact over lunch, as we eat some sort of paste at her favorite Indian Restaurant and drink watered down lemonade. There is nothing but Margaret thinks that there is something. She tells me that her parents would never fail to pay a phone bill on time. She mentions a place called New York as if I ought to have heard of it, and is clearly unsettled by my noncommittal response to the word.

"New York! You remember New York!"

I don't answer but rip a piece of Pita bread in half and load both halves with shredded lettuce and some sort of cheese.

We walk along 21st Avenue not talking. I try to enjoy the silence, the sunshine, the fact of the asphalt under my feet. I notice the chestnut trees planted alongside a chain link fence and then stop outside a Starbucks and grab a few free newspapers from a box chained to the No Parking sign. I read the headlines while Margaret brushes her hair out of her eyes and tries out a smile.

"Good news and bad news," I say and hold up the papers. One is a neighborhood paper that focuses on local businesses and city government and the other is called "New Connexion" and is really just a catalog for New Age services in town. "Industrialists threaten to roadblock Lincoln Neighborhood," I read. "And yet, on the other hand, we've got this report where a coroner affirms the reality of life after death."

Margaret stops walking and puts her hands up to the chain link fence, grabs it, and stares out at the concrete pillars of the Marquam Bridge, at the rust colored cars rolling along the top level. "I grew up in a cult," she says.

I look through the chain link fence, try to follow what she's following, but I don't see anything there worth pondering. It's just sun bleached newspapers and weeds and, off a bit further, the overpass. I put my hand up to my face to shade my eyes from the glare off of the concrete.

"I grew up on a commune in Durango. You know Durango?"

"Where the cliff dwellings are?"

Margaret nods and we step away from the fence. We head west, make our way to the end of 21st, to the point where the street the highway cut through, to another chain link fence with a cement wall behind it. We can't go forward so we stop again and look at the highway, at the ramp for the bridge. We're close enough to smell the exhaust from passing cars.

"There was a junk yard near our community, near the big house where my parents had set about making a new, peaceful, and loving community. Just through the woods, maybe a half mile in, there was a clearing where the county dumped old refrigerators, cars, wire baskets, radios, bleach bottles, and a million pieces of something made of brittle plastic.

"When was this?"

"I was six, so this was 1991."

"A hippie commune in 1991..."

"No. This wasn't a hippie thing, it was more of a cult thing," she explained.

"It would have to be."

"I remember going to the dump with the other yoga kids. We saw fairies out there. We all saw them."

"Fairies? You mean like flying elves?"

"They were eating bits of rusted metal, flitting about the automobiles."

"Just around the cars?"

"No. They were all over the dump, turning bits over, looking for rust and filling up on the flakes they'd find."

I count the number of red vehicles that pass for a minute, maybe two minutes, in order to buy some time to respond. I count thirty-five red cars and then let out a breath and ask for more information.

"What do you want to know?"

"How big were the fairies? How many were there? What happened next?"

It was a long time ago. All she can remember is that they had wings like an insect's, not pretty wings at all, and that they had long hair and big eyes.

JIGSAW NATION

"And they ate rust."

"When we went back to the house to tell our parents they all believed us. They believed us, really and truly believed. But they weren't really interested."

"What do you mean?"

"There were too many other miracles going on. They had hash brownies and mind control sessions with the leader. Fairies were just one more thing," she says. She stops looking out at the highway and turns to me instead. She opens her mouth, closes it, and then opens it again.

"My roommate says I'm shallow. That my spiritual life is just a show."

"Why? Did you tell her about the fairies?"

"I'm a cliché."

Margaret has seen fairies but now she finds herself siding with her detractors.

"New age bullshit," she says.

"But maybe not."

"No. It's true. There can be no miracles. That's not how it works."

I don't really disagree.

"But at least I remember New York. At least I remember the Post Office."

We're back at the Starbucks and while Margaret drinks a Chai tea, I drink coffee from a tiny mug and explain it all to her.

"The system," I say, "is your friend."

Winston O. Link worked in advertising for thirty years. From the late '20s to the mid '50s he produced thousands of commercial photographs. His work decorated promotional brochures, Quarterly Reports, magazines, and newspaper advertisements. He photographed beauty pageants, parades, restaurants, politicians, bars of soap, lady's hygiene products, and more. Nothing about his professional life was outstanding. It was all standard, the kinds of images that aren't meant to be seen but rather absorbed. Link believed in producing subliminal effects. Link believed in advertising.

"The system was O. Link's friend because after thirty years of working on other people's images, after cranking it out, he was able to make his own," I say. "The system gave him the skills he needed, equipped him with a special ability."

"What kind of ability?"

"He could create an aura around anything he aimed his lens at. He made his subjects appear as something more than what they really were."

I tell her that what he aimed his lens at, in the end, were trains. But not just trains; Link created dreamscapes. Using artificial light, choreography, and perfect timing Link made new worlds—realms where steam engines not only dominated but also unified. With the full participation of the railroads he was able to document the decay of rail transport and somehow turn this decay into a fulfillment. His images of working class women struggling with their kids in sooty train stations, his old men with vacant eyes, his employees in ragged conductors uniforms or overalls, were transcendent. The death of rural America was represented by Link as a promise, as a myth, a new social contract. Capitalism with a human face.

"He sounds like pure evil," Margaret says.

"We wouldn't be here. We wouldn't live the lives we're living, without him. America would be ordinary without Link and people like him. We would have sunk into the actual."

"The system works?" Margaret asks.

"Yes."

"Even without fairies or junk yards or mail delivery? Even without New York City?"

"It works. These things you're talking about don't make sense. They don't work."

Margaret finishes her Chai and throws her disposable cup away.

"Trains. Transport. Vision." I tell her. "Links. Photographs. Images." It dawns on me that I'll have to get up early tomorrow. I've got to get out by the tracks at Sunrise and get my shots.

Or I could stay in and try to get the images I already have to fit together.

"The system works," Margaret says.

But listening to her say it now I find I don't believe her. What system? Works in what way and for whom?

"We just had the only opinion poll that matters, and our ideas won. I've earned political capital with this election, and I intend to spend it," Bush says.

I have to take new pictures, start over. The problem is that I can't figure out when, can't find the schedule for the California Zephyr. I can't find the schedule online, can't find any mention of the Zephyr in Train magazine or in my Amtrak Encyclopedia, or anywhere. I look in the index again, hunt for the word California, and I can't even find that. I can't find it and I can't remember what it means.

California. California. California. California.

What kind of wind would a California Zephyr be? I look up the Amtrak schedule again and find what I'm looking for. The Idaho Zephyr runs from Indiana to Carson City and then up along the beaches of the Pacific Ocean to Idaho.

JIGSAW NATION

On the TV a technician wearing Buddy Holly glasses holds a cell phone up to his ear.

"Can you hear me now?"

The Verizon checkmark appears in the middle of the screen and is followed by a map of the United States with red lines shooting out in all directions. Verizon reaches everywhere, from Idaho to Virginia.

"Can you hear me now?" the technician asks again, and then smiles at the camera.

At the library I'm checking all the doors, making sure everything is secure, holding my flashlight like a club, when Margaret taps on the plate glass window. She's leaning over the shrubbery and pressing her palms against the glass, leaving marks.

It takes a moment to key in the code and unlock the entrance.

"I need a ride," she says. She wants to go home, back to New York, and has already purchased airline tickets on her student credit card. $1200 for round trip tickets to NYC and back to the Springs. And she'll miss the winter finals.

"You going to take them when you get back? Have you talked to your professors?"

"I don't care about that."

"I'm not off work until 5am."

She just looks at me, doesn't even bother to make a case. Her plane leaves in two hours.

"I just got here," I tell her. She doesn't respond. "I'll have to call in and get a replacement."

She actually bought two tickets to New York. New York? This makes no sense to me at all. We aren't even sleeping together, but she wants me to go with her. And I don't tell her I won't go, not at first. We're waiting for her plane in the gift shop across from the gate.

"You can wear some of my brother's clothes. He's about your size. Or maybe Dad will lend you some clothes."

I pull a toy airplane across a display table, pressing lightly down on it so the mechanism inside catches. I press down so it will roll forward when I let go.

She opens a box of Trivial Pursuit cards on a shelf next to the exit. The cards are dog-eared.

"What country is the Hellenic Republic?" she asks.

I shrug and let the airplane go. We watch it roll across the table and onto the tile floor.

"I'm not coming with you," I tell her. "I don't want to go."

She acts like she didn't hear and flips the card over to read the answer.

"Greece," she says. "Who created Winnie-the-Pooh?"

It's ridiculous. Does she think I'm going to blow my finals, lose my work-study job, and risk my future because she's got a cute smile? I don't want to go. The prospect of going to this mystery zone makes me anxious and queasy. On instinct alone I know I shouldn't go. There is something wrong with the destination.

"Who created Pooh? C'mon, you ought to know that one."

"Disney?"

"No. A. A. Milne," she says.

There is a snow globe with Pikes Peak inside. I pick it up and shake it.

"What was Elvis Presley's first film, in 1956?"

I refuse to answer and watch the artificial snow twirl around behind the plastic bubble instead.

"What Polish Astronomer demonstrated in 1512 that the sun is the center of the solar system?"

"I don't know," I tell her. "Was it Bishop Berkeley?"

"Where do Tangerines live?"

"New York?"

They're boarding her flight, starting with the disabled and children.

"Reconsider."

"Why do you want me there?"

"Because I don't know what's going on, or what I'll find. I can't reach them, my parents or anybody else, on the phone," she says. "I'm scared. Please come with me."

I take the trivia card from her and read the last question.

"How many ghosts appear to Scrooge in Dickens's Christmas Carol?" I ask.

"Three?"

"Four," I say. "You forgot his partner."

The flight attendant announces that Flight 1242 is now boarding first class passengers and we walk back across the hallway to the gate. The LED sign above the flight attendant is broken, it's blinking off and on, and while the flight number and departure time will occasionally flash by, the destination is a jumble of random red dots, just a flickering of light that can't be deciphered.

"You're not coming with me?" Margaret asks when her row is called.

"Why do you want me to go? Why not somebody else? Why did you waste all that money?"

JIGSAW NATION

She blushes and then picks up her carry-on bag, a leather tote bag with a shiny silver zipper.

"The money doesn't matter. It's on card, on my Dad's card and he'll pay it automatically. He'll just be glad I used it to visit home," she says. Margaret turns to leave, but decides she has one last thing to say to me before she goes, and turns back. Her face is red but I can't figure out if she's still blushing or if she's about to cry. "I thought you cared about me, you know? I thought a boyfriend would work out better for this trip than a girlfriend. Guess I was wrong."

I don't have a response, find that I'm blushing too, and then wishing I could change my mind. I would like to run after her, to join her on the plane, to sweep her off her feet. Instead I just watch her board the plane and walk back to the gift shop, watch her from the entrance. I feel awkward, embarrassed.

Margaret gets on the plane, the flight attendant closes the doors, and the LED sign flashes the flight number one last time and then turns off.

The flight attendant locks the door and then walks behind the counter and announces that Flight 1103 is pulling up to the gate now and that they will begin boarding momentarily. The LED sign comes back to life, displays the new flight number, a new departure time, and the destination.

Flight 1103 is going to Dallas.

I suddenly feel queasy. The plane Margaret boarded hasn't had time to leave the gate, couldn't have departed yet.

"What about the flight to New York?" I shout. Then I walk across the aisle and step up to the counter. "What about the flight to New York?" I ask again.

"The flight where?" The flight attendant looks at me like I'm going to make trouble, like I'm a problem.

"What about flight 1242?" I ask.

She types the number into the computer and I let out a sigh. What kind of game is this?

"Flight 1242?" she asks.

I nod and then point at the door, walk over to the plate glass windows and point out at the airplane, but it isn't there. The plane Margaret boarded is gone, just like that. Disappeared.

The flight attendant looks up from the computer screen.

"I'm sorry, sir. There is no flight 1242."

I'm standing in the Colorado Springs airport, by the escalator, and I'm watching the steps roll up toward me and disappear into the floor. I'm trying to remember something. I suddenly flash on the fact that I don't know why I'm waiting, what I'm doing at the wrong escalator, why I'm at the airport at all. I'm holding a Trivial Pursuit card and I read off the answers on the back while the steps roll in the wrong direction, as the steps roll toward me.

"Skiing. Copernicus. The Dead Sea Scrolls. Love me Tender." I drop the card at the top of the stairs, maybe somebody else will find it and know what do with those answers. I walk to the other side and ride the steps down.

Walking up to the attic I notice the photos of the presidents that Dad hung on the wall. They've been up there forever, but I don't usually look at them. At the bottom there is a black and white photo of Eisenhower, and half way up there is a color picture of Richard Nixon looking almost friendly. At the landing there is a picture of a smiling if slightly apologetic Gerald Ford and a photo of an angelic, airbrushed, and vacant Ronald Reagan.

I climb to the top of the stairs and realize that the Bushes were excluded. Either my father never met President Bush or his son, or he abandoned the project, or he had other reasons not to hang their portraits. Instead the hall outside the two rooms in our attic is decorated with trains. Pages ripped from calendars, a steam locomotive moving across a prairie was the pinup in June, 1972. A diesel engine in a train yard is from December of 1985.

I open the door to my train room, reach around to flip the light switch, and find the room empty. The room is empty but it takes me a second to figure out what it is that's missing.

There are marks on the hard wood floor, where the table legs were, and there is a small pile of discarded track in the far left corner, but the train table, my city, the six mint condition HO engines, and nearly sixty passenger cars, are gone. The whole world I created—my plaster mountains, the paper roads and miniature traffic signals, the matchbox cars, the plastic people, and all the rest of it—has evaporated. The room is empty except for the dust that floats through the sunlight.

I stand in the middle, in the empty space, and stretch out my arms. I'm surprised how easy it is to move around in here now. It was cramped in here before. I stretch out my arms until I'm sick with it, until the absence jumps on me and I can't stretch out any further. I'm not big enough to fill this space.

I get down on all fours and inspect the marks of the floor, the scratches. I fumble around with the little bit of track in the corner and discover that it's oversized, O gauge. This is track from my father's set. There is nothing to be done with it. It's oversized and clumsy.

JIGSAW NATION

The streamers are missing. Did mom take them down or were they never there at all? Dad is spreading margarine on his toaster waffle and staring at his glass of orange juice; he flips hair over his bald spot, absently patting the comb over back into place.

He looks up as I enter the kitchen and stops eating when I stride over to him. When I stand next to him and cross my arms he stops like he's surprised.

"How did it go with that girl you were talking about?" he asks.

I put my hands on the table, getting my fingers sticky with the maple syrup that has dribbled off his plate.

"What girl?" I ask.

"Didn't you say you were going to take a girl out with you on your next photography expedition? How's the panorama coming along?"

I'm not interested in this conversation. "Dad, where is my train?"

"I'm sorry?"

"My HO gauge model of the Idaho Zephyr, where is it? And not just that, where is the table? The whole set is gone. Not just that engine."

He doesn't answer, but starts cutting his waffle into bite sized pieces.

"Where is it?" I ask again, incredulous.

"I didn't think you were interested in my model train," Dad says. "If that's what you're talking about I think it's upstairs in one of the storage closets."

"What? Dad, I spent ten years on my train set."

Dad eats some more waffle and pats his hair again. "I'm not sure I understand what you're saying. You said something about an M-track? What is that?"

"Amtrak?"

Dad shrugs. "Have I ever shown you my old 8mm films of the old freight lines that used to run through the Springs?"

I walk away from the table, go to the kitchen sink to wash my hands. I use dishwashing detergent to wash the syrup off.

"Don't you remember anything?" I ask.

"I've already shown you the films?"

"Yes. Of course you've shown them to me. You've shown them to me about a thousand times. I'm asking you about my train set, upstairs, in the attic. What happened to it?"

Dad looks genuinely puzzled; he looks at me like I've seen him look at mom so many times. Like he feels sorry for me.

"Don't worry about it," I tell him. "Forget it."

"I'm sorry."

I sit down across from him and start eating the breakfast he's put out for me. I stuff a large piece of cold waffle into my mouth, use a sip of juice to help swallow it down, and then put my fork down again.

"Let's forget it. I think that's the best thing we can do," I say.

Everything good about America arrived by train. I really believe that. The laying of rail from one coast to the other brought everything else: airplanes, automobiles, color television.

America clicked into place back then, fit together like cars latched by their couplers, like tracks on ties laid down solidly in the dirt. But all of that is gone. It's all evaporated, disappeared in a puff of steam.

JIGSAW NATION

Waking Waco
By Cody Goodfellow

On the day they thawed Rydell "Waco" Peabody, all but two of the crew at the Rip Van Winkle's Tasty Vittles franchise called in sick. Of those who did show, one couldn't read, while the other was too young to remember what their charge had done to merit becoming the world's oldest surviving meatsicle. Once they'd waded through the excesses of Waco's rap sheet, signed special liability release forms and strapped on the standard gear for handling a Red package—Kevlar smocks, face-shields and cattle-prods—they were sorely tempted to either delete the schedule and feign ignorance or dump the package off its gurney. But they were bored and none too bright, and business was slow, and a load of corned krill patties was earmarked for Waco's berth in the freezer, so they went ahead and revived a man the Texas and U.S. Supreme Court had once unanimously decided to freeze until science found a method of punishment cruel and unusual enough to fit his crimes.

The Supreme Court had neither the supremacy nor a U.S. to back up their sentence anymore, and most of the dastardly acts he'd perpetrated weren't all that felonious in the Texarkana Confederacy. Three weeks ago, the Free Provisional Assembly had repealed the Rip Van Winkle Food Corporation's tax-exempt status, on the grounds that private enterprise should undertake the storage of dangerous criminals out of a sense of civic duty, or not at all. The clerks were supposed to check his vitals, pump him full of glucose and Relaxon, chat him up a bit about current events and turn him loose.

For thirty-five years, Rydell Peabody lives in an eternal instant of half-sleep. His body floats on the meniscus of 0 Kelvin degrees, icy molecules from the heart of a comet, a snowman-Waco giving the world the finger.

But fast food cryogenics, like most street-level technology, is far from an exact science; nobody has been home for quite some time, but the lights in Waco's attic still burn. His brain, suspended in a quantum temperature barrier, is kept just a few degrees warmer, enough for the crystalline gray matter to conduct electrical impulses, but not to secrete chemical reactions to them. Corpsicle Waco is a tuning fork, mutely resonating to the supernova of molecular activity outside. The constant, keening vibration of single hydrogen molecules sublimating out of the microscopic chinks in his freezer roars through his helpless brain like tinnitus at rock-concert volume. The subsonic aberrance of atomic piles and shake mixers, the subliminal tremors of wireless (D'y'all want Soylent Grits with that?)microphone chatter, the feedback loop of the last visual impression of his warm life–a button on the bulletproof vest of the Governor as he gave Waco a final thumbs-up (DON'T MESS WITH TEXAS) -- would have driven a rational man to kill everything that moved, and Waco wouldn't be here at all if he was a rational man.

As it turned out, Waco couldn't suck air on his own, let alone defenestrate anybody. Not that he wasn't pissed off. The teenaged fry-jerk stammered out that, by Texarkana law, Waco's face and hands had been tattooed with a numeric barcode, so the world would see him for what he was. The other jerk stood facing the wall, because he hadn't been trained to use the prod, and he'd fogged up his face-shield too much to find the ON switch.

And when the shuddering punk had hosed off his layers of necrotized skin, he squeaked, "Oh, Jesus on a Cheez-It." They showed him a mirror, then backed off. Jesus on a snack cracker didn't begin to do justice to what he saw.

Waco wasn't so out of it that he didn't recognize the telltale signs that somewhere on his long sojourn of frosty penance, he'd been thawed and organ-jacked. A wiggly T of puckered scar tissue graced his torso like the initial of a superhero, the crudely stapled folds bleeding as they hadn't been allowed to after the operation. "X-ray me right now! Some balls gonna boil, I tell you what!"

The snapshots showed the sleek silhouette of a suite of Sony surrogate organ modules where his God-given innards once were. Where Waco's sick little heart once pumped black blood through his villainous veins was a piece of Tupperware with "Hecho En Mexico" stamped on it. Only his lower GI tract was still organic.

Balls boiled.

Waco walked out on the streets, bound and determined to mess with Texas.

He had steeled himself for the love/hate of his hometown, for the mixed signals born victims broadcast to predators. He found no parades of protestors, no paparazzi lurking behind the polystyrene golem of Rip Van Winkle, no hard-bitten County mounties waiting to escort him to the city limit.

JIGSAW NATION

A convoy of monster trucks waited at the drive-thru window for baskets of flash-fried mystery vittles. In about an hour, the automated counter service would run out of food and the two teenagers would be missed, but by then the customers would have eaten the evidence.

Before he got to cooking, Waco persuaded the punks to open his file and, sure enough, he'd been shucked out and shipped to a hospital ten years ago by order of Webley S. Harpending, his lawyer. Not the state, but his very own lawyer.

The Tupperware-guts thing stuck in his craw, but still and all, there was a lot to be thankful for. After thirty-five years, Waco was out, not a day older than when the governor threw the switch. The judges, the lawyers and the shrinks were dead or rotting in retirement homes, and Waco was still big as life and breathing their air. But after a sentence of dreaming the dreams of a TV dinner, Waco's sense of purpose was a little fuzzy. He needed to sit down and wrangle things into perspective.

The road before him was an Interstate twenty miles outside of Waco, a nice idea that served its purpose when taxes were collected to maintain and patrol them, and there were places outside of Texas and Arkansas worth driving to. Now, the highway was nothing but a vague arroyo of gray pebbles, smashed to moon dust by the wheeled cruise missiles that rode it. Apparently, when the national infrastructure folded, people had sunk their tax savings in vehicles that could drive on the surface of the sun without getting a flat, and let the roads be damned.

On the corner, a good old boy sat in a lawn chair beside a sign that touted the slips of paper in his hands as Star Tour Maps. He had stumps for legs, and a cap with DISABLED WAR VET–2ND BATTLE OF NEW ORLEANS on it.

Waco bought a map with the fifty cents the manager of Rip's was ordered by state law to give him to make his way in the world. He scanned it once--something stank.

He commenced to gritting and throbbing when he saw that his daddy's trailer, where he'd flossed the smegmatic folds of his parents' flabby necks with monofilial wire from his junior high shop class, wasn't even designated. "This is no damn good. Whycome you ain't got my house on here? This thing's historically nearsighted as all hell."

"If'n you know where y'all lives, y'all don't need the map, do ya?"

"Don't you know who I am?" He clutched the front of his Rip Van Winkle foil hospital johnny, which he still wore, since they no longer had his clothes. "I'm Waco Peabody, you dumb suck."

The good old boy blinked. "Who?"

"Why you no-account charlatan," Waco growled, hoisting the hapless vendor up with blue fists still freaking with cryogenic ague. The good old boy's ass was so fat the lawn chair stuck on it, pointing into the sky like an antenna trying to get a pirate shitkicker station. Waco lofted him, fat ass, stumps, lawn chair and all, into the path of a Desert Stormer motorhome that bore him away for a few miles before the windshield wipers sensed the drag and scraped him off.

Waco sat on the curb behind the sign and, with a ballpoint pen from the gutter, colored his house in on each and every map in the vendor's stack. There was no space to pen even a thumbnail synopsis of his epic saga of woeful misguidedness, so he settled for scrawling in, "Birthplace of Waco Peabody, THE most feared mass murderer of the 21st century." He managed to sell four maps to passing tourists while he corrected them, but nobody would cough up a dollar to have their picture taken with him. He brooded as he ate the sloppy-joe he'd made for himself out of the less stringy of the two fry-jerks.

A white van stopped at the light on Waco's corner. He goggled at its porcupine array of antennae, at gun-turrets and blisters of blowback armor and a refrigerator unit sticking off the side like a limpet mine. Under the logo of a hot rod wheelchair, it said PIKE'S PARAMILITARY AMBUNAUGHT SERVICE.

If anyone knew where Waco's guts went, it'd be doctors. Waco got up and sidled around to the driver's side, rapped on the opaque panel where a window should be, and struck a suitably fetching roadkill pose.

"Whattayawant?" a voice painfully like the drive-thru intercom crackled from the speaker on the roof.

With his hand up over the tattoo on his cheek, he grumbled, "Say, buddy, can you roll down yer window? I need help."

"Are you injured?"

"Yeah, man, I think I got a busted kidney."

"How's the other one?"

"Good as gold, I reckon. Say, anybody in there?" The back of the ambunaught dropped open and a paramedic wheeled a gurney out. He lay Waco on it and trundled him into the van and they took off, sirens blaring.

The paramedic palpated and probed Waco's abdomen, his face wrinkled with confusion. He pressed a cold stethoscope against Waco's chest, frowned, then pulled back Waco's smock. "Jordy, stop the van! This sumbitch is plastic!"

Waco caught the paramedic's hand before it could get the trank gun from his belt, and bent it six different ways before giving it back.

JIGSAW NATION

The van stopped on a dime. The paramedic's howls were cut short as he kissed the bulkhead, leaving Waco free to reach into the cockpit and take hold of the driver's neck. The individual vertebrae grated between Waco's fingers, stopping the driver's frantic jabbing at the Emergency Send button on his radio.

"Stop that, or I'll kill you before I want to. That'll piss me off even more, an' I'll have to go after your family just to get some closure."

"I don't wanna die, mister–"

"Fine, Jordy, is it? Well, I just got sprung out the freezer, an' I'm a little weak in the head, so I'll cut you a deal. If you wanna help out–"

"I wanna help, I wanna–"

He squeezed the neck bones like hot craps dice. "Don't talk while I'm issuin' an ultimatum. Where was I? Oh yeah, I need to know some things, but if you piss me off, they won't find enough of you to make a decent sandwich."

"I wanna–"

"Shut up. You know where a guy can get a set of innards, real ones?"

"Sure, what do you need?"

"Works. I need everything. I want new ones, good ones, no wetback or Oriental shit. You know two or three fellas can fix me up, don't ya, Jordy?"

"Sure. Just–just let go my neck, an' I'll drive you there, fix it up."

"Real peachy, buddy."

Waco sat back and looked over the corrected Star Map. None of the names sounded familiar, but the body counts gave him a hard-on.

The whole back page of the map had an ad for the Fields Of Freedom Theme Park. See the Battles of the Branch Davidian Compound and the Siege Of Austin Re-Enacted Hourly. The world's largest outlaw museum, the world's largest Bar-B-Q pit, rides for the kids. He sucked in air over his teeth and felt the chill of the freezer crackling inside him. At the bottom of the ad was a logo for the Freedomland Corporation; under it, he found his name was on the star map after all.

Webley Harpending, CEO
Rydell Peabody, Pres. & Chairman of the Board

The last few frozen synapses in Waco's brain thawed and started calling his favorite tune, clearer than ever, as if some muffling barrier had melted away. His resolve was naked and clean like never before.

Waving the ad in the driver's eager-to-please face: "I wanna go here."

Waco was different.

The streets were the same, the brown Brazos still flowed through town like a lazy mudslide, and the sun still fell on it like a rain of baseball bats.

Those unmistakable staples of Texan architecture--the drive-in, the church and the liquor store/gun shop--were, if anything, thicker than ever.

But something felt wrong. Maybe it was that the few mad-dog fools out on the streets were doing to each other a lot of the things that got him frozen. Maybe it was the total absence of anything like police, highway patrol or state troopers anywhere. Maybe it was all in Waco's head, but it couldn't do more than cop a feel before it got pushed out. His brain was a revenge gland, pumping kill hormones like an Alaskan pipeline tapped into the ninth circle of Hell.

Waco had been betrayed by his lawyer, by his hometown, by the criminal justice system. Sure, he'd served his time, but even they had to know he hadn't been rehabilitated. Far from it: if anything, he felt more clearly attuned to the hunt than ever. He could rape and pillage in his sleep. Had they so little respect that they'd turn him out without slapping a tracer or a parole officer onto him? Knowing he'd repay their treachery in the only coin he carried, why let him out at all?

A crackling blast of pink noise erupted from one of the blinking boxes set into the dashboard. "Oh shit," the driver hissed. "Cops." He flipped a switch on the steering column and a monitor winked to life on the heads-up display above the windshield. Sure enough, a vehicle dogged their tracks, armed for bear with all manner of crazy gadgets, but still, unmistakably, a police cruiser.

"Pike Ambie Unit 2733, this is Deputy Benteen of the Greater Waco Corporate Militia. You got a passenger, answers to the name of Peabody?"

Jordy reached for the transmitter, jerked away as Waco's foot caved in the face of the radio. Sparks spat, and pink noise went red, then dead. "We ain't talkin'."

"They gonna pull us over." His voice wavered between dread and relief. One way or another, this would all end soon.

Waco felt relief too, albeit of a very different kind. At last, somebody here knew his name. "Not if you want to live, they won't."

"They'll try to EMP us–"

"What?"

"Electromag pulse. They'll try to fry our electrics, but we're hardened against meltdown. Still, it'll scramble the navigator and the blowback armor something awful."

"Then keep driving, or the van ain't gonna be the only thing scrambled up awful."

"You don't understand. They'll carpoon us–"

JIGSAW NATION

Before Waco could ask, it happened. On the monitor, a projectile fired from a tube on the cruiser's undercarriage and filled the picture, even as the ambunaught rocked on its shocks with the force of something hitting the rear bulkhead very hard. A steel spear stuck out of the wall just below the camera, a duranylon cable trailing back to the cruiser, which was suddenly swinging back and forth on the road like a little kid trying to bring a crank-eyed mustang to heel. The ambunaught didn't stop, but it slowed down, wheels spitting gravel as the driver fought to keep speed.

"Drive faster, you geek! If you think that cop'll save you—"

The cruiser's undercarriage lit up again, this time lifting it up on a cushion of fiery dust. Pitons shot into the road, holding it fast. The cable jerked taut, and the chase became a tug-of-war. The ambunaught whipped around on the road, fantails of pulverized concrete obscuring the anchored cruiser.

Jordy fought the wheel with both hands, standing on the accelerator. Beneath them, the ambunaught's power plant throbbed and screamed in overdrive. Racks of medical equipment toppled in the back; glass shattered, sending a fresh wave of eye-watering hospital smells into the cab.

Then, suddenly, they were loose. The cruiser's pitons tore away a huge chunk of roadway, and hurtled into their rear end like a ball on a rubber band whacking into a paddle. The rearview camera showed only snow, and for a second, Waco thought they'd been knocked all the way to Alaska. Jordy fiddled with the controls until he could find a camera that wasn't smashed. The cruiser lay on its side, its nose buried in the back bumper of the ambunaught. Only its blue and red lights showed any sign of life.

"Drive," Waco said, and sat back to try to think.

Waco was startled out of his reverie by a sudden motion from Jordy. A hand waving in front of his face. He snapped it at the wrist and drove one rigid digit into the owner's right eye, all the way up to the imitation catseye stone in his graduation ring from the Brownsville Vocational Correspondence University.

"We're here," Jordy gasped, and died.

"Shit-fire, son, that's all you had to say." He pulled the keys out of the ignition and tried them on the storage lockers.

A few minutes later, he climbed out in a straw Stetson, flak vest and clean hospital scrubs. He carried some newfangled model of beltfeed shotgun over one shoulder and a paramedic's tackle box over the other. He chuckled when he saw that most of the police cruiser still dragged behind the ambunaught, like a dog on a leash tied to the bumper of a long-haul semi.

Edward J. McFadden III & E. Sedia

The ambunaught was parked in the loading zone of a parking lot that stretched all the way to Oklahoma. Evidently, his little tourist trap was quite the going affair. Noting that he was parked near the statue of Tim McVeigh, he ambled over to the ticket booth. He cut the line to the front, where a squawkbox by the turnstile welcomed him to "those thrilling days of yesteryear, when freedom was outlawed, and outlaws fought for freedom," and to please insert his credit card.

"Paramedic, buddy. Big disaster in the park. People hurt, prob'ly dead."

The squawkbox went dead. The windowless ticket booth opened up and a doughy kid's face leaned out. "We ain't heard nothin' up here. Who's hurt?"

"You, for starters." The shotgun burped and turned the ticket booth into a dribble glass. The line waiting to get into Freedomland turned tail and scattered. Waco hopped the turnstile and scooted across the plaza, shotgun raised in a standing invitation to dance. At last, he saw cop uniforms— dozens of them, sifting out of the panicked crowd like ants out of sugar. Guns trained on him, a few even took potshots at him, but Waco ducked into a knot of tourists and wove his way through their dragnet faster than you can say "human shield."

The hostage of choice, a middle-aged fatbody in a muumuu, prayed and gobbled funnel cake while he lugged her over to a souvenir kiosk. "Map of the park, please."

"I ain't got 'em here. Go back to the entrance booth... Sweet Lordamighty–" this last when the clerk looked down the barrel of the shotgun.

"Where's the head office, son? Where the big cheese hangs his hat?" Suddenly, the fat lady stopped eating and sagged in Waco's arms as some motivated security guard asked himself, *What's one fat lady more or less?* and shot her.

The bullet knocked the wind out of Waco, but the vest stopped it. Bringing the shotgun around to cover the plaza, he was startled by a booming voice that rolled over the park, freezing the fleeing tourists in a cryogenesis of perfect calm. It was the Voice that always boomed out to announce the seventh inning stretch of a desperate daylight crime. The negotiator. Rydell was in no mood to negotiate, and he made this clear by winging some guy who cowered under a bench with his ass in the air.

The voice shouted, "Rydell Peabody, stop shooting! Rydell, stop it, there's no reason for this! Leave those people be! Damn it, boy, this is a theme park, not a wild west show!"

JIGSAW NATION

"Web, you twofaced, no-account lick of shyster shit! Come out and show your face, before I kill all your guests!"

"Let me talk to him, Web. Rydell? Can you hear me? Why don't you put down the gun and come over to the office, so we can talk this over civilized-like, just like back in the old days?"

Waco had always been prey to voices in his head, voices that told him 'Kill mama,' or 'get money,' or 'hostage time,' but even as he obeyed them, he knew the voices were just that. They hadn't exercised any godlike power over him. He just liked their idea of a good time.

This voice, however, coming out of every squawkbox in the park, telling him to lay down his weapon and sit down to parley, *did* wield a godlike power over him, because it had always been the one voice in his head he tried to drown out: the one urging him to reason, the one that had been blessedly absent throughout this otherwise fucked afternoon. It was Waco's conscience, broadcasting for all to hear over the P.A., and it was not to be denied.

Waco lugged his overstuffed human shield to a door with a blinking light above it, like the voice from inside his head suggested. After scanning for an ambush, he slipped through the door, propping it open with the limp body of his hostage.

The door opened on a network of service tunnels that ran beneath the entire theme park, so the Imperial Wizard and Lee Harvey walking characters could enjoy a moment's fresh air without kids' rubber bullets plinking them in the ass. Rows of monstrous costume heads–Nat Turner, Osama Bin Laden, Al Sharpton--hung on the walls like trophies from a safari.

The corridors were deserted but for a canister vacuum cleaner at his feet. He was about to shoot it, when the vacuum spoke in the voice he hated and feared. "Waco, I know you've been through a lot, and things are very strange for you right now. I always wanted only the best for us, and I want nothing more nor less now. I want you to trust me. Follow the escort."

Waco jogged after the retreating vacuum cleaner, down into the maze of service tunnels. Fleeting glimpses of fearing, worshipful eyes flashed by as he passed into carpeted halls decorated with soothing waiting-room paintings. The escort ground to a halt before double oaken doors that swung open like temple portals as Waco rolled in SWAT-style and pointed his shotgun at everything.

The room was massive and plush, a reception hall that could have housed a tennis match, the lines of force converging on a cyclopean desk before a screen that reminded Waco of the flimsy modesty curtains on tracks around hospital patients.

A very old man in a pearl-gray suit sat on one wing of the desk, his neutral gaze on Waco and one finger poised over the Naughty or Nice buttons on the desk control console.

"Rydell, you should've come with the police escort we sent for you. It would've been a lot less trouble. But then you never could stay out of trouble." The voice came from behind the curtain. "I'm sure you remember our lawyer, Webley Harpending." The lawyer waved his free hand and nodded. Waco smelled as much confusion and desperation on the lawyer as he felt himself.

"An' you're the fella that 'personates me so good. You throwin' your voice again, or are you behind this here curtain?" The curtain retracted before Waco's grab for it, and Waco stepped back.

The space behind the desk was filled with an array of machines. Towers of blinking lights and pumping cauldrons of weird liquids reached to the ceiling and sent tubes and cables into the wall behind them. At the center of it all was an aquarium full of wires, twirling in the faint cyclonic current around a single gray blob, no bigger than half a baseball. Its shriveled folds were impaled on the wires; tiny strobing flashes flowed out of the blob in time with the pulsing of the lights. The mastermind behind the theme park, behind Webley Harpending and the skillful manipulation of Waco's sweetmeats and vestigial psyche, was a big booger.

"What the fuck are you?"

"You don't remember anything, do you? About our crimes, the trials, the sentence, any of it?"

"I 'member just fine... but right now it's a mite fuzzy. Still a lotta icicles in there, yet, I reckon. What do you mean 'we,' booger? Where do you get off pretendin' to be me, right to my face?"

"I am you, Rydell. I'm the part of you that was worth saving, the part they cut out to save me from the evil you did."

"Maybe I better explain," Harpending cut in. "When we first, ah, met, there were a lot of states fighting over the right to execute you, but the two finalists were Texas and California. Now, America was still one big country in those days, but even then, states had different ways of settling with ne'erdowells like you. California had a whole posse of psychologists with a battery of tests to decide whether you were fit to stand trial, so the Feds let them have first crack.

"After about six months, they came to a decision. They couldn't call you crazy–psychotic, yes, but you knew you were doing wrong. I had to slap a gag order on you to keep you alive that long. Then this neurologist from a big company up north came to me, saying you suffered from brain damage."

"Limbic system disorder," the booger corrected. "Our higher cognitive functions–our superego, if you will–was paralyzed whenever you became violent. EEGs showed that in your killing rage, cortical activity in me was suppressed to negligible levels, while the rest of your brain was bathed in endorphins. You were able to shut me out; thus I, as your higher consciousness, was not responsible for your bestial actions."

Highbrow talk like that made Waco see red, especially when it was coming from his own brain. He growled, "If you *was* my brain, you could've pulled back on the reins. You liked it as much as I did."

"No, Waco. It was hell being inside you. I was a hostage to your basest desires, bound and gagged whenever I tried to stop you. Every human being has a guardian, the better angels of their nature, to tell them right from wrong. A short-circuit in us allowed you to lock me up whenever you felt like it. There was no question that you had to be put down for your crimes, but the state would be committing murder if it allowed me to die with you.

"The neurologist proposed an experimental technique to separate us, and Webley got the court to approve it. They surgically removed your forebrain–me–and hooked me up to a heuristic artificial intelligence that replicated everything the rest of the brain was supposed to do. You baffled modern science by surviving without any ill effects, but I wasn't surprised. You never needed me, anyway.

"You can't imagine what that felt like. Like one of Dickens's orphan waifs, rescued from a black pit of neglect and abuse to stand in the sunlight of a loving foster home. I was free at last to build the kind of life I'd only dreamed of, but I had a long way to go."

"Back up the shitwagon, brain of mine. You said California and Texas both wanted to kill me. I don't need my brain to tell me I ain't dead, and I sure as shit ain't in California. What gives?"

Webley Harpending cut in again. "Mr. Peabody hasn't been told too much about that. After he was removed from you, the state of California couldn't go and kill you, so they extradited you back to Texas to do their dirty work for them, right before the war. That's where I pulled out all the stops. I showed that even though you were still a menace to society without higher brain functions, that as the body of the unfortunate Mr. Peabody, you were property. The state could keep you off the streets, but they couldn't destroy you. So they froze you."

The brain made a throatless noise and retook the floor. "Web and the software company saw that I was tutored back to normal capacity, and I just kept going. Without a body and all its sick desires to fulfill, my potential was unlimited. But my upkeep was expensive, and after the software company had wrung all the publicity they could out of my rehabilitation, they wanted to pull the plug.

"We decided the only way I was going to support myself was by cashing in on our former notoriety, so we put together a little museum. We couldn't get the state to turn you over for display, so we did the next best thing. A VR tour of the short, bloody life of Waco Peabody, the most feared mass-murderer of the 21st century, conducted by the brain of the killer himself. A little theme park started to grow around it, and the rest is history. Over the years, we phased out the exhibits of our own shameful past, replaced with the kind of revisionist spectacle about the war that plays well out here. We became respectable."

Waco thumped the hollow plastic tub in his chest. "Somebody better tell me what happened to my plumbing, I'll tell you what."

"Naturally, startup capital for Mr. Peabody's venture was scarce," the lawyer said, "so we got a writ allowing us to harvest your organs. But the artificial set you've been retrofitted with should serve a lot longer than you'll need them."

"I saved you the stomach, because I remembered how much we liked to eat," the forelobe murmured. "It was one of the few things we enjoyed together."

"And now I'm paroled, you gonna put me in a cage for tourists to chuck goober-peas at, right?"

"I wanted only for us to be together again, Rydell. I want us to start over again. I want to be partners."

Waco's voice was choked with–God help him–self-pity. "Why? If I was such a burden to you, and you've got it so good now, why bring me back?"

Harpending took Waco's limp arm. "Rydell, artificial brain technology has come a long way since you and Mr. Peabody were separated. The lower-brain functions that once filled an entire room can now be fit into a man's skull. Your essential personality can be downloaded into new wetware, without the, ah, faulty wiring that your, um, brain has."

"He means we can be together again, Waco, just like we used to be, but as equals. You won't want to steal and kill anymore, but you'll learn there's more to life, and we'll learn to be proud of ourselves, for all the good we'll do."

Waco leaned against the desk and just let all the air out of his lungs without making a sound.

"Web didn't want me to ask you, he didn't even want me to thaw you out, and legally, I was within my rights to go ahead with the operation. But I wanted to ask you, so I pulled a few strings to get you let out. Ever since we were separated, I've felt something missing. It's black from all the evil we've done and the evil that was done to us, but it can be redeemed. I believe there's more to you than the will to hurt, and I believe you want to be redeemed too."

Waco sat very still and quiet and thought it over, for all they knew. "So I'm yours to carve up like a swayback mule, is that it? With your book-learnin' and your sob story about, 'Waco made me do it' in one breath, and how I'm your car, with no will of my own, the next. This lawyer's got your head all spun around, 'Mr. Peabody' sir, I'll tell you what. Yeah, I want to be together, again, but let me show you how it's gonna be—"

Waco kicked Harpending in the groin and lunged for the tank, unscrewing the lid as the crumpled lawyer drew a gun. "I told you he wouldn't understand, Mr. Peabody."

Waco fished around for the nodule of brain like the last pickled pig's foot in a deli jar. "You're *my* brain, you do what *I* say–"

"Maybe it's better this way, Web. So long as we're together..."

Waco disconnected the matrix of wires running into the flaccid lump of forebrain. He held it aloft for a moment as Harpending's bullets stitched his back. "Where's your fancy words now, Mr. Brain?" He stuffed the mushy morsel into his mouth and bolted it down like a prairie oyster as he slid to the floor at the foot of his brain's big fancy desk.

"Now who's smart?"

The Texarkana Confederate Assembly couldn't be bothered with another trial for Waco Peabody the mass murderer. They simply resuscitated him, pumped his stomach, made sure he understood the situation, and sentenced him to die by automated vivisection. In a feat of political brinkmanship, however, they sidestepped the unpopular execution by deporting him to the Republic of Southern California, where he weathered nineteen mandatory appeals and starred on a highly rated reality show, *Death Row Survivor*, before dying of complications from gout and cirrhosis.

The law firm of Harpending, Sawyer and Beane, as trustees of the Peabody estate, saw to it that the frozen contents of Waco's stomach were enshrined in a monument at Freedomland until the day that medical science could revive the acidic soup which was all that remained of Rydell Peabody, solid citizen and respected businessman.

Edward J. McFadden III & E. Sedia

Return To Nowhere
By Ruth Nestvold and Jay Lake

Clevis Blackburn looked down at the I-84 bridge over the Snake River. On his side of the river, the First Oregon Cavalry checkpoint was quiet, orderly, big trucks idling in a long line as bored troopers checked papers and inspected the undersides of trailers. As if anyone was going to sneak back *into* the United States.

On the other side, the Idaho side, the checkpoint was less organized, a muddle of pick-up trucks and rope lines and three or four competing militias arguing with each other and with the westbound drivers. It was "Real America" over there, as the huge banner strung from scraggly pines proclaimed from the east bank of the Snake. The town of Ramey spread out beyond, fire-blackened stretches of buildings reminding Oregon and the rest of the west coast of what the Free States had fled the previous year.

Real America, alright, Clevis thought. He'd already survived one march to freedom. Only a madman would go back and try again.

Or a loving fool.

He figured himself for a madman.

"Come on," said the guide, a *coyote* who'd spent years running bored farm boys and frustrated students, as well as slaves and dissidents, across the northern border into Canada, back when there was a United States to flee. From there they would make the arduous journey across the Yukon to Russian Aleskaya; while the Canadians had been happy to turn a blind eye on the Underground Railroad to Russia and Freedom, they were economically interdependent with the United States and couldn't afford to harbor escaped slaves themselves.

Now, since the secession, the journey was much shorter, only to Washington or Oregon or California.

JIGSAW NATION

Even so, going the other way was a curious trip, the man had told him over an egg breakfast that morning, because no one ever wanted *in*.

They'd both pretended the *coyote* didn't know who Clevis was.

A magazine cover. *The Economist*, out of London. Though England is a political and military backwater, Albion still plays hosts to some of the finest analysts and educators Old Europe has to offer.

There is a photo, digitally morphed and mosaiced into something like a cross between a Flemish masterwork and the tiling in a Roman bath. It is an image of a homely black man with a lazy eye and a missing tooth, rendered majestic by the magic of an ex-pat Japanese art director and the miracle of Photoshop. The headline reads: *The Last Slave in America*.

Clevis hates the picture, what it makes of him. He hates the headline more. If only it were true.

He is far from the last slave: there are still too many in the states that didn't ratify the Emancipation Proclamation, the states that had not seceded when it became obvious that the XXVIIIth amendment to the Constitution would not pass.

At least two of those slaves are still in the idyllically named and idyllically situated Estes Park, Colorado—an old woman and a young child.

The *coyote* passed him a thermos as they sat with their backs to a pair of boulders on the east side of the river, out of sight of border patrols. The little Zodiac raft was well-hidden in a cottonwood break down by the water below them.

"You have those fake papers?" the older man asked.

Clevis patted his shirt pocket and took the thermos gratefully. "I'm prepared."

The *coyote*'s expression told him how little the smuggler believed that.

Clevis poured himself a cup of the strong, black coffee. "You forget that I know very well what it's like over here."

The other man looked away, his gaze catching on a tumble of salvia and creosote. He spat a wad of something mildly disgusting into the dust to the right of their feet and took back the thermos. "Nah, didn't forget. Just wanted to make sure *you* remember."

Mostly Clevis wishes he didn't have to remember. Remember what had happened to Doreen. Remember Lindy sick, too ill to travel. His child, leaving his child...

No.

But he had done it, had led hundreds of slaves disguised as tourists to Rocky Mountain National Park, over the mountain passes, through desolate areas of Utah and Idaho, to freedom in Oregon.

His wife is long dead.

But her child--their child--is alive.

And still a slave.

He walked the back roads toward Boise. The Interstate might have been faster, hitch with a trucker, but a lone black man in ragged clothes would be a far more ordinary sight on the two lane blacktop. Highway 52 to 16 to 44 and on down into the big city.

The underground railroad didn't run so well in reverse, but Clevis knew names and safe houses. He didn't need to be hidden away, not for this part of the trip, but he needed places to stay. Slave hunting wasn't the business it used to be, even back during the days of his childhood on the Colorado prairies, but there were still die-hards and bounty hunters looking for darkies heading west. The political failure of Emancipation had been largely symbolic--slavery had been foundering on economics for three generations.

Now, walking east deeper into slave country, he was nobody. A nobody with papers saying he belonged to a tech combine in Longmont, Colorado, and was authorized to return home after a long-term assignment doing militia tech support near the Blue Frontier. As long as one of the three or four people in Idaho who actually read *The Economist* didn't pass by, Clevis figured he was safe enough. Thank God the Red fetish for repressing slaves extended to a lack of photo ID.

It was already early fall, and Idaho was high enough in altitude to have that slight scent of winter. Clevis' hands ached, in the bones along the back of the palm, which told him cold was coming.

An old rust-colored truck with farm plates chugged past, then shuddered to a halt on the side of the road. A thin, tanned man with iron-gray braids leaned out the driver door and stared back at Clevis before shouting, "You looking for day work, boy?"

Clevis kept walking, shook his head. "No, sir. Heading home."

"Where's home, boy?"

Clevis got closer and realized that the driver was not white, but Indian. Free, in a sense. "Colorado, sir."

"Hmm."

They met eye-to-eye, the old Indian staring intently into Clevis' face the way no white man ever would have, except maybe a cop. "I got to run over to Pocatello tomorrow or the next day. Good sight closer to Colorado than here. You help me today, I'll give you that ride."

There wasn't a graceful way to get out of this, Clevis realized, and Pocatello was at least as far as he could hope to get in two days' walking and hitching.

"What kind of work?" he asked.

"A darkie, being fussy?" The Indian laughed. "Nothing that'll hurt your hands, Mr. Blackburn."

Clevis was in the truck before the Indian's use of his name registered. But the engine was rattling and the radio was blurting some twangy Red State standard, and they were off.

A photograph. Of darkies, which is rare. Most folks won't waste film on slaves, and they're not allowed identification. There's a couple with a baby, standing in a field with mountains behind them, flat and tiny in the photo but from their shape those peaks must be tall.

Clevis remembers a fat white hand holding the photo. Folding it. Creasing it. Taking a lighter to it, and laughing when the darkie danced his agony.

He has trouble remembering his wife's face anymore. Like the photo, she is just an ashy blur to him now, a shape in the darkness that he still wakes up looking for after all this time. Clevis worries that someday he will forget her name, too, though he has never forgotten for a moment the blinding fire the love of her makes in his head and in his heart.

Fire. It always comes back to fire and flame.

In Pocatello, the Indian, Sam Edmo, dropped Clevis off at the intersection of Main and Center, an odd look in his eyes. But he had given Clevis no sign that he was with the underground railroad, and Clevis wasn't about to take the risk of betraying a safe house.

"I suggest you grow a beard," Edmo said. "Darkies may all look the same to white men, but some do look closer than others. And some even read foreign magazines."

Clevis nodded, but before he could slam the door of the truck, the Indian reached across the empty seat with a small, wrapped package, which he pressed into Clevis's hands. "Avoid Utah. And stop by Fort Hall next time you're in the area."

"Thank you, sir," Clevis said, closing the rust-colored door and stepping back.

He didn't want to open the package here at the busy intersection, so he walked a block on Center Street to Arthur Avenue and turned left. The western foothills of the Tetons loomed in the distance, and picturesque buildings from the previous century lined the street, but Clevis saw little more than the curious stares of the people who passed him.

Not enough darkies in this damned town.

A block before he reached the safe house, Clevis's steps slowed; even from this distance, it looked deserted, most of the blinds lowered despite the clouds in the sky. He turned left on Benton, back in the direction of Main, doing his best to appear unconcerned.

Was that an unmarked cop car down the street?

Clevis swallowed and forced himself to keep walking at a normal pace, when what he most wanted to do was break into a run. Pocatello wasn't safe anymore, and Sam Edmo hadn't known it either. If the Indian had meant him harm, he could have turned Clevis in himself and collected the reward.

Clevis had to get out of town, fast.

In the distance, a train whistle sounded, increasingly shrill as the train neared. The tracks were just blocks away--all he would have to do would be to find a freight heading for Wyoming.

But not Utah.

He picked up his pace, angling for the tracks, still trying to look casual for the cops who might be behind him.

A minute's walking brought the Northern Pacific coal train rattling past, hopper cars stretching in a line toward the short horizon. It was running empty toward the Wyoming mines, then. Even now, after secession, the Blue States and the Red States had interlocked economies.

If he lived so long, Clevis would find a way to end that, too.

The train was slow, moving at speeds respectful of Pocatello's dozens of grade crossings and massive switchyard. He glanced over his shoulder to see if the cops had followed him to the right-of-way. Then he ran, though it pained his ankles to scramble on the cinder ballast of the tracks.

No way Clevis would run as fast as the train, but he could run fast enough to snatch at a ladder without having his arm torn off. As long as he didn't stumble, and fall under the wheels, or get dragged by one of the hopper cars.

Then it was pounding feet and breath like hammers in his chest and one iron rung slipped by and here came the next and he leaned, grabbed and was jerked off his feet, nearly breaking his wrist as a bullet spanged off the metal of the car right in front of him.

Clevis twisted in surprise to see two men--cops? --pistols braced, trying to shoot him off the rail car.

JIGSAW NATION

It was a hopper car, with a little triangular space at the end behind the ladder, over the coupler. He ducked into the meager shelter even as the hollow metal rang with three, four more shots.

Out the other side? Or huddle? All they had to do was get in their vehicle, outrun the train, and call in to stop it.

He couldn't do anything about that. It would take several miles to halt the train, so once it started braking he would have time and places to jump.

Clevis stepped rearward, into the matching triangular shelter of the next hopper car. No more bullets drummed off the high metal sides. He swung out on the far side of the train from the shooters, scrambled up the short ladder, and rolled over the lip of the car, sliding down the riveted metal to jar painfully against the discharge doors at the bottom.

He didn't hear train brakes squealing.

Hopefully the blessed thing was going to Wyoming. He didn't recall any coal fields being worked in Utah. Copper and silver, yes, but the abundant black dust already smearing his clothes and hands testified that this was indeed a coal car.

After catching his breath and settling himself with a small prayer to the God who had long ago abandoned him, Clevis drew Sam Edmo's package out of his coat.

It was about the size of a book. Somewhat smaller and slightly thick. Though it appeared to have been wrapped for mailing, there was no address or postage on the outside.

He tore open the wrappings, prised apart the taped-together cardboard. Inside was old tissue, salvaged from some other purpose, wrapped around something small and relatively heavy.

When Clevis plucked off the paper, a medallion fell into his hand. He turned it over and over.

One side was stamped with the image of some building, surrounded at the rim by the words, "Boulder, CO Labor Exposition 2003".

The other side had a three-quarter profile of a woman, surrounded by the words, "Queen of Labor and Noble Service."

The face...

He dropped the medallion in his shock, then scrambled to recover it before it became wedged and lost in the hopper doors beneath his feet.

Memory rushed back to him, a storm of pain and regret. It was his wife's face--the blur vanishing like ash on the wind. As she might have looked if she'd lived these past five years, instead of rotting in a Colorado grave, body separated into pieces by a white man's axe in the name of posse justice.

"No," Clevis whispered, laying his head against the sloped side of the car. The rhythm of the rails made the metal vibrate, made his skull vibrate. "No."

The engine whistled then, somewhere far ahead, the cars shuddered as the train began braking in earnest for a stop.

Here, the train tracks ran right next to I-15, probably the first place the cops would be looking for him. But on the other side was the Portneuf River.

Which was still his best bet.

The right side of the car then. He scrambled to the rim of the hopper car, keeping his head low, and waited for the train to slow down enough that the fall wouldn't kill him. At the earliest possible opportunity, Clevis slipped over the edge of coal car, tucked his knees up against his chest, dropped, rolled, and ran, hoping the face on the medallion wouldn't steal his purpose and his concentration.

He headed back in the direction of Pocatello, figuring the search would be least likely there, following the river and hiding in the underbrush along the banks as much as possible.

He was in luck. After perhaps fifteen minutes crashing through bushes and trees when there was no one around to see it, and trying to walk casual when there was, he spotted a bridge ahead. None too soon. Behind him, in the direction of the Idaho border, helicopters circled in the sky above the stopped train, their orbits growing ever wider.

Helicopters for a runaway slave? The expense would be almost more than his value to the company that still officially owned him here in what was left of the United States of America, ostracized and morally corrupt superpower. He didn't want to think about what the helicopters meant, didn't want to think about the medallion in the pocket of his pants.

What he had to think about was Lindy, left behind with her grandmother in a safe house in Estes Park. Lindy, with her mother's strikingly hazel green eyes in her dark face and his own gaunt build--all achingly beautiful on her.

A girl for whom life as a slave would be an especial hell.

Clevis made the bridge without mishap and turned left, crossing as casually as he could manage, given the panic that was flirting with the edges of his mind and turning his stomach to knots. The road passed a scattering of buildings that claimed to be the town of Portneuf, luckily sleepy and unaware.

And ahead at the only intersection in sight, a rust-colored truck waited.

JIGSAW NATION

A shred of a newspaper clipping, undated and yellowed with age and creased with fold lines and wallet-grease, tacked to a cork board in a small town in coastal Oregon. The spidery, wandering hand of someone who learned to write as an adult has written in smudged pencil in the narrow white space along the side, "Estes Park Trail-Gazette." The other margin reads "C's 4rth grade gradyuashin." There's no photo of course, not on a column torn from the weekly "Colored Highlights" page.

followed by a performance that this reporter can only characterize charitably as unusual. One young man, Clevis Blackburn (of the county labor pool), recited the Declaration of Independence. It is always amazing to see a Colored person achieve such potential, even if only through rote memorization, though the nerve of the young man's teacher in allowing him to recite that particular document cannot be allowed to pass without remark. In a more seemly display of their own history, other youths in the Colored graduating class then demonstrated how a cotton gin could

Clevis clambered into the seat next to the Indian, hesitant, in fear of his life and his safety but needing the help. "Funny running into you here again, Mr. Edmo."

"Ain't it though?" The older man started the engine, peering into the sky. "Don't like the look of those helicopters."

"Neither do I."

Edmo gave a rustling noise that sounded vaguely like a chuckle. "Sorry about the misunderstanding back there in Pocatello. I thought you'd be taken care of."

Clevis nodded, smiling. If he was going to be trapped in a rust-colored pickup, there were worse people to be stuck with than Sam Edmo, with his gaunt poker face and dry humor and iron-gray braids.

The Indian turned the truck around and took the road south.

Clevis shifted uncomfortably, torn between the need for safety and the need for trust. "I thought you said to avoid Utah."

"Circumstances change." Edmo kept his eyes on the road, as if pits were likely to open up and swallow the truck. "And the more immediate circumstances to avoid right now are those helicopters in the sky to the east."

A dark child runs through knee-high grass, chasing buzzing locusts that leap skyward fast and high as any toy his granddaddy ever carved. He laughs at the mountains around him, their heads as white as anything that is good and proper in life.

Jumping over old tires and the trash of three generations of his town, he runs past a straggled grove of trees and cannons off a white man who stands, legs apart, arguing with a darkie.

In little Clevis's experience, darkies never argue. They just say "yessir" and "nossir" and look at the ground a lot.

"...going to have to--" the white man is almost shouting, but stops to scoop up Clevis.

He's never been touched by a master before, and he begins to cry.

"Hey, hey, little man," says the darkie. It's someone Clevis recognizes but doesn't know, from over at the county. That slave comes to their church sometimes, and meets with the pastor and deacons after services while Clevis's momma ladles out punch and Clevis plays in the sanctuary away from the grown-up words. He reaches to take Clevis from the white man.

"No," says the white man, holding Clevis away from his body to meet the boy's eyes. "Listen, son."

Clevis shivers.

"There's no one here. Never been no one here. Never will be."

"Yessir," Clevis mutters.

"Future's coming, boy. Never forget."

Then Clevis is off and running, but now he knows he will sneak down to the tiring room and listen to those grown-up words. Listen for the sound of the future, though even at his age he knows it will mostly be bullets and dogs.

Clevis dozed, dreaming of his wife's face in places they had never been before, of fat white men striking out medallions in order to torment him, a darkie that half the world knew. He shuddered awake as the rhythm of the tires changed.

Edmo was exiting I-15 into a town called Virginia—pride of Bannock County. Clevis caught a glimpse of a sign for US-91 toward Logan, Utah.

He must have slept an hour or more. What was Edmo doing? Not selling him out, certainly.

"Why are you taking days out of your life for me?" Clevis was going the wrong direction, after all -- the helpers dedicated to the underground railroad sent those who sought them out to the north or the west, now that Washington, Oregon and California had seceded. Or northeast, in those areas of the country closest to the states that had once been New England.

Sam Edmo gave that rustling noise again, that Clevis chose to think of as a chuckle.

"Mr. Blackburn."

"Clevis."

"Mr. Blackburn. You are nothing less than a legend in these parts. While I ain't devoted my life to The Cause, I know enough who have, and I know about you." Edmo's words were slipping deeper into a Red State pattern that stung exquisitely of old home and childhood. "Ain't so many of us would turn down a chance to participate in a legend. 'Specially not one we believe in."

Clevis dug the medallion out of the pockets of his pants. "And what about this?" Bitterness, unwanted, unneeded, crept into his voice. "Is this part of the legend?"

"Ain't got no idea what that's about, Mr. Blackburn." Edmo sighed, puffing out his cheeks. "It was give to me by Mi— someone, from the railroad." The old Indian took his eyes off the road briefly to glance sidelong at Clevis. "Someone. Who told me to watch out for you coming east. Wrong-Way Blackburn, they're calling you."

"And if it wasn't you that found me?"

"I reckon there's a million of them coins out there, Mr. Blackburn. They don't ever make just one or two."

He stared at his wife's profile. Someone wanted to make sure he didn't turn back. Had they struck the entire series, just to get his attention?

Not that he would ever turn away from Lindy. No matter what.

Edmo stopped the truck just south of Franklin, Idaho. He left the highway, followed a logging track into a stand of second-growth forest.

"There's checkpoints at the state line these days," the Indian told Clevis. "You could head east, for Wyoming, but I wouldn't without a good map and a local guide." He shrugged. "Which I ain't got either one of, sad to say." Edmo reached under the seat and pulled out a Big Chief tablet, like a schoolchild might have carried. "But I do have something for you."

He pulled down a ballpoint pen clipped to the truck's sun visor and began to write, with the quick, flowing script of someone who corresponded often and well. Clevis watched, fascinated. Words flowed from people and back to people, the true magic of the world. He wouldn't have picked Edmo to be such an enthusiastic user of pen and paper.

Edmo finished his note, signed it with a flourish, then dug in the glove box for a little leather sack. He pulled out a document seal and clamped it on the bottom of the tablet page, squeezing the handles with a clacking noise.

"Tribal notary," Edmo said with a grin, then carefully tore the page out and handed it to Clevis.

It was a handwritten ownership document, claiming Clevis as Edmo's personal darkie, under the name of Clarence Edmo. Sworn by Teton Sioux tribal law, according to the seal.

"Don't know much about Indians," Clevis admitted.

"Still got sovereignty. For now. This'll stand for anyone who isn't of a mind to tear it up and tell you they never saw it."

Clevis knew nothing would hold up before that kind of white man.

Edmo handed him a knitted cap with an Ottawa Senators logo. "Wear this, walk with your shoulders down, and for the love of God man, if we get separated, head east as soon as you can. 89 goes out of Logan toward Bear Lake, but you'll want 30 out of Garden City."

Clevis took his new papers and his hat, shook Edmo's hand, and got into the back of the truck, preparing for the border crossing as a good darkie should.

At first Utah was an anticlimax. The militia at the border looked at Edmo, barely glanced at Clevis, and waved them on.

He stayed in the back, wondering how far Edmo would take him. Could he get Momma and Lindy out as the Indian's slaves? Estes Park was a long way from Edmo's home ground. Somehow it didn't seem likely.

They drove along the edge of the Wasatch-Cache National Forest, an upland expanse of hilly pines that walked along the taller mountains beyond. It was cold in the back, but Edmo had horse blankets amid the tools and bits of tack, and Clevis wrapped himself tight and daydreamed of better, warmer times.

Despite Edmo's warnings about Utah, the state seemed asleep. The tribal seal on Clevis's papers didn't appear to impress anyone at the checkpoints they reached, but he and Edmo kept getting waved along, making up miles it would have taken Clevis days and days to walk.

There wasn't trouble again until Sage Creek Junction, just a few miles from the Wyoming border. From there it would be a haul across the high, dry southwest corner of Wyoming, then on into Colorado. Assuming they made it out of Mormon country.

Sage Creek Junction was where he learned why Utah was so dangerous.

A news story over the wire. Datelined Portland, Oregon. Headline: "Famous Abolition Activist Goes Missing." Speculation that he was abducted or murdered by Red State security teams. The theory that he's slipped back over the border.

JIGSAW NATION

Accusations of journalistic irresponsibility fly: if Blackburn is back in slave territory, the media has practically told the Red States he's coming.

The Interamerican Reconciliation Commission, meeting in permanent session in Saskatoon under Russian and Canadian auspices, promises an investigation. The highest levels of government stir into action.

In the Blue States: "Where is Clevis Blackburn?"

In the Red States: "Who the hell cares about a troublesome darkie?"

But even slaves read the newspapers, some of them.

Flat as sin but more boring, Sage Creek Junction was tawny yellow almost as far as the eye could see, all the way to where the horizon was interrupted by foothills.

And between them and the horizon to the east was a string of what Clevis had first thought looked like lamp posts and could now see were rotting corpses on display, a tribute to and reminder of Utah justice.

As Edmo's pickup neared the few rustic wooden buildings that comprised the town, the old Indian slowed to the posted limit of only 20 mph. Clevis resisted the temptation to hide under the blankets and did his best to take in his surroundings with what he hoped was a vacant stare, the knitted cap low on his forehead. He remained with his back leaning against the right side of the truck bed, knees up beneath the blankets and his hands dangling between them.

Four heavy-set men with baseball caps over closely cropped hair stepped into the road, forcing Sam Edmo to stop. The biggest of the four pushed his dirty green cap up a bit on his forehead. "Hey, Injun, that a runaway darkie you got in the back of your truck?"

Edmo leaned out of the window, one hand on the steering wheel, engine idling. "If he were a runaway, why would I be headin' east with him?"

"Yeah, why are you headin' east with him?" another man asked, punctuating his question with a massive wad of spit and phlegm in the dust between his feet and the pickup.

"Going to a pow-wow in the Ute Reservation in southern Colorado," the Indian said without blinking an eye. "Don't see any reason why I would have to do without him there."

Pow-wow. Clevis barely repressed a grimace, but Sam Edmo seemed to know what he was doing, because none of the white men blocking their truck made any sign of reacting to the silly fake-injun vocabulary.

"The Uintah Reservation is south," the first man said. "No reason to come through here to get to Colorado."

"I'm Shoshone-Bannock from Fort Hall in Idaho." Edmo shrugged. "Gotta go through either Wyoming or Utah or both to get to the Ute Reservation."

A third man in black overalls pulled out a pocket watch and flipped it open. Something glittered in the bright fall sun, the light glancing off what looked like... a medallion.

"I don't know about you three, but m'first wife's a mean cook, and today's her turn at the stove." He glanced around, eyes not resting on Clevis, who watched half-lidded from beneath his knit cap. "Any of you see any reason to hold the Injun up any longer?"

The biggest one with the dirty green hat scratched his head for a moment and then pulled the brim down to just above his eyebrows again. "Nah." He stepped back and waved the pickup through. "Have a good pow-wow, red man."

After the rest of the men moved aside, the truck started forward again. It wasn't until Clevis took a deep breath that he realized he'd been holding it.

As they rolled past the baseball-capped farmers, the one in the black overalls examined his pocket watch again, allowing the sunlight to catch the gleaming surface just as Clevis came level with him.

A medallion with the image of his wife's face, glinting in the late afternoon sun. In the hands of a redneck Mormon with more than one wife.

Who may just have saved their lives.

Once they were waved through the checkpoint at the Wyoming border, a mere five minutes after they'd left the rotting corpses behind them, Edmo pulled off at the side of the road to take a leak, and Clevis joined him.

At least even here in the Red States, a black man could piss at the side of the road same as a man of any other color.

"I hear they're lookin' harder for you now," Edmo said, shaking himself off and zipping up. "Made a call while you were in back, told 'em I won't be home for a while. My daughter said some damn liberal newspapers running stories about you slipping back into slave territory."

Just what he needed.

"Idiots."

"My thinking exactly." The Indian grinned. "At least those folks back in Utah don't read liberal Blue State papers."

Clevis rebuttoned his jeans. "Except maybe one."

Edmo headed back for the car. "Ah, you saw that too."

"I saw that too."

JIGSAW NATION

"May be good for us, you know--Wrong-Way Blackburn got himself a following. Never know when that might come in handy."

"Like it did five minutes ago," Clevis murmured. Halfway to the rust-colored pickup, he stopped. "Go back to your daughter, Mr. Edmo. If it's getting more dangerous for me, I've got no business dragging anyone else into this."

Edmo gave him a long, thoughtful look. "I'd argue with you if I thought it'd do any good at all, Mr. Blackburn. But if there's any man in these United States who can find his own way, it's you." The old Indian took a deep, shuddering breath. "I reckon if you think that's best, that's what I need to let you do."

They shook hands there, by the side of the road, and Clevis headed east and south, stepping into the long miles back to Colorado.

In the days that followed, Clevis met little that worried him. There were the ordinary kindnesses and cruelties of the road, rides given and threats offered and sometimes, rarely enough, food or a little cash.

Once or twice he thought he saw the copper flash of a certain familiar medallion, but a conspiracy of silence seemed to have settled over the Red States with respect to whatever was really happening in his life. To his wife.

She was dead.

He'd buried her himself.

What was he doing?

The mountains, the forests, the high-altitude farms and ranches and nearly-ghost towns and crumbling highway bridges gave him no useful answer at all. He was returning for Lindy. He knew that. If she'd passed away, word would have reached him. Hell, it might have been news.

He was not the last slave, after all, no matter what The Economist might call him. He was just a man. A father.

(A husband.)

Going to fetch his daughter home.

That thought sustained him past the questions and over the miles, across the southwest corner of Wyoming and, without any event whatsoever, into his native Colorado. All the hatred and violence of Idaho and Utah seemed to have melted into the studied indifference to darkies practiced by the entire American heartland.

Here, he was nothing more than mobile furniture. A tool with thumbs. A fixture that possessed the power of speech, when it was convenient for a white man to speak to him.

And he was going home.

So the miles wandered by beneath his feet, in the back of work trucks, in old cars filled with darkies willing to give a ride in exchange for news or rumors. In this manner, Clevis finally came back to Estes Park.

After crossing hundreds of miles without incident worse than some thrown beer bottles, Clevis found himself on Highway 63, walking among mountains whose names he'd known in his youth. The city of his birth sat in a sort of high-altitude bowl, surrounded on all sides by peaks already banded with snow, their arrayed ranks of sentinel pines silvered as if with age.

This was the country of his heart. Though he understood now what had been robbed from him as a child, they had never taken away the beauty in which he lived. The beauty had sustained him, the Heaven-high arch of the sky, the sweeping crags, the rolling plains in which the town nestled.

This was the country of his love, too, where he had courted Doreen in long walks through the tall grass, in a borrowed car driven carefully up the high meadows of Rocky Mountain National Park, by moonlight in the chill summers.

"What you doing, boy?"

Clevis startled out of his reverie to find himself staring at a cop. A familiar cop. A hundred yards ahead of him a cruiser idled on the gravel edge of the road, a Crown Victoria with enough chrome and lights to be its own sunrise if it were dark.

And this cop was Reggie Barnstone. White kid, his own age, used to run with the darkies on the weekends making trouble. Screwed the darkie women, too, confident no one would tell.

He had false papers. Edmo's papers. Barnstone would know exactly who the hell Clevis was, if he bothered to think through what he saw and what he remembered.

"Walking into town, sir," Clevis mumbled, watching the road. There was no point in fighting Barnstone, even if Clevis had had the strength and training.

No darkie ever bought freedom on the flat of a fist.

Then the question he'd been dreading. "Don't I know you, boy?"

Clevis held his silence long enough to be respectful, not so long as to be sass. Though sass was always what a white man said it was. "Don't reckon so, sir. I'm sorry, sir."

Barnstone dug into his pocket, pulled out a copper medallion, began flipping it from one finger to the next in a lightly-closed fist. It was a coin trick he'd had when they were all kids. Clevis never did understand why it impressed the girls so much.

He knew that medallion. And he knew Reggie was clear on whose face was stamped upon it.

"You might be from around here, boy," Barnstone said. There was a careful edge in the cop's voice now, not the flat challenge of before.

Think, man, Clevis told himself. *He's offering you a way out. Otherwise he'd already be busting your head.* "Could be, sir," he said, his voice neutral as he could make it. Then, a chance on what was really going here. "A man's memory might change over time. His history might change over time. Sir."

"Might. Might could change at that." Barnstone cleared his throat. The medallion flashed in the afternoon sun. "So... what kind of trouble would bring a man who'd long picked up his feet back here to our dusty little mountain paradise?"

"No trouble, sir." Quickly this time, step into the question. Stay ahead of him. "Just family. Not looking for nothing but a little old history. Then I'll be dust, sir."

"Dust." The medallion vanished. Into his fist, Clevis knew. Simple stage magic. "Dust is good, boy. Stay low."

Barnstone turned and walked back to his cruiser. Clevis shuffled about six paces behind, not wanting to overtake, not wanting to stand dumb as a signpost. When Barnstone got to the Ford, he tugged the door open, then turned to meet Clevis' eye.

"Be careful, Wrong-Way. More riding on this than you know." The medallion flashed again, spinning in the air toward Clevis. He caught it as the cop slammed the door. The cruiser dropped into gear, then Barnstone pulled a 'u,' spraying Clevis with gravel and more dust.

He stood, the second medallion in his hand, convinced he should just go home right now.

What the hell was going on?

In the distance, there was the familiar chatter of helicopters.

Five miles from Lindy, and they're coming for me. Damn me for a punk-ass white kid.

His daughter was not going to finish growing up in this place. No matter what.

A flash of skin in the high mountain sun, a laugh, a herd of elk, a secret smile. A few moments as close to perfect as moments can get.

Then the two white kids who stumbled upon them. Or had they followed?

They made Clevis watch. Doreen had gone somewhere far away in her mind, but she still saw the way his hands clenched at sides while one of them held him. She looked him straight in the eyes and gave a short shake of her head.

And the anger began to build.

But if there was one thing a slave learned in order to survive, it was how to channel anger.

The helicopters in the sky meant he couldn't go straight to Momma, pick them up, and head west. As if he ever could have done that.

The safest place until he figured out what to do would be where there were a lot of darkies–below-stairs at one of the many resorts nestled up into the mountains rising up on all sides of Estes Park.

Clevis pulled the knitted cap lower on his forehead and turned down Highway 34 where it curled around the north side of Lake Estes on the edge of town. The help at the first lakeside lodge turned him away with a shrug, but at the second, they let him in with hardly a word.

A young woman with high cheekbones and skin so black she looked African handed him a uniform in shades of green and brown. "The whiteys pay the least amount of attention to the darkies on garbage duty. Jim's at the end of the hall -- he'll tell you what to do."

"Thanks kindly, ma'am."

A slight smile lightened her stern features. "It's an honor helping the famous Wrong-Way. None of us want those choppers to find what they're looking for."

Clevis was slowly being overcome by a sense of awe -- where had all these people come from who knew him, knew about him, were willing to help him? How had be become a figure for people to rally behind?

Here in Estes Park, the medallion with the face of a dead woman was nearly as common as coin, and soon Clevis knew he would have a small army at his back when his preparations had been completed for smuggling Lindy and Momma away. Of course, only a few of them could vacate their posts at the Lakeshore Inn at a time, and then only with a good excuse, but slaves nowadays had a freedom of movement unimaginable a hundred years ago.

Ah yes, so much to be thankful for.

After a week collecting garbage, Clevis was nearly ready to make his move. The presence of the helicopters had diminished, and he and those who carried medallions had scouted his mother's house, counting the unmarked cop cars and noting when shifts changed and the numbers were lowest. From a distance, Clevis watched as his daughter left for school in the morning, watched and forced himself not to go to her, even though his arms ached to enfold her thin body, feel her fidgety child's warmth again.

During the long, hushed discussions in the slave quarters, they had decided to get Lindy and Momma away separately. Clarice, the stately young black woman he'd met the first day, had visited Momma already and warned her; while Clarice was getting Lindy away after school, Jim would pick Momma up to "go shopping."

Clevis was emptying garbage cans into the big bins near the service driveway when he saw a rust-colored pickup with Idaho plates pull into the parking lot of the lodge.

He couldn't help himself--he stared.

"Hey, darkie, what you doin' standin' around -- you need more work?"

Clevis dragged his attention away from the familiar truck and pulled down the brim of his cap with a deferential nod to the white supervisor. "Nossir. Sorry, sir."

The supervisor looked at him more closely. "What's your name, boy?"

"Leon, sir." There were three Leons at Lakeshore, making it one of the least suspicious names here in the lodge.

"Get back to work, Leon, or you'll end up thinking garbage is the sweetest thing you ever smelled."

"Yessir."

After the supervisor left, Clevis began to go from room to room emptying trashcans and searching for Sam Edmo. He found the old Indian in a small ground-floor room without a view.

"Having a nice vacation, sir?" Clevis asked.

"Ain't a vacation, really," Edmo said. "Need to pick something up."

"Here in Estes Park?"

"Down by the fairgrounds. Then I'll be heading back to Fort Hall in Idaho."

They exchanged a long look, and Clevis nodded. "Good luck, sir, and have a good trip back."

If Sam Edmo could get Lindy and Momma out fast, their biggest worry would be solved.

The Colored school was in the southeastern part of town, away from the desirable tourist property in the foothills and around the lake. It consisted of simple prefab units, worn and discolored with age, discards from some temporary government project but still good enough for the children of the Colored labor pool. The buildings should have been replaced when Clevis was a child, and now here was Lindy going to the same school.

The air was clear and crisp, a perfect fall day, sunny with a hint of cold. Clevis watched the door from the comparative safety of the bushes along the edge of the overgrown playground, feeling his heart wrench, knowing he would soon see his beautiful young daughter again--and this time, he would hold her and talk to her.

And put her in danger.

No, he couldn't think about that. He had to get her away, and they had done everything they could to keep her safe.

The first children were coming out of the door and Clarice had appeared to pick up Lindy, when the sound of helicopters blossomed in the sky again as three cop cars appeared around the corner, squealing to a halt in front of the makeshift school building.

How had they known?

The children who had already left the building were cowering in a small huddle, and those just leaving froze in the doorway.

Lindy.

Car doors opened, uniformed officers appeared, and there was a staccato of slamming doors punctuating the more continuous rhythm of the choppers above.

Lindy stood on the wooden plank steps of the prefab building, staring at the cops with her classmates.

Don't go to her, Clarice!

Two of the policemen scanned the faces of the kids and then moved towards the stairs while the other four stayed near their cars. They were heading straight for his daughter--they hadn't known, they were just trying to draw him out, use the most effective weapon they had on him.

They reached the stairs and one of the cops took Lindy's bony shoulder in his meaty paw and forced her down the stairs.

It wouldn't help her at all if he came out of hiding, but how could he not?

Lindy cried out, tears starting in her eyes, and before Clevis knew it, he was dashing across the playground with the scream of rage that had been choked in his throat since that day in the high mountain meadow, that day of sunlight and pain.

"Daddy!"

Handguns came out of holsters and rifles were lifted to shoulders, but Clevis couldn't bother with that now. Voices called out for him to stop, to give himself up, voices far away from the world of his daughter's tears and the white man with his hand on her, far away from the rage that consumed him.

JIGSAW NATION

As he neared the school building, the other children scattered. The cop who had been manhandling Lindy let her go to reach for his own gun, but he had barely gotten it out of his holster when Clevis tackled him.

"Run, Lindy!"

And then Clevis was rolling on the ground with the thickset cop, slamming his fist into his face, arm-wrestling him for the gun. He could hear more shouted commands, feel hands on his arms and shoulders, trying to pull him off, all somewhere outside of the haze of anger that had him in its grip. And then he had the gun, and the cop beneath him was screaming, bleeding, while Clevis pounded him with the butt, and the rest of the cops pulled him off their buddy.

His arms were yanked behind him and handcuffs clamped on. Panting, Clevis looked around.

No sign of Lindy or Clarice.

Through the fog that was slowly leaving him, Clevis felt a fierce joy, a hope he couldn't contain: his daughter had gotten away. Edmo would see to it she made it to a safe house and to freedom, he knew it.

And then they threw him to the ground and started kicking him.

He woke up in a cold cell, on a hard pallet between gray walls, every inch of his body aching. Breathing was a stabbing pain, and he wondered how many of his ribs were broken.

A key rattled in the lock and he turned his head to the door of his cage.

"Doc here to see you," said the burly guard. "Though I don't see why, since you're hangin' sure enough after what you did to Frank."

"Protocol needs to be followed," came a soft voice behind him. "And we can't make a martyr of this particular slave or we'll have more trouble on our hands than we can manage."

She stepped out from behind the guard and into his cell--and Clevis's breathing suddenly became even more difficult.

It was a white woman with the face of his wife.

"Can you take off your shirt, Mr. Blackburn, or should the guard assist you?"

Clevis was still staring, incapable of replying. Green eyes, high cheekbones, a long nose with a patrician bump on the bridge. Doreen's nose had been wider, but otherwise it was the same face except for the color of the skin.

The guard came to his bunk and yanked him up. Clevis screamed with the pain.

"Answer the doc when she speaks to you, Darkie." His breath was garlic and old tobacco.

"That was unnecessary, Mr. Gibbon," the white ghost said, her voice cool and professional. "We have to see that this man survives until his trial."

"Darkies don't need no trial," Gibbon muttered.

The doctor grimaced. "Unfortunately, this one does."

Clevis finally found his voice. "I can get my shirt off myself."

The doctor moved to his side with her black bag and snapped it open. "Good."

As he began to unbutton the shirt, Clevis thought he had promised too much. Every movement sent shooting pain through his chest, and he could only peel the shirt slowly from his aching body–and in the bloody patches, the fabric stuck to his skin.

The doctor swabbed the wounds so she could pull the material away, and he was able to see her name tag. Varin. The name of the family that had owned Doreen's parents before turning their slaves over to the Estes Park labor pool because they were more trouble than they were worth.

Doctor Varin began probing his chest with cool, capable hands, while Gibbon looked on, sullenly massive.

"Wince and cry out," she murmured near his ear.

Clevis was so surprised, all he could do was suck in his breath.

"I never knew I had a sister until she was dead," the doctor added in a whisper. "I don't want the father of my only niece to die the same way."

With those words, she prodded one of his aching ribs where the skin was mottled with bruises. It was easy enough to follow her directions; other than his scream when Gibbon yanked him up, Clevis has been holding his pain in.

"Again."

He gave another yelp, and another, as she prodded down his chest and around his back.

Dr. Varin stepped back and folded her arms in front of her chest, looking at him critically. "As far as I can determine from a superficial examination, at least half his ribs are broken. We have to transfer him to the hospital facilities in Longmont--it's a wonder a lung wasn't punctured."

Gibbon grumbled, sounding as if he was about to spit out a chaw on the spot. "Good riddance, I say."

She shook her head and pulled out a cell phone. "You heard what the chief said. There can't be any suspicion attached to the authorities where Clevis Blackburn is concerned. He may just be a runaway slave, but he's more famous than either one of us."

The guard snorted. "No justice in the world."

JIGSAW NATION

"Hello, Officer?" Dr. Varin said into her cell. "We need to arrange for transportation of the prisoner to a hospital." She paused, listening to someone Clevis couldn't hear. "Yes, that would be fine. Goodbye."

She flicked the phone closed. "A police car will be here in about fifteen minutes. Do you think you can walk, Mr. Blackburn?"

Clevis nodded mutely, and Gibbon came forward with handcuffs. Standing was a shaky business, but not as painful as breathing. The guard snapped the cuffs on his wrists and together they shuffled out of the cell and down a short corridor with cells on either side; Estes Park was too small for a large jail facility, and besides, that wouldn't be good for tourism. Clevis was dying to ask about Lindy, but he couldn't say anything with Gibbon gripping his elbow.

Another guard opened a further cage door, and then they were in the entrance hall of the small jail where the windows were larger and autumn sunlight streamed in like a gift that Clevis had to squint to accept. They pushed him down on a hard wooden bench. It was an effort just to keep sitting up straight and breathing regularly.

"Any news of the runaways?" Dr. Varin asked the guards while they were waiting for the police escort. Clevis could have gone down on his knees in thanks.

The second guard shook his head. "Best forces are on it, though. Won't be long before we get them back."

Drive far and fast, Sam Edmo, and God keep you safe.

Then there was the sound of a car pulling up in front of the building, and the guards were yanking him to his feet again and taking him outside, Dr. Varin leading the way.

Reggie Barnstone got out of the cruiser parked at the curb, sunglasses hiding his blue eyes. He folded his arms in front of his chest and leaned against the vehicle, looking every bit the mean sonovabitch.

"The prisoner needs to be taken to the hospital in Longmont," Dr. Varin said.

Reggie nodded, his expression unchanging, and opened the rear door. The guards hustled him in none too gently. The car door slammed behind him and Reggie got in the front seat and started the car.

"Forget about the dust, Wrong-Way," Reggie said as they turned east on Highway 36. "You're here for good now."

Clevis's hopes sank. For one wild moment when he saw Reggie emerge from the cruiser, he'd thought, maybe, somehow they'd arranged for him to escape and get back to Lindy.

"What's left of these United States needs the direction someone like Wrong-Way Blackburn will take it," Reggie continued. "I think you'll find something there on the back seat next to you."

Clevis looked down. Tucked into the crack where the seat cushion met the back was an unmarked envelope. He picked it up with his manacled hands and tore it open. Inside was a key.

Reggie glanced at him in the rearview mirror. "Prisoners can be a violent lot. Not all of them get where they're supposed to go."

The key fit the lock on the handcuffs perfectly, and they opened with a small click.

Clevis grinned. "How badly you need to be beaten up, old buddy?"

His one-time pal grimaced. "I knew there was a reason I shouldn't've volunteered for this job. Maybe we should just roll the car."

"Might be better. Don't know how much people will believe with half my ribs cracked."

Reggie nodded. "I'll run us into a tree. By the way, got a message for you from some old Injun. Says you should visit Fort Hall sometime."

Clevis's heart opened up like the manacles he'd just taken off his wrists. "I think maybe I'll do that."

JIGSAW NATION

The Man From Missouri
By Patrick Thomas

"I can't believe we're actually going slaving. It's like something out of the history books," said Stan, cradling his shotgun and staring out onto the deserted night streets of Wilson's Creek.

"More fun than you can shake a stick at," replied Jasper.

"And so close to home. Hell, we walked the whole way here from Pea Ridge."

"Missouri's right next to Arkansas. Why, you'd rather go all the way to Africa like the ole days?"

"Hell and damnation, I don't want to go to a whole continent of jigaboos. Bad enough they're walking around free up here with the Yankees. I just wanta thank ya for including me. How many times ya done this again?"

"This is the fourth time. Used the same towns for the last two. They haven't wised up yet. Easy as taking candy from a baby," said Jasper, grinning ear to ear. "Better. No one yells at you for hitting a negro in the face to make him shut up. This is my new calling and there's good money in it ever since the Confederacy conscripted most folk's slaves for the factories."

"Well, there is a war on," said Stan.

"In Europe, not here," said Jasper. His views on the war were well known by anyone who'd slow down long enough to listen. As far as Jasper was concerned, President Henry Ford had a soft spot for Hitler ever since he got that Grand Cross award from the Nazis back in '38. Ford was pushing 80 and Jasper wondered if the man still had all his marbles, although he couldn't dispute the man's business sense. Ford turned around the economy by using all his assembly lines and factories to supply Germany with weapons and tanks. Jasper took pride in the fact that the Confederacy had made the best armored vehicles in the world ever since the CSS Manassas and CSS Virginia helped us kick a little Yankee ass in the War between the States. Jasper just worried that Ford might decide to send soldiers over there, and the Nazis fight wasn't the Confederacy's.

Jasper got his mind back to the task at hand as he heard footsteps. "Shut up. Someone's comin'."

A large black man, well-muscled and topping out over six feet walked down the street. At first glance, his pace and gait was casual, but on closer examination his eyes seemed to be squinting as if searching the shadows for something.

As Jasper and Stan watched, they worried their prey would be too far out of reach. Despite Jasper's boasting, the streets had been barren. This was the first person they had seen all night and the path the black man was walking would keep him too far away to snatch without betraying their position. Getting caught would probably get them lynched.

Unexpectedly, the black man veered across the street directly in front of the alley they hid in. It was the opportunity they had been waiting for.

"Freeze, boy. We got a coupla scatter guns pointed at the back of your head. You so much as twitch, we'll blown your nigger scalp clean off your skull and into the next county," said Jasper.

The man froze, but his face reacted oddly, smiling for an instant so brief it barely seemed to exist before turning to stone as if he was staring into the head of the Medusa.

"Git yer hands up and git in this here alley. What's your name, boy?" said Stan, his posture straight for the first time in years, propped up by the feeling of power that came along with holding a gun on an unarmed man.

"Virgil Mullen," he responded softly.

Jasper smacked Stan in the back of the head.

"Jasper, why'd ya hit me?" asked Stan, his drawl high and whiney. The curve in his upper back had returned and his shoulders slumped forward.

"Ya don't ask him his name, cause it don't matter anymore. Whoever buys him gits to name him," whispered Jasper.

"Sorry, I wasn't thinking," said Stan.

"Big surprise. Tie his hands behind his back, rope his ankles and gag him," said Jasper, tossing the smaller man some cord.

"How's he gonna walk?"

"He ain't gonna walk until we get some more. When we're done, you can untie him and he can hoof it then."

"Gotcha," said Stan. As he started to wrap the rope around Virgil's wrists, he pulled his own hands back. They were covered with something wet and sticky that shone black in the moonlight. "Tarnation, what the hell's on his hands?"

Exasperated and shaking his head, Jasper moved closer to exam the liquid. "It looks like blood. Boy, how'd you get blood on your hands?"

"You mean spiritually or physically?" asked Virgil, the smile daring to stay longer this time.

JIGSAW NATION

The butt of a shotgun snapped up, smashing Virgil in the back of his head. The black man stumbled forward, then caught himself.

Stan's posture indicated he was more than willing to do it again. "Think you're a wise guy? Answer the question, boy or I'll give you more of the same."

Virgil held back his instinctual response and didn't lunge at the white man. "Killed a chicken earlier. Wrung his scrawny white neck in my bare hands. I guess I didn't have a chance to wash yet."

"Scrawny white..."

Jasper put a restraining hand on Stan's shoulder. "Finish what you were doing. We don't want one to git away while we're wasting time here."

Stan finished tying Virgil and the pair returned to the vantage of their hiding spots, where they waited until shortly before dawn. Not another soul came down the deserted road in all that time. Angry and frustrated at his small catch, Jasper still chose to leave rather than risk being found in the town. Under cover of darkness, they made their way through fields and forests toward safety in Arkansas. They moved at a quick pace for hours before they stopped to take a break.

"I don't understand it. The last couple of times, I came away with at least five in less time. Boy, where was everyone?" asked Jasper, pulling the gag free. Virgil ignored him, so Jasper punched him in the breadbasket. "I asked you a question, boy."

Virgil looked over at Stan. "He must be talking to you, 'cause I'm a man, not a boy."

Jasper smashed his fist into Virgil's nose. "Don't mouth off at me, boy."

"I ain't your boy. You want me to answer you, you use my name."

"No nigger's going to give me orders. I'll show you who's boss here," said Jasper, boxing Virgil's ears, then kicking him behind him legs, forcing him to drop to one knee. "You answer me or I'll break every bone in your body."

"You won't be able to sell damaged goods and that's what this is all about, isn't it?" asked Virgil.

Jasper kicked him in the ribs. Not wanting to be left out, Stan did the same. Boots bit into flesh for over two minutes.

"You ready to talk now, boy?" asked Jasper, a sadistic smile shining on his face.

Virgil's only answer was to spit equal parts saliva and blood onto his tormenter's pants. Jasper lifted up his gun butt to smash in his face, when Stan grabbed his hand.

"Look Jasper, I admit I liked the idea of an adventure and all, but I did this for the money. Ya kill him, I git nothing. What's the big deal? Use his name. This time tomorrow, he's sold and is someone else's problem."

"Fine. Virgil, why the hell weren't there any other people out tonight?"

"Curfew. People have been going missing at night, town decided to do something about it," said Virgil.

"Looks like the baby's not giving up the candy so easy anymore." Stan snickered.

"Shut up," said Jasper, smacking Stan. "What were you doing out then?"

Virgil shrugged. "I was out visiting a lady. Her husband is due back in the morning and I wanted to make sure I didn't run into him over breakfast."

Stan laughed lasciviously, but quieted at a glare from Jasper.

"Hopefully the others did better," said Jasper.

"This is the meeting place. Shouldn't they be here by now?" asked Stan.

"They're running late. We'll wait another half hour. Meanwhile gag the nigger back up," said Jasper.

An hour came and went with no sign of the missing members of the slaving party.

"We can't wait any longer. Never know when a Yankee patrol might stumble by. They'll have to make it back on their own. On your feet, boy," ordered Jasper, unhappy at the failure of his enterprise.

Once back in Pea Ridge, they headed for Jasper's barn and put Virgil in chains. The pair waited until nightfall for the other hunters to return, but they never did.

"Damn Yankees must have caught Tom and George. I told them ta be careful."

Stan asked, "Ya gonna cancel the auction?"

"Ain't got a choice. One slave ain't enough to auction," said Jasper.

"That mean I ain't gonna git paid?" asked Stan.

"You'll git yer money. Barry Jackson always tole me he'd take any slaves I want ta bring his way," said Jasper.

Virgil's eyes became more focused and his body tensed at the turn of the conversation.

"The Colonel bought most of the last batch anyway, didn't he?" said Stan.

Jasper chuckled. "All the women and about a fifth of the men. The auction just helped jack up the price."

Virgil exhaled a breath he hadn't realized he'd been holding and visibly relaxed at the news.

"You ready to be sold, boy?" asked Jasper.

"I'd prefer you sell me to your wife or your mother. They both stopped by while you two visited the outhouse. They gave me quite a ride. Told me it was good to finally be with a real man. Although they wouldn't call me by my real name either. They just kept screaming "Oh God". I guess I gave them quite the religious experience. Said they wouldn't need to go to church for a month," said Virgil.

Crimson faced, Jasper charged forward grabbing a pitchfork mid-lunge. "Yer dead!"

Stan reached out, barely stopping him from skewering the black man. "Ya kill him, you're paying me out of ya own pocket."

Jasper held the points of the pitchfork against Virgil's throat. "It would almost be worth it, but business is business. Gag him and check that chain. We'll take him over to the Colonel's at first light."

It was almost eight the next morning when they arrived at the Jackson Plantation. They had cleaned up Virgil and had only taken the gag off after multiple threats and a brief beating.

They were met at the entrance by Jackson's house slave. "Morning, gentlemen. Are you here to see the master?"

Jasper nodded. "Jacob, tell the Colonel that we brought a present."

Jacob gave a nod that was practically a bow. "Certainly. Please wait in the parlor."

The men entered the house, putting their shotguns in a rack in the foyer before entering the parlor. A few minutes later, Colonel Barry Jackson strolled in smiling and wearing the grey uniform of the Confederacy, but the smile disappeared when he saw the single black man.

"Jasper, why do I see only one slave awaiting me?"

"Barry, we ran into some difficulties. The Yankee towns are getting wise to us. They started a curfew. We think they caught the rest of the boys. We were lucky to get this one."

"No females?" asked Jackson, his voice tinged with disappointment.

"No, but certainly you haven't used up the last batch yet?" said Jasper, smiling.

"The last one gets her chance today, so I was hoping for something fresh for the weekend, because I'm heading out for Richmond on Monday," said Jackson.

"War business?" asked Stan, anxious to show he was in the loop.

"That's on a need-to-know basis and frankly, Stan, you don't need to know. What do you want for this one, Jasper?"

"Well, I knew you needed a strong hand for the fields so I brought him straight to you, without even considering putting him up for auction. I think five hundred should cover it."

"Five hundred? Jasper, have you been out in the sun too long? The highest I paid before was less than two hundred."

"But those raids had gone off without a hitch. I lost two good men on this one and I'm going to have to tell their families. I don't want to show up empty handed. Those men each deserve their fair share and I plan to deliver it to their kin."

The Colonel sighed. "I see your point. I see he's shackled like the other men." The Colonel walked up and examined the prisoner. Virgil stood rigid and staring straight ahead. "Seems strong, but he's got some attitude."

"Barry, ya have to understand these niggers have lived their whole lives with the illusion that they are the equal of white men. That kind of self-deception doesn't just up and disappear over night. Ya gotta beat it out of them."

"I guess you're right. I'll give you three hundred for him."

"Four fifty."

"Three fifty."

"What don't we meet in the middle and call it four hundred?" said Jasper.

The Colonel nodded. "Done." Stan let out a rebel yell, but fell silent as the stares of both Jasper and the Colonel fell on him simultaneously. "Jacob, please get these gentlemen four hundred fine Confederate dollars. They'll pick it up from you on their way out."

"Yes, massa," said Jacob, bowing practically to the floor.

"Oh and Jacob, bring in the girl as well."

"Yes, massa." Jacob left.

"Can I offer you gentlemen a drink?"

"Don't mind if I do," said Stan.

"Bourbon, neat," said Jasper.

"Oh, bourbon sounds good," said Stan, rubbing his hands together and licking his lips.

"Stan, make the drinks. Pour me two fingers of bourbon," said Jackson.

"I'll take three fingers. Make sure it's in a clean glass," said Virgil, speaking for the first time. As he spoke he bent down, as if he was tying his bootlaces.

The Colonel's jaw dropped. "Excuse me? Are you so very stupid or so simple that you don't understand your situation here?"

"I understand perfectly. It's the three of you that don't seem to comprehend what's happening. You crossed the line."

"Nigger, we warned you not to backtalk the Colonel. Now it's time to pay the piper," said Stan as he stepped forward with his hand raised to strike.

Virgil pulled a hunting knife out of his boot, jumped up and slashed the man's throat. Stan make a gurgling noise as blood bubbled out of his open trachea and dropped to his knees. Without hesitation, Virgil sprinted to Jasper and wrapped his chain around his captor's throat.

"Move and I'll snap your neck," promised Virgil. Looking at the Colonel, he added, "You move and I'll plant this knife in your chest up to the hilt."

"Human necks don't break as easy as a chicken's," said Jasper through gritted teeth.

"Don't I know it. What do you think happened to your friends? Well, the first one anyway. I cut the second's throat with this very knife. You were too stupid and confident to even check me for weapons because no black man could possibly be any smarter than you." Jasper lunged away, but Virgil used his chains like a choke collar and reined him in. "Take out those keys and undo these shackles, and you might live a few more minutes."

The Colonel rushed toward the parlor door, and Virgil threw the knife, hitting the officer in his right hamstring. Jackson collapsed to his knees with a scream.

"Don't try that again."

Jackson whimpered and held his bloody leg.

Virgil yanked the chains again. "Hurry up with those keys."

Jasper pulled them out of his pocket and undid the left shackle, but before he could unlock the other one the keys clattered to the floor. "You want me to get those?"

Virgil shifted the chain so he held it with his left hand, controlling Jasper as if he were a dog on a leash. "Go ahead."

Jasper bent slowly, reaching for the fallen key ring with his left hand, hiding his right as it reached for a boot knife of its own.

Jasper stabbed back trying to plant his blade in Virgil's thigh, but the black man was faster. The knife only grazed him. Virgil hauled back on the chain, throwing Jasper backwards to the ground. With his free hand he grabbed Jasper's knife hand and smashed it repeatedly into the hardwood floor until the blade fell free. Keeping Jasper pinned, Virgil plucked the knife up. The Colonel was crawling toward the door. "Freeze or I throw this one next."

The Colonel froze. Jasper tried again to pull free.

Virgil stood and dragged him to his feet.

"You don't want to do this, boy. You'll never get away with it," said Jasper.

"I still don't see no boy here."

"Virgil, you don't want to kill me."

"Sure I do. Of course you could try begging for your life."

"Please don't kill me. I got a wife and kids."

"So do I. I don't remember you caring enough to even ask about it," said Virgil.

"Sometimes I can be a little brash and I apologize for that. You'd find out I'm really a nice guy if ya got to know me," said Jasper.

"Don't have the time or the stomach for it," said Virgil as he tucked the knife in his waistband. With a smooth motion he took hold of Jasper's jaw and the back of his neck and spun it to the side and up. It made a snapping noise. Jasper's eyes got wide. When Virgil let go, his body fell limply to the floor. It took him several seconds to get the keys out from under the corpse and free his other wrist.

The Colonel cowered on the floor as he watched Virgil come toward him. Getting a hold of himself, Jackson used the wall to pull himself up until he was on his feet.

"I guess the Yankee Army found out about our planned invasion of Washington and they sent a nigger spy to capture me, huh? I knew the US wanted me bad, so I guess you think you'll be the one to bring me in? Ain't going to happen. Just how do you think you'll be able to manage to get me back over the Mason Dixon line, boy? Ain't no way I'm going to keep quiet for you. Soon as we come in hearing of a white man, you're going to be caught."

"That ain't the plan at all. And the Mason Dixon line don't come this far west, but I guess a well educated Confederate gentleman like yourself already knows that."

"You want to argue technicalities at a time like this? If capture isn't your mission, what is? You going to torture me here to try and get the plans out of me? The Confederacy trains its officers to resist torture. You'll never get me to talk before someone notices I'm missing."

"Won't come to that either. I ain't a spy."

"Then why..."

The door opened and Virgil spun, pressing the tip of Jasper's blade so it gently bit in to Jackson's Adam's apple as he watched the door.

"It's just one of the new slave girls. The one I told Jacob to get. I can get rid of her," said Jackson, his secret hope that the slave would tell someone and help would come.

A small girl, barely into adolescence, slowly walked in staring only at the floor. Jacob had discretely waited outside.

"Listen dear, come back in an hour."

At the words, she dared look up. That was allowed. When her eyes took in the scene, she received one of the greatest shocks of her life.

"Daddy?"

"Daddy?" repeated Jackson. He blanched as the reason for Virgil's infiltration suddenly became deadly clear.

"Looks like I don't need you alive anymore," said Virgil.

"Wait. The information I can give you will make you a hero back home," said Colonel Jackson.

"Only a fool wants to be a hero," said Virgil. "But I guess it would be better to know than not."

"The Japanese will attack Pearl Harbor at the same time our infantry and armored divisions hit Washington..." started Colonel Jackson.

Virgil took a pen and paper and wrote down the details.

"That's everything I know. You'll let me live now?" "Can't do that after what you did and what you were about to do." Virgil pointed at his daughter with his eyes when he spoke.

"But you promised..."

"I didn't say any such thing. Honey, please turn your head and close your eyes for Daddy," said Virgil. She did as asked, so he slit the throat of the man, careful to aim the spray away from him and his daughter.

The killing and the dying both done, Virgil wiped his hands clean on a couch before sweeping his little girl up into his arms and whispering calming words into her ears. "Everything's going to be okay now that Daddy's here."

He let her see the body, before walking into the attached bathroom.

Coming out, he used a sponge from the tub to paint a warning on the wall in Jackson's own blood.

"STAY OUT OF WILSON'S CREEK OR I'LL BE BACK."

Looking down at his daughter, he took her hand in his. "Let's find everyone else and go home."

Jacob gave the pair no resistance as they picked up all the guns in the foyer and exited. Instead the house slave walked into the parlor and saw Jackson bloody and dead on the floor. Calmly, he pocketed the four hundred dollars he was holding and picked up the bottle of bourbon, drinking straight out of the neck. He kicked his former master several times, careful not to get blood on his shoes.

Stopping only to gather a few personal affects, Jacob ran to follow the man from Missouri and his daughter to his first chance at freedom in fifty years.

The Switch
By Darby Harn

I go down to the tavern under the bluffs at seven sharp, just like the man said to. If she's not there tonight, I don't know what I'll do. I don't have any more money for the hotel, and I can't go out on the streets because of the curfew. I'll end up in jail or, worse yet, one of those camps, if they find out where I came from. If I don't find a way to get across the river tonight, I never will.

I must have crossed that bridge a hundred times as a kid, when Mom took us on trips down here in the fall to see the leaves change. Didn't take a minute. Now it's blocked on both sides by spirals of barbwire and concrete barriers. They built a wall five foot high of sandbags along the riverfront, as far as the eye can see. Gun nests everywhere. It looks like the beach front in every World War II movie I've ever seen, and this is the new border of America, right here where Iowa, Wisconsin and Illinois meet.

The government controls most of Iowa, along with more or less the entire country except the states that for some reason or another all border water; the Pacific states, a few states around the Great Lakes, and the upper northeast down to around Pittsburgh and over just north of D.C., though I haven't heard news from there now in about four months.

Atop the bluffs on the other side there's this old sign that used to sell beer, but now says in big red letters OF THE PEOPLE, the motto of the rebel states. I'm surprised the people on this side haven't tried shooting out the lights. I don't dare linger on it too long. I smile at the soldier standing on the corner, ask him if he's warm enough. He just nods, and I cross the street quick as I can. I stand outside the tavern door until I get through my coughing fit. Just gets worse all the time. I should see a doctor maybe, but I can't trust anyone here. I'll feel better once I get over and can relax for once.

I go on in. There's hardly anyone inside. I ask the bartender for my usual, not that he knows it, and as he takes my change, he nods discreetly toward a table over by the jukebox, where an overweight woman a little too big for her seat sits alone with her drink. I take my beer and wander over, pretending to look for a song to play.

"The guy behind the bar said you could help me."

She sets her beer down and looks at me a long moment, this woman the same age as my mother. It was her birthday a few weeks ago. I thought about calling. She wouldn't have answered. I should have called.

"Pick something loud and sit down."

I pick a crappy heavy metal song from the 80's and take the seat across from her as she signals the bartender for another. The chair creaks as she leans over the back of it with her money held out, and I find myself concentrating on the mish-mash of her clothes — the green holiday sweater with sequined trees, the red trucker hat with white block letters B&T something or other, and the burgundy sweatpants.

"I need to get across the river. Can you help?"

"Maybe," she says. "Where you trying to get, honey?"

"Elizabeth."

"What's your name?"

"We don't need names."

"Alrighty. Where you coming from, then?"

"You won't hold it against me, will ya?"

"You got this far."

"California," I say. "I was a student."

"You're a long way from California, honey."

"Don't I know it."

I've been hitchhiking for days. I didn't think anyone would help me if they knew I came out of California, so once I got out I made up a new point of origin every place I stopped. Vegas. Salt Lake. Denver. Kansas City. Omaha. I used the same story about family I was trying to get back to, and they took me as far as they could. Out in those infinite plains of Kansas of Nebraska, you'd never know there was a war on, save for maybe the rings of jet trails in the sky you'd sometimes see, bombers circling rebel targets.

It's a little hot in here, so I take my cap off. "Honey, you know you're losing your hair?"

I pull the cap inside out. A ball of my thin, dry hair rolls out. I pull the cap back on.

"Stress," I say.

"You must have been scared out of your mind."

"I guess so."

"How did you get out of the west?" she asks.

"Red Cross van. Going east, once you get past Barstow, it's sort of no man's land. They were driving all up and down 15, all the way into Nevada, so I volunteered."

"Is it true what they say about Vegas?"

"The desert out there looks like those pictures from Iraq, remember? When they were going down the road to Baghdad and there were smoking Iraqi tanks and trucks and bodies everywhere. That's what it's like from L.A. to Vegas."

"Good lord."

I don't know why I'm telling her all this. She could turn me in to one of the soldiers. She could just shoot me right here. I don't know if I believe those stories, though. I don't know what to believe anymore. Ever since this started, I feel like I've been sinking in quicksand. All of us. The more you struggle, the more you sink.

"And that place, I don't know, where they keep the nuclear waste out there in the desert? Didn't they—the rebels, I mean—didn't they try to capture that?"

I shrug my shoulders. "We don't get much news."

"So what's in Elizabeth?" she asks.

"My mom's funeral."

"I'm sorry."

"Sorry to hear that, or sorry you can't help me?"

"What makes you think I can help you?"

"He said you could. I just need to get over the bridge. Please. Please, help me."

She takes a swig of her beer as she considers it. "You know where the South Switch Junction is?"

"I can find it."

"Finish your beer and then walk down by there. There's some old boxcars stuck out on the tracks there. Pick one and hide inside. I'll meet you at eleven."

"What about the curfew?"

"Don't get caught."

I settle up and then leave. I don't know if I can trust her or not. She could be setting me up, but then I don't know how much choice I have, either. Choices don't exist anymore. You do what you have to do to survive, to save your country from itself, because you believe empire is not our destiny, endless war is not our destiny, because you believe that this government--this perversion of America—cannot fight both the world and itself at the same time.

JIGSAW NATION

I follow the river walk as far as I can down south of town. I pass the railroad bridge halved by mines or bombs, disemboweled rungs of barbwire fence that didn't quite do it spewing into the water below. I love trains. I wish America still loved them. One summer in college I rode the trains all over Europe. The best was Ireland, especially the day we left Dublin for Belfast. I knew we'd passed into the North without being told. The North is more colorful, I said out loud. The man across from me looked up from his game of solitaire and laughed. And how they all compete, he said.

A crown of pink clouds rings the horizon all around as the sun sets and the sky reflects the city lights, leaving only a little circle of stars right overhead. It's almost like looking up out of the bottom of a jar. I'd laugh if it weren't so sad, if this weren't happening to dozens of other cities all over the country. The river provides a natural border but in other places there are walls and fences and towers with armed men in them like prison watchtowers.

The day after we got to Belfast I went on a tour designed to show off the city, but most of all, the parts they warned you not to go. I had this fairy tale image of Ireland in my head, born out of the stories my grandparents used to tell me, but it evaporated that day. They call it the Peace Line. It looks like the wall of a concentration camp, thirty feet high, made of iron, a coil of barbwire topping the entire length of it. Gun towers on the corners. It's no even divide; the wall carves through backyards like a scar, cuts people off from the givens of a regular neighborhood--the grocery, the newsstand. It makes every trip to get supplies a running of the gauntlet. It's our little Berlin Wall, the guide said, and chuckled.

Most houses facing the wall were abandoned, except a lone one I remember, with a fence like the net protecting the crowd behind home plate at a baseball game going up over the back of the house. A line of green, white and orange flags hang from telephone pole to telephone pole, the same sequence repeated in paint along all the curbs, the palette of all the disturbing murals, but there was no color. The faces were as gray as the sky, as the streets littered with trash. A boy stood on the opposite corner of us in nothing but green shorts and dirty tennis shoes, subject for our voyeurism, our rubbernecking.

I felt sick. It's the price of empire, the guide said, sounding a little rehearsed.

What is? I asked.

Terrorism, he said. It's the only way the little guy can fight the big guy. Fleas on a dog.

I protested, saying that terrorism killed innocents. I even broke out some Gandhi I'd learned the semester before. What difference does it make to the dead, I asked him, whether they were killed in the name of totalitarianism or the holy name of liberty and democracy? You just wait, he told me. You just wait 'til it's your streets and your trains and buses and your people, you'll see what all difference it makes.

I get to the switch. No one's around. I find a little place out of the cold in one of the old rusty boxcars moored on the tracks. I climb in and try not to cough too loud. I close my eyes and wait for eleven o'clock.

"You out here, honey?"

I stand up in the dark, my legs all cramped up from pins and needles and the ugly cold. I cough and it sounds hoarse and deep, worse than before. I climb down out of the car. Now she's wearing a Packers jacket. I'd smile if the muscles in my face weren't frozen up.

"You hungry? I brought some cookies."

She hands me a stack of chocolate chip cookies wrapped in a paper towel. I devour them while she unfolds a clean and pressed army uniform from her book bag.

"Where did you get it?" I ask.

"I made it," she says, with obvious pride.

I take the uniform from her. It seems real enough. The gold buttons, the badges, all of it. The badges she says she took from a frame on the wall at the UAW. They come from Vietnam and Desert Storm, but in the dark people won't be looking all that close. I take off my coat and try to put it on over my clothes but it won't go. I take off my sweater and jeans, and shiver my way into the fatigues.

"Your color isn't good at all, honey."

"It's freezing out here."

"That's not what I mean."

"Just tell me what to do."

She hands me a badge of the American flag with a Velcro strip on the back. "This goes on your left shoulder. In your right pocket is the same, but of the rebel flag. Switch them when you get over."

"And how am I doing that?"

"Down at the switch they have a guard post," she says. "They change shifts at midnight. You walk down there and relieve the man on duty. Don't say anything. Just salute and take your position. If they make you, they'll shoot you."

"Jesus."

"Wait an hour and then start walking across. Ice is thick enough now. Should be anyways."

"You gotta be out of your mind," I say.

"You ain't a shittin'. But it's the only way. This is the shortest distance right here. Across the way on that little peninsula like is the nature reserve. If you can get across to there, you should be alright."

"This is it? This is how you help people? What do you do when the ice isn't frozen?"

"I ask them if they can swim."

"For goodness' sake..." I come all this way. Told lies to get here. What's one more? "Won't they know something is up when they come to relieve me in the morning?"

"No."

"Why?"

"My son has the morning shift."

"I- I don't even know your name."

"I thought we didn't need names?"

She's nothing like I thought. Most people I've met along the way haven't been. Makes you wonder. No. It's just that false American hospitality. Underneath it there must be layers and layers of hatred for people like me.

"Bonnie," she says. "Name's Bonnie."

"Thanks, Bonnie. I wish I had some money or something..."

"Just eat your cookies. You got a few minutes yet."

I finish off the cookies as she tells me she used to come down with her Dad as a girl when he went fishing and how no one fishes the Mississippi anymore, except for bodies. I can see the anger on her face. The gross disappointment.

"What do people say out here?" I ask. "About the war?"

"Ain't much of a war, is it? They trade a couple shots across the Mississippi every now and then, but it's just for show. Half the boys won't fly those planes. They won't drop bombs on their own people. It will end soon, you'll see."

"On your terms?"

"I don't know about my terms, honey, but I do know you guys don't have a leg to stand on."

"I don't know about that."

"You're just a couple states, separated by the rest of us. You don't even have an army, not really. You're all acting like a bunch of terrorists, if you want to know the truth. Blowing up bridges and convoys. It ain't right."

"I'm sure King George said the same thing about Americans when they dumped his tea in the harbor."

"Why bother? It's not like you all have war in you. Isn't that why you up and quit on the rest of us, you didn't want to be part of a war to protect your own selves? What are you supposed to do when someone attacks you?"

"Remain true to yourself," I say, trying to stay quiet and not let my voice rise.

"You gotta get dirty sometimes," she says, shaking her head. "Nobody wants war, I know. But you can't just sit back and let people roll you over."

"We didn't. We seceded."

"You picked the wrong fight."

"Maybe. History will decide."

"See, that's how you are. You're all content to sit back and let history decide. We can't afford to."

"Why are you helping me then?"

"I got friends over there, too. Family. It's been hard on all of us. Well. You plan on staying?"

"I don't know. Don't know if I'm welcome."

When I decided to stay in California, Mom wouldn't answer the phone anymore. Dad tried to reason with her, but she believed what 'we' were doing was wrong, and I was a traitor. I only intended to stay a while to prove my point, whatever it was, and then go home. I wanted to be with my family. But by then getting back was nearly impossible.

I can't believe it's been five years already. Seems like just yesterday Judy woke me up real early, before the sun was up, screaming hysterically, "They did it! They did it!" I'd never been to New York. I always meant to go.

We watched the news all morning and all day, as we did years before on the eleventh. It felt so much the same but worse. We thought there would be more bombs. The order to evacuate San Francisco came around noon our time, but by then leaving was impossible; all the roads were jammed. So I stayed put and watched the news. The President came on in the evening. I remember the tears in his eyes, and the fear. He kept looking off camera to someone throughout the speech, as if they were feeding him his lines. He enacted 'emergency powers'—even though he was due to step down in a few months, he said he would remain in office until such a time when he felt the crisis was sufficiently passed.

We never went to bed. Late in the night Judy got through on her cell phone to a friend of hers in Boston.

"They're all going there," she said to me, her face the same color as the TV after watching it all day.

"They who?"

"The wounded. They're just walking. She's at the hospital, my friend. She said there's not enough beds. Burn beds, you know. For the burns."

"In Boston?"

JIGSAW NATION

"In the country."

"How many?" I asked, as she handed me the phone so I could try home again. "How many wounded, Judy?"

"A million. She thinks probably a million."

The next day we let them have it. There were three bombs, I think, but we never knew for sure because that same day the president declared martial law. They gagged the news. They started rounding people up, not just suspected terrorists but the people protesting the president. The day Judy left to try and get back to Michigan someone told me we seized the oil fields in Saudi Arabia. Fear overcame us all. You were left with a dizzy nausea, like you needed to throw up but never could.

I don't quite know how it started, only that I woke up one day and a number of states had threatened to secede if the president didn't return the government to the people. He refused. There were arrests. He sent the National Guard into Chicago to quell the riots. Hundreds of people died. A few days later, I read a paper that said "NEW YORK, BLINDED AND BURNING, LEAVES UNION." And that was it.

She checks her watch. "Fifteen minutes. You gonna be alright? Think you can make it?"

"I'm tough enough."

"Oh, don't take all that too personal," she says. "I don't know who I am, saying you got to do more than you are, after coming all the way across the country like you did."

"That's kind of you."

"How long did it take you? To cross?"

"I'm not sure exactly. Week, week and a half."

"And the funeral is tomorrow morning?"

"Mm-hmm."

"They held off that long for ya'?"

I cough a little. More blood this time. "Seems like I'm just going to make it."

She looks at me funny. "Sure was considerate of 'em."

"It really was."

"Bet you'll have a lot to tell 'em all. Where all did you say you'd been to?"

"Vegas. Salt Lake. Denver. Kansas City. Omaha."

"What you'd say your mom died of again?"

I start to say, but then I forget. So I just smile. "Thanks for all your help, Bonnie. I really appreciate it."

She knows. She knows she's made a mistake by helping me, I can see it in her eyes. We all have this same look to us these days. They asked for volunteers. We all knew whoever accepted this mission would never come back. All I wanted was to get back home. They said the person who did this would end the war, save the country, be a hero. I'm dying. Radiation sickness. Heroes don't die of radiation sickness.

I hug her. I don't know why. I feel sick again. I'm afraid I've made a terrible mistake. Maybe it's just this thing I have, or my fear. It eats me alive inside. I have become the thing that created the monster I now try to kill. Does that make me one? Wars aren't fought between angels. At least wars since the first one. I am a monster. The price of empire is terror. The price of terror is choice.

"I wanted to be a teacher. I wanted to teach kids."

"You better get going now," she says. "Go on."

I let go of her and leave without saying another word and hurry down the tracks, down to the switch. The soldier stands under an old semaphore, smoking a cigarette. He's young, not even twenty maybe. He sees how sick I am.

"You're gonna catch your death out here, buddy."

"Gotta do what you gotta do."

I smile and salute him. He does the same and walks off down the tracks into the dark. I did it. Just like that. I take up his position and wait. I wish I had my coat. It's so cold. After a while I get to where I don't even feel it.

After an hour or so, I set out on the ice. I walk as softly as I can, avoiding the places where I can see the scabbed over scars of previous cracks in the ice. Under my shoes the snow makes an annoying sound like rubbing two pieces of Styrofoam together. The trees on the Illinois side get bigger and bigger. I feel so weak now. I just want to get home. It will be so nice to be home. I imagine there will be a lot of people at the funeral. Flowers and banners and me in my uniform. A flag maybe too. A hero's funeral.

JIGSAW NATION

Down In The Corridor
By Robert Lopresti

The doorbell rang at 1:24 A.M. Joe Vargas slipped out of bed as Marian shifted and muttered in her sleep.

He put on a robe, wondering what it was going to be this time. Interruptions came more nights than not, but most of them were phone calls from panicked citizens needing money, a lawyer, or a place to stay. Anyone who knew how to find his residence had to be an official visitor, and therefore someone bringing a more serious problem

He peered through the peephole and saw two soldiers in U.S. Army uniforms. They looked bored, which was a good thing. Their pistols were holstered, and that was even better.

He opened the door on the chain. "Yes?"

The shorter one–black, maybe thirty, sergeant stripes–was the spokesman. "Consul Vargas?"

"That's right."

"You're needed at T.H.Q. One of your citizens is under arrest."

"Give me five minutes," he said, and shut the door in their faces. There was no reason to let the soldiers think they could stroll into the consul's residence.

As always, his clothes were laid out in his home office so he could dress quickly and leave without waking his wife. Let Marian put off her worrying until the morning.

He left her a scribbled note and went out. Vargas was thinking about what the sergeant had said and, like any diplomat, he was parsing it out phrase by phrase.

You're needed at T.H.Q.... That was standard enough. *One of your citizens is under arrest.* Nothing surprising there.

But why not say, *A citizen has been arrested and needs you at T.H.Q.?* Because if that had been the case, it would have been a phone call, not a special invitation by soldiers.

An official had summoned him because the prisoner himself was unwilling–or unable? –to do so. Perhaps some Westerner had been beaten unconscious, and now Vargas was being brought in to hear an elaborate and unconvincing explanation. It wouldn't be the first time.

The soldiers had come in a Humvee. They held a rear door open for him, respectfully. Their good manners made him more suspicious.

Vargas remembered the first time he had been summoned like this, almost three years ago. The soldier at the door that time had leered at him and spoken with mock concern. "Sorry to bother you, your Excellency. I hope we didn't wake your husband. We just caught a whole truckful of wetbacks trying to sneak up from Mexico. They claim they're refugees headed to Fagtopia, so why don't you come down and see if any of them are your type?"

And that was back in the good old days, when the P.S.A. and the U.S.A. were officially allied in the Arab War. That battle was over now and President Jeb Bush seldom made a speech without mentioning such buzz words as "past mistakes," "indivisible brotherhood," and innumerable references to Lincoln, the restorer of the Union. You didn't need to be a trained diplomat to think he was setting the stage for a war to retake his country's lost regions.

And suddenly the soldiers had been told to be polite? Vargas smelled a rat.

The consul's official residence was a mission-style home in Kensington. To reach Territorial Headquarters the Humvee had to go south on 15, giving Vargas a night tour of a big chunk of the city. It was a view few people got these days, because the curfew forbid the roads to civilians after dark, except for those who drove the trucks that endlessly rolled goods across the length of the Corridor.

Of all the weird geographies created by the Blue Liberation–in the U.S.A. they called it the Secession, or even the Great Treason–none was stranger than the San Diego Corridor.

Washington could never have permitted the Western states to split off without holding onto a link to the Pacific Ocean, something south of Alaska. As desperate as George W. had been to settle the ever-growing riots in his homeland so that he could concentrate on his expanding war in the Middle East, he could not yield without a western port. In order to come into existence, the Pacific States of America had had to give up the four southern counties of California.

The citizens who lived there had expected to become a separate state, but instead, nine years later, they remained occupied territory. Their leaders complained bitterly about being treated like enemies, pointing out that three of the four counties had voted Red in 2004. That color was far deeper now, since tens of thousands of Republicans had moved south at the time of the Secession.

But the leaders in Washington, on the rare occasions when they responded to protests at all, simply pointed out that the Corridor was vital to homeland security, and no truly patriotic American would complain about a little inconvenience.

Vargas watched the steady line of troop carriers and oil tankers and eighteen-wheelers booming up and down the highways. Every mile or two the Humvee passed another guard tower, machine guns bristling. In some parts of the Corridor, like Palm Springs and Orange County, you could go days without seeing a soldier, but here, in San Diego itself, barbed wire and automatic weapons were facts of life.

Marian hated the Corridor, and he couldn't blame her. When they met, back in Los Angeles, she had thought marriage to a diplomat would be wonderful. Seeing the world sounded like a great idea. She was a painter, after all, and a painter could work anywhere.

But if you went outdoors in the Corridor and tried to paint a landscape you could expect soldiers to show up, demanding to see what you were doing. And possibly confiscating the work on the off-chance that that particular palm tree might somehow have military significance.

Welcome to life in the U.S.A., Vargas thought, sourly. A memory tickled the back of his head: something a diplomat named George F. Kennan said, back in the Cold War. It went approximately like this: *The worst thing the enemy can do is to make us more like them.*

If that were true than everything he saw outside the Humvee was Al-Queda's victory. Look at the fruits of 9/11: denial of legal rights to anyone the government suspected of terrorism. Cutting off public information. Torture of prisoners. Religious intolerance. Even the retreat from democracy–it was the revelation in late 2005 of massive voter fraud in Ohio and Florida that had turned the radical pipe dream of Blue Liberation into a mainstream platform.

All of these were ways the U.S.A. had taken to copying Al-Queda, in order to fight Al-Queda.

"We're here," said the sergeant.

The headquarters complex had taken over most of National City, a suburb of San Diego, convenient to Interstate 5 and the harbor. The federal troops loved the name of the town because, as one soldier had told Vargas, with a smirk, "it ain't no city, and this ain't no nation."

Once out of the Humvee, the soldiers led him to the main building, a squat and ugly monstrosity of granite. They moved faster than he liked, and he struggled to keep up.

At the entranceway he walked through the metal detector. The guard frowned. "I'll have to take that cell phone."

Vargas stared at him. "Since when?"

"Visitors can't have cell phones inside T.H.Q. That's always been the rule."

Maybe so, but it had never been enforced against diplomats before, not that he'd ever heard. Whatever was going on here, Washington didn't want it known until they were good and ready.

Vargas complained, loudly and at length, but eventually handed over his phone. If he hadn't made a stink they would have wondered why.

He hoped they would go to the Military Governor's office. He respected General Crawford, a by-the-book man who wouldn't take nonsense from his enemies or his own bosses. Vargas was sure no prisoner had ever been tortured with Crawford's knowledge or permission. Of course, the general had no control over what went on in the Homeland Security compound over in Imperial County.

But the soldiers did not lead him upstairs to the Governor's office. Instead they went straight down to the cells. The sergeant opened the door to a small meeting room and gestured for him to enter. Inside was a long narrow table with half a dozen chairs. A photograph of the third President Bush smiled down from the far wall. There were no windows.

Bill Takeshi was sitting at the table, an empty yellow pad in front of him. He leapt to his feet and greeted Vargas with a smile as broad as it was insincere.

"Señor Vargas!" he said with apparent delight as they shook hands. "How wonderful to see you again. I only wish the circumstances were better."

Takeshi was a Japanese-American man, forty and ambitious. He was prematurely gray, and his intelligent eyes sparkled behind horn-rimmed glasses. His official title was Special Assistant to the Military Governor, but Vargas thought of him as the Commissar. His role was to pass suggestions from the White House on to General Crawford, suggestions that were expected to carry more weight than orders from the Pentagon.

Takeshi was also a master at the veiled insult. Take *señor*, with its suggestion that Vargas represented a third world country, instead of four former states of the good old U.S.A.

The way to react to that kind of insult was not to notice it. "Always a pleasure, Mr. Takeshi. But before we start, I have to make a protest."

The Special Assistant looked startled. "Did those soldiers get out of line?"

JIGSAW NATION

"They were fine. But the entrance guard took my cell phone."

"Really?" He frowned in false astonishment. "They aren't supposed to do that. Rest assured I'll get it back to you. Please have a seat."

Vargas made a show of reluctance, not wanting to appear to give up too easily. But the fact was that if Takeshi wanted to stall some news, Vargas needed to know what it was as fast as possible. So he sat down.

Takeshi peered over his glasses, managing to give the impression that he was taller than Vargas, which he wasn't. "Our border guards caught one of your citizens smuggling drugs in from Mexico." He shook his head with mock patience. "As you know, we try to be good neighbors, Señor Vargas. If your people stay on I-5 all the way to your side we generally ignore whatever trouble they might be bringing with them. But some of your kids think they can take advantage of that, and we do reserve the right to stop them and check."

"Of course." This was old news. He was still waiting for the kicker that had made it necessary to send troops to his home in the middle of the night.

Takeshi leaned forward, his face so solemn that the smirk only showed in the corners of his eyes. "This *particular* citizen of the Pacific States says her name is Cindy Weisbeck."

Vargas shook his head. "I've never heard of—" His eyes widened. "As in *Richard* Weisbeck?"

The Special Assistant nodded solemnly. "She says her father is the governor of Southern California."

Of Aztlan, Vargas thought automatically. Only Uncle Sam's boys would call the new state Southern California. "I need to make a call," he said. "I want that phone back now."

Takeshi nodded. "Absolutely. But before I go hunt it down, don't you want to know what kind of drugs she was smuggling?"

His smugness made Vargas brace himself. What was it? Heroin? Crack?

The Special Assistant picked up a cardboard box from another chair and held it out. It was short and wide, about 25 centimeters on each side. Vargas took it gingerly and opened it.

Four plastic pill vials, each with a printed label from a Mexican pharmaceutical company. Each label read the same: AB87.

Sweet Jesus, Vargas thought. *Now the shit really hits the fan.*

"We found this carton hidden in the trunk of her car." Takeshi looked solemn. "As you understand, these are very serious charges."

"Was there anyone in the car with her?"

"I'm afraid not." This time his smile seemed genuinely sympathetic. "Be easier if they belonged to someone else, wouldn't it?"

It sure as hell would. "I need to make that phone call. Right now."

"Oh, yes." The Special Assistant frowned. "I'll get your cell phone immediately. You said the guard had it?"

"I need it *now*."

"Absolutely."

"And when can I see her?"

"If you'll just wait here—" Takeshi backed out, still promising the bring the phone and Cindy Weisbeck, in that order. Vargas had a feeling only one of them would be coming.

After the door shut he waited a full minute to see if anyone was planning to pop in to keep an eye on him. When no one did, he reached down and unbuckled his belt. He was then able to slip two devices out the belt's lining. They were long, narrow, and made mostly of flexible plastic.

"Good for the posture," the techies had told him when they fitted him for it in Seattle. It wasn't comfortable, that's for sure, but he had figured it might come in handy someday, and now was the day.

He snapped the pieces together and had a cell phone.

The room was almost certainly bugged, but the odds were that no one would be listening until the girl arrived. He had to take the chance.

Vargas hit button 4 on his speed dial and woke the Secretary of State of the Pacific States of America. He could hear a grunt as hands fumbled with the phone. "Locke here. 'Lo?"

"Mr. Secretary, this is Joe Vargas, down in the Corridor."

Gary Locke took a breath and seemed to come fully awake. "Of course, Joe. What is it?"

"We've got a problem, sir. They say they caught Richard Weisbeck's daughter trying to smuggle drugs in from Mexico."

The former governor of Washington let out a low whistle. "Do they definitely have her?"

"I'm in National City right now, sir. Takeshi has gone to get her. Of course, I don't know for sure that it *is* Weisbeck's daughter—"

"Of course." There was a pause as Locke thought it through. "I'll have to wake the President."

"Yes sir. You should know, they confiscated my phone. I'm using my emergency line."

"Huh. So they don't want the news to get out until they – what?"

"I assume they want to announce it themselves, sir. To the press, or to you."

"Or to Governor Weisbeck."

"Exactly. There's something else, sir. The drug she was allegedly carrying was AB87."

Another pause, longer this time. Vargas suspected that Locke was trying out a dozen things to say, and deciding none of them were adequate.

Finally he said, "You remember rule number one, Joe?"

"Of course, sir."

"It is still your main concern. Keep me informed."

Vargas remembered the first time he had heard about rule number one. It was three years ago when President Barbara Boxer had called him to the Green House in San Jose.

The President of the P.S.A. had looked tired. Rumor had it she was in around-the-clock negotiations by video, trying to settle the war in Asia that had taken up most of her first term.

"Joe, have a cup of coffee. I've heard very good things about you. You were born in Mendocino, here in Redwood, weren't you?" She offered a smile that was partly ironic and partly apologetic, something you got used to in the P.S.A. It meant, "I know that when you were born there was no state called Redwood, but we split California into two parts and we had all better get used to it."

"That's right, Ms. President. And I studied political science at University of Aztlan." To show he could also use a name that had changed. It had been U.C.L.A. when he was there. "But the Liberation happened just after I got my M.A. and I joined our foreign service."

"And for the last year you've been our deputy ambassador to Japan. Your boss speaks very highly of you, Joe. But I'm hoping to take you away from him."

He had figured it was something like that. Marian was hoping for someplace in Europe, within visiting distance of the Louvre or the Prado. "Whatever I can do, Ma'am."

She smiled. "Officially this position would be a demotion, but in reality it's probably the fourth most important post in our foreign service. Have you figured out what I'm offering you?"

He swallowed and nodded. "Consul in the San Diego Corridor."

"Exactly." Boxer sipped coffee and looked at him thoughtfully. "Why is that job so important?"

It felt strange, sitting in the office of the President, being quizzed like a schoolboy, but Vargas understood that she needed to know how much he already knew.

"If the U.S.A. wants to start a war with us, the Corridor is the easiest place to do it. There's conflict there almost every day."

Boxer nodded. "And now that it looks like their fight with the Arab States is dying down, and our problem with North Korea may be over soon–that's confidential, Joe."

"Of course, Ma'am."

"With luck, Kim Jong Il will be on trial in China within a month. They're as tired of his antics as we are. If that nuclear bomb hadn't been a dud..." She shook her head. "But if there are no wars to occupy Washington's attention they'll be thinking about ways to get the Blue Nations back."

Vargas nodded.

"I asked Secretary Locke who to select for the consulship. I asked Lou Zelaney—" The former consul, retiring because the stress of the job had wrecked his heart, so the rumor went. "Your name was at the top of both lists. You know what quality I was looking for most, Joe?"

He shook his head.

"*Calm.* I need someone who can assess a situation and give me accurate information, while not making things worse. Rule number one is no provocations, no excuses for them to start a fight."

She stood up, holding out a hand to shake. "Keep things *calm* down there for us, Joe."

Vargas had the phone back in his belt about two minutes before the door opened and Takeshi came in, followed by a young woman in prison orange, and a female trooper.

The Special Assistant gestured generously. "Miss Weisbeck, this is Joe Vargas, the consul from your government. We will leave you two together."

Vargas complained again about his missing cell phone. Takeshi promised to hunt for it as he led the trooper out. The door shut.

"Have a seat, Ms. Weisbeck." She was in her late teens. She had an expensive haircut, and careful make-up that was a mess now. She looked a little stunned, and was having a hard time keeping her chin from trembling.

"This room is bugged," he told her.

"I don't care. I've told those fascists everything already. I'm *proud* of what I did."

So it was like that. Teenage rebellion pretending to be political awakening.

Vargas turned his chair to face her and leaned forward, hands on his knees. He wanted to look like a friend, not an authority figure. "So tell *me* about it."

"I was coming up from Mexico on I-5. I thought they were supposed to let me through."

JIGSAW NATION

He shook his head. "They don't usually stop you, once they've checked you at the border, but under the treaty, they can. And of course, they identified you when you first crossed *our* border at Temecula, going south. I'm sure their satellites have been tracking your car ever since."

Her eyes went wide. Everyone had heard about what the satellites could do, but no one ever thought about them doing it to *you*. If they did, who would leave the house?

"Cindy, did they find what Mr. Takeshi told me? Four bottles of AB87s?"

The girl was starting to pout. Her arms folded across her chest. "Damned right."

He sighed. "Oh, Cindy."

"Don't you get like that, Mr. Consul. I was trying to do some good. To *help* people!"

"Is that right? How much were you going to charge your friends for each pill?"

She sat up straight, glaring. "This isn't about *money!* This is about human rights!"

He might be able to work with that. Misguided charity. "So you were going to give these pills for free to poor people in Los Angeles?"

"No! I was going to give them to doctors here in San Diego!"

Vargas felt his blood pressure going up. He couldn't blame her for the sentiment, but lord, she had no idea how much trouble she was making. "And you told Mr. Takeshi that?"

"No. But I told the soldiers who caught me." She folded her arms. "Do you know how they treat women in this country?"

Oh yes, he did. But all she knew was what she had seen on TV. "How do you think they treat drug dealers?"

She looked at him with scorn. "I'm not a dealer. This wasn't *heroin* or something."

"No. It was a morning-after pill. Which you were prepared to distribute in a country where abortion is illegal."

"It's a bad law."

"So you can do whatever you want, because you're right and they're wrong? Isn't that the way *they* think?"

"A woman's body is her own—"

"Cindy." Something in his tone shut her up. "They can send you to jail for twenty years."

She swallowed. "My father-"

"You think he can protect you because he's the governor of a state in a different country?"

"Abortion is legal there—"

"But those pills aren't. They aren't legal in any of the Blue Nations; not P.S.A., or Superior, or New England. Or Canada, for that matter. Because they're a cheap knock-off of a patented drug, and they haven't been tested properly. So how is your father supposed to ask the U.S.A. to ignore an act that would have been a crime if you did it at home?"

Her voice wavered. "I was just trying to *help* people."

"Maybe the military court will keep that in mind."

Her eyes widened.

"That's right, Cindy. You'll be tried by the people you called fascists."

The rebel was gone now, replaced by a scared little girl. "Am I really going to jail?"

"I hope not. They've made exceptions before, for first offenses. If you videotape a confession, and an apology, probably with a condemnation of abortion—"

"Daddy will kill me!"

"Your father will be thrilled to have you back. Although he certainly may break our law about spanking children."

Vargas stood up and walked toward the door. It opened, confirming his suspicion that they had been listening since Cindy came in.

Takeshi came in, beaming like a sunlamp. "Forgive me for interrupting, Señor Consul, but I have excellent news."

"Is that right?" said Vargas, waiting for the shoe to drop.

The Special Assistant nodded enthusiastically as he sat down at the end of the table. "I've talked to people very high up in Washington and explained what makes this case special." He smiled at Cindy who frowned back.

"It was a first offense, after all." He opened his hands wide. "A case of youthful indiscretion. And, let's be honest, this child has been subject to a lot of very foolish lies and propaganda from her family and her country. Wouldn't you say?"

Vargas didn't dare to disagree. Cindy seemed about to speak but he put his hand on hers. *Let the man have his little victory, if the story ends happily.*

"What was their conclusion?" he asked.

"They have decided not to press charges," said Takeshi, still smiling.

The girl burst into tears. "Thank you! Thank you so much!"

Vargas didn't believe it was going to be this easy, but he had to play out the hand. "I think that's a very wise and merciful decision, Mr. Takeshi. My government will be very grateful."

"Well, we are brother republics, Señor Consul. I think it is appropriate that the eldest brother sets a good example."

"So, if I may take Ms. Weisbeck with me, I'll see that she gets out of your hair—"

"Oh, I'm afraid we can't allow that." Takeshi allowed his face to show surprise. "Miss Weisbeck is going to be with us for a long time. Probably eight months, I'm told."

Here it was at last. Vargas felt his heart pounding. It took every bit of control he had to keep his voice level. "What are you talking about?"

"Didn't Miss Weisbeck tell you she was pregnant?" He smiled. "Oh yes, my dear. You may remember you asked to use the ladies room when you arrived here? Our tests are *very* prompt these days."

"That's not fair!" said the girl.

"Is he right?" asked Vargas.

She didn't answer but the look on her face was enough. *Just when it couldn't get worse.*

"You have nothing to worry about, my dear," said Takeshi, who was enjoying every damned bit of this. "We have wonderful facilities for unmarried pregnant women. Don't we, Señor Vargas?"

He nodded, grimly. "I've toured the camps."

Cindy shrank away from both men. "This isn't *fair.* I don't even *want* an abortion. Just let me go home!"

Takeshi shook his head. "I'm delighted if you have truly decided to do the right thing by your child, Miss Weisbeck, but if that is the case, why are you smuggling these pills?"

"She wouldn't need them for herself," Vargas pointed out. "In the P.S.A. she could have an abortion legally."

The Special Assistant nodded. "Yes, practically up to the delivery date. We know all about your laws. That's why we can't let her go home."

"You don't understand," the girl said, shaking her head. "Abortion was the first thing I thought of when I realized I was pregnant. But I figured out right away that it wasn't what I want. Not at *all.* And that made me think about all the women in the U.S.A. who don't *get* to choose. I thought about how awful it would be if the government was deciding this for me."

What they used to call a radicalizing moment, Vargas thought. *Just the sort of thing to make an overprivileged rich girl turn rebel.*

"The American government is trying to protect human life," said Takeshi, and his face was grim. "If you truly want your baby to live you should be grateful to us for being willing to take care of you."

She was crying again. "But I don't want to have the baby *here.* I want to go home. Mr. Vargas, they can't make me. You can't let them—"

Vargas barely remembered what he said after that, a string of meaningless promises that he would do the best he could. But there was no way the U.S.A. was going to let her go. They would be reluctant to let *any* pregnant teenager escape their tender care, but a Governor's daughter? Not a chance. Think of the propaganda.

But, no. They weren't after mere propaganda. They were hoping for something even better than that.

And that, of course, was why they had taken his cell phone. They wanted to tell Governor Weisbeck the good news themselves, not let President Boxer cushion it, reason with the man, keep him from doing something crazy.

Something *provocative*.

When Vargas left the room Cindy was staring at Takeshi, who was talking to the female soldier, something about a *suicide watch*. At the front door the guard handed him his cell phone, apologizing for the confusion, not meaning a word of it.

Vargas stepped out onto the stone steps of the building and flipped open the phone. The Secretary of State answered on the first ring. "Joe? How is she?"

"Pregnant."

There was a pause. Locke's voice, when it came, was grim. "The president wondered if that might be the case."

One advantage of having a woman president, Vargas thought. *It never occurred to me.*

"They're dropping criminal charges, sir, but they plan to keep her in a Choose Life Camp."

"Much better P.R. then sending her to prison."

"Takeshi made sure I heard that she was going to the Eagle Mountain Camp."

"Isn't that in the Corridor?"

"That's right, sir. Just east of the Joshua Tree oil refineries. There are hundreds of those camps all over the U.S.A., but they're putting her in one ten miles from our border."

"Of course," said Locke. "It's an open invitation to Weisbeck to try to rescue his daughter. And he's in command of the Aztlan State Troopers and the Guard..."

Vargas shook his head. The temptation, knowing the sort of indoctrination and humiliation his daughter would be undergoing, would be damned near overwhelming. But any sort of raid, much less a real attack, would be exactly the provocation Washington had been waiting for. They would have their war and the P.S.A. would have started it.

"What are we going to do, sir?"

JIGSAW NATION

"We're already doing it, Joe. The President has decided, and I concur, to carry out Plan 6."

Vargas felt as if the wind had been knocked out of him. He had to lean against the wall of the armory. *Martial law...*

"Mr. Secretary, do you really think..."

"Only in Aztlan, Joe. And not for long, I hope. If we can convince Weisbeck to step down temporarily, just until we can get this straightened out..."

Eight months, Vargas thought. *Until Cindy has her baby.*

Locke almost seemed to be pleading with him, begging him to understand the decision. "We can't leave him in charge of the State Troopers, or the Guard down there. Not while his daughter is being held in that camp. You see that, Joe?"

He saw. That was the worst part. They were absolutely right.

Within a few hours there would be P.S.A. soldiers running the Aztlan state house in Bakersfield, P.S.A. troops patrolling the streets of Los Angeles, and the president was right. It had to be done.

He gazed through the barbed wire at what was left of National City, once a peaceful suburb of a lovely place called San Diego. He looked at the watchtowers, the spotlights, and always, always, the soldiers with guns.

The worst thing your enemy can do...

Vargas terminated the call. He stumbled down the steps and found two soldiers walking toward him. *House arrest,* he thought.

But no. It was the same men who had brought him here a few hours ago–it felt like days. The sergeant frowned at him, looking honestly concerned. "Sir? Can we give you a ride home?"

Home? Vargas wondered. *Where the hell might that be?* But he followed them back to the Humvee, and into the morning of what promised to be a very long new day.

Edward J. McFadden III & E. Sedia

Homecoming At the Borderlands Cafè

By Carole McDonnell

We are sitting, my folks, my brother Charlie, and I, in the Borderlands Café in Wommack when this '32 Datsonaki drives up... and this young guy — a little younger than me — gets out. He doesn't come into the café, though. He stands beside the car, in the falling snow, talking to a woman who's half-in, half-out the door. From what I can see by the streetlight, she's young too. No more than twenty, twenty-one on the outside. But the weird thing is that she isn't white like him. Or like us. She's black, real pretty, with what looks like a baby in her arms. But neither of them is moving. They're just staying there not moving for a good five minutes like it's a showdown or something. And the snow's falling all around them.

After a while, the woman pushes the car door wider and puts both feet out the car. She does this real awkwardly, like she knows she's in a place where God knows she doesn't want to be, but for whatever reason, she's trapped and she's gotta do what she's gotta do.

And from where I'm at, a window near the café entrance, I can see that yeah, it *is* a baby she's holding, a newborn probably, 'cause she holds the tiny bundle like she's afraid she'll drop it, the way my cousin Chrysta used to hold her baby when she first brought him home.

The guy takes the gal by the waist, holds her like she'll break or shatter if the Wyoming wind even touches her face. He lifts the blanket off the baby's face, takes this quick look and smiles, then rubs the girl on her shoulder. When I see this, my chest tightens. Cause it's obvious they're together and that's not something you see in our town. Not since the secession.

Being the wife of one of the largest ranch-owners around, my mother gets involved in all kinds of Christian charities. She belongs to the Border

JIGSAW NATION

Society and the Relocation Council and has helped more than her fair share of escapees but now she shakes her head and glances up at me. "Christ, Mike!" she says. "This don't look good, don't look good at all." And, unfortunately, I know what she means.

Ma's got a nervous smile on her face. Obviously, she's trying to smooth things out between her and me by picking on somebody else. It's the wrong way to go, though. I'm still thinking about the way she and my cousin got closer and closer to each other by lighting into Nona and me. I take another sip of coffee and try to get Nona off my mind.

We're all staring through the window at the couple. Except Dad. He seems to be making it a point to look in the other direction. Dad's kind-hearted; too kind hearted, if you ask me. And he stresses out about things way too much.

"Let's hope they're just on vacation," Mom says. "Out here trying to soak up some local color. You know how those Columbia folks look at us, like we're backward or something."

Dad nods. Not because he really agrees with what Mom said. Heck, an interracial couple–a black person–ain't gonna cross the border and enter the Confederate Republic just for vacation. But I suppose Dad feels he's got to do something. And nodding is something. He's looking at me and I can just see the tiniest bit of shame in his eyes. Like he's remembering the argument about Nona and he's dying to apologize for everything that's happened... and now this.

"His hair's real short," Mom says, looking out the window. "Like our preacher's kid. That type usually have a pony-tail or something."

I don't ask her what type. We all know what she means. My brother Charlie says, "They don't look like the type to shack up together. And the way he's holding her as they come up them stairs, she's his wife all right. I keep thinking I know this guy."

I'm thinking the same thing too. Or maybe I know his family. Something keeps just almost coming to the edge of my mind; his name is on the tip of my tongue.

They approach the café's top step. Then the girl stops suddenly, turns around and retraces her steps. She opens the door of the Datsonaki, gets back in and sits down. She glances at the baby and shakes her head. For a second or two they are two silent people staring at each other in the snowfall. Then he starts pleading with her. A real tense discussion, you can tell. Cause she's shaking her head real adamantly. Like there's no way, but no way, she's gonna come into the café.

We don't see a lot of mixed couples around here, and we're not like some of the other states in the Confederate United Republic. It's not like they're gonna get killed or lynched or nothing. But it's tough just the same. And although it's weird enough that they're an interracial couple, it seems to me that they're arguing about something bigger than merely coming into this café. I don't know any blacks. You got to go to Laramie, or Cheyenne to see them. But I watch Cosby when it's on. The Confederacy ain't as bad as the folks in Columbia might think. Sure everyone's segregated, but it's all equal and the Platte County school district is pretty good about African-American History Month.

The kid says something and the gal stops talking, like what he said hit home. She shrugs, opens the car door and once again walks to the café steps.

Wommack has all of two hundred people. Everyone knows everyone else. But like I said, no blacks. There's an Indian reservation in Lander, about two or three hundred miles away. Where my ex-girlfriend Nona lives. But no other minorities. It was pretty awful after the secession and some of the whites weren't real keen on having minorities around. So the Pakistanis and the Arabs and, of course all of the blacks, left town. Some – even the religious ones—went to Columbia. Tough choice, but I guess they felt they'd take their chances.

So by now the couple's come through the door and everyone starts stealing glimpses at them. I say 'stealing' because that's what it feels like. Like our eyes are robbers, stealing their comfort.

The odd thing is how the café kinda divides itself. The middle-aged folks, those born in the early days of the secession, well, they all have this angry look on their faces. They're not making any bones about hiding how they feel about this couple intruding on their café. The real old-timers, though, the ones who lived in the former United States, they're better at not staring. Not that they want them here or anything, but they're trying to make the gal and the guy feel comfortable—after all, they must be damned uncomfortable—a mixed couple in the middle of Wommack—but this is mere etiquette. And we're all pretty uncomfortable. So the middle-aged folks are staring and the old folks keep talking to each other, staring at their coffee and out the window and at the plastic Home Interiors pictures on the wall. But we all know what's what. As for the teenagers and the elementary school kids, they can't keep their eyes off her. She's black and none of them's ever seen a black girl in person before. I mean, they watch the video music channel on bootleg satellite even although it's forbidden, and they see black people singing and dancing and talking on some of their stolen VIDS. But that ain't exactly like having a black friend down the block, is it? And I, although I finished eating a couple of minutes ago, can't seem to rise up from my table. All I can think is, "If I get up now, these two are gonna think I'm prejudiced." And God knows I'm not.

The funny thing is that the girl is staring at everyone too. She gives the entire café this once-over, a quick sweeping glance, as if we're all members of the Klan or something. I know the look; my Shoshone girlfriend was a master of it. I tell myself that if she's anything like Nona, I pity the guy. Because these sensitive minority women are definitely a piece of work. So after glaring around at everyone, this gal stares out the window. Like she's already summed us up. The guy orders for them. He doesn't look at the menu, just tells Sandy the waitress what he wants. Then he asks a question which I can't quite hear although their table is two tables away from us, but Sandy nods. She walks away and after two minutes, Yvonne, the owner walks in, shouts real loud, "Well, damn, what're you doing back from California? Married, uh? This your kid?" So there's all this hugging and kissing, and Yvonne's trying her darnedest to be friendly to the girl, but the girl's just staring out the window as if not looking at us will make us white folks all disappear. And for a moment I find myself getting angry at the girl: heck, if she hates and fears us Confederate whites so much, why the heck is she here? There're black towns she and her husband can stop at. Then I remember the lynchings that happened in the first months of the secession. They happened in places like Idaho and Iowa, not here in Wyoming. And all of the lynched weren't black. But still, I can kinda understand where the gal's coming from. So I let my anger against her subside a bit, but not much. Like I said, all these touchy minority women are all the same. And she's reminding me more and more of Nona as the minutes go by.

So then, about ten minutes later, this older couple comes into the café. They stop at the counter and give the place a searching look. I recognize them as the Garrisons who own a ranch by Wheatland. Dad turns pale. Like almost white. And his left hand's rubbing his forehead. And suddenly I recognize the guy who's been making us all uncomfortable; it's Bradley Garrison. My cousins went to school with him. And I tell myself all Hell's gonna break loose. More reason for the girl to get nervous. The Garrisons are hardliners. And Bradley bringing home a black wife is about as upsetting to them as, say, my wanting to marry Nona was to Mom. I think of the way Mom and my cousin, years of mutual anger dispelled, tore into Nona and me on New Year's night when I mentioned we were gonna get married. I still remember the hurt on Nona's face when she saw me just sitting there, not defending her. Not saying a word.

My brother Charlie looks at me, like he's looking through me. And I can tell what he's thinking, that at least Bradley is not a coward. I remember

Brad from high school. No, Brad has never been a coward. I want to say to Charlie, "If Brad's not a coward, what's he doing back here then? Don't tell me he's homesick." Cause everyone knows the United States of Columbia has started cracking down on conservative believers. And if Bradley were so gol-darn brave he'd have stayed where he was instead of escaping back here.

Marjorie Garrison looks around the café until she spots her son. Her face falls farther than the floor when she sees him. She nudges Hank, her husband, and together they walk towards Brad and the girl. And now, I'm feeling sorry for the girl. Because I know Marjorie Garrison. I know what she said about me and Nona. Me and Nona of all people, and damn, we aren't even related to the woman. Without anyone telling me, I know this gal's gonna get reamed. I feel Mom's eyes on me. She's giving me that look of hers. Like I'm still thinking about Nona or something. I turn to my brother and say, "Well, I have to go. Big day tomorrow, remember?"

But Charlie is still pissed that I allowed Nona to leave. He just sits there eating his sausage as slow as you please. And he tells Yvonne to get him a slice of apple pie topped with whipped cream.

Of course, I could get up and leave. I could take Charlie's car, let the folks drop him off. But, like I said, Mom can see through me. And she's looking at me like somehow this thing with Bradley and the girl is a mirror reflecting my own life.

So there I am watching Bradley and the girl and the Garrisons, and wishing the world would end, or at least that a hole would open up in the floor and swallow me up or something. And by now, it's clear there's some kind of war on and everyone in the café has taken sides. There's the hard-line contingent and there's the 'let me just pretend nothing's happening' contingent. Looking around at the faces, I can pretty much tell which side most folks are on. Because it's a small town. I already know how most of my neighbors think. Wommack people might like gossip. And we're all God-fearing. And many of us are racist as all get-out. But we all hate tension, especially family tension.

Hank Garrison, Brad's dad, is a born peacemaker. The first thing he does is extend his hand to hold the baby. The girl gives him a look and then reluctantly hands him the baby. Hank takes the kid and pulls the blanket away from its face. I catch a glimpse. A pretty little girl with lots and lots of dark black hair. She's got a pink sweater on and wrapped up so snug and warm. He loosens the blankets a bit, like he thinks the baby's overheated or something, and rests the little girl on his shoulder.

But Mrs. Garrison... she's got this victimized look on her face. As if the baby's some Black mugger in Denver who has not only assaulted her family, but raped it. Her arms are crossed in front of her and she stares into space as if she's waiting for an apology.

Mom turns to me. "Poor Mrs. Garrison," she says, shaking her head. "I feel for her. Brad going off and marrying someone... who wouldn't fit in here. It's sad. So disrupting to the family."

I nudge Charlie. He glances at me, says nothing, then returns to his pie.

At this time, the café TV blares on. Real loud like. I turn and see Yvonne's hand on the controls. The blare of the TV subsides as the volume is turned down but we can still all hear. The news is on. It's the African-American news channel out of Cheyenne. Separate-but-equal all the way, but it's not the news channel most folks in Wommack usually watch. All the same, the news segment is so devastating we all have to watch. Some earthquake and tsunami has killed 80,000 people in Southeast Asia. The destruction is terrible. The cameraman focuses on a weeping Hindu man. A voice-over says the man is crying for his kids who were swept away by the flood. I'm not a crybaby or nothing but seeing this guy, all I want to do is cry for him. Tears just flow down his face and it looks like the guy's never gonna stop crying. But behind me I hear someone say, "Serves them right. They have too many kids anyway. The world sure has heck ain't gonna miss 'em."

My brother Charlie rises suddenly from his seat. I grab him by the hem of his plaid shirt and plunk him back into his seat. That'd be all I need: my brother socking some guy over something that's none of his business.

"These women who seduce innocent white boys," Mom says. "Think of all the heartache they cause. Our boys are so innocent, they don't know life. And these women are so free with sex—"

"Christ, it's late," I say. "Got to get back and—"

"Get back and do what?" she interrupts me. "It's not like you do anything. Either you're at Nona's or you're sitting around the house wasting your time. You have to find yourself a purpose, son."

I don't answer her because I know she's right. It's not like I'm lazy or anything. It's more like I don't quite have a fix on my purpose yet. And certainly it's not sitting around following cows all day long.

"It's like," she continues, "our boys mistake the wiles of these women for love. They don't know you've got to share the same culture, the same race to really understand what love is. Brad made a mistake. Look what it's doing to his poor mother. If you ask me, the sooner he divorces her, the better it'd be for all concerned. He could find a good wife, a nice white girl."

Mom is nothing if not a master of overkill. I want to tell her to shut up, that I got the point a long time ago. But coming out and saying something as obvious as that would only cause trouble and make it look like we're some troubled family. And that's what this dinner is about, right? The fact that we're all one happy family with good values who all love each other. But Mom's supposed to be above all that; after all, she's the Chairperson of the regional Relocation council, but as usual she hates it when things aren't clear-cut. A white boy belongs in the white areas and a black girl belongs in the black areas and nothing's going to convince her otherwise. So even though they're obviously fugitives, she's turning the other way.

The Black anchorwoman switches to a new item: the persecution in Columbia against religious parents. It's gotten worse. In the past, Conservative religious parents were merely asked "questions" about their beliefs. If the belief or values of the parent didn't measure up to the liberal beliefs of the federal government in the UCR then the child would be taken away. Now, however, the government is doing away with the questions. Records and past deeds, are used against new parents. Their children are taken away from them within days of leaving the hospital.

I'm looking at Brad now, and feeling sorry for him. I think I know him. At least I know myself. He'd be as lost and as unhappy without his girl as I am without Nona. It'd kill him to have her leave, kill him to marry some white girl, some woman he isn't a tiny bit attracted to. And by now, I'm so mad at Marjorie Garrison, Mom, and bullies in general, that all I want to do is stand up in the middle of this café and tell them all to get a life. What the heck do they want Brad to do? Go back to a place that accepts him and his marriage but will persecute him for his beliefs? It's hard for people who don't fit neatly into categories. Wonder what Mom'll do if I marry Nona? Wonder what the local council'll do? Heck, Mom's their boss; maybe she'd lighten up, create some programs to bring the races together. But what if she doesn't? Would I want to live on the reservation? Heck, Ma might change her mind. But later, rather than sooner. And what would Nona and I do in the meantime? Be living sacrifices? Live among the whites and suffer just to prove a point?

I tell Charlie to get up. "My ass is killing me from all this damn sitting."

"You're not finished eating yet," he says.

"I didn't say I was finished. I said I gotta stretch my legs."

"Don't go hiding out in the john," he says and moves his legs to let me pass.

I start walking towards the Garrisons and Bradley and his wife. I don't look behind me because I know Mom's gonna give me one of her looks. When I reach the table, Brad smiles at me so kindly that I feel like crying.

JIGSAW NATION

"Remember me?" I say. "Mike McMasters. You went to school with my cousin, Bobby. Heard you went to some college in California. I went to UW in Laramie."

"Bobby's cousin? Yeah, I remember. How you doing?"

"I'm cool," I say. "This your wife?"

"Yeah," he says. "Jody. Met her when I went to New York."

"New York, uh?" I stretch out my hand. But she doesn't take it. She gives me one of these if-looks-could-kill stares, takes the baby and walks out of the café into the cold. Lord knows what they've gone through in New York.

"You went there to teach, right?"

He nods.

I shrug. "Guess you had to give that up, huh?"

A sigh escapes his lips as he turns to glance at the exit door. "I could take the daily mocking and sneering," he says. "Not Jody though. But the liberals seem intent on destroying us, not just our livelihood but our lives."

His mom is staring at him but she's not saying anything. Just staring as if he brought all the trouble on himself.

"I seen some of their television on satellite," I say. "Seems we Christians are all cruel, hateful, ignorant or deluded."

"A curse on the land," Brad says with a half-smile. "I don't know. I guess I thought it was my purpose to do something for our people across the border. Some guerilla fighter, I am, huh?"

"You tried," I say.

His mother groans but says nothing. Her glance passes me and darts towards my mother who sends back a reassuring nod.

"But like I say," Brad continues, "I could put up with all the emotional persecution and the cruel stuff they say about us in the media. Even when they started forbidding Bible-believers to work in teaching, medical or the legal professions. I learned to hide my faith. I went to the home churches instead of the liberal mainstream ones. But then we had the baby. Well, the minister at the church we attended–you have to attend one of them to look like you believe in the liberal agenda–well, he saw us reading a Bible together when he visited Jody in the hospital. He was gay and you know how hateful they get about the Bible. Next thing you knew the government people came trying to take—" he bursts into tears. I try not to flinch but I suppose I do just a bit. Cause it's hard to see a Wyoming guy cry. Besides he's telling me—a relative stranger—his life story. And we Wyoming rancher types just don't go crying like that. Seems like such a New York touchy-feely kinda thing to do.

"You can come on over anytime," I say. And I realize I'm trying to find some way to tell him that I'm dating a full-blooded Indian girl from the Reservation and I'm probably gonna be in the same boat as him one of these days. I gesture towards the door. "Jody can come too."

"She's kinda tired," Brad says.

"I understand. Long trip from New York. Anyway, call me when you can. We Christians are all one family." I write my name and number on a napkin. Then I walk away.

I'm getting a lot of looks from my fellow patrons. Mostly angry ones. These folks may read their Bible, but most of them are as racist as they come. But among the hateful glares, there are a few of approval, and this surprises me. Heck, who'd think one could find even one understanding heart in this place? But people have sons and daughters and life gets complicated, I guess. I find myself thinking that Brad must've had moments like this in New York City where unexpectedly he'd meet some Christian and they'd give each other some secret sign of reassurance.

Mom looks like she could kill. When I return to our table, she says, "You're trying to embarrass me, aren't you?"

And all I can think is: Mom wants me to marry someone like her. And the thought of marrying a woman who from day one has been taught that the world revolves around her pretty much sickens me. I could see my future and what I saw didn't look appetizing.

"Give me your car keys, Bro," I say. I'm looking at Dad when I say this. And he's trying to evade my eyes. But I'm thinking that maybe I was born into the world to fall in love with Nona and to help people like Brad and Jody. "You hear me, Charlie? The keys."

"Why you need them?" he says, biting into his apple pie.

"I gotta go see Nona. Gonna ask her to marry me."

At this Mom starts coughing, like she's choking on her own bile or something. But Charlie doesn't mind.

He throws me his keys. "Tell her 'Hi' for me."

JIGSAW NATION

Places of Color
By David Bartell

Delicia made a conciliatory prayer of thanks for her mixed blessing. Her son Daniel was finally imprisoned, another black male statistic. But at least he couldn't hurt anyone. Driving home from the courthouse in Philly, she felt free for the first time in years. Though her soul ached for Daniel, it was also relieved from the agonies of disempowered responsibility and disappointing motherhood.

The apartment was quiet. She lit incense and put on some Al Jarreau. Now she could heal for a while. But what to do? She could move to one of the seceded states, New Jersey, perhaps, or New York. She'd always wanted to go to Mozambique to trace her roots, but she didn't want to do that alone. Her sister had gone with her as far as Brazil, but refused to go to Africa. Who else would possibly go with her on such a pilgrimage? James? Perhaps he was back in town.

The thought of James whisked her mind from adventure and grounded it back to the domestic. They had only been on a few dates, so going with him abroad was a long shot, but she was interested in him. He might help take her mind off of Daniel. Delicia picked up the phone. The dry smell of sandalwood thickened the air, luring her away again. She bit her lip and hesitated, but loneliness won out. She spoke his name into the mouthpiece, softly, so that the autodialer would recognize the name she had trained with such warmth.

"James."

She fidgeted as the phone dialed. There was no way to make such a call without tipping your emotional hand, she decided. When she felt young, she told herself there was nothing to lose. When she felt old, she told herself the same thing, only with more urgency. At the moment, she did not feel young nor old. She just felt nervous; free, but nervous.

"Hello?"

James was back from a trip to the Republic of Hawaii where he'd been upgrading some kind of computer system, and she was elated by his enthusiasm over her call. They dined that night.

Bahia was a favorite restaurant of hers, a *churrascaria* with the Brazilian cuisine of her parents, and quiet corners bathed in flickering orange light. It was in D.C., so they didn't have to carry visas. That was the only good thing about the States refusing to let Maryland secede. James scooted her chair in for her, the thin, soothing voice of Joyce crooned in the background, and she melted into the evening.

"This is perfect."

"I haven't been to Georgetown in ages." James sat down next to her, instead of across, and smiled. "You look great."

"Please sit over there," Delicia said, "so I can see *you* better." At the moment she wanted to study him, and not be distracted by the possibility that he might try to hold her hand at some point.

He moved.

A dusky waitress arrived, continually flipping hair out of her eyes. She set a basket of cheese bread balls on the table, augmenting the ambience with a pleasant, doughy odor. "Can I bring you each a *caipirihna*?"

"No thanks." Delicia ordered red tea.

"Latte," said James without hesitation. No alcohol, a good sign. More than that—too good to be true. No HIV, no herpes, no criminal record, great paying job (even if the clients were mostly military), never married, no kids. Tall and lean, with thick eyebrows, James looked a bit like Lionel Richie. He was a class act.

"How's Daniel?" he asked.

Delicia was delighted that he remembered her son's name, but was wounded by the sound of it. "Let's save that for later."

"Oh. Sure thing."

"So how was Hawaii?"

"It's no triumph for the locals, if that's what you're thinking. The whole place is Asian, you know. They were only Blue before the split so they wouldn't have to be Red."

"Well, that comes as a surprise."

"It's just classic Balkanization. Aside from the military bases, Hawaii is becoming Third World."

"Developing World," she corrected. "But how can you stand being on a military base?"

"Tripler is a hospital. They have better health care than most private ones."

"Maryland has good hospitals."

"Of course, but again, the best ones are military. The telemedicine system I just helped upgrade is cutting edge stuff. They can monitor a guy's vitals anywhere in the world, and remotely administer drugs or even a defibrillator charge from a medipak."

"That's horrible!"

"It's a miracle. It's war that's horrible."

"Well, thank God there aren't any at the moment."

James smiled again. "Amen to that."

Delicia smiled and looked at her tea. She could feel herself blushing. So James was a praying man, it seemed. She had been comfortable with him from the start, and now she automatically shifted into a higher emotional gear.

"They just put Daniel in prison," she said.

"Oh—"

Dinner arrived, butternut squash soup and steak *rechaud* for her, a huge sampler of skewered meats for him, complete with a tabletop grill to complete the slow grilling. All to cover the awkward moment. They ate over small talk. Delicia was ready to laugh, and made sure that she did. James seemed to be having a good time too. Delicia put down her fork, and wiped her lips.

"Finished?"

"Just slowing down." Delicia was more interested in the craft of the meal than the quantity. After years of anguish, she had finally convinced herself that she was not overweight. Her legs were just born pudgy, that was all. The rest of her was as slim as her younger sister Phydariel, if not so buxom. She was savoring her steak, and she would finish it. Besides, desserts were not good at Bahia. "You know," she said, "I've been thinking of moving."

She watched the whole of him for any reaction. He noticed, froze for a moment, then laughed, wiped his mouth and put his napkin on his lap. "I see! Where were you thinking of moving to?"

"Well, since I am no longer responsible for Daniel...."

"I'm so sorry. You were going to tell me about him."

"Yes, well. Daniel is in prison."

"Look," he said, "if you don't want to talk about it..."

"No, I do."

She spoke quietly of how Daniel had fallen in with the wrong crowd— easy to do in Prince George's County with no father to speak of—and how his gang had worked out a smuggling scheme back and forth over intra-national borders.

"All that was perfectly legal before the Blue States seceded," James said. "I wouldn't consider your son to be a criminal."

"The story does become more sordid." Don't move too fast, she reminded herself. She raised an eyebrow and puckered her lips, a signal that this time she really wasn't going there. If things went well, she would have her chance.

"Then lets talk about your moving," he said. "Let me guess. New York?"

"Don't get me wrong. I really love Maryland. It was Blue, you know."

"Of course. But since it borders Washington, you can't expect that the U.S. would let it go. Just like Pearl Harbor, and San Diego."

"You're raising your voice." She reached across the table and took his other hand, and they both smiled and blushed a little.

"Sorry," he said.

"Let's have a prayer of unity." She closed her eyes, and James did likewise. She knew he would peek, but she was pleased that he was cooperating, particularly in public. "Dear Father and Mother God," she began, and then paused. That's the time he would peek, and she paused to give him a chance to do so. She was who she was, and he might as well get a good look while she prayed:

"Please bless us now and bless this food. Please bring unity to these two souls who come to you with heads bowed. Bring peace and strength to Delicia Deslandes. Bring wisdom and success to James Washington. And please breathe your spirit upon Daniel Deslandes, who so desperately needs your guidance, and make him to see that he needs that guidance, so that he may be receptive of it. These things we beseech of thee. Amen."

"Amen," said James, whose eyes were actually closed when Delicia opened hers prematurely. "Thank you."

Delicia had not sought to test James, but if she had tested him, he'd have passed. They arranged to meet again soon, and drove home separately. Delicia prided herself in always resisting first temptations.

She burned to call Phydariel, to confide and seek affirmation. She was overflowing with James, and had to tell someone. But she disliked chitchat, and even though her relationship with James was on solid ground, she wanted to be sure first. Phy was likely to try to douse Delicia's elation with her wet-blanket realism – a good check and balance, but it was too soon for that. Also, Delicia considered it her burden to always counter Phy's sardonic outlook with more positive thoughts. Phy had a lot in her, and some day Delicia would find a way to bring it out. But for tonight, she went to sleep with her date fresh in her mind, committing it to her spirit.

JIGSAW NATION

Delicia returned to work after taking time off to go to Philadelphia for Daniel's sentencing. Energetic voices on the car radio were talking about cultural tribalism and mass migrations over state lines, with the intention of sounding important, as opposed to making sense. Too much talk, she thought. That's what got us into all this in the first place—melodramatic rhetoric fomenting phony debates. She turned it off. Music or silence, and reading only when she needed to know something. Words were too powerful, too addicting, too deluding. It was better to project one's thoughts than to broadcast them.

She had trouble focusing on her work. Her boss, Mr. Schiller, was out, the next newsletter wasn't due for weeks, and her assignment was to visually represent something called the "Finlandization of Pennsylvania". She preferred hand painted art, but this one definitely required a computer. It was a chronic lament; even the Association of Small Art Galleries she worked for did most of their promotional work in digital pointillism.

In the following weeks she saw James several times, and while a deep love was wisely patient, she grew more and more attached to him. He treated her magnificently, and on one occasion, while they were strolling a new art exhibit at the Freer, he stopped her by a marble column.

"I just wanted you to know," he said, "I am not seeing anyone else."

Delicia smiled and sparkled and took in a breath. Smell of oil paint. Time to confide in Phydariel. But first, James. "You are wonderful," she said. Then she stammered a little, not because she was nervous, but because she had to rein in her words. James was as slow as she was in relation building, and she matched his caution. "I think things just may work out between us."

They held hands for the rest of the day.

In the evening they parted, and Delicia called her sister. There was no reply, so she left a message.

She stayed up late surfing the web to try to decrypt "Finlandization of Pennsylvania". She gathered it had something to do with D.C., while demographically Blue, being fettered by the Federal government. Maryland was Blue, but denied secession. New York was true Blue, and Pennsylvania was somehow caught in the middle. Thinking of a possible visual tie-in, she looked up the meaning of the cryptic nickname "the Keystone State." A couple sources cited Pennsylvania as a sort of historic bridge between North and South. She decided to portray it in sick shades of running purple in her graphic. The alliteration was fittingly awkward as well— "Purple Pennsylvania". She started to sketch a map with her pencils of color.

If she were to move, Pennsylvania was a possible destination. Since the Split, Maryland had become almost unbearable to her. The suppression of honest opinion, the hypocrisy, the heavy-handedness of the authorities, the intolerance of local flame radio.... The peaceful, let's-just-get-along neutrality of the Keystone State appealed to her. Moreover, that's where Daniel was.

On the other hand, there was James. Could she live happily in Maryland, if he were in the picture? Would he consider a move to somewhere more idyllic?

The phone rang. Phydariel must be home, she thought, but when she answered, it was James.

"Well, hello!" she said, slinking into her lounge chair and crossing her legs over the padded arm. "What a pleasant surprise!"

"I just wanted to say good night."

"Aren't you the thoughtful one?"

"I do know how to treat a lady."

"Do tell."

"Tell what?" He sounded nervous.

"Never mind. Thanks so much for calling."

"Listen, Delicia, I was thinking of a little trip, making it a whole weekend. Are you free this weekend, or next?"

Her eyebrows fell. It was just what she had wanted to hear, but it wouldn't do. "I visit Daniel every Sunday."

"You can make an exception for this."

"An exception for what?" she said, inadvertently using her hands-on-hips cadence.

"It's a surprise."

"James, it sounds lovely, but I'm not going to put myself before my son."

"Oh." James sounded confused. "I thought you told me you were going to look out for yourself for a while."

"Yes, I did say that. But with you doing that, I don't need to worry about it."

"Okay, then do it for me."

"James," she said, in her softest, and sweetest voice, the one that people thought was too saccharine to be genuine, but was all natural.

"Yes, hon." It worked.

"Listen to us. Here we are falling in love, and talking smack to each other."

"Well, I didn't mean to talk smack, but-"

"Neither did I."

"Delicia --"

JIGSAW NATION

She gave him a power hug, and sighed in his ear. "Let's change the subject. What color would you say Pennsylvania is?"

"What color would I say Pennsylvania is?"

"I like to think of places as having colors. Brazil and Mozambique are both green by day and orange by night, for example. My mother's house was red, green and gold, like Christmas. And Heaven is blue, of course."

"I never thought of places having colors, but I'd have to say that Pennsylvania is green."

"May I ask why?"

"The game of Monopoly. Pennsylvania Avenue was one of the green properties."

"Isn't that interesting? Lately, I've been thinking it's purple."

They continued on a bit of an edge, and after they hung up, Delicia frowned. The good-bye had been uncomfortable, and they had made no plans for a date. Something had gone wrong during the conversation, but Delicia had no idea what it was. She suspected James didn't know either.

She looked at her sketch. During the call she had doodled unconsciously. The doodles were just little chevrons, like birds migrating from state to state, shading from red to blue. Pennsylvania was dotted almost in half-tone by her tapping pencil. She'd have to start over, in earnest, tomorrow. She went to sleep thinking of a patchwork of elephants and donkeys walking in opposite directions across Pennsylvania, merging into one another like a drawing by M.C. Escher.

Saturday was a rainy September day, and Delicia and Phydariel went shopping. When they were teenagers, they could spend the whole day at the mall. Now so many of the good stores were in outdoor strips that they had to zip around, slogging through crowded parking lots and getting soaked. They loved it. Delicia told her sister about James, about how well things were going, and about the odd friction the other night.

"I've met James," said Phydariel with a mischievous smile. They'd just stepped out of the car into the rain, and she knew Delicia would be in suspense until they could dash into a store.

Delicia glared as they entered. "That was cruel, Phy!"

"Sorry!" The sunniest smile you could imagine. Then she added, in a Katherine Hepburn drawl, "Really Ah am." Unlike Delicia, whose sweetness was always authentic, however incredible, Phy's was nearly always the opposite. Growing up with peaches and cream for an older sister will do that. Phy could perfectly mimic the winsome, and she was fully aware that it was as transparent as glass. "Anyway, you knew I met James, at happy hour at Chili's, remember?"

"Oh, that's right. I forgot, because I didn't even know him then."

"Well, you should have seen him, smoking a big cigar and drinking a *presidente* margarita. The girl he was with slapped him on the cheek, right in front of everyone!" Phy laughed at the memory.

"You're kidding! What did he do?"

Phy shrugged. "Whatever it was, that was the end of them. I actually wrote his name down afterwards, so I wouldn't forget. But he wasn't interested in me."

"I just wonder what he could have done to deserve that slap!"

"You know men like that. Too good to be true. He's the perfect gentlemen, until you get close. Then his immune system kicks in, and tries to eradicate you. He might actually love you, but his immune system thinks a woman is a germ."

"Not James."

Phy laughed again. "Dee, you got a lot to learn. He's not married, but he's a bachelor. Think about it."

"Oh, I've learned, many times over. James is different."

"May be," Phy said, again with the drawl, but Delicia knew this time Phy meant what she said. She had been impressed with James too. "Sis, let's get shopping."

The women had a system in which they would work from opposite ends or sides of the aisles, with subtle gestures and glances communicating concepts such as "how about this one?", "wrong size", "try it on", or "have you lost your mind?" They rifled through a bargain rack of summer dresses, watching a man doing the same. They exchanged knowing smirks. The man was yanking the hangers, taking a quick look, and replacing them, with all the flourish of Delicia and Phy.

"He doesn't even work here, but he's sorting them by color!" Phy said with glee.

"So what should I do?" Delicia asked, still troubled.

"Leave him alone. He's gay."

"No, I mean about James."

"I was talking about James."

Delicia lost her composure. "Don't go fixing your mouth to say a thing like that!"

"Oh ho! No denial! So you haven't slept with him."

Phy laughed even louder, and no amount of scowling could straightjacket her sister's face.

Delicia chuckled in spite of herself. "He is most assuredly not gay!"

When they were done, and had given up on the clearance racks, Phy took her sister's hand. "Here's what I would do," she said. "First of all, stop worrying."

"He's just too good to lose."

"Well, if trouble comes, let it come. Have it out in the open. Then you have a better chance to work it out."

"Mmm." Delicia smiled flatly to show she understood, but wasn't quite on board. Conflict had never worked for her in the past, though Phy was making sense.

"Oh, and one more thing. For God's sake, don't move away. If you break up, *then* you have my permission to move."

Phy could talk a great game, and was usually right. The funny thing was that her own love life was always a mess.

There was nothing worth buying, so they darted back through the rain. Streaks of water not only pounded from above, but when they rebounded off the pavement, they leaped right up Delicia's dress. She slammed the car door to fend them off.

"Thanks Phy."

There was a scare in which Delicia feared that Daniel would be extradited to New Jersey, and in a flurry of visits over several week's time, it became obvious that James had little interest in her son. He said he was interested, of course, and that someday—*et cetera*, but actions speak louder than. The extradition fell through, and Delicia turned her eye back to James.

"During all that trouble, you never once went with me to visit."

"You're being unfair," he said. "Things at work have been in flux. I'm on call."

"That's why you have a sat phone."

This was the inevitable chink in his armor she dreaded. After four months of serious dating, she knew there were issues. They were minor, and she did not understand them, but she knew they were there. All in all, though, she considered their relationship to be ever deepening. "Durable" was what James once called it. That word stuck with her because it was limiting, though she knew he hadn't meant it that way.

And after all, Daniel was her son, not his. Why make things hard on James, and scare him off with the responsibility? By the time Daniel got out, he wouldn't be a minor anyway. So chink in armor or not, it didn't matter. No one was aiming arrows through it, so why should she? Any man could be brought down by the right woman, if she wanted to do it. "Let them be men" was a lesson from her mother she had never forgotten.

Everything else was as close to bliss as one could hope, and yet, she felt in a corner of her heart that they would never marry. This she ignored, washing it away with a sigh. Optimistic, but prepared.

In December she accompanied James to his company's Christmas party in Rockville. The Presidential election was still fresh in memory, and the booze had loosened many tongues. In the spirit of the moment, Delicia let her guard down.

"Isn't it rather ridiculous to even have elections," she said to one man, "since the U.S. is effectively a one-party state?"

"You must be Bluish," said the man, who was obviously tipsy. "Why is it that you people keep insisting that diversity made America strong, when obviously it was the unity of the States that made our nation great in the first place?"

Delicia mentally bit her lip, but smiled. Though incendiary, the "you people" part she could overlook. She had grown used to that long ago. What disturbed her was that she had caused the man to bring it up in the first place, and now she felt compelled to restore the peace. She composed a reply: "Oh, I agree with you! It took a lot of strength to bring such strong unity from such diverse backgrounds." She thought that was pretty clever, seeming to agree while actually driving her point deeper.

Meanwhile James had seen trouble out of the corner of his eye, and stepped in to defuse it. "Excuse me, Carl," he said, steering Delicia off by the shoulders to meet someone else. "Remember, nearly everyone here is Red or Redder. Our customers are all government, mostly Defense."

"That doesn't give them the right to bully us."

"Aw, don't sweat it so much. It's just politics."

"It's occupation."

"Yeah, okay, whatever. Just don't go there *here*, okay?"

Delicia smiled, and gave him a kiss to cool his lips. She had already cooled with the abruptness that others often mistook for disingenuousness. "I'll be good."

"I apologize for some of these folks. Carl there is drunk."

"Don't worry about that. I'm not moving away, just because of some boor."

"That's my baby."

She stepped back to make solid eye contact. "Things might be easier, though," she said slowly, "if you worked somewhere else."

James tensed up, and set his jaw. His eyes darkened, and he took a deep breath to speak, but stopped when his boss approached them. Introductions and mingling followed.

"James is on the fast track," his boss told Delicia while James was off getting some bottled water. "My Christmas present to him is a promotion to V.P. He doesn't know it yet, so you won't spill the beans, will you?"

"No. No, I won't."

Until the party, Delicia had no idea how illustrious James's reputation was within his company. He certainly had a high opinion of himself, and often cited important work as his reason for frequent overtime, but some part of that she had felt was simply pride – something she was unwilling to deny him by prying. When James returned, she beamed with pride of her own.

Vice President!

Winter did its thing, the new U.S. president was inaugurated, though nothing changed, and James did not receive his vice presidency.

She did not raise the issue for a while, but finally gave out and told him that his boss had personally told her about the promotion. "He promised," she said.

"There is some big shake-up coming down."

Delicia laughed at his mixed metaphor.

James darkened. "What's so funny?"

"Never mind."

One rainy day in March James called her at work. His voice sounded bewildered, both excited and depressed. She was sure he would say that he'd been laid off.

"Our office is moving," he said.

"Well that's a relief. I'm assuming your job is safe?"

"Yeah. They're finally making me a veep."

"That's wonderful! James, I am really thrilled —"

"Hold on now." Something was wrong.

"What's the catch?"

"We're moving out of the state."

"Oh, no. Somewhere really Red, right?"

"No, they're taking us to Oregon."

"Oregon? Who's moving to Oregon?"

"All of headquarters."

"They're closing the office in Lanham? Why would they do that? All of your contracts are with the government, which is right next door."

"Everyone is singing the Blues. The bottom line is taxes. Since the Blues have no military to speak of, their taxes are almost half of ours. That's a big incentive to locate there. If you think about it, it makes sense. It's the game of Twister. You know, right foot red, left hand blue, move to where the taxes are lowest."

"So Uncle Sam simply outsources to his nieces and nephews."

"You got it."

Delicia tightened her lips. "Oregon is pretty far away. Are you going?"

"This is huge, Delicia, it's everything. I'm going."

"When?"

"I'll be moving over the July fourth holiday. I'd love it if you decided to come too."

Delicia was stunned when they hung up. She phoned Phydariel just to let her know, but wasn't ready to really discuss it.

James was early, coming home before sunset, while Delicia prepared a candle-lit dinner for later. He forced a smile as he came in and saw it. His eyes seemed too tired to notice that she was wearing an evening dress of Kente, and make-up.

"Tired?" she asked.

"Dead. Do you mind putting out the incense?"

"It's a potpourri. 'Nubian Sundance.' What's the matter, you don't like it?"

"I never liked that stuff, especially while dinner is cooking."

"I'm so sorry. Why didn't you tell me that ages ago?"

James did not answer, but stripped off his jacket and tie, throwing them over an armchair. Then he sat at the table and rested his head on his hands.

Delicia tended to dinner, homemade lasagna. She thought that Nubian Sundance oddly went well with the first heady scents of Italian cooking. "What does Oregon mean for us?"

"I want you to come, Dee, but I know about you and Daniel. Would you leave him?"

Delicia could not look him in the eye. "What do you want me to say? That I'll leave my son when he needs me most?"

"Now *that* I have to take issue with. I've never even met the boy, but I've heard you speak with him. I don't know who's in the bigger prison, him, or you."

She looked him in the eye. "What is that supposed to mean?"

"It means that you've basically locked yourself up with him. No! You know what, Dee? You're locking him up too! He's in two prisons—one made of bars, and one made of your rosy-assed expectations. It's too late to be that kind of mother to him."

Delicia boiled, but as always, contained herself. "Daniel is my son, and I will *always* be there for him."

"He doesn't need you to always be there. He needs to be a man!"

James stalked to the bedroom to change. Delicia left him alone. Sometimes you had to stand behind your man. Sometimes he had to find his own way. She could do that with James, but Daniel was her baby, and the possibility of him failing again was unacceptable.

JIGSAW NATION

When dinner was ready, James returned, holding a plastic bag. He was aloof, as if nothing was wrong. A phony air, she thought, to protect them both. She didn't like it. He gave her a long hug—no kiss—and sniffed the potpourri. Hey, she could put on airs too, though she felt sick to her stomach. James was right – the combined smells of Africa and Italy stank.

"This is really hard," he said, "but I'm going to make it a little easier on us both. I'm moving out."

"Why?"

"I love you dearly, but we're just heading in different directions."

Delicia smiled instinctively. A pit dragged on her stomach, and pulled the ends of her mouth down, and she had to force the smile again. *Courage, always.* "I'm surprised to hear you say that. I changed my mind about moving away because of you. Now you're the one who's moving, for no real reason!"

"I'm sorry. We should have talked this out sooner."

"Talked what out? You aren't telling me anything, other than you love me but you're leaving."

"Whenever I start to tell you things you don't want to hear, you either turn it around in denial, change the subject, or give me a hug. You don't want to talk anything out. I bet you don't even know you are doing it."

"Well, you're not going anywhere without telling me now."

"Look, Dee, I love you dearly. You know that. This hurts us both, and I don't want to hurt you any more. But I've got to do my thing."

"There was something wrong from the very beginning, wasn't there?"

"Early on, yeah."

"Well," she said, taking in a breath and fighting tears. "Since you aren't going to tell me what the problem is, I guess I will never grow from it."

"Here," he said, giving her the plastic bag. "This says it better than I can."

"Oh really?" She could be the Queen of Snide when she borrowed some of Phy's excess Latin blood, but this time it was hard. "Is this a parting gift?"

"No, it's nothing really."

She opened the bag and pulled out a white T-shirt with a black and white print on it. "It's an Escher!" She laughed a bit. "You know me so well."

The print showed the famous depiction of birds migrating in opposite directions, the black ones going one way, and the white going the other. In the middle they melded in gray patterns of almost-birds. "It is a bit droll," she said, "but I understand."

He made a visible effort just to hold up his head. "Some things are just black and white."

Delicia turned away and gazed out the window. The frugal Sun withdrew a golden beam from behind spring clouds that mottled the sky in jigsaw pieces a thousand shades of gray. They looked like a celestial chart, and she studied them, wondering which cloud would turn orange first, as the retiring Sun reappeared beneath them.

The first orange one, that's where she would go.

JIGSAW NATION

Juneteenth

By K. M. Praschak

Several minutes after Bill Reynolds made his racetrack-worthy left turn out of the grocery store parking lot, he remembered the birthday cake on his back seat. One glance at the floor behind him revealed a blurred purple flower and streaks of frosting on the top of the box.

"Nikki shouldn't have ordered the whipped topping anyway." Bill hated talking to himself, and the sacks had about as much to say to him as his ex-wife, so he turned up the radio and winced at the stream of national security warnings for the next few blocks.

His kids were due for his birthday dinner at six, but when he saw the empty driveway down the street, he suspected it would be another night of flipping among the sports channels and a fistful of defrosted burritos. After he parked his car, Bill noticed the neat row of picnic benches lined up in his neighbor Gus Bowden's yard. Gus caught him looking and waved with a pair of tongs from his enormous grill. Next to it, the smoker puffed and a waft of barbecue scent straight from heaven blew in through Bill's open window.

"You got a day off for Juneteenth? That's right, it's your birthday. Happy Birthday, Bill." For as long the Bowdens had lived in the neighborhood, they'd hosted a large family gathering to celebrate Juneteenth, the unofficial holiday that commemorated the end of slavery. A lot of the white people in the town ignored Juneteenth, which had started in post-Civil War Texas and spread to other states over the years, but Bill had always made it a point to throw down some steaks in his own yard and share a few beers with his oldest neighbor.

Bill got out of his car and grinned. "I took the day off—my kids are coming in. You having family over again this year?"

"Yeah, those daughters of mine are bringing my grandbabies to show off since school's out. This knucklehead here is helping me until I get some real help." Gus slapped his oldest grandson in the belly with an oven mitt.

"Cut it out, Papa Gus. All this red meat is bad for you anyway."

"Pork's not red. Neither's those hot links you keep snacking on, Sylvester Augustus Bowden." Gus snapped his fingers. "Bill, Wanda got you a birthday card."

"She did?" Wanda had died almost three months earlier thanks to a heart attack. Bemused, Bill took out his mangled cake as Gus scooted into his house.

"You know Nana," Sylvester said, grabbing a bottle of water from the cooler. "She liked to be prepared. There's a whole stack of Christmas cards ready to go in her desk, too."

Every year, Wanda had delivered birthday cards to everyone in the family. She'd only stopped bringing one for Colleen two years ago, when everyone had been glued to their TVs to watch the Secession Riots.

"How many people have you got coming down?" Bill leaned against the pecan tree in his yard for some shade.

"Enough." Sylvester rolled his eyes as he offered a beer to Bill. "You know we're demolishing a whole rain forest with all these paper plates. How's Nikki? Is she going to be here soon?" Sylvester and Nikki had grown up together.

"Soon, yeah." Bill sighed. "She's driving by herself all the way from Boston. I told her not to do it, but she wouldn't let me buy her a plane ticket."

"She's always been stubborn like that," Sylvester said. "Always wanted to make her own way."

"Sounds like Wanda," Gus said as he rejoined them. "She missed your Nikki when she went east -- they were teaching each other how to knit. Ugliest baby blankets you ever saw." He held out a cream-colored envelope. "Lord, that cake needs help."

Bill set the cake on top of the car trunk in order to open the birthday card. "No one will care about the cake five minutes after they eat it."

This prompted Gus to shake his head. "Nah, appearances matter. You don't live more than thirty years with Wanda without fixing a few fancy cakes and getting hollered at for it. Did Miss Nikki order it?"

"On the computer. All I had to do was pick it up and drop it." Bill rolled his eyes. "She'll kill me when she sees the cake this way." He now regretted his fast escape from the grocery store.

"Sylvester and me can take care of this," Gus said. "You watch the meat."

Bill watched as Sylvester took charge of the cake. "I don't mean to put you to any trouble." He hadn't exchanged more than a few words with Gus since Wanda's funeral. In the years before that, Wanda had been the one who checked up on the kids and sent them pies and cakes during the holidays. He and Gus had talked about football and the weather and the cost of college. The older man's sudden burst of friendliness caught Bill by surprise, as a lot of people in the town had isolated themselves in the last few years since the Secession.

"No trouble at all." Gus chuckled. "Anything to keep Miss Nikki from exploding. Do you remember the time she and this guy here took my truck out?"

Bill remembered. "She still won't touch a stick shift." He took up the grill fork and his cell phone. "Thanks, Gus. Sylvester."

"We'll just be a minute or two. You remember how that girl put a dent in my fender with that big orange boot of hers?"

Still snorting, Gus led Sylvester inside. Bill turned on his phone and punched the button for Nikki's number. After he got her voice mail, he grinned. "What's this about beating up Mr. Bowden's truck? Call me later."

A wave of smoke made Bill cough into his cell phone as he called his son Nat.

"Happy Birthday, man. You okay?" Nat sounded distracted. "I meant to call you earlier, but a protester broke into the building and we got evacuated."

A chime broke in. "This call is being monitored by Eager Ear—your security is our security. Dial 911 to report suspicious activities."

After the announcement stopped, Bill spoke again. "I'm watching the neighbor's barbecue." He wiped his mouth on his sleeve and decided to watch another beer for Gus, too.

"Someone moved into that place across from you?" Nat asked, again at a distance.

Irritated, Bill adjusted the lid to the smoker. "No, this is the next door neighbor. Remember Ms. Wanda, who gave us birthday cards every year?" To his shame, Bill didn't know Wanda's birthday, though he'd attended her funeral and had sent a fine pot of lilies to the house.

"Oh, you mean the uh, African-Americans." Now boredom lined Nat's tone. "You should get out to the club more, Dad."

"I'd hoped to spend time with my children today."

Bill heard the impatience in his voice and wondered how his oldest son would take the hint.

"Nikki better not get you a cake with whipped topping. Did you get the golf clubs I ordered for you? Hang on, Benton -- I'm almost done."

"The golf clubs came last week." Bill clicked his tongs together and reminded himself to auction the clubs online. "Sounds like you jumped the gun on my party."

"No ice," Nat said, put out. "How many times do you have to be told? Sorry, Dad. Can't make it out of the city today—I've got to help the senator with a fundraiser tonight and there's a bunch of committee members to ride herd on for the mass deportation bill that's coming up. Let's try to catch up in a few weeks, okay?"

"What about your brother and sister?" Bill asked, flipping a slab of ribs with some savagery. "They wanted to see you, too."

"Zeke started hitting me up for money the minute he heard I'm flying out to San Diego next month and Nikki is handling some stuff for me in August. Let's talk Thanksgiving soon, all right? Catch you later, old man."

Before Bill could say more, Nat hung up on him. "Thanks for the golf clubs." He hadn't played at the club since the guys found out he'd voted the wrong way during the last presidential election. Nat still didn't like to talk about it, but unlike the club members, he'd thawed out since the Secession.

Managing the grill and the smoker made Bill think of Zeke, his middle child. Instead of finishing his degree in political science, Zeke had moved out to California, where he now ran the kitchen of a popular waterfront bar.

"Hey," he said when Zeke picked up the phone. "How do you like your baked potato again?"

"Don't talk to me about carbs, Dad." According to Nikki, her brother had lost almost forty pounds and his sense of humor in the last seven months after unearthing an ancient stack of health magazines.

"This call is being monitored by EZEars—" Bill pushed 7 to shut off the announcement.

"I've got steaks soaking in the fridge. Or if you aren't doing red meat this year, I can make my famous chicken nachos."

"Your nachos are an environmental disaster, Dad. Anyway, don't worry about it." Zeke sounded too casual, a sure sign of evasions to come.

"What's up? When you going to get here?" Bill kept his hundred other parental questions bottled.

"Er, I won't make it there until tomorrow." Zeke inhaled over the noise of bells ringing. "The dealership won't honor my warranty because I bought my car in another country and Wendy can't get money into my account until after she gets off work."

"Who's Wendy?" Bill resisted the impulse to beat the grill to death. "Where are you? If you're close enough, I can come get you."

"I don't need you to rescue me, Dad. In fact, I'm doing pretty okay by myself here." This time it sounded like cheering in the background.

"You're at a casino, aren't you?" Bill gave the air a vicious swat with the grill fork. "You said you'd stop with the gambling two years ago. Are you smoking that crap again, too? If you get one more arrest, you won't be allowed back into the state for five years."

"Calm down, will you? I'm passing time until my car's done. I'll win you a big gold teddy bear for your birthday, how does that sound?"

"No thanks. I expect you down here by noon tomorrow. Don't do anything to tick off the highway patrol this time."

"It's your birthday, Dad—wish me luck."

"I wish you wouldn't end up behind bars this year." Bill hung up on his son and jammed the cell phone into his pocket.

"Whew, you must have been talking to that boy Ezekiel." Gus uncapped a beer and offered it to Bill.

"I guess so." Bill drank down a quarter of the bottle. "Colleen brought home the wrong kid when she went to the hospital with Zeke. He never took after either of us."

"He grew up trying not to be his big brother and succeeded," Gus commented. "Sylvester's upstairs messing with his scanner and computer to fix up your cake extra special. Remember the year Ezekiel ran around with them dreadlocks? Wanda finally cornered him and gave him a haircut."

Bill laughed and took another swallow of beer. "He never did tell me who cut his hair for him. Sounds like I owe a lot to Ms. Wanda."

"She liked fussing over kids, even if they weren't ours," Gus said, taking charge of the smoker and grill once again. "I'm the same way, that's why I got Sylvester. He's still agitating at me about going to one of them northeastern colleges. I'd have an easier time sending him to another planet, the paperwork is so bad. Not to mention the money. Nine out of ten of them fancy universities double the tuition if you're from one of the Old States."

"I heard on the news that the state school is going to make it harder to admit new students," Bill said. "You're lucky you got Sylvester in when you did."

"I'm just thankful he didn't get picked up by the military yet," Gus said. "He and his attitude wouldn't survive basic training, let alone two years in a ditch in Europe or Korea. Well, who do we have here?"

A blue SUV pulled into the Bowden driveway and Gus surrendered the grill fork back to Bill as he walked up to the four newcomers, who swarmed around the older man.

"Papa, I told you I'd help." The woman about Bill's age waved. "How you doing, Mr. Reynolds?"

"It's good to see you again." Bill hunted for the lady's name and gave her a hangdog grin when he couldn't find it.

"Belinda, this must be the first time ever you've been early to a barbecue." Gus patted his daughter's back as his grandchildren made a beeline for the house.

"The border cops stopped the folks in front of us, but let us through, thank God." Belinda squeezed her husband's hand. "David, do you remember our neighbor Bill Reynolds? He came to Mama's funeral."

"Of course." David had a firm handshake. "Thanks for helping out my father-in-law. Let me take care of that for you." He relieved Bill of the grill fork.

"My pleasure." Bill felt self-conscious as Gus and his daughter continued to catch up with each other. "I better get ready for my kids to get here."

Gus broke off in mid-stream. "I'll have Sylvester bring over the cake when it's done."

"Thanks."

Like a restless ghost, Bill made his way back to his own house. With its four bedrooms and two bathrooms with stubborn plumbing, the house didn't fit him anymore. He felt comfortable in the kitchen, where he'd moved his biggest TV. After he found himself another beer, he settled in front of it.

The Secession had wrecked the playing schedules of hundreds of teams. Many of the colleges, faced with the prospect of securing all the paperwork that travel in the United States now entailed, had elected to trim down their seasons. A large number of Democratic States officials had gone as far as to call for a boycott of the US in protest of its repressive security policies. All around, it made for lousy baseball, basketball, and football.

Bill stared at the bottom of his empty bottle and speculated over who had sucked down the American dream. Outside the kitchen window, he saw Belinda's kids running around the pecan tree and Sylvester approaching with the cake balanced in his arms. He hurried to the door to let the younger man inside.

"Took longer than I thought, but it worked out." Sylvester held up the cake for Bill's inspection.

He'd printed out small pictures of Bill's kids at different ages and glued them to sticks which he'd inserted all over the cake to hide the worst of the damage. A young Nikki stood in front of a flag that still had the right number of stars.

"Your grandma would be proud." He got out of the way so Sylvester could put the cake on the counter.

JIGSAW NATION

Sylvester stared at his creation and shook his head. "We're lucky Papa Gus didn't throw out my yearbooks in one of his cleaning fits. I better go help him—he wants to tell Aunt Belinda how to make Nana's potato salad. Neither of them are going to get it right."

"Well, I appreciate it." Bill grabbed the digital camera off the top of the fridge and blew the dust off it. "Let me get a picture of you with the cake for Nikki before we demolish it later."

The younger man shrugged and picked up the cake again. "Papa Gus said you and Nikki and the boys are welcome to sit down with us. In case the grill and smoker didn't tell you, we got plenty to eat."

In spite of the invitation's sincerity, Bill couldn't bring himself to say yes. "If Nikki doesn't make it in too late, we'll drop by to say hello."

A police siren cut the awkward silence. Both men hurried to the window and saw the police car pulled up behind Belinda's SUV. The Bowden family members waited by the grill and smoker as the heavyset figure of Chief Rait stepped out.

"Let's see what's up." Bill led the way out the door as Rait leaned over to stare at Belinda's license plate.

"Good afternoon, Chief," Gus said with a tight smile as Bill and Sylvester joined them.

"Fine weather for a barbecue," Bill added, wary about the hooded look in Rait's eyes.

From what Bill had learned about the new police chief through the papers and the gossip, Rait combined inexperience and a misguided zeal for the recent defense restrictions handed down from Congress. Three lawsuits were already pending against the city thanks to some arrests he'd pursued.

"Looks like some of you folks are from Illinois," Rait said, staring at each of them. "You're a long way from home. Let me see your paperwork."

"No one's doing anything wrong," Sylvester said in a sullen tone.

"Our travel papers are in the baby's diaper bag," Belinda said. "David and I will go get it." Holding her baby, she shooed the two toddlers in front of her into the house.

"My daughters and their families are visiting for a few days, Chief." Gus fanned himself with his tongs. "I dropped off the visitation notice at the station yesterday morning. Can I get you some lemonade? Sylvester, get the man one of those red cups."

"He can help himself to it," Sylvester said, kicking the pecan tree. "It's what the government's for nowadays."

Giving Sylvester a glare that could cut meat, Rait drummed his fingers on the SUV's window. "It's been a quiet day and I expect it to stay quiet. Curfew's at ten, understand?"

"He understands, Chief Rait," Gus said, taking Sylvester by the shoulders. "We all do."

The police chief gave Gus a satisfied nod while Belinda came out of the house alone, rummaging through the diaper bag. He took the papers from her shaking hand and studied them with an attention to detail that made Bill shift from foot to foot and Sylvester glowered.

"Everything is in order." Rait handed the papers to Belinda. "Keep your hands to yourselves, your mouths shut, and don't forget to turn around and go home at the end of the week."

"We'll do just that, Chief. Thank you."

After Rait returned to his car, he caught Bill's eye. "Mr. Reynolds, you haven't been to any party meetings lately. People at the club are wondering about you, too."

Rait's upraised eyebrow made Bill's stomach gurgle. "I've been working a lot," Bill stammered. "My son sent me new golf clubs — I'll have to make more of an effort to play."

"A few of my men will drop by to pick up your donation to the campaign fund later in the week."

"I'll have the check by the door. Thanks for reminding me about it." Bill plastered on a smile and prayed for the man to go.

All of them save Sylvester waved as the chief pulled out of the driveway. As soon as the car made a turn out of view, Gus attacked the cooler and started handing out beers.

"I'm having one of them science fiction show flashbacks to the Sixties," Gus said, wresting the cap off the beer. "Didn't we do this forty-some years ago, Bill? This time, you one of us."

"I hope that's the last we see of that little man." Belinda returned the beer to the cooler. "Let me check on the babies, then we can find the chives for that potato salad."

"Not chives, I told you. Look at that smoke rise — Sylvester, take the tongs." When his grandson didn't move, Gus swatted him. "Come back from dreamland before something burns."

"Why did you put up with that?" Sylvester snatched the tongs from his grandfather. "Why we got to be nice to a man that treats us like we're the dirt on his tires?"

"Watch the news, son. That fool's going to get himself thrown out of office soon enough."

"Maybe," Bill said, thankful for the beer. "Rait's so busy seeing bogeys everywhere that he's going to wear himself out keeping normal people like us in line. Sad to say, chances are some other zealous super-patriot would take his place, though."

Sylvester threw open the grill. "I don't want to warp back to a time when people didn't have the right to be who we are. Freedom's starting to smell a lot like burned pork if you ask me."

"College kids," Gus said, dropping his bottle into the trashcan. "Always point out what's wrong without bothering to try to put anything right first."

"What can I make right?" Sylvester demanded. "Look at all them states that got fed up and left us behind." He yanked down a streamer hanging down from one of the pecan trees. "We got no reason to celebrate Juneteenth if we're all headed to slavery again."

He crunched the streamer into a ball and threw it into the trashcan, then stormed off behind the Bowden house. Gus looked heavenward and rolled his eyes.

"You want me to watch the meat again?"

Gus handed over the tongs and grill fork. "Slavery. That boy's got a good imagination, wilder than your Nikki's. I should put all his energy into a pill and sell it."

"He'll settle down in a few years," Bill said, preoccupied with the charring landscape on the grill. "Most kids do."

Without answering, Gus walked inside his house. Once Bill finished checking the coals, he took out his cell phone and dialed Nikki's number.

"I'm away right now, but leave me a message and I'll get back to you."

"Me again. Your brothers can't make it, talk to you later." He hung up before the security message could kick in.

Later in the afternoon, another SUV drove up the street. Sylvester appeared in time to help his Aunt Gussie and her family unload her vehicle.

"Bill Reynolds, how are you?" Gussie kissed Bill's cheek. "You better be staying to eat with us. Mama always said you were the skinniest man alive."

Bill looked at his watch and his expanding waistline. "My daughter is coming in. Actually, she's kind of late."

"That Nikki," Gussie said, shaking her head. "We met up with her at a gas station a few hours ago. She wouldn't take a ride from us, though."

"Is she okay?" Bill's heart started to pound and Sylvester crowded in to hear.

Gussie patted Bill's back. "You're still in insurance, right? You'll be okay. Didn't she call you?"

"I left a few messages for her. What happened to Nikki?" Visions of his little girl in jail or in a hospital hammered him.

Honking from a pair of cars made them turn around. "She heard us talking about her."

Nikki's dented hybrid car pulled into Bill's driveway. All of a sudden it felt like the whole neighborhood filled with people. Sylvester eased the grill fork out of Bill's hand and waved at Nikki.

"I got it, go on now."

Nodding at Sylvester, Bill made his way through the crowd to his daughter. Up close, he saw the bruise on her forehead, not quite hidden by makeup. He also noted the dented front fender and the broken left headlight.

"Hi, Brat," he said. "You run into some trouble?"

"Not much." Nikki reached into the car and pulled out a gift bag. "Happy Birthday, Daddy."

Instead of taking the bag, Bill folded Nikki into a bear hug. "Thanks for showing up, kiddo. I was starting to get worried. Let me get your bag and we'll go inside."

"There's only my purse," Nikki said in a subdued manner.

"Okay." Bill sensed he shouldn't press for details yet. "Anyway, there's a place in town that can get your car fixed up before you have to go back. Consider it an early birthday present."

Nikki flinched. "I'd rather take a plane back to Boston, Dad. Or maybe I'll stay here awhile."

"Who's going to sample this potato salad for me?" Gus held out two bowls as he walked through the yard. "Nikki Reynolds, tell Belinda that chives are wrong."

"Chives are wrong," Nikki said, slumping her shoulders. "Oh God."

"Nikki, what's wrong?" Alarmed, Bill caught her as she sagged against her car.

"Get her a drink, Sylvester. Make the lemonade the way your nana liked it."

The young man sprinted into the house while Nikki took a handkerchief from Gus.

"I thought I could do it," she said in a choked voice. "I balanced myself on the fence and fought to make everyone my friend, all-American or not." Nikki made a fist over her cracked headlight. "Instead, I get mugged by a bunch of middleschoolers in Illinois, a pair of skinheads in Missouri beat up my car thinking I'm a rabid liberal because of my license plates, and a highway patrol guy threw my laptop into the bushes at a rest stop twenty miles from home. That's what's wrong, Dad—and you can't fix any of it."

JIGSAW NATION

Bill felt a lump in his chest, but couldn't find the words to tell Nikki it would be all right. Behind him, Sylvester shoved a glass of lemonade that smelled of bourbon at Nikki, who gulped it with a grateful look.

"Drink that up," Bill said. "You'll feel better after you eat, too. I bet Gus makes great potato salad."

"Better than Belinda does. Let's make some plates, everyone."

"I'm sorry," Nikki said, gulping for air. "I didn't mean to ruin your day. It's Juneteenth, isn't it?"

Gus grinned. "You can't ruin nothing, Sunshine, except those baby blankets you and Wanda made."

Belinda scowled. "Papa." Her youngest child clutched her blanket and wailed.

"Sylvester's dog didn't like 'em and he's colorblind—ow. Come over to the tables when you're ready, Bill."

"Thanks." In the intervening exodus, Bill memorized a spot of mud on his wingtips until Sylvester tugged on his sleeve.

"Let me bring your cake out." Sylvester smiled at Nikki. "You're going to like it."

"Sounds exciting." Nikki shook her glass. "You'd like the campus, Sylvester."

"Maybe, maybe not." Sylvester ambled into Bill's house. "I'm thinking the state college is good enough for me after all."

To Bill's eyes, the woman sitting in front of him looked like a battered older version of the Nikki he'd raised.

"You going to be okay?" Bill asked. "We might be able to get you in to see the doctor. What time is it?"

"It's nothing a few days asleep won't cure," Nikki said, rising to her feet.

"You can't stay asleep forever." Bill knew his son Zeke would never wake up from his terminal case of Everything's Okay -- a disease most of the country suffered from. "No one should climb a fence if he doesn't expect to fall down a few times."

"You want me to go back, don't you?" Nikki threw up her hands. "I'm not Nat and this isn't baseball, Dad. I can quit the game if I want."

Bill narrowed his eyes at her. "If that's how you feel."

At that moment, Sylvester arrived with the birthday cake.

"Check it out." Nikki caught sight of one of her own pictures and grimaced. "Dad, you found the worst pictures for that cake."

"Blame me," Sylvester said. "Let's park it on a table before it gets dropped again."

"Again?" Nikki followed Sylvester. "Why again? Is that Zeke in a skirt?"

"It was his Polynesian era, remember?" Bill sat down at one of the tables with them and picked up the image of his son. "If Zeke makes up his mind about who or what he wants to be when he grows up, the world will end within five minutes."

"Zeke's fine," Sylvester said. "He's one of them folks who are okay as long as someone's there telling him what to do."

"I notice that approach didn't exactly work out for our country," Nikki said with a yawn. "Driving through from Boston, it felt like a road trip through a few hundred countries instead of parts of two."

"Once the cake is cut, you can't put it back together again the same way."

Bill shrugged, thinking of his ruined sports seasons, the fractured clientele of his insurance company, and the feral regard of the police chief earlier, while overhead a spy drone wobbled across the sky. Freedom's as fleeting as a slice of cake in this warm June sunshine, he thought. No wonder people needed to celebrate Juneteenth after the original Civil War.

Gus appeared with a plate heaped with thick slices of meat, along with baked beans, corn on the cob, and hefty doses of potato salad. He set the prize in front of Nikki and gave her a stern glare.

"Don't go telling me you're on one of them diets you and Wanda always moaned about."

Nikki lifted a rib the size of a baby's arm. "No, sir. I'm home and I'm eating till I fill up my cavity. Then we're having my dad's birthday cake."

"That's our girl," Gus said.

Some Juneteenths would last forever and later ones might mock the freedom slipping out the grasp of the average American family. Watching Nikki and Sylvester laughing over their food, Bill resolved to talk to both of them about heading to Boston, to discover if they could find a Juneteenth celebration there next year. They'd invite Nat and Zeke and Gus. Maybe even Chief Rait, too—he'd be a good man if he hadn't been trained to fear shadows, Bill thought.

"Can I borrow a cake knife, Gus?"

Another birthday, another cake, someday another country. Juneteenth would return. Tasting hope again, Bill didn't mind the whipped topping.

JIGSAW NATION

The Patriot

By Erin Fitzgerald

The year before Ohio finally joined the Freedom Republic, Mark Bloom's father locked himself in the basement for a month. He wanted to know what imprisonment was like. More specifically, he wanted to know what it would be like if he was sent to jail. The most trouble Mark's dad gotten into before he started going to secession rallies was a couple of speeding tickets.

He had time to go to lots of secession meetings after he got laid off. They were usually at the town hall, or in the room at the library with the carved wood eagle statue.

Before he began his sentence in the basement, he sat Mark down across from him at their tiny kitchen table. Mark's dad had a spiral notebook and a mechanical pencil. He rubbed his hands together and at that moment Mark remembered, as he sometimes did, that his dad was littler than he was. Mark's dad glanced at him quickly, put on his glasses and got to business. "I'm going to need you to bring my meals," he said, drawing a line through an item.

Mark nodded. His dad's notebook was open to a penciled list. It was so faint that Mark couldn't read it at all, even if he squinted.

"I also need you to stay out of trouble." One of his friends must have told him not to leave that out while making his plans. Mark's dad knew perfectly well that Mark never had opportunity or reason to get into the kind of trouble his friend meant. When Mark wasn't at home doing laundry or playing video games, he was at Youth Group at church.

"Yes, Dad," Mark said. "What kinds of food are you going to want?"

He flipped further back into the notebook and took out a photocopied sheet. "Anything from this is fine. Don't worry about nutrition or food groups, prisons don't and I want to duplicate the experience as much as possible."

Mark glanced through the list. Canned fruit, cottage cheese, low-end cold cuts. Dinner rolls. Kool-Aid.

"I'll also need you to flip the lights on and off," Mark's dad went on. "How's 7 a.m. and 8 p.m. sound?"

"Fine," Mark said. "But Dad— "

"I know what you're going to say," he said without even looking up. "But this is important to me, son."

Mark thought about telling the Youth Group what his dad was planning. The Adult Mentors were always saying that you could go to anyone on the Teen Leadership Council with any of your problems and no one would judge. They'd all had special training before taking their positions so that no one would ever laugh at your problems. They brought someone in special from Cleveland every year for their Leadership Retreat, just to cover that topic.

So Mark told Anthony O'Donoghue about it, in between Wednesday Weekly Meditations. He was the Social Justice Activity Representative, so he seemed like the best choice.

"Wow, Mark." Anthony pushed the button to rewind the meditation tape. "All this time we figured you'd come to us about your mom dying and all that. I mean, we got to talking about it one time and we figured if that happened to any of us, we'd all be basket cases."

That was when Mark started realizing Anthony wasn't going to be much help, because his mom shot herself with her father's Army pistol when he was six months old. And he didn't remember any of it. But Mark kept going, because he'd spent four years supporting other members of the Youth Group through Tylenol overdoses and groping uncles, and wasn't it his turn to get some help?

"So what do you think I should do?" Mark asked him.

Anthony flipped over the tape. "I'm as interested in secession as the next person but locking yourself in your basement to see if turning to acts of sedition are worth it? That's just... well, pardon my French, but that's fucked up. You could always turn him in to the police, I guess." He stepped back to shout over Mark's head. "Everyone? We're going to walk to a favorite place from childhood with Jesus in a couple of minutes... so go pee now if you need to, I'm not waiting!"

After Mark's dad started collecting unemployment, he had gotten very precise. That was why he had the notebook and the mechanical pencil, and the careful lists. That was why he'd quickly become an important member of the local Freedom Republic group. There were always people calling the house asking him to take notes, collect money, come over to the community room and join an envelope-stuffing party.

JIGSAW NATION

The change was fine, except when Mark and his dad's ideas of a chore well done were not the same. Mark came home on the last day of school and found a stack of folded coveralls on the basement stairs. Without thinking about it, he put them in his dad's dresser. Then his dad came back from his meeting and got mad because the coveralls were for the basement, they were part of the preparation, and how could he count on Mark to get things right when he was going into the basement less than a week from now?

"You do your job and I'll do mine," Mark said, even though he wasn't really sure what his job was.

Then Mark's dad calmed down. He reached up and patted Mark on the back, something else he'd learned how to do since he got laid off. "That's really all we can do, isn't it?"

Moments like that made Mark feel a lot better.

The day came, and some of the Akron Freedom Republic committee came by to see him off to the basement. They'd all been at the house at one time or another, Mark was used to bringing them beer and pretzels before he went off and did his own thing. Mr. Nadelsky, who was on the Freedom Republic Flag Committee (Midwest), brought his daughter Brianna. Brianna was Mark's age. They didn't go to school together because she was home schooled, and she wasn't in Youth Group but Mr. Nadelsky never said why. And even though Mark knew that the Activity Leaders say there are polite ways to ask, there just never seemed to be a right time.

Mark had never seen Brianna before. She was pale and bony. She sat at their kitchen table, hugging her knees and reading a book while Mark's dad went through his checklist one last time.

"What you're doing is remarkable," Mr. Nadelsky said to Mark's dad. "It's brave. I wish everyone who wants what's best for our families had the opportunity to do what you're doing now. To find out for themselves what little individual sacrifice has to be made in order for us to reclaim our heritage as a whole."

Brianna laughed, and they all turned to look at her. She glanced up. "What? Oh, sorry. The book. Bad timing."

Mr. Nadelsky nodded and began to make a stack of things to carry downstairs.

Mark looked at the spine of Brianna's book and made out faint words on its maroon cover. The Federalist Papers. Their eyes met, and she winked.

The next day, Brianna was waiting on the front step when Mark came home from school.

"Forget something yesterday?" Mark dug out his keys.

"Only to introduce myself," Brianna stuck out her hand. "Brianna Nadelsky, aspiring republican. And you must be a silent but loyal arm of the confederate movement."

"I'm not silent all the time. Want to come in? I have to feed my dad."

Mark wasn't expecting his dad to change much over the month, if at all. But after just one day he was pale, and through the bookshelf Mark saw him blink rapidly when he flipped the overhead light on.

Mark banged on the water pipe, as his dad had asked him to do from time to time. "Lunch." Brianna sat on the steps and watched as Mark put the plastic tray and paper plates his father had bought at the discount club on the floor, and pushed them under the bookshelf with a broom handle.

"Thank you, guard," he answered, and Mark heard the tray slide closer to his side of the bookshelf. Mark glanced at Brianna as if to say, did you want to talk -- but she shook her head. Whatever reason she was there, it wasn't to give his dad encouragement. So Mark told the prisoner he was welcome, and Brianna followed him back upstairs.

There was still some breakfast mess to clean up from the morning, so Mark started in on that. Brianna sat down at the kitchen table, saying nothing for a while.

"Did you want cookies?" Mark said, just to break the silence. "I think we've got chocolate chip."

"Mark," Brianna said with such seriousness that he froze. He couldn't even turn around to look at her.

He tried to blow it off, though. "That's my name."

"How do you live this life?" she asked, in that same voice.

"What do you mean?"

"You work, and you work hard," she said, and Mark heard her stand up. "And yet, you have no reward that I can see. Not even an abstract one."

Mark put a cup in the dishwasher. "He's my dad." When he straightened up, he felt Brianna's hand on his shoulder. She turned him around to face her. Mark saw that her eyes were two slightly different colors. Blue-green, green-blue.

"You need to realize your true potential," Brianna said, and she kissed him.

A couple of years before Mark had gone to a Youth Leadership Conference at Woodside Lake because one of the Teen Leadership Council members had won a week at Space Camp, and it was at the same time. At the

JIGSAW NATION

Conference they made you bunk with people you didn't know on purpose, so that you'd be exposed to more perspectives. The only perspective Mark's bunk cared about was the one belonging to a guy from Parma named Oscar who said he'd gone all the way with his au pair.

"Dude, aren't you like too old to have one of those?" one guy asked.

Oscar laughed in a way that sounded knowing to all of them. "My brother isn't."

"Where was she from?" someone else wanted to know.

"Belgium." Oscar smiled and put his feet up on the cabin table. "And, like, Belgian girls are the best."

"Are you Belgian?" Mark asked Brianna.

She laughed and kissed him on the nose. "If I defined myself by mere ethnic ancestry, we wouldn't be here now, would we?"

"I suppose not," Mark said, and pulled her over to him like he'd always seen guys on TV do after they've scored. Brianna smelled faintly of newsprint.

"Where were you yesterday, bro?" Anthony said. "We needed someone to paint the trees for the mural in the Fellowship Room."

"I was busy," Mark said. Normally when a Teen Leadership Council member sought him out, Mark was pretty psyched and took the opportunity to give as much feedback as he could. But the day after Brianna came to the house, Mark just wanted Anthony to leave him alone. Mark wasn't even really sure why he was at Youth Group that day anyway.

Anthony leaned in and lowered his voice. "Everything going okay with your dad? Did you talk to him like I suggested?"

Mark blinked.

"You know, if you want some of us to come over and help support you, we can do that. We've done it before. When Linda Bly's parents wanted her to quit gymnastics we went right there and we got— "

"No," Mark said. "It's okay. I talked to him and everything is cool."

"Everything is cool," Anthony repeated, and clapped Mark on the back—not far from where Brianna had dug in her fingernails less than a day before. "That's awesome, champ. Glad to hear we helped you out. Since you've done so much for us and all."

Mark's dad liked living in the basement. He had a clothes bar down there that he could do chin-ups on, plenty of heavy things to lift like weights. He had ten years of Sports Illustrated back issues to read. "I'm really pleased with how this is going," he said. "I think this is making me even more resolved than I already was."

"Yup," Mark said. He didn't think guys in prison had any of that stuff but it wasn't like he was going to tell his dad that. Both of them were happy with the way things were.

"I just don't *understand*," Brianna would say while she took her clothes off, folded them and stacked them on Mark's desk chair. "Read a high school history book, even a poorly written one, and it's all there! States' rights were debated hundreds of years ago! How can you uphold the Constitution in its entirety except for one little part? That's just... hypocritical!"

"Yup," Mark said, and moved over so she could slide into bed next to him.

"And then HE says well, times change." Brianna sprinted across the room and burrowed under the covers quickly. "In that case, shouldn't we be revisiting the Amendments every year? Every month? Every day? Didn't we learn anything from Prohibition?"

"I guess not." Mark kissed her. It was still so weird, being able to kiss a girl without asking, without having to worry about what she'd think. And then there was everything else he didn't have to ask about. It made Mark laugh to himself when he wasn't paying attention, like when he was taking back his dad's plastic tray from underneath the bookshelf.

"Something funny you can share, guard?"

"Naw, Bloom," Mark said, flipping the light off as he walked up the stairs. "You really had to be there."

"Come over to my house this weekend," Brianna said on the phone very late that night. "My parents are going to a Marriage Encounter."

"What are those, anyway?" Mark had seen them in the church bulletin, but there was never much description.

"It's a religious retreat where it's okay to fuck." Brianna laughed. "We'll have our own retreat and skip the God stuff. What do you say?"

Mark's dad was starting to look better. A lot better, actually. The chin-ups and prison food seemed to be doing him good. He wasn't mopey anymore. Mark would come downstairs and his dad would be whistling and reading. He was also working on a drawing on the basement wall. It was a picture of a wolf.

"What do you think?" he said, stepping back so that Mark could get a good look.

To be totally honest, it wasn't very good. "You going to have it finished before your sentence is up?"

JIGSAW NATION

"I'd better." Mark's dad leaned over and gave the fur an artistic smudge. "Maybe after I get out of here, I'll take my own stab at a new state flag, huh?"

Mark had seen one of Mr. Nadelsky's flags when he brought it to the house one time. It turned out he had many, many prototypes.

"He's good with a sewing machine," Brianna said Sunday morning, when they were looking for ways to kill time. She had her parents' bedroom closet open and the flags were neatly folded on hangers. "He used to fix my play clothes when they got ripped. That's about the nicest thing I can say about him."

Mark fixed his own clothes when he was little. One time he burned his fingers on the iron when he was trying to put a patch on his jeans. After that, he just threw stuff out and asked for money.

"Every single one of these flags represents more than the Freedom Republic." Brianna stepped back for a minute and looked at them. She took out a green one with yellow trim. "He was working on this one when I told him I got into the Gifted and Exceptionally Talented program at school. He said, that's nice. Never even looked up from the sewing machine."

Mark was suddenly aware that his legs were really sore. "I thought you were home schooled."

"Not always." Brianna pulled the flag off of its hanger. It slunk off and trailed to the floor. They both looked at it for a minute, and then she smiled. "I'm still Exceptionally Talented, though."

If Mark ever had the chance to have sex on top of a flag again, he didn't think he'd be able to without feeling like he's about to get caught by the guy who made it.

"What in the hell?"

Mark turned and looked behind him. Mr. and Mrs. Nadelsky, still holding their luggage. At first, Mark felt like he was in a doctor's office. But he wasn't the only one naked, so that didn't last long. What's the right thing to do? Mark glanced at Brianna. She was in shock, no help there.

Mark cleared his throat. "I can explain..."

Less than thirty seconds later, the front door closed in front of him. Mark sat on the step and watched as his clothes fell from the sky onto the Nadelskys' lawn.

Long story short, Mark had forgotten to feed his dad. After missing a day of meals, his dad got worried. He planned an elaborate escape, and it went off mostly without a hitch. He ran up the stairs to home, only to find his son wasn't there. Maybe Mark had been kidnapped by the CIA, or the FBI? So Mark's dad called Mr. Nadelsky's voice mail, since that was the number below his on the Freedom Republic (Midwest) Crisis Phone Tree. And the Nadelskys cut their Marriage Encounter short to come home and help him find Mark.

It'd turned out Mark's dad was sort of right. But not really.

"Ah son," Mark's dad said when he came home. "Women either get you with sex or food. It's all wrapped up with a nice big bow, and then you find the bomb inside."

"I'm sorry I forgot to feed you," Mark said.

His dad patted him on the head. "It's all right, Mark. You've learned a lesson that every man has to learn for himself. And you were fortunate to learn it early. Some of us never do."

A week later, the same day Mark's dad got a contract job at his old company, Mark got a letter in the mail.

Dear Mark,

As you may have guessed by now, my parents have decided to send me downstate. There's a summer camp and a boarding school here that espouse their simplistic values. They're tired of my attempts to change their thinking, and this is how they've chosen to deal with it this time. It is easier for them to send me away than silence me.

What they don't realize, though, is that my work can be done here as well -- and perhaps more effectively! The other day I was bird-watching with a guy from Columbus and another one from Toledo, and we ended up having a very enlightening and rewarding teach-in. My goal, before graduating, is to give every student here something to think about when they go back to their cozy, secession-minded homes.

I miss you, of course. I appreciated how you were always willing to listen, and to think over the ideas I introduced -- that is a rare thing to find in anyone, much less people our age. So I hope that next summer I'll be able to return home from this place. Until then, though, there is work to be done here.

Keep the faith!
Yours, Brianna

"You seem pretty quiet lately," Anthony said later that day, as he and Mark were putting sandwiches into plastic bags. "Quieter than usual, I mean."

"Just thinking, I guess." Mark slid a peanut butter sandwich snugly into a bag.

JIGSAW NATION

"Anything you need to share with someone?" he asked. "I mean, sometimes we all need a sympathetic ear. I'd be happy to do that for you, or find someone with more training who will."

"Thanks, Anthony." Mark said. "I'll let you know when I need some counseling."

"Awesome." Anthony studied the remaining bags and bread. "Think we should make more sandwiches? People seem to get more hungry on Day Excursions than they do at regular meetings."

"Might as well." Mark reached for the jar of peanut butter closest to him—one of the two he'd brought, one of the two he'd taken home for a few minutes before he went to Youth Group.

Anthony reached for the other one. "You know, I'm sympathetic to the convictions of vegans and the discrimination they face in the world. This natural peanut butter is going to do a lot to enlighten the others. Good thinking!"

Mark smiled, even though he probably shouldn't have. "Like they say, you have to start small."

Seconds
By Seth Lindberg

Darkness.

Flashes from the brush ahead of them, accompanied by an odd popping sound. Gunfire? he thinks blearily. "Get down! Get down!" someone's hissing nearby. A dark figure in front of him, flinching downwards as another series of cracks echoes through shadows.

Kevin Marshall blinks. Where? What th—

The figure turns. "Jesus, Marshall," the figure whispers. "Whatchoo spacin' for?" Panic, panic in his voice. The figure turns and with a heavy hand pushes him firmly into the dirt.

Crack-crack. Kack-kack-kack-ka-kack.

They wait, tense. Seconds pass.

Crack ka-kack.

Silence. Marshall remembers to breathe. He tries to do so slowly, without noise. He instinctively clutches on to something he now realizes is a rifle of some sort. Finger on the trigger. No one on his side seems to be shooting.

They wait, for what seems like forever. Sounds of talking from somewhere, perhaps further along the ridge. Through the gloom several figures begin to move, holding rifles like theirs, barrels pointed to the ground. Their helmets hang jauntily on their heads. One of them is smoking a cigarette.

Marshall's trying to remember what the hell is going on. The figure in front of him is Jackson, this much he's pretty sure. Chang's nearby, Nomura and the others are just a bit up front, by a stand of trees that had to have been growing since before the devastation.

The figures walk along a known pathway, perhaps an old road. A few grasses and some trees grow through the cracks, nothing else.

Jackson's slowly eased himself onto his back—a big risk, Marshall realizes: anything could happen, a twig cracking, anything—and has cradled his rifle on his stomach, pointing out to the line of figures walking past. Marshall's just doing his best not to keep his ass too far up in the air. Where am I? he thinks. What the hell is happening?

Why does this seem so familiar?

JIGSAW NATION

"Fucking nervous as shit," one of the figures down in the clearing says in a lazy drawl.

"You heard the Lieutenant," another says, sounding defensive. "They've been known to crawl up this far north."

"Fucking partisans," another sighs. That figure stops, glancing at the treeline suspiciously. He's only about twelve or so feet away from them. Marshall doesn't know if the figure can see him. Marshall turns, looking at Jackson's face. Set, tense. Teeth clenched, finger on the trigger. Waiting, waiting.

"Those pussies wouldn't dare go this far into Frisco." Frisco meaning these Guardsmen aren't from around here, Marshall thinks. Recruits from somewhere else. Midwest, maybe. He closes his eyes and imagines sunlit fields of corn, stretching out as far as the eye can see.

"Well, I heard *something*," says the second. Bright red ember of a light from the cigarette, Marshall can see a bit of his face. Widely-spaced eyes, pale features. A bit overfed. Young, maybe in his late teens.

Kevin Marshall and the others wait, not moving. He can feel his leg cramp up, he aches to move it but is just too terrified. The chatter between the guardsmen begins to trail off into a mix of sounds, as the figures move away.

Far away, two cats yowl in an atonal chorus.

Marshall and company just sit there, tense. Waiting for someone to relax. Kevin decides to stand, and Jackson follows, warily, his rifle down and his stance wide. He sees other figures ahead of him rising up into crouches, one figure behind him.

A hand is raised up ahead. Come *on*, it motions with a flick of the wrist.

They make their way quickly but cautiously to one side of the road, letting it wind upwards on the hill. Reaching the top, they see a low, flat concrete building with some more soldiers outside. Probably a ton inside. An armored troop carrier sits, guns pointed south. Generators rumble.

The squad creeps around to one side of the hill. From here they can see all of the north part of the Peninsula–the ruined buildings of downtown San Francisco, spires stretching halfway up, skeletal framework twisted and torn in places. Trees grow through the concrete in city blocks, a grid of roads can be made out barely through the foliage that now covers the ruined city. North and east is the Bay Bridge, collapsed from shelling. Warships sit in the Bay; thin, sleek monstrosities.

To the north, Sutro Tower rises defiantly from the hills like a three-fingered claw attempting to scratch the sky.

"Fuckin' beautiful, huh, Marshall?" someone whispers.

Marshall doesn't think so. He just feels strangely sad about it all.

Kevin Marshall woke groggily to the sound of his alarm clock. His wife reached up to press the snooze button, and he lay there, too tired to get up, too awake to fall back asleep.

Another one of those dreams, he thought. He sighed, heavily. He twisted and stretched, his legs painfully stiff. He sat up in bed, willing himself to get into the shower. He sat there, like that, until the alarm rang again and his wife wearily and silently slipped out of bed and into the bathroom.

He fell back asleep without realizing it, waking up when Marienne kissed him on the cheek. "Huh?" he mumbled.

"I'm gone, babe. Off to work. You should get up, too."

"Tired," he said.

"Yeah, me too. But you don't want to be late. Remember what your boss said?"

"Yeah."

He watched her hips sway as she stepped out of the bedroom. She'd gained some weight since their marriage. To be expected, he guessed. He didn't have room to complain about it–he'd gained weight as well.

It took effort to stumble into the shower, let the hot water fall all over him. It felt wonderful, luxurious. As if the water was scrubbing off years of grime and sweat from him.

He hated the dreams. They made him feel completely alone. He hated the idea of this second self out there in the darkness, he hated everything about it. He'd given up talking to Marienne about it—another subject he avoided with her. Each time he tried he became sick of the politely-worded suggestions of therapy. The misunderstandings, the lack of interest. She worried about the dreams only because she worried about him. She had no desire to understand them for what they were.

He wished he could stay forever in that moment in the shower when his body became used to the hot water. But life had to roll on. To work, to work.

His body ached to sleep. He kept thinking to himself: To work, to work.

On the bus to downtown a large woman sat down next to him, and Kevin glanced over, recognizing her but not knowing where. She had a small, pinched nose, dark eyes and features, and her face set in a tight frown. She had headphones on and Kevin could just barely hear the Stevie Wonder songs coming from it.

I know you, he thought. But where from?

Seconds passed. He blinked. She glanced over at him, her expression vaguely curious. He looked away, not to be rude. Pressed his face against the window and watched the rows of houses and buildings drift past.

JIGSAW NATION

Glanced over again, as she got up to leave. She cocked her head slightly, shouldering a bulky purse, and suddenly with that gesture the memory flooded through him.

Night, it was night. They shined the flashlights up at the dangling corpses.

Kevin stared at the woman as she nonchalantly brushed past someone standing in the center isle.

"Remember the faces," Jackson said to Nomura, the kid who'd joined up a few weeks before. "They were heroes."

Kevin Marshall had flashed the light up at the face of the sole woman of the five hanging bodies. Remember. The way her tongue hung out of her mouth, those sightless eyes, the dried blood and dirt on her swollen face.

Kevin swallowed, forcing himself to turn and look away. The woman got off the bus and wandered back into the fold of the city.

Sometimes going to work was all about pretending you were somewhere else. And sometimes it was like running an obstacle course while blindfolded. Today wasn't so bad, as obstacle courses go.

When he got home he flipped channels for a little while until Marienne came home. They waffled on pizza for a while, settled on two Lean Cuisine microwave dinners, and ate in front of the TV.

"Wake up," says Jackson.

Kevin Marshall blinks, groggily. He feels exhausted to his bones. He'd been sleeping in some weird position: now one leg is numb.

"Wake up," Jackson repeats, with some urgency.

"I'm awake, I'm awake," Marshall says. "What's going on?"

"Nothin'. You were tossing and turning. You been having those dreams again?" Jackson's face in the darkness is a mask of concern.

Marshall nods. "Yeah, you too?"

Jackson grimaces. "Not in a while, thank God. Come on, the wake's about to start."

He gets up, punches his leg a few times, then picks up his rifle and limps in the darkness to where the fire is. The dark shapes around the fire has to be his squad. Where are they? Somewhere in the Peninsula, no doubt. The tall Redwoods rise up around him, like ancient, watchful spirits.

"Sergeant," his squad mutters to Jackson. "Captain," they murmur a bit more respectfully to him.

Marshall nods to them, then looks around. The faces show up stark in the flickering firelight, like they were already ghosts. Already dead. He tries to compose a speech in his head. Who died again? he thinks. Damn, should have asked Jackson.

"We're here to remember Nomura," he says after a few minutes. He tries to conjure up Nomura's face, but can't. "He was a good soldier, and young. He fought hard and bravely, he fought for you guys." Kevin looks around. People nod and make small noises. Marshall steps back.

Jackson steps forward, and the fire plays across the angles of his face. His gaze is scarecrow-intense. "God took Nomura, like he takes so many of us. It's all part of His plan. We can't forget that. But meanwhile, we have a battle to fight. We have a country to take back from those god-damned rednecks. We're all counting on each other now. We got to." He grunts and steps back.

The soldiers reminisce a bit, uncomfortably. It used to be a good ritual, but these days too many are dying. Now it just reminds people of things they want to forget. Someone passes around some grain alcohol he bought on the black market, people drink and look up at the stars. There are so many.

One of the new recruits walks up. Evans, he thinks. She hands Marshall a small but heavy shiny metallic box. "Here," she says. "Nomura would have wanted you to take this."

Marshall blinks. "What is this?"

"Mp3s. Over ten thousand of them. It's on a hard-drive. It's Nomura's collection. His entire life. Almost like his soul." Pause. "He idolized you, you know."

It's too heavy, he thinks selfishly. *It'll weigh me down.* Seconds pass. He musters up some kind of false modesty instead. "I can't take this."

It takes a bit of convincing, but Evans eventually decides to take it instead.

Nomura had died in a retreat action, Marshall remembers. A pitched battle with fresh National Guardsmen with shiny new rifles, they look like bull-pupped M-16s, auto-lathed from some base in the deep South. There were a lot of them, but the Guard was running. He remembers shooting one in the back. A blonde kid. Went right down.

Then they heard the sound of aircraft, and decided to take off. Whole companies of partisans had been lost to napalm attacks, once the Guard forces had decided burning half of California was a better moral option than losing. Their squad has shitty Chinese-copied Stinger missiles, but they tend to break down, and no one knows how to fix them. And no one wants to find out theirs is a dud when a jet is screaming towards them dropping clouds of pure flame.

As soon as they started retreating, Nomura went down. One minute, it's an orderly retreat, the next, shrapnel and fire everywhere. Marshall took a split second before deciding not to go back for him. They listened to his screams die down as the jets thundered above them, the shrieks of planes piercing the sound barrier, drowning out human anguish like an axe hacking off the branches of a tree.

Darkness.

Flashes from the window outside the apartment. Kevin Marshall woke in a cold sweat, his wife mumbling and turning over in her sleep, pushing her back against his side. He slid out of bed, careful not to wake her, and peered blearily at the clock. 4:30 AM.

He scratched his head. He'd woken up right at 4:30 AM before, from one of these dreams. Maybe it had some meaning. Or maybe it meant nothing at all. Maybe it was just some coincidence, just like the dreams, and his brain was feverishly trying to figure out the differences, put it all together, make it all work.

He opened the blinds and peered down at the street. Several patrol cars had their lights flashing, surrounding a car, but the cops out seemed in a jovial mood, cracking jokes with the person Kevin could only assume was the driver of the car.

Kevin frowned, watching the scene unfold. He caught movement out of the corner of his eye, and turned to see Marienne rising up, unable to discern an expression from her shadowy form.

"What is it, hon?" she asked.

"Dunno," he said, still thinking about the dream. "Nothing, I guess."

He made his way back to the bed, and turned into the way Marienne was sleeping. She made a pleased sound, and weakly pulled his arm over her. He could feel her under his arm, falling back into deep relaxation, and soon he did, too.

"I love you," she said, her voice dreamy and pleased.

"I love you, too," he replied automatically, without thinking. A half second later, he thought to himself, I do, though. I really do.

Marshall and Jackson share a cigarette at the safehouse down in Redwood City, patrolled by Guards and supposedly safe from the fighting. Downstairs people are making improvised explosives. With the bomb-making, smoking's a poor idea. No one stops them, though.

Marshall holds the rolled cigarette in his hand, he closes his eyes and inhales, feeling that rush of nicotine and God knows what else Jackson put in. He feels the poison in his lungs. It feels good. It adds some sort of unearthly clarity. He exhales, and watches the smoke drift upwards.

"Gimme that blunt, bitch," Jackson says, mock-irritated.

Marshall inhales again, then grins and hands it over.

"Christ, Kev. You smoke in your dreams?" Jackson asks, before taking a puff.

"Nah," Marshall says, his voice ragged. "Not that I remember, at least."

"Sure as hell must be a dream, then," says Jackson with good-natured charm. "I can't even see you goin' a few hours without one." He sighs, exhaling a cloud of blue-black smoke, then passes it back.

Marshall inhales again, then says, "You smoke in yours?"

Jackson looks away. "Eh. Don' know. Don' care."

"You think any of the others have these dreams? Chen? BT? Evans?"

"You ask 'em, you so curious," says Jackson, irritated. "Bet they don't, though. Bet they don't even have dreams."

"I saw someone in the dream, you know. Someone I saw out here."

Jackson looks over, faint alarm on his face. "Oh yeh?"

"Yeh. Dead chick. One of them Bear Flaggers, the ones that got hung."

Jackson looks away. He shakes his head. "Shit. Bad stuff, that. Fuckers got caught in the wrong place at the wrong time. She dead in the dream?"

"No," says Marshall, then he inhales. The smoke feels good. It feels certain. "Just hanging out on the bus. Maybe going to work."

"Weird shit," Jackson says, without affect. "Pass me that blunt, already."

Weeks had gone by. Kevin Marshall was in the middle of working on a project proposal Sales was on his ass about and his boss had made some kind of 'action item', when one of his coworkers managed to spill coffee all over the desk and floor, and his boss came strutting in and had to show everyone he was in command of the situation. So, while everyone was standing around or grabbing paper towels to mop up the coffee, the boss called building services to get someone up to clean the mess.

He only barely paid attention, working the proposal, sweating under the pressure, some futile report that people would glance over, then toss aside just like all the other proposals he'd ever written. But if he missed one, everyone would remember.

He heard a clatter, someone exclaiming, and he looked up. One of the janitors was looking over at him, a bucket at his feet. Kevin peered at the man for half a second. He looked familiar, but so... skinny, his shoulders slumped, an almost invariable twitch about him, a look like he was waiting for some unseen hand to smack him on the back of his head.

"Jackson," Kevin said, blinking.

Seconds passed. The janitor stuttered something, glancing furtively at the door. "I guh. I gotta. I gotta go," he mumbled, then shambled off.

JIGSAW NATION

Kevin rose, taking a step to the door. The other janitors sighed in exasperation, then spoke in annoyed tones in Spanish at one another.

He moved quickly to the doorway, poking his head into the hallway. "Hey!" he shouted. He saw the janitor's form make it to the elevator, slipping into one. He looked hunched over as he moved, his head ducked.

The translator's name is Arthur, but he doesn't look like an Arthur. Cold winds are coming off the Pacific, and the slender guy's shivering and moving in some slow dance to ward off the cold. The stars don't glitter tonight: instead the fog is high, rolling above them, like clouds whose stomachs you could reach up and rub.

Marshall's unit stands around, bored and fidgeting, mumbling under their breath. They're uneasy, they've been on a run like this before, but he thinks mostly they don't like that he's forbidden them from smoking, afraid the cigarette lights would attract any attention. Old, run-down pickup trucks sit, three of them, up about fifty yards away.

"Glory to the revolution, huh?" Arthur says cheerfully, then laughs.

No one responds. Finally someone grumbles. Arthur gives the shadowy partisan a steady glare, then glances over at Marshall for support.

"Don't give me that revolution crap," Marshall breathes. "We ain't you commies, we ain't Bear Flaggers, either."

"Yeh," Jackson says. "We Seconds." He shoulders his Kalashnikov and yawns.

"Seconds," Arthur says sullenly. "More like second-placers."

Marshall just looks away, peering out into the cold and dark waters. He shrugs. "A well-regulated militia being necessary to the security of a free state..." he starts in bland tones, but lets his voice drift off. He would argue with the guy, but he just doesn't care.

No one talks for a while. They peer out into the sea. The minutes that pass dawdle to take in the scenery. Arthur just hops from foot to foot. Then, suddenly, winking lights. Marshall turns, squinting. He can just make out the black form out there. The submarine, arrived on time. Well, he thinks. Hot damn.

Marshall walks down the beach, someone's got a light and is flashing back to them in Morse code. All according to plan, yet he feels tense tonight. Or maybe he feels tense every night.

An hour later, his squad's staring uneasily at the small boats that have come up on the shore, and the crates various Chinese PLAN sailors are quietly sliding on to the beach, dropping unceremoniously onto the sand. A stiff and tall officer stands in a pressed dark uniform. Even in the cloudy moonlight, Marshall can see how smooth and sharp his cheekbones are, how even and chiseled his features look, how haughty his gaze appears to be. And he can tell from the wary glances the sailors are giving him, they either don't like him, or he's some weird political officer and not to be trusted. The translator speaks to the officer in hushed undertones, the rhythm of Chinese sounding strange and peaceful to Marshall.

It takes far too long for Marshall's taste for the crates to be unloaded. Sullen-looking sailors break them open: in the moonlight weapons gleam. Arthur speaks slowly to the officer, bowing low while the officer's eyes glitter, watching the squad.

Jackson slips one of the weapons out and holds it up. The ammo clip is in the back, handle near the front, the rifle's all angled lines moving forward. It has a dull gleam in the dispersed moonlight.

"Whoa," someone says.

The officer smiles. He turns to Marshall. "Queue Bee Shzee," he murmurs. "Type-Nine-tee-Fahve." He intones this slowly, speaking from his diaphragm. It takes Marshall a moment to realize he's speaking in English.

Jackson's sighting the shadowy hills of Santa Cruz, his face hidden in the darkness. "Type-95, huh? Pretty sleek."

"I'll say," one of the squad murmurs.

They must want the Feds to know they're arming us, Marshall thinks, calmly. *Put the fear in 'em, or something.* He narrows his eyes in thought.

Jackson slips the clip out, then snarls. "Fuck."

"What?" Arthur says, querulously.

"These bullets ain't a standard caliber. We got much ammo for this?" A search of the crates is made. The People's Liberation Army in their effort to supply the partisans with the best and latest in armaments had forgotten to supply any reasonable amount of ammunition.

Jackson just sighs.

"Shit's useless after one fight," says Evans, mournfully.

Marshall turns and gives Arthur a cold look. "Tell 'em we can't use 'em," he says.

"But-" Arthur starts.

"Do it," Marshall says.

Arthur sighs. He stammers out a communication to the officer. The officer reacts like a two-day old fish was just dangled under his nose. His teeth gleam angrily in the moonlight. The officer barks back, Arthur drops down, chanting, *"Duì bu qǐ! Duì bu qǐ!"* Marshall can catch a look of unbridled fury framed by those beautiful cheekbones of his.

JIGSAW NATION

"What's going on?" Marshall asks, catching the change in tone. He tries to sound bland, disinterested. The officer turns to scrutinize him.

Arthur looks up. "He... uh... he says it's offensive that we won't take his weapons. He's... he's getting pretty pissed off, Marshall."

Marshall sighs. He glances at Jackson, Jackson shrugs. "Well," Marshall says. "Tell him it's elite weapons, not meant for us common soldiers. But I'll take one to show the others, and as a sign of my position." He had no desire to lug one of those useless things around. But it seemed like a good compromise.

Arthur nods, then turns, stammering out the request. The officer nods, crisply, then gives Marshall a look of newfound respect. Marshall tries to respond in kind, but knows his performance is lacking.

Hours later, they've moved over the ridge of the San Andreas hills, north of Santa Cruz, a little north of Felton and just south of Ben Lomond. Here the hills shade the area from the heavy winds off the Pacific, but deposit all the rain and mist down on the hills. Redwoods rise up all around them; they sit on the back of their trucks and smoke cigarettes, sharing some decrepit alcohol made in a still up in the refugee camps along the Peninsula.

Somewhere out in the trees, an owl makes a mournful cry.

"Cell leaders won't be happy," Jackson says.

"Fuck'm," Marshall says, moodily. He looks at his hand. The gold wedding band sits on his ring finger, a reminder of happier times. Of Marienne, when she was alive. He frowns, then eyes the QBZ, the sleek and modern rifle sitting in his hands. So light compared to the heavier rifle on his back. He looks at his unit, rifles on their backs and across their laps, or resting against the truck. Kalashnikovs, hunting rifles. Scavenged M-16s from Guard units. The QBZ seems so out of place, so modern.

"Somethin' on your mind, Boss?" Jackson asks, carefully.

"Saw you in my dream, Jackson," Marshall says, looking at the rifle.

"Yeh?" Jackson says. Marshall can almost feel his grin. "Was I some pimp, some ladies' man? You saw me across the street, I bet. My cool and calm personality hit you across the face all the way from there."

Someone nearby laughs. Seconds pass, then Marshall gets up, eyeing the redwood trees. Such giants, here long before the United States was ever a country, before any Bear Flag Republic, before the white man came, before they pulled black men with them to work the fields, yellow ones to build the railroads. They'd be here long after.

The clouds have cleared up, this late at night. He can see starts through the cover of the trees. He lifts the rifle up, firing at the stars. The noise is tremendous, the smoke stings his eyes, casings flashing shell casings fly far too close to his face. It's a hissing, angry buzz, like the death rattle of millions of bees.

The clip empties in seconds. Leaves fall, some animal screams in the darkness. There's the sound of branches breaking, but nothing falls to the floor. He gets the spare, puts it in. He can hear the hushed silence, followed by whispers from the squad behind him. He levels the gun up, aims at nothing but up.

He pulls and holds down the trigger. The gun empties, a loud retort. His eyes are tearing up. It has to be the cordite. Has to be. He looks down at the QBZ, this pinnacle of modern Chinese military engineering, then tosses it into the trees.

He turns, hardening his face as he walks back to the truck. "Come on, people," he growls. "We go."

"Kevin, you're dreaming again," he heard her say.

He blinked a few times, then rose up. "Sorry," he mumbled.

Marienne gave him a fond smile, looking tired herself. "I'm getting in the shower. Get yourself some coffee," she commanded. "You'll be late for work."

Work, he thought, blandly. He frowned. Jackson. He had to know. The dreams... they seemed more intense these days. He hardly knew which was real anymore. Was any of this happening? Or was that... terrible world the real world?

Seconds, he thinks. Second-amendment. Well-regulated militias. The second amendment that had to do with keeping and bearing arms. Marshall... *Kevin* scratched his head. All confusing, what he remembered. The second world and this one had similarities, but they ended in confusion. Both had foreign-born actors as governors. Kevin still had one, but in his dream the actor got shot. Assassinated. A fight with the Federal government over something stupid... heating oil or something. State workers pulling down the Stars and Stripes, leaving only the State Flag of California flying, with its bear and red star and the words "California Republic" emblazoned on it, never changed since it was raised the first time in 1846.

Rioting in San Francisco, Castro district. California National Guard units called in to keep the peace. Pictures on the news of them sobbing, laying down their rifles. Vandenburg AFB occupied, US Marines defiantly patrolling San Diego, chaos on the Eastern Seaboard. Pacification. Kevin's dream-recollections seemed cloudy when it came to outside of the state, like only wisps of memories kept their form. With an Army called to foreign shores to protect vital interests, it fell to weekend warriors to keep the peace. They failed. The Seconds arose as a reaction, along with other rebel groups, some still around and some long gone. The Seconds aimed to kick out Guard units, keep their rifles, negotiate from strength for a peaceful transition to a government that would welcome California back with open arms. They failed.

The Guard had all sorts of names, Kevin remembered. Reds. Feds. Cornfeds. Nats. Guards. Dogs. They trained to aim for the leg in hit-and-run combats: get the Guards hurt, but still talking, still able to bitch. Don't kill one, make them pissed. Backed in the corner, though, you shoot for the face. Avoid the chest. Avoid their body armor.

They measured out life in scavenged coffee spoons. Every detail taken care of, nothing overlooked. You went hungry sometimes. Sometimes you stood in long lines in refugee camps, getting ladled porridge from 17-year-old farmboys you tried to shoot the night before. Sometimes you robbed a house for the cause. You did what you had to.

Kevin hated it. He never wanted to go back.

He found Marienne applying makeup in the bathroom mirror. He slid up behind her and snaked his arms around her waist, leaned down and closed his eyes, smelled her neck, felt her warm body in his arms.

"Mmn," she said, sounding absent. Distant. But pleased.

He tugged her towards the bedroom, a sudden impulse. It wasn't that he wanted sex, well, he did. But there was some terrible intimacy he wanted, some way that sex lets you fall apart and it's still okay.

"Oh, jeez," she said, sounding annoyed. "We have to get to work."

"I don't want to go," he mumbled.

"Well," she said pragmatically. "Neither do I. But we have to. Bills and all. We need to pay for this place."

"This place?" He opened his eyes and looked around. "We don't need it. Let's leave." He yanked at her waist again, a little more urgently.

"Honey," she said, her voice rising. "Come on, I'm applying makeup." When she frowned, her mouth creased into wrinkles he hadn't noticed before. "Maybe later tonight," she said, conciliatory.

Kevin was silent. "Nah," he said, feeling defeated. "Never mind." He went to a closet and looked for a tie, grabbing one, any one. It didn't matter which: no matter how different he thought they would be, they all ended up looking the same to him.

He found Jackson at work. Hunched in some back room, shoulders slumped, body sagging as if slowly drifting to the floor. "Jackson," Kevin says. "D'you remember me? From the dream?"

Jackson's dead brown eyes looked up. Kevin saw recognition in them, saw his own silhouette in there, somewhere, some distant reflection. "Dream," Jackson intoned woodenly. "Don' know no dream. Leave me alone."

"You know who I am, Jackson." Kevin walked over, warily.

"Don' know who you are. Leave me alone." Jackson's eyes drifted away to look in another direction, ignoring Kevin's steady gaze.

He followed Jackson home on the bus. Jackson lived nearby, under the shadow of the projects in the Mission. Kevin walked slowly, his hands in his pockets. Jackson had to know he was being followed. But he ambled on anyways, his shoulders slumped, defeated.

For some reason, Kevin lost his nerve, then. He walked around the block, then doubled-back and ended up in a bar, moodily working it over in his head. He had to piece things together. He had to set the first and second world straight in his head, at least. Maybe stop having those dreams. Or at least understand them.

He saw a cigarette machine in the corner. Awful stuff. He stared at it a moment, then bought a pack, grabbed some matches from the bar.

Fortified with liquor, he walked back to Jackson's place, banged on the door. While waiting for an answer, he lit a cigarette, cupping his hand so the match's flame wouldn't die out. A scarecrow-looking woman answered, her eyes darting back and forth, as if reading prose on his face. "What do you want?"

"I'm here to see Jackson," Marshall said, glancing up and inhaling.

"He's busy."

"I'm seeing him anyways." He stepped, or rather lurched through the door, brushing the woman aside. The cigarette tasted awful. He hated it. He inhaled again, and stepped down the hallway, looking in every room until he found Jackson.

Jackson looked up from the television set. Marshall stepped in, sniffing the air. Something smelled bad here... like chemicals or exhaust fumes. He looked different, somehow: like some animatronic version of him, or some computer graphic representation. All movement and form and nothing else.

His eyes glittered, like doll's eyes. "Marshall," he said, suddenly, and smiled. "Man. It's you. Without the cigarette..." He glanced away, his voice drifting off.

"Jackson," Kevin said. He furrowed his brow. "You remember the dreams, then?"

JIGSAW NATION

"Remember 'em? Hell," Jackson said. He leaned forward, resting his rake-thin arms on the chair. "Them nightmares, they plagued me. But I found somethin', finally. Somethin' that'll fix it good."

Kevin blinked, stepping back.

Jackson's voice sounded hollow. "You know what they do to you, Marshall. Don' lie. They killing you like they killing me." His smile was stretched tight on his face. "You don' wanna live with those memories. No one should."

He looks sick, thought Marshall. Like a dog that needs to be put down. How could someone thrive in hell, and wilt and die here? It didn't make any sense to him. No sense at all.

He shut his eyes for a moment, and a flash of an image from a dream hit him, like something he'd been doing his best to forget, could never forget. Stripping the bodies from those Alabama boys, the 20th Special Forces Group, the elite guard units. Those girls. Who knew who raped them, really. Who knew who did those things to them. But the twentieth, they paid. The bodies of the men hung in awkward ways, the burns on their faces from where the muzzle-flash of rifles had seared their skin black and red, it was like looking into the face of chaos itself. The battle was over in only a few panicked seconds, the pain continued long after.

Marshall flinched, and opened his eyes. He took a long drag off his cigarette, and coughed.

"I know that look," Jackson said, hollowly. "I saw you *flinch*."

I can't help him, Marshall suddenly thought. It's beyond me. There's nothing I can do. The only one I can help is myself. It felt selfish to think that way, but it was a desperate kind of selfishness. It made some inner sense. He started backing away.

Jackson's face twisted from some hateful rage inward, he looked down at his hands. Marshall could see a tear falling down his face. "I just want... I just want..." the man tried to get out.

It's not him, Marshall thought, desperately. It's not him.

At that moment, the scarecrow woman returned, hissing and screeching protectively, shouting empty threats about the police. It was all the excuse Marshall needed.

Marshall returned to the apartment a little late, smelling of cigarettes and beer. Marienne looked up from the kitchen, concern and growing suspicion on her face. "Kevin," she said softly. "What happened to you?"

"It doesn't matter," Marshall said. "It doesn't have to. I have you," he said, simply.

It could take seconds to destroy everything he knew, everything he cherished. That space of time after the retort of a gun, those variable seconds when the world shifts one way or another. His safety, his time, his precious life could be dashed in some instant, a shot from someone's hand, a plane in a building, a desperate act by some crazed loner or a world leader. The world was never safe. It had never been safe. That was an illusion, but the illusion worked. It kept things going, it kept people going to work, to work.

It didn't matter either way because the foundation of life was still there, inside and out, and nothing could take it away. Marshall thought he could feel it flowing through him from the contact of his bare skin against Marienne's neck, but maybe that was his imagination.

"You smell awful, Kevin," Marienne said. "Let's get you cleaned up."

Kevin sits on the beach, watching the waves of the Pacific crash into the rocky shore. Jackson's there, yelling absently as the squad hovers around the open engine of their cheap sport utility vehicle, trying to figure out how to take out the computer wiring and just let the engine run itself. The waves batter on, endlessly, back and forth, as the tide comes in once again.

"Beautiful," Kevin says.

"Whatever," says Jackson. They sit there for a spell. "Any dreams recently?"

"Yeah," Kevin says, and smiles a private smile. "You?"

"Nah," says Jackson, his voice easy but still just as hard. He's glancing down the beach with a practiced look, alert for any signs of a Guard column from the south. They sit like that for a while. "When you met me... in your dreams..."

"You were sick," says Kevin, frowning. "I told you that."

"But was it... like cancer?" asks Jackson, uncharacteristically vulnerable.

"Like cancer," Kevin repeats, watching the waves. "It's not important. You and I, we could die any minute, or step on a land mine, a random mortar attack, anything. What does it matter how you die?"

"It don't, but..."

"It don't. Let's go, Jackson. It ain't important." He gets up, walking to the truck.

"But..." says Jackson, furrowing his brow. "Which one's real?"

Kevin turns back. "You know what I think?"

Jackson nods.

"I used to think this world was the second world, and the other one was the first. And then, the other way around. But now I think, maybe they're both second worlds to each other. Maybe neither one is real. Maybe it doesn't even matter."

"What does?" Jackson asks.

Kevin just shrugs, splaying both hands out to the other man, wide and expansive, as if taking in the whole ocean into his fingers. Then he turns, barking out orders to the rest of the squad. They groan and start to complain, until Jackson starts angrily growling, Come on! You don' want those Cornfeds to catch you with your ass sticking out, bent over some damned SUV! Let's go! And the partisans bleed up into the San Andreas hills in ones and twos, disappearing into the ocean and the fog, until Kevin is left all by himself.

He stops, pulls the ring off his finger, inspects it, smiling softly to himself. He turns out to the water and throws it as far as he can, watching it glitter like a star until it hits far into the darkened waves, washing it away to sea with the calm and methodical manner it wears against the land, ever onwards, pulling sand and rock and souls and dreams into its murky depths, lost and yet lovingly tended, for ever and ever.

Edward J. McFadden III & E. Sedia

Mission Control
By Tara Kolden

Depending on how you looked at it, there were either very many or relatively few places you could hide something on a craft like the Calypso II. When Raymo's Dodgers cap went missing, he started looking in the obvious places like his personal locker and the zippered pouches that lined the small space they used as an exercise area. When it didn't turn up there, he considered the laboratory, where row upon row of identical compartments held their various experiments and gear, and whatever else Farraday had decided to squirrel away.

"You took my hat," he announced to Farraday, who was unzipping an instant meal in the tiny galley behind the cockpit. Farraday was in socks and boxers and no shirt, which wasn't strictly up to code by either NASA or FSSRA standards. His only other adornment was a coy expression in which Raymo read guilt, although it was hard to tell because Farraday was upside down.

"Don't be an ass. What would I want with your hat?" Farraday spun himself in a lazy half-circle until he and Raymo were eye to eye.

Raymo knew responding would be useless. He'd find the hat eventually, or Farraday would give up the prank next time he needed help with the guidance system. Their next trip to the moon's surface was in only eight hours, and that would offer ample opportunity. If he faked a crisis, got Farraday good and worked up, he could offer his technical expertise in exchange. Farraday was one hell of a pilot and a theoretician, but not much when it came to the rest of the on-board systems. He styled himself a loner til he got himself in trouble, and then it was *Go team!* Raymo had played the game with him enough times in training, to be sure.

He kept his mouth shut and looked out the small galley porthole. Below them, the Copernicus Crater moved past like a watchful eye.

"Console yourself," said Farraday. "Have some beef jerky." He lobbed a sealed packet in Raymo's direction, and both men watched it turn sluggish cartwheels across the galley. Raymo caught it easily and hesitated briefly before opening it, in case Farraday thought he could be bought off. Farraday had been plying him with the stuff almost from the moment they reached their target orbit. Raymo was reluctant to admit how much he liked the jerky, which was a rarity where he came from. Now that most beef was imported from the Free States and taxed to death once it crossed the border, in the NUSA you made do with chicken.

In fact, the Calypso's galley was a cornucopia of delights. Even in their dehydrated, concentrated, or otherwise manipulated states, the meals on board represented more tantalizing options than most of the grocers in Raymo's hometown. He couldn't remember the last time he'd tasted corn, or eaten so much wheat flour instead of the rice products more common in California. Farraday watched him at mealtimes with obvious delight, needling his crewmate with stories of cheap milk and wheat bread so inexpensive you could buy five loaves at a time. But the Texan had his moments, too. He tore into their salmon rations with unbridled enthusiasm, and although Raymo said nothing, he thought of the plentiful fish supply back home and allowed himself a smile. Food had never been a factor in his becoming an astronaut, but sometimes joint ventures between NASA and the FSSRA came with surprising perks.

"You're not getting tired of that stuff yet?" Farraday asked. He'd finished his own meal and was pawing through one of the galley lockers, picking out and discarding various silver packets.

"Looking for dessert?"

"No," said Farraday, "just something to break the routine. I can't believe we have five more days of this. The results of the next landing are going to be just the same as the one we did yesterday, and the day before that, and the day before that." He shook his head. "We're ready for the geology crew now. Let's drill this sucker."

Raymo looked again at the grey expanse below them. A vast and pockmarked plain filled the tiny porthole. It was a constant marvel to him that an object as familiar as the moon could take on such an alien perspective when viewed from close orbit. You thought you knew it, but you didn't. Now they were passing over a jagged mountain range. In the shadow of the peaks, a sprinkling of lights stood out. It was ILMC-1, the first drilling base set up by the FSSRA. Soon, if the rest of the data they collected checked out, there would be another.

"Concentrated peas," said Farraday, making a face. "Nobody likes concentrated peas. Hasn't anyone told Houston?"

Raymo looked over at the packet Farraday was holding. It bore the same NASA logo and tiny United-American flag that were embroidered on the sleeves of his flight suit. "That one came from us."

Farraday pushed it at him, making a noise of dissatisfaction. "Tell your people to cut that one from the menu." He steadied himself against the frame of the galley locker and sized up his crewmate. "Unless it's some kind of delicacy where you come from."

"What are you worried about?" Raymo asked. "This is the last joint mission on the roster."

"Huh. Safe from peas soon."

"Maybe for all time. Did you know they're cutting our funding?"

Farraday nodded. "I'd heard rumors. But can you blame them? You gotta turn a profit out here, just like anywhere else."

"It used to be about more than money," Raymo mused. "It used to be about the science. You don't miss the thrill of discovery?"

Farraday snorted. "All I'd miss is the paycheck. That's why I'm here, buddy. That's why I'm here." He looked at the clock mounted in the wall between them. "Time for the instrument check. Why don't you go discover whether this piece of junk will hold together for another five days, huh?"

Raymo consulted the mission notebook that dangled beside the porthole. "You're right. I'll be back for this." He nudged the jerky toward Farraday and pushed off the wall, swinging himself through the narrow hatch that led from the galley to the control center.

The instrument check was a long process, and one Raymo had done so many times in the past that as he typed his passcode into the Calypso's computer, his mind was anywhere but on the task in front of him. The energy cells, oxygen, and guidance system all checked out, and as each reassuring ping registered on the main screen, Raymo fantasized about new and better missions. Survey chores like this one didn't excite any passion in him. He wanted to go further—maybe Mars—but a manned trip of that complexity was sadly out of NASA's reach. And while the FSSRA did have the resources for such a mission, they weren't about to invest them in something that promised such spare monetary returns. He didn't like Farraday much, but he had to admit the other man was right.

Raymo gave the command for a perimeter sweep and let the computer perform its analyses. One by one, the Calypso's outer hatches and windows appeared in a list on his screen, all of their seals intact. But during the final pass, a yellow warning light registered on the panel above Raymo's head.

Raymo rechecked the system, then clicked on the communicator.

"Pasadena, this is Calypso II."

The second of dead air that always preceded command contact made him uncomfortable. Finally the communicator came to life. "We read you, Calypso. Go ahead."

"I'm picking up an unidentified object off the starboard cells. Do you have it on your systems? Over."

Several clicks sounded from the communicator before anyone spoke up. "Raymo, son, you find yourself a little green man?"

Raymo smiled. "Is that you, Cole?"

"That's an affirmative."

"So what if I have? Check your own data, you'll see what I mean."

There was another break in communication, and another series of clicks. Cole's voice was all business when he returned. "Negative, Calypso, we're not seeing anything down here."

"Look again," Raymo insisted. "Maybe ten yards off the solar cells. It's tiny, whatever it is. But you should be able to pick it up."

"Negative, negative," another voice broke from the communicator. "We got nothing here. Suggest computer malfunction, Calypso. Over."

Raymo adjusted the volume on the communicator. "Is that you, Houston?"

"Roger, Calypso. Nothing on our systems."

Raymo made sure his line was closed before he swore. Communicating with two different command centers was a definite drawback to joint NASA-FSSRA missions. You never knew how many people were on the line, or how many opinions were coming into play. Hearing the dismissive tone in the Houston command voice, Raymo wondered if taking part in all this had really been worth the beef jerky.

"Still nothing here," came Cole's voice. "All quiet in Pasadena."

"You're sure?" said Raymo.

"Run the check again." This came from Farraday, who had poked his head through the galley hatch. His brow furrowed as he took in the vast control board and the angry yellow button that was lit up in the otherwise dark panel over Raymo's head. "You can never be sure with this thing. Damn piece of junk."

"Free-American made," Raymo reminded him, but Farraday ignored the jibe. Both of them hovered above the console as Raymo reprogrammed the diagnostic tool. The warning light remained lit.

"Right off the solar cells," Raymo repeated. "We could see it out the starboard window in the lab, except the thruster's in the way. Let me reset the exterior cameras."

He was talking to himself, and to the crackle of puzzled impatience coming from the communicator. Farraday had propelled himself rapidly through the hatch that led to the laboratory pod.

"There's nothing," Farraday called. "I'm not seeing a thing."

Raymo couldn't see the other man, but he could hear the growing agitation in his voice.

"Probably just space trash," said a voice over the communicator that sounded like Cole's. "What are we getting worked up about? There's still nothing showing up on our systems down here."

"Also negative here. Houston over."

"It's throwing our computer totally out of whack," Raymo replied. "I'm registering extreme density. This isn't loose tinfoil, guys."

"Where is it?" cried Farraday. He'd turned on the communicator in the lab, and now his voice bounced unevenly around the control center, emanating from both the communicator and the lab hatch in unsettling stereo. "Why haven't you queued up the external cameras? We should be able to look at the thing, at least."

"I'm working on it!" In a moment the moonscape that had taken up the starboard camera scope dissolved into static and then reformed into a blurry image of the solar panels and the stars beyond them.

"Can't you focus?" called Farraday.

"Still working!"

At last a tiny, glittery object could be seen at the edge of the solar panels.

"It's closer now," said Raymo. "Much closer." His stomach did an involuntary flip. This, he thought, was what discovery felt like.

"What the hell?" cried Farraday. "It's on top of our cells."

"Houston," said Raymo, "request permission to intercept."

"Negative, Calypso. We suggest a wait-and-see. If it's not showing up on our systems, it could be dangerous. Houston over."

"Pasadena?"

Cole's voice was calm. "You can reach it with All Thumbs?"

Recollecting the Pasadena lab's joke name for the Calypso's retractable arm, Raymo momentarily forgot the tension that was mounting along his spine.

"Yessir."

"Well then," said Cole, "I suggest you go for it."

Farraday squeezed himself back through the lab hatch and put his hand on the communicator's toggle switch. "Wait a minute! Houston? Did you copy Pasadena's last command?"

"Roger, Calypso. Houston stands firm. Maintain your present orbit and continue observation."

Farraday crossed his arms and shot Raymo a look of worried appeal. "You're not going to go against orders, are you?"

"I have my orders."

"You don't!"

Cole's voice crackled over the communicator. "Play nice, boys."

JIGSAW NATION

While the two astronauts eyed each other, a rainbow of new lights appeared on the console. Something began to chime.

"What is that?" cried Farraday.

"Houston, Pasadena, we're losing power. I'm switching to the backup battery." Raymo flipped a switch that extinguished several, but not all, of the new warning lights. The steady chiming continued.

"Roger that, Calypso. We can see your backup battery engaged. Pasadena over."

"I'm going for it," Raymo announced. He flexed his fingers and settled them around the joystick that controlled the retractable arm.

"I think you should leave it," Farraday insisted. Once more, he disappeared into the laboratory.

"Negative!" A more authoritative voice had replaced the initial controller speaking for Houston. "Do nothing until you have confirmed orders."

"Pasadena here. Houston, they have to get whatever-it-is off the solar cells. They can't run the rest of the mission on battery power alone. It's that, or abort. Over."

For a moment, all Raymo could hear was the pounding of his own heart and the quiet whirr of the retractable arm as it powered up. Then Houston was back on the line.

"It is not the policy of the Free State Space Research Administration to jeopardize a mission in pursuit of unconfirmed UFOs. Calypso II, power down the retractable arm and run another systems test. All data here still suggests this is a computer malfunction, and nothing—"

"Where is it?" cried Farraday. "I can't see it! Is it really on the cells?"

"Farraday," said the Houston controller. "Farraday, can you confirm?"

"I think so, yes!" he shouted from the lab. "I can't see it out the starboard windows, but it's coming up on the camera. Tiny. Silver. Moving slowly."

"Pasadena," Raymo declared, "I'm going ahead. Over."

"Grab it," said Cole.

"Do it now!" Farraday shrieked. "It's eating into the cells."

"Confirmed, Calypso. We're registering damage to the starboard solar cells. Better get on it. Pasadena over."

The sweat on his hands nearly made Raymo lose his grip on the joystick, but slowly he maneuvered the retractable arm into what he thought was the correct position. The guidance screen that showed the mechanical limb unfolding from the Calypso's belly was wavering in and out of focus, so he was forced to move the arm blindly.

"Are we close?" he called. "Farraday, can you see the arm?"

"Yes, very close," Farraday replied.

"Come on, you." Raymo knocked his free hand against the guidance screen, which flickered into momentary clarity. "I can just... reach it..."

"Now!" cried Farraday. "You've got it!"

Raymo squeezed the trigger that closed the giant fingers of the retractable arm, and he thought he felt a light pressure in the joystick as they clamped around the mystery object that he could not quite see in the malfunctioning guidance screen.

"Yes!" cried Farraday.

"Got it," he told the communicator.

"Affirmative," said the Houston controller. "Starboard cells are back to seventy percent efficiency and climbing. Good work."

"Pasadena here. We can confirm that."

Raymo allowed himself to exhale for the first time in what felt like hours. "What now?"

"Tag it and bag it, son." Cole was matter-of-fact over the communicator. "Let's find out if all that fuss was for nothing."

Breathing slowly to steady his heartbeat, Raymo moved the arm back toward the ship and toggled the switch that opened a series of storage bays on the starboard side. "I'm putting it in an isolation chamber now. Then we can take a closer look."

Raymo switched on the automatic control that linked the retractable arm to the storage bays and let the Calypso take over. "Easier than picking berries," he sighed, abandoning the guidance screen. A dull thud let him know that the maneuver was complete, and a light on the console in front of him confirmed that the storage bay was secure. He reset the arm, and listened as it slowly folded itself back into its niche on the underside of the craft.

"Farraday, are we good?" he called.

Farraday's head appeared in the laboratory hatch. "We're good, but you're a klutz."

"What do you mean?"

"You squeezed it too hard, man. It's leaking out of the storage bay."

Raymo looked at him quizzically. "That can't be. The system just confirmed it. The seal's unbroken."

Farraday shrugged. "See for yourself."

Raymo pushed past him into the laboratory, and propelled himself to the starboard window on the far side. Outside, small globules of green matter were floating past the Calypso, some of them almost close enough to touch.

"Jesus."

The communicator interrupted his amazement. "Calypso, this is Houston. Can you give us your status?"

"Raymo found himself little green men, sure enough," Farraday answered. "Then he pulverized them."

"Say again, Calypso? It's organic?"

Raymo consulted the lab computer. "Storage bay 4 is registering organic material. That's affirmative."

"Calypso, this is Pasadena." Cole's voice shook. "Raymo, put on your headset. Move to secure channel."

"But sir—"

"I don't care if it's against regulation. Do it."

"Roger that," Raymo replied. It took concentrated effort to tear his gaze away from the window. He pulled himself back into the control center, leaving Farraday alone in the lab with mouth agape. He opened one of the lockers beneath the console and came up with a headset. He looped it over one ear and plugged it into the communicator, blocking out a congratulatory message from Houston control that was coming in over the public line.

"Raymo, can you hear me?" Cole's voice grew clearer as Raymo adjusted the communication channel.

"Yes, I hear you."

"Did you secure a sample?"

"Yes."

"And you're sure it's organic in nature?"

"Not certain," said Raymo, "but I think so."

Cole breathed out heavily. "Good work, man. This could be our ticket out of the hole. They'll have no choice but to fund something as monumental as this. I've already sent word to the prime minister. No more piggy-backing on these ridiculous mining ventures with the FSSRA. You've done us a real service today, son."

"Thank you."

"Back to public channels," Cole told him. "No need to ruffle any feathers."

"You got it." Raymo tore off the headset and ran a hand over his sweat-slicked forehead. On the communicator, a voice from Houston control seemed to hesitate.

"Say again, Calypso?"

"I said it's a hoax!" Farraday insisted. "He's taken you all in. I don't believe it!"

Raymo pulled himself partway into the laboratory, where Farraday was mid-tantrum. Farraday glared at him.

"You think this is funny? This idiotic joke? You get everybody on the ground worked up over a stupid prank?"

Raymo ducked as Farraday let fly with a notebook, which spiraled across the space between them. Farraday began ripping pencils from their Velcro holders and throwing these, too, at his crewmate.

"What are you talking about?"

"This is your idea of humor?" Farraday cried. "Rigging the computer system alarms? Monkeying with the external cameras. It's peas!" He cupped his mouth against the lab communicator and bellowed. "It's his goddamn concentrated peas!"

Raymo ducked another flying object, one he recognized as his Dodgers cap. "Unprofessional!" Farraday cried, pulling papers from their holders and littering the air with them. "Immature!" He ripped an air hose from the wall and let it go, making it dance crazily around the lab. "We invite you to join us on a fact-finding mission, and all you can do is sabotage it? No wonder your space program is failing. Houston was nothing until the Free States of America took it over. Stupid... New-American... idiot!"

"Farraday," Raymo pleaded. "It was no joke."

"It was peas!"

"It was not."

Farraday was red-faced. He thrust a finger at the starboard window. "You look at that and tell me it isn't concentrated peas."

Raymo looked at the window. Several green globules had collected on the outside, and he was willing to admit that they resembled something out of the Calypso's galley.

"It's no joke," he insisted. "I didn't put that there."

Farraday's next breath became a sigh. "Well, I'll give you credit. It was a good prank. And maybe I deserved it—a little—because of the hat. But I'll tell you—"

"Calypso, this is Pasadena. We have an airlock breach in the laboratory. Can you confirm this?"

The laboratory computer, like the control console, began to light up with alarms, and a shrill warming bell hammered in the starboard wall.

"Look," said Farraday, extending a hand to his crewmate. "Enough is enough, all right? Why don't you make it all stop."

"Because I can't," said Raymo.

Behind him, the starboard window began to melt.

JIGSAW NATION

State of Blues

By Gene Stewart

Sure, I'll tell you. Why not?

He had one of those soap opera actor names, Derrick Trent or something. That alone did it for me but then he opened his mouth and started demanding things in a loud, flat bray suitable for a donkey on crank. Entitlement stressed every syllable and posed him primly. A core certainty that merely by demanding he would move everyone within earshot to scurry toward meeting his slightest wish made him seem almost comical.

Almost.

What galled was how smug he was when his pasty face turned to me and said, "Well?"

He wasn't, not after I was done with him. Well, that is. He was more like hospitalized and unlikely ever to be the same.

Had he not been a Homeland Insecurity officer I might have gotten off with a warning. Well, maybe a few months in the slammer. Because he was one of those Nazi thugs, though, I drew twenty-five years to life with no chance of parole.

Breaking out is hard to do.

I worked at my prison job of making Bonsai trees for wealthy housewives in retirement communities and kept a low profile during food riots and hunger strikes. Never understood starving yourself to protest a lack of decent food, by the way. Must be an Irish kind of thing. I also didn't get throwing around what little food they did give us. How did that help? I mean, it wasn't as if media cameras or lawyers or anyone ever saw inside those places.

Being Scottish in ancestry I learned to like the maggots. Extra protein was nothing to sneer at in those cesspools run by for-profit government subcontractors. They skimped on everything possible and then cut it down some more, every penny begrudged if it had to be spent on fulfilling their contract. I swear they wouldn't be happy with one hundred per cent profit; they'd demand an extra ten or twenty percent for their trouble.

It was during my fifth year that the country split. We were told about it on the PA system. Warden Carlysle bellowed out a statement from the junta. It said we had to pick what category we fell into, reality or belief.

Most of us didn't believe a thing and hated reality so it was a choice that made no sense to us. We found out on scuttlebutt that it meant you had to decide whether to call yourself a believer in some religion or a nonbeliever.

Seems the religious right had finally had enough pretending to tolerate anyone but themselves. Not that they ever did a very good job of it. But still, they'd finally gotten fed up and now they basically said, fine; anyone who didn't believe in their guff could damned well go live in the blue states.

We asked around and best guess was that blue states meant the northeast, the great-lakes states, and the west coast.

Well hell, some of us figured. We'd rather not be surrounded by religious maniacs with redemption in their walnut-sized brains and a branding iron in either hand. Far better to go with reality; at least then you knew where you stood.

First impressions can be deceiving.

I was shipped out on a bus three days after I'd handed in my form with the Reality box checked. I hadn't been fed for those three days. Guess they took one look at the Reality-Based choice and figured why waste food on the likes of me.

Good thing I had a stash and knew where some others were. I managed to eke out a living on chocolate and peanut butter but it makes you sick after awhile.

The bus ride was long and thirsty. No water, no rest stops, robotic driver, doors welded shut, windows sealed, and AC set at about 90 degrees F. Guess what the F stood for.

From Louisiana, where I'd run afoul of the Home boys by being on a list of people who may or may not have gone to grade school with some kid named Omar who may or may not have been A) Islamic, B) Black, or C) Anything Else We Don't Approve Of. Came and dragged me right out of the grease pit where I had been changing the oil on a beautiful vintage Buick Skylark.

I broke that soap-opera-looking fed's face and some of his other bones, too, and finally they tasered me and I did the jitterbug and fell over and they beat me blue and purple and tied me up for the trip to the pen. Trials happen these days only for the rich, and then only as a kind of Noh play, formal and meaningless, to entertain their friends.

Nine years later I'm still wearing those coveralls I had on that day, by the way. Clothes are strictly optional in for-profit prisons. The only concession is any article of clothing you might need to do whatever slave work that prison performs.

Slave labor is what prisons are all about. Few outside the system know that. Ask any CEO though. He knows where to find workers that make NAFTA slaves look like overpaid vacationers.

I was hoping realists would be more reasonable about things like feeding and clothing us. Or giving us medical attention. In Shreveport Pen we were told basically to pray if we got hurt or sick. It was amazing to us how harshly God treated us. A cut finger could get infected and soon there goes the arm, and since that was done without anesthetics or even a clean saw — they used one of the rip saws from the lumber workers unit, I swear — well, few survived the new and better infection if shock didn't kill them first.

God's will.

In the bus we were better off, before some of the cons who couldn't take the heat puked. After that it was getting kind of uncomfortable. When the first one died of heat stroke or thirst or whatever it was, well, let's just say the body dumps things it doesn't need once it decides to end the synergy, and gasses are among the first to go.

Several guys broke fists trying to break a window for air.

We rolled into the Garden City Pen around midnight and the cons lined up like school kids to be the first off that bus. Me, I bided my time. What did I care? I'd been in the hole in Shreveport. Nothing about that bus ride bothered me much. To me it felt like tough faith, same as always.

"You men get in there and walk through the showers. Fresh clothes at the end."

I didn't believe it so I walked through clothed. They decided at the far end my clothes were clean enough that I could keep them. That's how I outsmarted myself out of a new pair of overalls but that was okay.

"Anyone here who doesn't want to be? This is a reality-based facility. No religious activity or speech of any kind will be tolerated and violators get one warning and after that you will be taken to the nearest red state border and dropped off. If you think that means freedom, I suggest you look at what's hanging from the crosses and lampposts on the other side of the border. Every single one of those corpses claimed to have religion."

Some coughed, some laughed, and some of us just looked down at the dust, wondering what it tasted like and how soon we'd find out.

"We recognize that some of you men are irredeemable."

Whatever the hell that means, I thought.

"We also recognize that some of you can be recovered and rehabilitated."

A big black guy stepped up and announced the hell if he was going to let himself be rehabilitated, could he please be nailed to a cross right away? This got a laugh but not from the self-important prick giving the welcome speeches.

"Very funny. But the few of you who do manage to work your way out of prison will find a good life can await you. It's up to you."

"How come no prayin'?"

He looked up from his clipboard but the screw was unable to spot who'd asked this. He smiled. "We tried separation of church and state and couldn't keep the cross-infection down. So we cut off the church part to make the body politic healthier. In practical terms it means no religion at all, of any kind, in public or in private, will be tolerated and any that is discovered will immediately be rooted out." His voice got softer. "Besides, men, you'll find that living rationally is far better anyway. No more superstition, no more lies, no pie in the sky promises of rewards later, none of that dogmatic goose-stepping."

Guy sure could talk, I thought. If he's getting through to even a third of these cons, it's more than I could believe. I piped up with, "No hope, you mean?" He didn't spot me.

When he stopped yapping, I was shown to a cell cleaner than any I'd ever seen. It even had a mattress on the slab. A sit-down toilet, too, not just a slit to squat over. And a sink with hot and cold water, even a bar of soap. I could not get over it and kept waiting for the beating, the cockroaches, the rats.

"We hit the jackpot," a lot of the guys kept saying.

As I said, first impressions can be deceiving.

"Why so many cams?" someone asked.

I told him, "A watched pot never boils ever."

He didn't get it and asked if it was true. "Yeah, it's true. Them old sayings ain't around for nothing."

You guess it in one if you realized I got taken into the guard shack for a reeducation, cause I broke the no religion rule. Seems any old saw like that one is considered superstitious, which, apparently, is religion's godfather. So they taught me. I still don't pretend to get what they mean by that.

All I knew was I had to cut them sayings my mother drilled into me when I was a kid. If I didn't, I would break the rule twice more and after that the next one would land my ass outside the prison on the other side of the border, three feet inside a red state with a cross and nails measured just for me.

That night I wondered if there was any place left in the world where someone can just live. I mean live without anyone else messing with you.

Reminded me of what I heard about the Eskimo. Turns out, the ice all melted off and they all ended up in Canada and Alaska and on welfare. This translated into oil pipeline slavery or relocation camps or prison work.

Inuit guy told me this. And what rang a bell was him saying at the time, "They can't just leave us alone so we can live. Got to put their rules on us and then their boots."

I knew what he meant.

Wild places all belong to companies that call them raw material. Can't live in them anymore. Nowhere to run, it meant. Even if I could earn my way or break out of prison, there was nowhere I could go to get out from under the thumb of big government of one kind or another.

Oh sure, space. Become a miner or welder for food wages, and be even more trapped by the conditions than the rules.

Under pressures like these is it any wonder a lot of us just sort of went nuts? Some got religion or lost it. Some found out they were king of this, or some space alien princess. Some even turned off somehow and became human beanbags, nothing but filler inside, never talking or moving on their own.

Most of that kind died quick with no water.

I kept wondering where I could find that I could be where they didn't constantly push it at me. Someplace I could live on my own and ask for nothing from any of them. Some place where I would never be bullied or even asked about what ever the government thought mattered.

Tropical island was a popular dream but I knew they were all in rich boys' pockets.

Came time when I was working in the prison library—big difference with red state prisons is they have no libraries—and ran across a book with a picture in it of a place called Mammoth Caves. Said it was caverns, not caves, and told the difference, which is that caverns go on and on, caves are just sort of a scoop out of the side of a mountain or hill or the ground.

Okay, so it's clear I had to get there.

Mammoth Caves was in a red state, though. I did not want to go back to one of those, ever. Reality might suck cause it's indifferent and all, but the religious types are just plain cruel.

I started looking for other caverns. Turns out there are lots of them. Even where I was.

You'd have to plan long and hard. You'd have to have supplies and access to more. You'd need water and coats and such. Says in caverns mostly it's in the fifty-five degree range. Sounded cool and inviting to me.

I'd need lights, meaning power, meaning mostly batteries. In my dreams I strung lines tapped into city grids but those were just dreams.

Planning how to get all that stuff arranged, hauled, and stowed, all without being noticed, in a cave, took up a lot of time. I realized no way could a man do this alone, so I recruited. Took my time, picked men only once I was sure. Tested them by telling them all kinds of other things first, see what they did with them. If they proved out, I got them near the truth and kept them at arm's length. You never knew.

Still, eventually I had a dozen handpicked men who could do the hard work needing done to make a cavern livable. We could escape, hide for a while, raid the stuff we needed from nearby cities, then just go underground.

We would have picked the holidays for making our move, but there was no more Easter or Christmas or any of those. Without the gloss of religion most lost their draw. No one cared about much but time off, and they took that randomly in blue states. Every worker was entitled to three weeks off any time they wanted to take it, no questions asked.

Basically there was no time when the prison was down to a skeleton crew. This meant we needed a diversion.

Fire worked only if they gave a damn about the people who might be burned. In that robot prison no one cared at all. The people were inconveniences, in fact. I'm surprised they didn't have a fire every year just to clean things out.

Flood might work with the electronics all over. We thought about that awhile but eventually realized they'd just shoot off the flow outside the prison if they had to.

Riot ended up being the only damned choice for a while. Trouble there was, if there was an uprising of prisoners, the guards just backed off and let the robot prison do its thing. Knockout gas that killed a good fifteen percent was considered a good choice. Periodic blasts of brain-busting noises administered at random intervals until everyone was in his own cell was another.

And then I realized something. The one thing the blue states offered, other than books and education, that red states didn't bother much with, was doctoring. And if enough of the population got sick they'd have to bring in doctors. And line us up for them in the commons area. Surely they wouldn't schlep a doctor to each cell; that would be too much even as a joke.

Food poisoning.

And one of the guys on my crew had access now and then to the food portal, where they brought in the stuff made by the factory across the valley. Another of my guys could get his hands on pesticides used to keep brush down around the prison.

Seemed like our only plan, so we decided why wait?

They fed us in our cells. We rarely had any commons time anyway; only encouraged trouble. If we had none, I would not have been able to recruit help.

As it was, the sounds of guys puking their guts up in every cell within earshot was music to my ears. That was until I heard the lock down clang through the prison.

Seems we were not to be herded to a doctor in the commons. Seems in fact that robots had analyzed the poison and were issuing antidote via each cell's food slots. Many chose not to take it.

It was thirty-five years later that I got out for good behavior. That was two, three years ago. Yeah, three. I was seventy-three and rehabilitated, they said. From having maybe gone to school with someone maybe called Omar who might have been something or other. Yeah, thanks, society.

You know, I've visited a few caverns in blue states since getting out and I got to tell you, I could live in one. No kidding. If only someone would take me seriously about how it can be done. Guess I'll be underground soon enough anyway.

Well, got to get back to work, these hedges don't trim themselves, Ms. President. And thank you kindly for the water.

Edward J. McFadden III & E. Sedia

Victory Without Honor
By C.J. Henderson

"Sleep sweetly in your humble graves,
Sleep, martyrs of a fallen cause;
Though yet no marble column craves
The pilgrim here to pause."

—Henry Timrod, Ode Sung at the Occasion of Decorating the Graves of the Confederate Dead at Magnolia Cemetery, Charleston, S.C., 1867

The recalibration took just a minute—far less time, actually—but tensions stayed high, for even the smallest handful of seconds was enough to stimulate a disaster. A minute in Proven Time could turn into a thousand years if a lost object were discovered and claimed by the residents of some OtherWhen. As the missing canister reformed in the Locator, many unconsciously held breaths were finally released in unison.

"Get it opened and get it checked," shouted the Time Coordinator on duty. "And in case anyone needs this explained to them, I mean *now!*"

The verification team knew what the woman in white meant. One did not lose twenty-one nuclear devices—

Lose...

Twenty-one...

Nuclear devices...

And not make certain that upon rediscovering that which had been "misplaced" that all of that which had been misplaced had been un-misplaced down to the last smoldering atom. The verifiers poured into the recovery area the second the greens started flashing, hurling themselves at the Locator platform with an unbridled urgency.

JIGSAW NATION

After all, the scouting threads had indicated both discovery and tampering while the devices were lost. That meant that someone, somewhere in the murky recesses of time gone by had opened the canister and had removed things—mucked about, rifled through, gone over without understanding but with impunity—some blindly lead hands from anywhere between the First Dark Ages and the Second had done a bit of juggling with enough atom-ripping force to devastate a score of major cities.

"How do these things happen?" The military attaché in charge of the recovery strained to keep his wits about him. "How can they be allowed, this kind of, of... I want it clear that this was not our fault—you know that."

"We know, general," answered the tech in charge, wearily but sympathetically. "This was our screw-up, no question. Which is why we've moved as much heaven and earth as needed to get your property back to you unchanged. That is our job here, you know, to make certain absolutely nothing interferes with upper case 'p,' upper case 't,' Proven Time."

And then, as the two men watched through the protective glass, a sudden shift in body language on the floor told the tale. All the devices were intact.

All the devices were *intact*.

And then, just as suddenly, a ripple of discovery washed over the verification team and tension leapt from body to body once more. The general's mouth went dry, his eyes widening as if simply staring harder could make him privy to what was happening on the other side of the time-protective glass. As all attention in the recovery area focused on the Locator pad, the woman making the forward inspection began pulling her arm from inside the weapon's canister as she shouted out, "There's something extra in here. Something that doesn't belong!"

The piercing sound of alarm sirens shattered the tension, throwing everyone within hearing into a numbing panic.

"Explain your findings for the time committee."

The head of Verification Team 7 looked somewhat apprehensive. It was one thing to report to fellow techs and spatial movement wonks, the Time Coordinator thought, but to wag tongue at norms, that was not something to which she had ever looked forward. Still, it went with the job, and so she said, "To be as brief as possible, here are the most immediate and direct facts. First, all the devices were removed from their canister in the past -- at some point during the last months of 1864.

"Second, their manuals were studied, and one device was apparently taken partially apart and reassembled.

"Third, after that, the devices, in the hands of the Army of the American Confederacy, were then repackaged, and buried some seventy-five feet underground. No problem for our retrievers, of course, but certainly sufficient to keep them out of the hands of anyone else."

Relief flooded about the conference chamber. Before it could become too wide spread, however, the general asked, "They said something had been placed inside the canister, something extra—from the time where it was lost. What was that all about?"

"What was discovered," the woman in white answered, "was a manuscript. We have gone over it, calibrated the language to current time understanding, and done complete verification. I can report that it dates out as authentic to the period. No one else was privy to the devices or ..."

"No, I haven't made myself clear," responded the general. "What was this manuscript all about?"

The woman in white fidgeted slightly, then composed herself once more and replied, "It's a transcript."

"A transcript of what?"

"The document records the debate within the Confederacy over how best to use the nuclear weapons in their struggle against the North."

A strange noise filtered through the conference room. No one really talked to anyone else, but everyone had some sort of buzzing noise to make before they thought better and settled back into the appropriately approved awkward silence. Indeed, the woman's words stopped most everyone in the room until finally the general, after looking both to the left and then the right for anyone who might be ready to say something, ventured;

"I think I'd like to see that."

It was several days later when General Gordon MacMurdy, senior military attaché to the Pelgimbly Institute for the Advanced Sciences, the center from which all time travel whatsoever was directed, knocked on the door of his old friend, General Cooper Reynolds Finch. After a few minutes of pleasant banter about old commands and current family members, Cooper got them to the point.

"You know I always prefer a direct engagement. Have you got this thing with you?"

"Not the original. That's off being fought over by libraries and museums and the such... but I do have a copy."

Cooper held out his hand.

Gordon pulled a sheaf of folded pages from his inside jacket pocket. Instead of handing it directly over to his friend, however, he held it just out of reach, saying, "I want to impress upon you, old buddy, that you are about to become privy to one of the most interesting military decisions of all time." The general shifted in his seat to find its most comfortable position, then added, "The time people, they tell me this whole thing happened at the end of the conflict. Now think about this for a moment. It's a year after Gettysburg. Sherman's already completed his march to the sea. Southern resistance has been all but obliterated. And then, out of nowhere, seeming like a gift from God, the power to end the war in their favor was handed to them."

"Well, Gordie, it's not that easy... I mean, how do we even know they knew what they were dealing with? And, there's the problem of delivery, and — "

MacMurdy cut his friend off with a friendly waggle of the pages he was holding. Pointing to them, he answered, "Forget it, Coop; they knew what they had. The early part of the transcript shows that they read the manuals and doped out the whole process. They might not have understood splitting the atom, but frankly, neither do I. Do you?"

"All I know," admitted Finch, "is you press a button and a city disappears."

MacMurdy waggled the papers once more, smiling as he said, "Yeah, so did they. The tacticians reporting to Jefferson Davis had detailed plans for smuggling the bombs into all the major cities -- D.C., Boston, Philadelphia, New York, et cetera. Their main proposal was to set one off in Washington, destroy Lincoln and the Congress that they saw as their real enemy, and then sue for peace."

"Well," asked Finch, "isn't that the whole story? What's so important about those papers?"

"First off, since no nukes were ever detonated in the United States outside of tests, and certainly none in the 1800s, we have to assume something happened to thwart the plans of those in the Davis War Room." Shaking the pages he was holding once more, he pointed to them, saying, "*This* is what happened. This is the response Davis wrote to his generals. They had argued the whole thing back and forth several times, and Davis had refused to use the nukes. So, basically it seems his men were planning to do it anyway, blow up D.C. and save the Confederacy despite Davis."

Finch sat listening — absorbing. It took a moment for the full impact of what he had just been told to sink in completely. The Confederacy, in the last months of the War Between the States, had been gifted with a decisive tool with which they could have repulsed their enemies quickly and thoroughly. The North would not only not know what had hit them, they would have done one of two things, for they only had two options -- to either immediately surrender, or to attack the South with all possible speed and force, killing everything in their path.

"Davis was in quite a pickle when he sat down to draft this document," MacMurdy said. Handing it over to his friend, he added, "I'm looking forward to seeing what you think."

Finch began to read as soon as the papers touched his hands. He did not speak, or even look up again, until he was finished.

I write here for posterity, for those unblemished, yet unformed generations that will follow us, and be molded by that which happens here, and indeed, by how we conduct ourselves in accordance with those happenings. We, the Union of Southern States, have been given an opportunity. Many are shouting what I feel to be premature hosannas as they claim this which has come before us to be a bounty delivered unto us by God the Father. Much as I might wish this to be true, sadly I have come to think that this is not so. I believe rather that the Almighty has sent us a test, and that we are in sore danger of failing this exercise which he has set before us.

The power to destroy, totally and utterly, it has been put before me, is God's, and God's alone, and with this notion I subscribe completely. But, when this fact is then perverted by the thought that if the power to destroy, totally and utterly, is then put into our hands to use as we will that it must have been put there by God Himself, I must respond by saying I feel faulty logic is at work.

A man might leave his belt cannon upon the table and leave the room. He might then become distracted in some manner and not return before his child comes across his loaded weapon. Just because he put the circumstances into motion where the child and firearm came together, does not necessarily mean that he wished for such to transpire.

Or equally, the same man, having told his child to not tamper with his weapon, might then contrive to leave it where it would eventually be discovered. Such could very easily be done purposely, allowing the child to come across the blunderbuss known to be the property only of the father, simply to see if his orders will be obeyed or disobeyed.

What I am saying here, is that God may have caused these weapons to have come into our hands. But his form in the shadows does not tell us that he wished for such to happen, or that if he did, that he wished for us to act on it. Suddenly having the power of the Lord our God does not immediately suppose we have in the same instant gained the wisdom to use such power.

As He told us in Romans, 19, "Vengeance is mine; I shall repay." And that is what we are talking of here, when we speak of wiping Northern cities from the face of the hemisphere—vengeance. To unleash such unholy slaughter is nothing more than the last assault of those who have nothing to lose. But, I say to this that we have far too much to lose to contemplate such a terrible choice.

There is a great and hidden danger here in seeing that which we wish to see simply because so doing is to our own advantage. As easily as this bounty might indeed have been dropped in our midst by our own sweet Savior, it could just as easily have been gifted to us by the tempter who besieged Him in the desert. We could be under the eyes of the Lord in this moment in the same manner as Job once was, and it would suit us well to remember so.

And, since there is not a man among us who would argue the thought that we are—all of us—constantly under the watchful eye of Heaven above, I say, as I have said since this business first came to our attention, that we must conduct ourselves as if our immortal souls were at stake here, for they most certainly are. We are not discussing a new type of cannon that will kill this or that number of soldiers on the battlefield. We are not discussing the mining of harbors, silent deceptions which steal the lives of brave sailors on both sides of this conflict.

No, we are advocating the wholesale murder of women and children. We are talking attacking civilians in their homes, and not only slaughtering them in their beds, around their dinner tables, at their work places and in their classrooms, we are talking about annihilating them. We are contemplating the elimination of entire populations—their total removal—snuffing them out completely, burning them away until they are but the ash of dreams. How can anyone think there is anything righteous about a people who would stoop to such horrors—for any reason what so ever?

Mark me, for I speak to you here that which none seem to want to face, the fact that we are contemplating cremating entire cities—of laying waste to hospital and church, to strangling the final breaths from grandfathers in their rockers and their grandchildren in their cribs. We are talking of reaching our hands out and closing them around we do not know how many hundreds of thousands of necks at one time, and choking them with barbaric animosity. We are discussing wholesale, bloody slaughter of the innocent, and it saddens me to my heart that every time we bandy about this idea, it seems to become easier for far too many of our company to accept.

It has been made plain to me that I can not do much more other than to state my case at this time. Those who have said they will make this happen with or without my approval are determined in their course to use one evil to offset another and I have not been able to dissuade them from this course. Wanting my blessing in this matter, however, they have allowed me this one last chance to propose a course of action of which I would approve. I have studied at this problem from many angles, and I do believe I have at last discovered a solution.

Therefore, I state here and now that I hereby approve of the leveling of Washington, D.C., as an example of what these weapons can do, but only under the following conditions.

First: the fact that twenty-one of these devices have fallen into our hands should make the mathematics of my proposal easier for many to accept. After the first weapon is detonated in the Northern capital, ten of the remaining weapons will be given to General Robert E. Lee and his staff for safe-keeping and for further, if any, offensive distribution.

JIGSAW NATION

The other ten surviving devices shall be sent to the North to clearly state our intentions. As all know, our desires to obtain peaceful, legal secession was thwarted at every turn by Mr. Lincoln and his Congress in their attempt to "preserve the Union," a corrupt and grasping Union dedicated to the carnal function of bleeding the South dry. Once D.C. has been wiped as thoroughly from the face of the world as both Sodom and Gomorrah once were, then I propose that we must relinquish half the surviving weapons.

A North living in constant fear of us will not be anything like a good neighbor. Once we call down all the forces of Hell upon the innocent, we shall never be able to drape such mantle over ourselves or our own ever again. We shall be the demons of the plains, and we shall be cursed and hated for as many generations as there are to come.

To prove our intentions, we must have as much courage in our mercy as we seem willing to have in our vengeance. Do we truly wish to simply live in peace, to continue our own way of life, or do we have some more sinister purpose clutched to our bosoms? I could go on at length, but the truth is here for all to see. This sad and futile war has torn apart families, divided churches and dragged the shroud of darkness across this land. Losing this hurtful conflict now will cause us great immediate suffering and humiliation. Winning it, however, in this monstrous fashion proposed, will harm us far worse.

We must not be the people that usher this nightmare into the world. The devices in question, it seems clear, were brought to us from our own future. No matter which hand guided them to our midst, the texts accompanying give clear year and title -- these things were created in the United States of America, in a year more than a century still untold beyond that which we know.

We are instructed to use those talents we were given at birth, to not hide them under a bushel. Foremost among these is our blessed ability to reason, and that is what I have struggled to do here. That is why, as stated above, I have presumed to act as God's instrument and order the leveling of Washington, D.C.

But, only after my conditions are met.

My first was for ten of the devices to be given over to the North. The second is this: I myself will take the bomb to the Northern capital. I myself will undo their gleaming monuments and their perfidious legislature in one swoop, offering myself as sacrifice to both sides and to He above who has put this choice before us.

It is a selfish, and cowardly demand, I know. But, if I am to be the man who ushers such a nightmare onto humanity's plate, I will not be here to see what type of world is created in response to so repulsive a meal.

This then is my proposal, gentlemen. I know you will do as you think you must. Every moment of every day each of us must do as we will, and thus I have done what I think best as well. If honor and decency still mean anything to us as a people, I would wish these twenty-one monumental temptations to be buried a hundred feet from sight, covered over with pitch and bricks, boulders and chains, anything that might keep them from human hand.

If our time has truly passed, then I say let us teach the future by the example of our dignity.

With my deepest sincerity;

Jefferson Davis, President

Finch held the manuscript for quite some time. He flipped through it after he had read it through once, revisiting numerous passages. MacMurdy did not speak as his old friend digested the document. Finally, however, Finch looked up from his desk and said, "Well, that was certainly something."

MacMurdy nodded.

"And this is no joke? I mean, we really lost twenty-one nukes in the time stream somehow, even if only for a few seconds, and this is what happened to them? Really?"

"When the Locator pulled the storage canister free, trace remains of soil, some kind of old-fashioned cement, tar, et cetera, were all found on the exterior, as well as a multitude of fingerprints, especially on the inside, of people dead for quite some time. White people, all males, DNA recognition... I could go on, but yes, Coop. Yes—it really happened."

General Cooper Reynolds Finch stared at the copies of the antique manuscript. As his eyes came up above the top of the pages to meet his old friend's once more, MacMurdy offered:

"I know, I wonder the same thing—how many people in that position, given such a choice, could have found their way to making the one he did. And then could have dragged along everyone else with him just through force of will."

"Amazing," whispered Finch. "Could have been a whole different world... imagine it, Gordie... I mean, just imagine if they had won." To which Gordon replied;

"They didn't lose the war, Coop... they won it. They were simply too honorable to claim victory."

Field Work
By J. Stern

Day dawned like a death sentence, everything grey and wet, a dull stonework diorama under a vast expanse of chilled, moist air, sky the color of slate. Something the Mexicans called 'las nieblas', some natural demon of obscurity. On days like these, it was best to huddle inside the mobile office, clinging to its promise of bright lights and hot coffee.

The Appalachian valley was beautiful on a good day, but this one was a drag. The valley was inhospitable, something bleak and dirty to be conquered, controlled, watched for signs of treason.

"Shit weather," remarked Green. His own home country of upstate New York was no better at times, its cold in winter a wolf, but on fog days he missed it often and loudly.

Nussbaum, slouched in the corner with his hat over his eyes, nodded at the newest outburst in mute agreement. He was from California, and much further from home, but he had a calmer demeanor, a more stoic attitude. He accepted all assignments, reports, and events with the same effortless aplomb. This and other traits had encouraged his swift promotion to Regional Command. He was the youngest officer in the division.

"God!" yelled Green, pacing around the long plastic table, passing mountainous stacks of loose documents, folders in disarray. "What the fuck did I ever do to deserve this?"

"Jesus," exclaimed Nussbaum airily. "You think you got it bad..."

Before he could finish, his point was made for him, as if some divine agent had put its seal of approval on his admonition. There was a pounding noise, the entire side of the trailer shook. Someone was knocking on the door.

"God damn it!" Green shouted, stalking toward the windowless single panel that was their entrance and their exit. "Stop it!"

JIGSAW NATION

He yanked open the door to reveal an old man standing in the mess outside, a scarecrow figure drenched pathetically in rain, its straw hair plastered to a face so gaunt that it showed the demarcations of the skull. This flannel-clad ghost, evidently a local, stared at them for a moment with its bloodshot eyes, shuffling its boots on the metal stairs, and then it spoke.

"Please," said the redneck. It was always the same, that single-syllable foot in the door, and then a volley of entreatments, cigarettes, food...

"I got a family," said the man. "I got to get to work." He didn't really look like a family man, but at least he didn't have 'the shakes', as it was known there, the marks of an alcoholic or a junkie, worn-out face, trembling hands. Still, there was something about him that didn't look too good. Green glared at the intruder who had interrupted his morning coffee.

"Don't you get it, you stupid hick? There's no oil left! There's no goddamn gasoline! You swilled it for years. God, you had a high old time, while all of your down-home country boys pissed around like kings, and now... now there's none left! Surprise, asshole! You're fucked!"

He was ranting, pacing throwing his hands up in the air as if to scatter confetti.

"You got the bus schedule, granddad," drawled Nussbaum. "Residents code page A15, A16."

"Bus's too slow," muttered the local. He shifted his gaze, full of uncertainty, around the trailer, then back to Green. In his younger years he would have pounded the yankee into paste for his insolence, but times had changed.

"Don't you," he said, his voice almost quivering, "don't you gov'mint folks have work for a body? Y'all need the lawn mowed?"

Green shook his head, speechless. Nussbaum craned his head up to take a look out the window at the grounds where government workers had installed the mobile office.

The site was a lot at the side of an on-ramp to the interstate, convenient for visiting dignitaries. The vestigial growth on the sloping banks that edged the lot was brown and dried into a thin stubble. The lot itself was gravel, eroding in the flood, a dire soup of pebbles and rainwater. The Californian slumped back down in his seat, pulled the hat back over his eyes.

"Whyn't you come back tomorrow?"

"Better do some work." Nussbaum looked up from his seat. "Start earning them greenbacks."

Green was already slouched into his seat by Incoming, headphones slung over his shoulders, fiddling with his Palm Pilot.

"You wanna go out in the field on a day like this?"

"Nup. Just check out some dossiers."

"Right," said Green. "I got one for you." He ripped off the headphones, swiveled, piloted the chair to the bench, and deftly plucked a thin red dossier out from among its fellows.

"Here." He threw it into his colleague's lap. "Little town about 30 miles south of here. Name of Elkton. They kicked out all the Blacks and Mexicans, burned the trailer, fenced off the town. Municipal Command was up on a raid in the mountains, came back, saw the smoke, got stopped at some... roadblock that these fucks threw up. Went south to Staunton. Replacements coming up from Roanoke, but that convoy'll take a day or so."

"What's their angle?" asked Nussbaum carelessly.

"Got a guy named, uh, Terri Horton. Stirred em all up. He says the Federation is a Jewish-Satanist cabal. Pick a side, you dumb fuck."

"Yeah. We've heard that one before."

"No kidding. They're all over these hills. Crazed on meth and years of neglect. Fucking lunatics. He's saying that when the last oil dynasty went down, that was some kind of international communist plot."

He slammed a fist down on the table, sending paper clips skittering everywhere, agitated by the intelligence presented to him on the crisp white forms.

"This asshole assumes there's some kind of 'International Communist Plot' from... Russia, or somewhere... after all the shit we've been through between now and when he was in fucking diapers. I don't think so, Horton! I think you're fooling yourself, you old hillbilly!"

He stopped, aware that he was shouting to someone miles away.

"Course," he continued in a lower voice, looking in Nussbaum's direction, "It's all got that undercurrent of self-pity. What else do they have to fall back on? All of those blowhards they used to believe in have failed them. There's no more magic mountain, nobody to pin it on. They finally came face to face with the beast."

"Hmm," said Nussbaum, playing with a bit of wire from one of the TelCom packages. He was attaching thin bits to the central thick cable apparatus used for marking urgent shipments. It looked like he was trying to make a little man.

"You know," said Green, "The thing to remember about this is, until recently, these guys were considered pretty normal. They had churches, held public office as mayors of small towns, went on television... they even had lobbyists. Never mind that not a fucking thing they said made any sense. People just went along with it. Guess they thought it was entertaining." The sarcasm was growing, becoming more evident in his voice. He stopped, growled under his breath. "Stupid bastards."

Nussbaum stood the thing up on the table. It fell over. He gathered it up and started fiddling with it again.

"Until the money ran out," continued Green, lost in a recitation of national events that was, for him, deeply personal. "What was it they used to say? Get a job. Get a job, asshole. Get a job and get off the street. Get a job and stop making noise. Get a job and be like me, strain in your traces till you die from the shit that you've stopped trying to solve. Yeah. That's what they said. While we all kept sliding all the way to the bottom. That was their answer. Get a job."

"Look," said Nussbaum in an uncharacteristic display of slight anxiety. "We've got jobs already. Can you stop repeating yourself? It's a small trailer, and we've got the rest of the day in here."

"Right. That's what I'm saying," replied Green. "Now it's the other way around."

"I get it already."

"Well, anyway, these guys are all fucked now. We're gonna break up that little slumber party with a couple of teams of Federal Marshals, and we're gonna send that flathead Norton to Guantanamo. See how he likes it."

All day they sifted through streams of information, documentations of tense communities, pressure points on the body of the local population, reports of intransigents and tiny riots against the analysts and peacekeepers sent down from the North to keep order. Everything kept shifting; flames of rebellion quelled in one hamlet sparked up in another; personnel were kept scampering along the interstates in their Smartcars, scouting for anything that required troop assistance, looking for lawbreakers in the far places of rural Virginia. In the eyes of the Northerners, it had always been a place prone to anarchy, a place where people acted without much thought, doing whatever they thought was best at any particular moment. As such, it had always been susceptible to exploitation, and under the Federation's multi-tiered economic plan, those who were raised there were doomed to second-class citizenship, barring grant recipients and prodigies that escaped their hometowns for the big city or the northern universities.

Around lunchtime, they heard that Bryant was coming down from New York, Bryant of the Second Precinct, Green's old chum from the charter school, the tall, fair-haired Irishman who had been a radio jockey, a fireman and a star athlete before turning his hand to the dynamisms of Regional Command. They got the communiqué around noon, and at three he showed up, barging in without knocking, rousing Nussbaum from a brief afternoon nap.

"Mornin', gents!"

Green was at the workstation playing Tetris, scowling at the rapidly descending red, green and yellow shapes, cursing at them and at himself in a nearly ceaseless mantra.

"Goddamn it, Dave!"

"Take it easy, pardner. Heard I was coming, dincha?"

"How's things?" Nussbaum grinned and offered a smooth West Coast soul shake that Bryant deftly accepted.

"Not bad, not bad. Inquiring minds want to know: how's the holler?"

"It's been better." The Californian shook his head without any real emotion. "Lot of trouble down there."

"Spots C22, D30, F11 and 19." Green threw a map over to the newcomer. It landed at his feet.

"Put a little effort into it, man." Bryant knelt down and picked it up in one quick seamless motion. "That was always your problem on the court. You could have beat that posh bastard from Crichton, remember? You just got lazy."

"Don't lecture me about laziness," said Green. "You were supposed to be here two days ago. I bet you didn't bring the supplies that Central ordered for us, either."

Bryant jerked a finger toward the door. "They're in my truck."

"Well," said Green, only partially mollified, "Who's gonna bring them in?"

The rain was harder, pounding down on the roof of the trailer.

"Jesus Christ!" Bryant snapped, staring down his old classmate, offended at the implication. There was a moment of tense silence.

"Nelson County," muttered Nussbaum.

"Huh?"

"Bunch of rednecks down there in little cabins off the pass," said Green, warming to the topic. "Each one with a little Winchester, maybe a gas mask, a can of pork and beans. Stupid little bastards hiding in there like mice, scrounging around on the side of the mountain. They think they're gonna do something, but they're not."

"Hey," said Bryant. "Donaldson wanted to know what you guys are gonna do about Elkton."

"We're sending in three units," said Green proudly. "Smoke 'em out."

"Look." Bryant shifted on his feet, pursed his lips. "You can't just use manpower for everything. We've got to downsize. That's always been part of the problem."

JIGSAW NATION

"Whaddya mean?"

"He's right," said Nussbaum. "The zeppelin army, bloated, sponging up dollars. Okay, so it was ridiculous before, but it always gets that way. The whole thing threatens to become too Spartan."

"Yeah," said Bryant. "Anyhow, it's in the works. We're scaling it down. We're gonna put em to work on hydroelectric, solar, conservation projects, biotech. They'll be the last to have the guns pried from their cold dead hands."

"Yeah, but these guys are well trained. They're ours. They'll put the same muscle into peacekeeping."

"Don't you believe it. Those guys are snakes. They'd turn all of it on its ear in a second if they could. Just like their old men... soldier of fortune deadbeats..."

Green muttered the last words, and fell silent, remembering all the pain and indignity of the dark years, when knowledge was as dangerous as a razor blade. Lost in memory, he stared at the map on the wall, while Bryant and Nussbaum forgot him and moved to the far side of the trailer, looking up surf gear on the net.

Presently, he snapped out of it, brightened and looked up from his reverie to the flags that hung on the wall, the pair of banners. Above was the traditional mantle of U.S. history, the Stars and Stripes forever, Old Glory unchanged and timeless. Below it was the Federation Flag, one white star on a blue background, a companion piece to its predecessors in Israel and the European Union, a slogan writ small across its base in triplicate, in English, Spanish and Latin.

Strength in Wisdom. Survival in Conservation. Prosperity in Cooperation.

"My country 'tis of thee," he said, and gave a long low chuckle before completing it, pronouncing each word with quiet relish through a cheese-eating grin. "Of thee I sing."

Seven o'clock, vespers, and the legions of the despondent, those hosts of local citizens let down by a haywire system, arrived to stand in line for the free soup and bread handed out by the Federation's soup kitchen. It hadn't stopped raining all day, and they came straggling in with evident dejection; most on foot, in slickers or carrying umbrellas, or with trash bags slung over their heads like hoods. Or they came in with nothing, looking like drowned rats. Old men, little children, young migrant workers recently deprived of their meager incomes. Families, single parents, pensioners. Blacks, Mexicans and Whites. Some of them were used to the routine, most had adjusted enough to go gracefully through the breadline of the Northern Aid Services, but there were always the others, wild-eyed and full of contempt for everything and everyone, but mostly for their situation. They were easy to spot; they herded themselves or their families into the building as if submitting to incarceration or the guillotine. They had not been able to reckon the loss of their bent idealisms, they had bought bundles of lies for so many years that the naked truth, staring them in the face, was an unacceptable intrusion.

Bryant leaned on a grey plastic shelf loaded with canned pinto beans, haphazardly punching buttons on his cell. Rodriguez tossed her sleek mane of jet-black hair away from her face, put one ringed hand on her slim waist, next to her belt, the items hanging from it like medals: the radio, the cuffs, the baton, and the Beretta in the unadorned black leather holster. She was a lithe, smooth-skinned beauty in a clean starched blue uniform, her feet encumbered by a pair of combat boots, laced up to her shins, with the legs of her trousers tucked into them. All of this gave her a distinctly martial appearance; the only things marking her as a civilian were her quick smile and easy manner.

"Poor souls," said Bryant listlessly, without looking up.

"Yes they are." She clicked her tongue in sadness. "You know, we got to have some compassion. We can't be like the old crew. You know?"

The only sign of reception was a tiny grunt, a little voiced outpouring of air. Bryant was deeply immersed in something that involved his phone, oblivious to the scene around him, the hordes of tired, hungry masses reaching out their arms to partake of the bounty of the new party, the fruits of the elections that had been so long in coming.

"Have you seen some of the crap that Green recommended?" she asked. "That New York scumbag. Who does he think he is, anyhow, huh? That stuff's not going down, fool. That's stuff's fantasy."

Bryant nodded. Everybody knew about the simmering rivalry between the hawkish Yankee and the half-Mexican Jersey girl born in a hospital in the San Fernando Valley. She still had her western accent, and memories of her father's parents, and uncles and aunts and cousins accustomed to the same hardships of breadlines and public housing, cheap transport and backbreaking hard work. Everybody knew that to Green she was just eye candy promoted by the latent lust of politically correct bosses. She resented what she had heard on the grapevine, and loathed him for his temper and his broad pronouncements on the strangers in his jurisdiction.

"You got to have the love, Eric."

He put the cell phone away, passed an eye over the line. It was mostly quiet, the people huddling there murmuring, accepting their meal in mute resignation or servile gratitude. He sighed.

JIGSAW NATION

"Yeah. It's tough times." His eyes darted to hers.

She flinched inside. Was he sincere, or just humoring her? To her, it was a given that all men wanted something; she found it hard to read them, to see who was a friend and who was an opportunist. There were some in her office who she trusted, but not many. "Who do you report to?" she asked. She didn't know him that well. His precinct was New York, hers was Jersey.

"Davidson," he said.

"Can you tell him that Lt. Brad Paisley in Hoboken put out a memo on Green? We're trying to get some of it vetoed at the brass level."

"Okay," he said. "Will do." He flashed her a smile, winked. "Don't worry, *cariña*, huh?"

She thought he could be trusted. "Thanks," she said, and walked away, without touching. She passed along the broad aisles between the tables. It wasn't uncommon to break up fights, or to calm down some slightly crazed consumer. They were in many cases broken people, with nervous minds, with tension in their stomachs, with wild fantasies driving them along. They had to be watched, as if they were children, and in a way, they were orphans of a collective dream that had left them bereft and unable to fend for themselves.

Many of them as they glanced up looked at her with awe, with a helpless respect for her beauty and her power. Their eyes were like the eyes of her people when they knelt in the darkness of small wooden churches, or when the crèche of the Maria traveled above them through the streets.

But on some faces she saw serpentine hate, as brutish and direct as the ferocity of a wild dog. They hated her because she was different, not just because of her uniform, but because she had earned it as a woman, as a foreigner, as a copper-toned child of the global south. They hated her because she symbolized the emergence of what they had always feared most of all, all of the bogeys used to drive them deeper into the grave that they dug for themselves at the end of the millennium. She was the Federation, the thing that took the reins when the horse had slipped its harness, she was what happened when the things that they had always taken for granted crumbled like a sandcastle on the Jersey coast under the changing tides of the Atlantic.

These were the people who had called her father a wetback, thinking that their nationality and citizenship had given them bright wings, believing in their own superiority with all the fervent devotion of cultists. *And*, she thought with a mix of emotions, *look at them now. Their world cracked in half, their collective vision folded into twins, and one now rules the other. It happened before, but then, history runs in cycles, and even though we can place these things in the realm of possibility, the thing is, we never believe in them until they happen.*

They hated her, and she tried to love them, but it was so hard. They were like children, like obstinate, wayward, maleducated and insufferable children, made crazy by their latchkey existence in a world of dreams. None of them wanted it: the divide down the middle of their great nation, like a dark, bitter Mississippi. Their 'revolutions' had been weak and half-hearted, the reasons behind them shattering into incomprehensible shards of self-interest and fear. The whole thing, in a way, had been based on fear, and she had been as afraid as anyone.

She left the hall and walked out through the slackening rain, out to the trailer where the fluorescent light burned against the coming night.

The trailer was empty, the men gone to guard the dinner, to lean on railings and boast about their rise as apparatchiks of the cause. She wanted to rest. Slumping down onto a stool by the blank screens, she continued her thought, gazing absently out at the night.

Everything happened so fast. They had been in a circle holding hands, and then suddenly, they were singing a different song. She heard it in her head, a catchy, jingle rhyme: Brooklyn's burning, Brooklyn's burning, look out, look out...

And the fire of natural responses from people unaccustomed to larger troubles than the thankless job or the problematic brother-in-law... she mused on and on about it, how they had scattered before the changes, the gasoline shortages, the job cuts, the tortured movements of the migrants, and then the rise of the Federation. The southerners and the mid-easters hated the Federation, gossiped about it endlessly in the corners of their homes and school and markets, but it brought them food, and it brought them a future, however dubious, and so they had to put up with it. It was their stern single parent presenting them before the cruel, quick reality of the outside world.

The rain was pounding harder again. She stopped thinking and listened to it. Within minutes, she had fallen asleep.

JIGSAW NATION

This Divided Land
By Michael Jasper

Once upon a time, not long from now, there lived two people who had fallen in love. Alan was from the northeastern mountains, and Zack was from the Midwestern flatlands. They met in the virtual world long before they ever met in person, but by their third shared linkup, each knew he'd found the person he'd been seeking all his life.

Unfortunately, the new border separated them.

Like most of his peers, Alan was too poor from a raft of college loans and the oppressive taxes to move away from his parents' three-room home just yet, while Zack still enjoyed the comforts of his family's sprawling house in the gated community in the suburbs. They were young, foolish, and in love, a potentially lethal mix for two men in this divided land.

A typical night together for them consisted of a quiet room, a screen, a connection, and a touchpad. Alan would often be doing something else on his system at the same time—traversing another world with a troupe of disparate peoples from around the globe, writing to one of his aunts, watching music, processing his photos of black mountains and frozen streams—while Zack was content just to chat with Alan; he had to stay focused and keep one eye on his bedroom door, should his father decide to check on him without knocking. The connection he and Alan shared was hacked and encrypted, but Daddy paid the bill.

Weeks passed, and Alan, the adventurous one, grew tired of the lack of contact. He suggested they meet halfway between the mountains and the plains, at the border. Zack, the timid one, went silent for a few days after that, making Alan wonder if he'd gone too far too fast.

He would later learn that Zack's father had gotten the monthly tracking statement from the sub-department of Government information, letting him know exactly where every member of the family had visited in the virtual world on his house's various connections. Daddy had wanted to know about a certain address in the mountains that had been linked to countless times in the past few weeks.

Zack lost his touchpad for that, and he had to cajole a new one from his mother on the sly. Thanks to a tip from one of Alan's online friends, he found a new connection to hack into. The setback had only made both of them more determined to meet at the border.

Alan took on the most risk, demanding to do so, because he wanted be the one to cross the border and enter foreign territory. He'd never done it before, though he'd come close once as part of his job before he was laid off, before he signed on for another year of state unemployment with benefits (his mother had stopped asking him when he was moving out when those government checks started coming in on a regular basis).

Alan already knew, after only a month and a half of being with him virtually, that Zack didn't have the fortitude to make a border crossing. He also had a feeling Zack was going to have trouble simply getting out of the house without tipping off his father, who worked long hours for a top multinational industry but always seemed to know exactly what his son was doing.

Alan loved Zack in spite of Zack's lapses into weakness; those lapses may have been part of why he loved him in the first place. Alan liked taking care of people, which explained why he was still at home, living off his monthly checks and paying just the minimum on his loan bills -- his father had seizures from the mercury dumped years ago in the lake next to the family home, and his mother was always off visiting her sister down south, where she wanted to move once Alan's father died and live off his money with lower taxes and no snow.

Alan downloaded his most recent check onto his money card, packed a backpack full of provisions, and drove his father's mud-spattered truck down the mountain, heading west to meet his soul mate in a foreign land. He tried to cover his fear of the other land with bravado, but even singing along with his satellite couldn't drown out the memories of the "family-friendly" lynch mobs and the "one-man, one-woman" marriage terrorists, to say nothing of the all-powerful government information department on Zack's side of the border.

Part of him wanted to see this place close-up, to try to understand how someone as perfect and funny and sharp as Zack could have grown up there. Another part of him wanted to snatch Zack away from there and take him to the mountains. There no one would bother them so long as they did their public service and paid their community fees and taxes.

JIGSAW NATION

And a growing part of Alan was scared witless at the thought of crossing the border. And his wits were about all he had left these days.

Zack left home with just his touchpad and his money card in his jacket. He signed out of house security claiming to be visiting a local faith-based center for the formerly homeless, where he'd been volunteering for the past year, on his father's suggestion. He drove the newer of the two Hummers his father bought him, bulling his way through the heavy noonday traffic on the toll interstate. He'd just get up to speed when he'd have to stop and wave his money card at a sensor stop, and the oversized cars and trucks around him would honk at his slowness. After being cut off three times trying to get off the five-lane, he took the first exit he could access, his nerves shot and his confidence dwindling.

On the bumpy side roads, Zack made his way east in silence, too afraid to activate any of the technology in his urban tank for fear of alerting his father—or the government information department—of his adventure. The penalty for being queer and out in public was a choice between chip implantation and five years in prison. Zack never wanted to have to face that choice in his life.

At the foot of the mountain, Alan left his father's truck at the recycling center, where they'd drain the oil and the tank of non-ethanol his pops had been meaning to filter for years now. He got on the free ultralight train and rode a nearly empty car down through the mountain pass and into the hill country. He grew more apprehensive with each mile of friendly territory slipping past.

He had his story memorized for the border crossing, and he went over it as the train car began to fill up with people, most of them white and unwashed, carrying children that clung to them like small monkeys. They were headed down to cross the border as well, providing cheap labor for the flatstaters who could afford such things, rich folk who demanded white workers now that all the non-natives had been sent back to Mexico and Africa and Canada. The children were especially in demand for their skills with dusting hard-to-reach areas and cleaning bathrooms.

Alan's story? He was going to work as a porter and butler for a young businessman named Zack. He had the contract loaded in his touchpad, though he was afraid to send it to Zack over the linkups they shared. Zack—Alan figured he could tell Zack all about his scheme after they'd met and had time to simply be with each other. His lips and arms ached for the touch of the young man he already felt he knew intimately.

While Alan slid down with ease toward their rendezvous point at the border, Zack was stuck behind an armored bus. The bus wouldn't let him pass, and it stopped often, forcing Zack to stop as well. A quick check of the satellite streams told him that the soldiers on the truck were patrolling the countryside for a group of protestors that had crossed the border, heading for the state capital. The soldiers would be shooting to kill, in that case.

At this rate, Zack would never make it to the station on time. He turned off the satellite streams, panicking that he'd been connected too long, and Daddy would now be tracking him. He wondered if he should just give up now, go back home, and be safe instead of risking everything out here. He touched the brakes again as the armored bus made another stop.

Alan's train was stopped by bored-looking soldiers at the closed border gates. They began checking credentials with pencil-shaped scanners, and when a soldier ran his scanner over Alan's card, Alan tried to smile and hold his hand steady. The soldier noticed, however, and he advised him to relax and to not believe the rumors about how horrible life was on the other side of the border.

Surprised by the unexpected kindness, Alan wanted to spill out the details of his story, but the soldier had already moved on. On wobbly legs, he walked out of the train car and got his first non-virtual look at the land on the other side of the border. Dead fields, black helicopters, and razor-tipped fences were what comprised his initial impression of this foreign land. He wanted to cry for Zack, growing up there.

Zack finally got free of the bus when it turned off, and he gunned the Hummer's engine. If he was late for this meeting, he'd never forgive himself. All his life, his father had paved the way for him, cutting him slack when needed, but this time he knew he was on his own. His Hummer roared down the two-lane road, bouncing over the potholes the road crews ignored, thanks to the toll interstates and gated community streets demanding all their attention.

The hell with Daddy, Zack thought as he continued picking up speed.

He realized his mistake the moment he heard the thunder of helicopter blades above him. Along with all his other online connections, he'd shut off his radar detection system. The instant he went eleven miles over the speed limit, a police helicopter nailed him. The chopper thundered down on top of him, as if its pilot wanted to land on the roof of Zack's truck.

The soldiers at the border had taken a sudden interest in Alan as he stood staring at the fence separating him from his lover. He'd caught sight of one of the scruffy men from the train talking to the soldiers at the guardhouse that was his last obstacle.

Alan watched with shock as the laborer pointed in his direction. He stood frozen in place, looking from the laborer to the soldiers to the fence and back again. All of his confidence drained out of him, and he wanted to run back to the safety and anonymity of the mountains.

Two of the soldiers came up to flank him as a man with gray hair and a black overcoat stepped out of the guardhouse. Alan saw, too late, the patch with the eagle on a blood-red background on the man's coat. The man was from the border patrol division of Homeland Security. Alan knew he was in deep, deep trouble now.

He tried to remember his cover story, but all he could think of was the deathly silence he'd encountered when Zack's father had cut the connection and he was unable to talk to Zack for just three days. He didn't want to face that silence again. He'd rather die.

The consult with the automated cop inside the chopper and the bribe to the pilot took Zack a good twenty minutes. By the time he was done, ticket-free but much poorer on his slice of Daddy's account, his false bravado had almost evaporated. He wondered if Alan was worth all this.

The chip implantation was supposed to be quite painful, and prison would be even worse now that guards could use torture again. All this risk for someone he'd never met in person.

And Zack was convinced the pilot had been looking at him funny in the two-way monitor of his Hummer—the pilot had seen right through him. The truth was evident on his face, he knew. He was breaking the law simply by showing his face outside.

With a supreme effort, Zack shook off his nagging thoughts and pressed on the accelerator, keeping his speed right at the designated limit. If he quit now, so close to achieving his goal, he'd just as well give up on life altogether. And he was not ready for that, not at all.

Zack was drawing close to the border—he could tell as the farmhouses disappeared and the crops and fields were barren or burnt up on either side of the road—when a beat-up Ford Excursion zipped up from behind him and sideswiped his Hummer. He stopped, panic filling him at first the thought of explaining this to his father and then at the thought of his growing tardiness.

Zack immediately regretted stepping out of the safety of his urban tank when he saw the zealous look on the driver (and the two friends of the driver) approaching him at a run. They wore suits and ties or dresses and Easter bonnets. Alan was too shocked to climb back into his truck. They were fundamentalists, and he'd seen them before, prowling outside the club were he sometimes went dancing and hoping to meet a guy.

They fell upon Zack like starved wolves on a lost sheep.

Alan had slipped free of the soldiers after far too long explaining his story to far too many people. The man from the Homeland border patrol wanted to know what Alan knew about a group of protestors, and Alan could only repeat his story and reiterate his complete lack of knowledge about anyone else.

That was the way he'd been trained to live—take care of yourself and your loved ones first. Anybody else was on their own. He'd never been to a protest before, and didn't plan on starting now.

But now he'd most likely missed his chance to meet Zack. The soldiers had kept him hidden away for too long, asking him the same questions over and over, and now Zack was surely gone.

Alan managed to take two dozen steps outside of the station when he drew up short, unable to move once again. On the other side of the border, he saw Zack. He knew it was him immediately. His lover was emerging from his Hummer, his face bloodied and bruised. Alan couldn't believe it -- Zack had made it. He wanted to drop his bag and run toward him and whisk him off to safety to heal whatever wounds had been inflicted on him.

Before Alan could reach Zack, however, five scruffy men and women on Zack's side of the border ran past and threw themselves onto the tracks in front of the westbound train.

In the long, drawn-out moment before the Homeland guns opened fire, Alan broke into a dead run, aiming himself at the gap in the open gate where the soldiers had just vacated. As he ran, he kept his gaze locked on Zack, and Zack did the same, both of them memorizing the solid reality of the other young man's presence, his solidness, his unique shape and mannerisms, and above all, his impassable distance from the other.

Alan made it one step across the border before a soldier took him down with a rubber bullet, and then the arrests began.

Five years later—or, to be more accurate, four years, two months, and three days later, time off for good behavior and therapy—Alan left the border prison with a pair of homemade tattoos and a badly damaged spirit. The only person he felt able to take care of now was himself, and that was just barely.

Zack's father, of course, had kept Zack from getting into any sort of trouble, much less prison time. Alan didn't begrudge him that; he just wished he could've gotten out sooner and not made Zack wait so long as his own hopes for the future began to fade. If Zack was still waiting at all.

The prison didn't have touchpads, of course, and Alan's had been taken from him after he was hit by the rubber bullet. He was aching for the actual touch of Zack, to the point where he wondered if he wasn't going mad from all the waiting.

JIGSAW NATION

After a long delay at the guard station—as they processed his now-ancient money card with the assistance of the security woman and a call to the prison to make sure he was legitimately free—Alan was facing the border gates once again.

His thoughts in prison had only been on getting out and starting a new life with Zack. Alan's own father had died two years into his sentence, and his mother had scooped up everything left of the family property in the mountains, sold it all, and headed for retirement down south. Even his aunts had stopped writing to him, and he held out no hope of ever hearing from any of his family again.

All he had now was Zack. As he waited for him, his bitterness grew along with his sense of desperation. He just wanted to be with the man he'd loved. They wouldn't make a huge scene out of their affection; even on this side of the border, he'd lived his whole life knowing he'd never get to hold a lover's hand or kiss a lover's lips in public without raising unwanted attention. He wanted something better than that, but he could tolerate smothering his feelings if it meant he wouldn't be alone anymore, and he'd never been more alone than he was right now, at twenty-five and feeling fifty.

Alan wouldn't have blamed him if Zack gave up on them, but Zack had found his backbone in the years since they were separated at the border by a matter of a couple feet. Zack had been living out of his battered Hummer, which was the last real possession he had left. He spent his days hiding out from his father and his old government information cronies, who'd gotten bitter when their department was chopped up and integrated into the rest of the sputtering government machine.

Zack survived because he belonged to a variety of groups who took turns gathering food, either as gifts from their contacts inside the gated communities (which had flourished and multiplied like caged rabbits) or as stolen bounty from the warehouse stores (which were in the process of imploding now that gated communities had their own marketplaces).

Zack's survival had been spurred on by the hope that Alan would be released early for good behavior. When the day he'd been waiting almost five years for finally arrived, he left the bags of food he'd packed for his friends and ran to his Hummer.

It was all he could do not to speed as he aimed his wheezing truck at the border, always the border, the damned border. During Alan's imprisonment, the border had grown porous as money for its protection was siphoned off into foreign wars and other financial sinkholes and graft schemes.

One of the pleasant side effects of this was that when Alan and Zack finally found each other at the border, they could walk across from one land to the other without risk of being harassed.

And truly, the energy expended when they touched would have been enough to light a small town for a year.

Later, inside the Hummer, they faced the question that had awaited them since their first interaction in the virtual world: *Where do we go now?*

Zack suggested Canada, while Alan hesitantly pointed back at the distant, invisible mountains to the east. Then he reconsidered and asked if Zack spoke any Spanish.

"We have to get out of here," Alan said. "We have to run away, find a better place."

Silence filled the Hummer for so long after he spoke that it felt like another any prison term. The moment they'd been waiting for had come and gone, and to Alan the future was just another wall instead for him, instead of a doorway.

Finally Zack spoke, a smile breaking across his face.

"I'm tired of running, love," he said, picturing them putting their backs to the wall and going in the opposite direction from it in this divided land. "What do you say we go meet my father and have a nice long chat with him?"

JIGSAW NATION

Abraham Lincoln for High Exulted Mystic Ruler of the Galaxy

By Edward J. McFadden III

"The dogmas of the quiet past are inadequate to the stormy present. The occasion is piled high with difficulty, and we must rise with the occasion. As our case is new, so we must think anew, and act anew. We must disenthrall ourselves, and then we shall save our country."

-Abraham Lincoln, Second Annual Message to Congress, December 1, 1862.

The bartender had been walking across the desolate hardpan for days, the bruised sky constantly shifting and caressing the barrier between worlds. Several times, forked lightening had streaked across the horizon and the bartender covered his ears, waiting for a deafening *crack* of thunder that never came. That's when he realized there was no sound at all. He could feel the wind on his face, but it produced no noise. His breathing echoed in his ears, the pounding of his heart sounding-off like a bass drum.

There was nothing on the horizon except menacing sky — no mountains, no forests, and no life. Sunlight had become a distant memory and even firelight would have been welcomed like a lover. The hardpan was unyielding and the bartender had not seen a plant, nor so much as a dead blade of grass, since he appeared in-between. Like a delicate string stretching across an infinite number of points in time, in-between is at all times everywhere, a twisted netherworld stretching across the countless dimensions of space.

The bartenders name was Skip, and he had walked through the dust and sand for more than a week, but was no closer to understanding his place in this strange world. There was nothing to distinguish the difference between forty feet away and four miles, and that lack of depth perception created chaos in his mind. He hovered alone on a stage set atop the world, and it didn't matter how far he walked, or how long he could coerce his body. Eventually he and his ghost would be forced to give up.

Skip's essence had partly survived in-between, his bodily energy having been sucked through a rip in space-time so small there are an infinite number of them. Some beings have an energy within them that will not allow their entire physical self to die. A type of shadow immortality, the price of which is the highest ever paid.

The bartender fell, his weakened legs finally coming unhinged. His head hit the sand with a soft thud, and he rolled over. Wisps of gray smoke streaked across the purple-black sky, the faint shadows of shining stars beyond. Skip closed his eyes hoping death would take him again.

"Sir, are you well?"

Skip's eyes flicked open. He could see the faint shadow of a man in a black suit standing above him, but when he turned his head the man vanished. Skip rose and rubbed the blurriness from his eyes. For an instant he focused and the man again stood solid before him. Skip blinked and the man was gone.

He blinked.

A distorted President Abraham Lincoln glared at Skip. The President's black beard writhed like a bowl of maggots, and his left eye had been replaced with a lens that constantly telescoped in and out. The real eye was bloodshot and barely visible within its shrunken black socket. His top hat ended in a point, and his coat with tails had become a cloak. Scaly snake-like hands protruded from beneath the tunic, and the president's cold red lips were twisted in a grin.

"Are you well?" Lincoln reached to lift Skip. "May I help you?"

Skip had been a bartender in New York City for more than forty years. He had poured more liquor then there was water in the small lake behind his house in Queens. His instincts were that of a worn battle soldier: guard constantly up, senses tuned beyond most human capacities. This, along with the block of ice in the pit of his stomach, made Skip jerk back, avoiding President Lincoln's touch.

"Yessssss," said Lincoln as he saw Skip pull away. The word slithered from Lincoln's mouth and the chill in Skip's belly spread to his fingers and toes, yet beads of sweat dripped down his forehead.

"What is this place? How did I get here?" The questions came unbidden, and the smile on President Lincoln's sick face grew wider.

"The first one's free," hissed Lincoln, and Skip jerked his neck back as the sound of the president's voice sent a jolt down his spin. "You are in-between, on a pathway from one point in physical space to another." Skip heard the sound of a servo motor as Lincoln's mechanical eye shot out, putting him under its microscopic stare. Silence continued to fill the open plane. In that moment Skip felt like the world had forgotten them. They were no more than ants crawling across a rock on a forgotten desert in a lost universe.

"What are you?"

President Lincoln didn't answer. His real eye appraised Skip as if he were a diseased animal that he was trying to figure out how to kill. "As I said, the first ones free."

"Sir, I have no money. I could pay you when..."

"I don't want money, you infantile little fool!" Skip stepped back, the president's good eye deepening into an even darker shade of blood red. "I want your vote!" Lincoln straightened, pulling back his shoulders and rising to his full height. His wizard's hat sat slightly cocked to one side, his black robe accented with a silver bow tie pushed out as if he were posing for a portrait.

Skip almost laughed, but didn't want to bring on the president's legendary wrath. It was common knowledge that Lincoln had fought doggedly in the Black Hawk War. Also, when Lincoln moved to New Salem as a young man he immediately began fighting with the biggest bully in town, Jack Armstrong, and threatened to fight the entire city if need be. A gentle man he had been, but tough and ruthless at need, and Skip didn't doubt that in the chaos of this impossible landscape the former president would crush him to powder if the fancy struck him. "What are you running for, sir?"

"High Exulted Mystic Ruler of the Galaxy." Lincoln smiled broadly, his mechanical eye rotating and purring. "If all do not join me now to save the good old ship of the Union this voyage, nobody will have a chance to pilot her on another voyage," said President Lincoln, forefather of the Old United States who had presided before the dark times and the fall of the Republic.

"How did I get here?" Skip asked again, his voice cracking apart like burning wood.

"Have you ever heard of the butterfly effect?"

"Sure," answered Skip, and as he spoke Lincoln seemed to fade for an instant, the black of his suit shifting to bright orange, his skin turning the color of dark chocolate, his beard hanging in purple strands below his knees. Skip blinked, and the image shimmered back into focus and the president was restored to his funereal parlor-like color and attire. "It's when one very small action has effects that become greater as time moves forward. A pebble thrown in the flat ocean can cause a tidal wave. The beating of a butterfly's wings can cause a hurricane."

"Hmm, well that's one way to explain it," said Lincoln, his cocky aristocratic voice adding to his mountainous presence. "Small events may have huge consequences and rash decisions sometimes lead to futility and darkness. It is with those words that I begin to tell you why and how you are here. Do I have your vote of confidence, sir?"

"You do, Mr. President," said Skip, the faint murmur of old patriotism stirring in his gut.

"The event that brought down your world, and thus destroyed that part of you that could not follow to this place, was as simple as one person drinking too much wine.

"Chad Beager, called Beef by his close friends, was supposed to spend the night reviewing Hickory County's final ballot for the 2000 Presidential Election scheduled to take place November 4, 2000. The format had been studied. Design concepts discussed and agreed to by all necessary parties, and all appropriate votes had been taken.

"But the printer's draft was late to the Florida Judges Office because Chad's son-in-law, who had 'won' the design contract, had been arrested for trying to smuggle two pounds of marijuana home from his Jamaican vacation in his carryon bag. Apparently, the moron didn't understand that a Hickory County Judge didn't hold much sway in a Federal Customs case.

"So it was that the proof arrived for the Judges final approval on the night of September 11th, 2000, and had to be to the printer the very next day in order for it to be printed and punch hole perforated, shipped, and dispersed to the various polling stations by Election Day. The deadline is mandated by law and if the judge had…"

"I know all this," interrupted Skip. "He went out and got drunk instead, then…"

"Would you interrupt George Washington?" the ex-president bellowed.

"Sorry, sir."

Lincoln's gazed drifted across the hardpan, and for a moment Skip thought Lincoln had forgotten he was there. They stood face to face, but the president didn't seem to see him any longer. His mechanical eye was fully extended, looking over Skip's shoulder. The breeze continued to blow, but only the sound of Skip's ragged breathing and the steady thump of his heard could be heard in the silence. The vast bleakness of in-between continued into nowhere, and Skip felt drained.

Then, as if someone had hit his 'un-pause' button, Lincoln's mechanical eye pulled inward, the servo motor buzzing. "Yes, he got drunk," he continued. "The next day, his eyes blurry with lack of sleep and impeded by swollen blood vessels, he barely looked at the form before he signed it and sent it off to the printer. That paper butterfly's flapping wings caused the nuclear winds that brought you to this place."

President Lincoln paused again, staring up at the purple-orange sky. Skip knew the history of the early 21st century as well as anyone. A stolen election and the United States alienated itself from the world, pounded its chest a little too hard, and September 11th changed the way people thought about freedom. The divided country became more polarized, and by 2016 the United States had become The Former Republic of the United States which encompassed the entire Old United States minus Pennsylvania and all points north, and the entire West coast including Alaska and Hawaii. Those states had joined Canada, taking their money and business northward.

As if reading the bartender's thoughts, Lincoln began reciting like on old victrola in his head had been turned on. "Secession is illegal, and I will do again what I have done before; use the collective will of our forces to impede such an act of heresy. Let us have faith that right makes might, and in that faith, let us, to the end, dare to do our duty as we understand it."

"To what end?" asked Skip. The sky had changed color to yellow-pink, but still no rays of sunlight broke through the thick layer of gloom. The bartender felt the urge to move on, to leave this relic of a bygone era alone amidst to emptiness of the barren plane.

Lincoln's mechanical eye extended further than it had before, and he seemed to have returned from his reverie. "All dreaded it, all sought to avert it...And the war came," said Lincoln. "It was only a matter of time before a foreign power took advantage of the divide, and who better than the Chinese?" Lincoln's voice was sad, and he removed his hat and bowed his head to honor the fallen.

"The Chinese attack came swiftly and caught what remained of the U.S. at unawares. They seized most nuclear sites, the White House, and the new Parliament Building in Toronto. The American people were scattered and divided, our country lost."

"OK, you done?" The contempt in Skip's voice was sharp and easy to detect. "I knew all that. Then we recaptured New York, parts of Boston and the coast as far north as Newfoundland. I had a small place on the east river. It didn't look like much from the outside, but it fixed up pretty good on the inside. Three kinds of beer—real shit, not the piss crap people made from potatoes or carrots—but real beer made from hops grown on the roof of the building. I had some wine, booze; things were starting to look up. Now I'm in this never changing barren shithole." Skip's reverence for the

President was gone. If he wanted his vote, it was time to Christ God earn it. "So how did I get here?"

Lincoln came forward, reaching out his arm and pulling Skip to him. "You know something? I know a guy who wants to open a place like that. This barren shithole ends, and a new barren shithole begins, but there are better places in-between than this, and I think you are destined for them. *Skip's*. That has a nice ring to it."

Skip thought it did to. "OK, maybe, but I need to know. I'm from New York Mr. President; you can't get me off topic that easily."

Lincoln laughed, and then fell silent. He pulled at his beard, his dark eyes examining the ground before him. "The Chinese used the nukes they had captured from the Former Republic of the United States to quell the uprising in the northeast. The first city to go was New York. You don't remember anything?"

Skip looked into the president's real eye, and saw the interior of his old bar. A smile crept across Skip's face as he watched himself serving Tony Greag and Jill Whiteker. The front window was dark, and several patrons hide in the shadows nursing their drinks alongside their sorrows.

Then the president's real eye flashed with white light, and his mechanical eye wrenched back into his head with a squeak of servos. "All because Chad drank to much wine. Had Thor won, the United States would still be going strong and my monument wouldn't be a pile of rubble." The president's head jerked like his mother had grabbed him by the ear. Skip turned slightly, and the president blinked out of existence.

Sunlight broke through clouds, which were now a myriad of color. Skip saw something metallic glowing to his left. Turning toward it, he took several hesitant steps forward and picked up the shining piece of metal. It was a small round pin with blue lettering on one side. Skip heard Lincoln's faint voice on the wind. "I'm true blue and I'll fight for you." Skip chuckled, a republican true blue? Then he pinned the **Abraham Lincoln for High Exulted Mystic Ruler of the Galaxy** button on his tattered shirt and continued across the desolate hardpan.

Out there he would start *Skip's*, and face the oncoming storm.

[Editors note: The author notes that some of the names of people and places in this tale have been changed to protect the guilty. Skip, his bar, and the world of in-between, are further explored in Ed's novel, *Shadows & Dust*.]

JIGSAW NATION

Rhymes With Jew
By Paul G. Tremblay

Diane rhymes words with 'Jew.' Silly, nonsensical rhymes in love with the simple rhythm, the hard monosyllables ending with lips pursing into the *ooo* sound repeatedly. As a child, Diane drove her mother crazy with it. Mom, in her English sprinkled with Yiddish, said her daughter was a *schlemiel*, said her daughter was giant pain in the *tuchis*, said she wasn't respecting their heritage, said people would think she was a *shikseh*.

It's approaching sundown on the Sabbath. Diane was too weak to go to Temple today. But she said a *Kaddish* for her long-deceased mother. Now in the middle of her tea, there's a knock on her door. Diane, this older-than-Abraham woman, who now forgets more than she remembers, finds two Jews (she notices the delicious rhyme) on her doorstep. Two young men she has seen at Temple, two young men said to be attending a secret *yeshiva*, two young men wearing tattered and worn suits (she knows the suits likely comprise their entire wardrobe), two young men wearing *yarmulkes*. She marvels at their *chutzpah* for being so public with their faith. Yes, she supposes there are still a few of them left. A few Jews. Mm, that rhyme....

The young men don't have to tell Diane why they are here. No need to talk about the new Homeland Faith taxes placed upon Synagogues and the purchase of kosher foods and all things Jewish are so burdensome, so aggressive, so clear in their message. Like so many young people, they are poor in pocket and in spirit. She knows they want to leave the Red States and go to the Blue, but they don't know how to leave and they don't know where the Blue States are. They haven't found the Blue in their libraries or on televisions and computers. Even their rabbi only has rumors, and of course, Diane's name and address.

Diane invites the young men into her home and offers them *bailies* despite the late hour.

She tells them, "Sit."

She tells them, "I'm not what I used to be, but I can still talk, and drink. We'll drink, fill our lungs with cigarette smoke and die sooner rather than later, if we're lucky."

Two weeks before the government grants and subsidies expired, Gail Goodwin (who had earned millions with home alarms and other personal security products) privatized and financed a social work department loosely affiliated with Charlotte State Hospital. One year after her start, Gail hired Diane despite her apparent status as grossly under-qualified. Gail wore turtleneck sweaters even in summer, jeans, thick glasses, and chewed gum to keep from smoking. Gail was always as serious as her sweaters.

This is how Diane remembers their first conversation:

Gail said, "I hate gum."

Diane said, "So do I. Makes me feel like a cow working a cud."

Gail said, "We live in the eighth poorest county in the country."

Diane said, "When I left the house to come to this interview, my mother said what I had on was a *shmatteh*, a rag. But I think I look appropriate, if not nice."

Gail said, "Racial, religious, and ethnic discrimination coupled with the price structure of consumer fashion makes it easy for poor people to appear to be middle-class."

Diane said, "Am I allowed to smoke anywhere in the hospital?"

Gail said, "Many of our clients believe they are a part of the disappearing middle-class. They have no job security. Everything they own is on credit. They are living one paycheck away from homelessness, but believe they are middle-class and they believe that what is good for government and corporations is good for them."

Diane said, "Could I have a piece of gum?"

Gail said, "While it's not difficult to appear economically stable, it is difficult for the poor to get enough to eat and to keep warm."

Diane said, "I have no prior professional experience in this area, only amateur experience. I've spent my lifetime in a family desperately trying to appear economically stable."

Gail said, "Obesity is the new disease of poverty because the poor can only afford to eat the wrong things."

Diane said, "My mother wants me to work here. She says I'd be mixed up, lost, *farblonjet* without this good work."

Gail said, "Recently, one client of ours ran naked through a local swamp, then emptied his shotgun into a small herd of cows that belonged to a neighboring farm, still pumping and shooting even after being out of ammo. We have too many clients who periodically exhibit the kind of violent behavior that warrants a stay in our hospital. But you know what? They recover after about two weeks of food. These people's nutritional needs are so far from being met that two weeks of hospital food changes them. Nine months out of the year they eat rice, cornmeal, sawmill gravy, maybe a vegetable if its summer, maybe fast-food if they have a little money, maybe meat from a stolen hog off one of the farms."

Diane said, "Pigs aren't kosher."

Gail said, "You start tomorrow."

This conversation may or may not have happened as described. It is more likely an amalgam of twenty-five plus years of her relationship with and memories of Gail. Regardless, the reciting of this conversation confuses the young men. They tell Diane they don't understand what any of this has to do with getting them to the Blue States.

Diane tells them, "Stop *nuhdzing* and hush up." She appreciates, even envies their impatience. Impatience means they hope.

She tells them, "In due time, you will hear what you need to know."

She tells them, "You will hear everything. You will hear about Sandra first." Diane pulls yellowed newspaper clippings from the top of her refrigerator. They shake in her hand but only because her hand is always shaking. An obituary paper-clipped to a short, two-piece article.

Unlike the graying memories of Gail, Mom, and just about everyone else who was important to her, Diane remembers Sandra.

Sandra's case report made mention of her $12,000 income working second-shift janitorial at a *William and Morris* office building. Her one-bedroom apartment rent was $1000 per month. Both income and rent numbers were the average for an adult citizen of the one-time textile city of Lawrence, North Carolina.

Winter, and the temperature had dropped below forty degrees. Drug paraphernalia littered the front-stoop and hallways of Sandra's apartment building. The case report made mention of Sandra having passed her last three random drug tests. Sandra was trying. Inside the building wasn't warmer than outside. Diane's breath was white exhaust while walking the hallways and staircases.

Diane knocked on door # 213. A young woman, a teenager, a girl (Mom would've called her a pisher) opened the door. She wore a moth worn-sweater concealing her cigarette-thin arms, and she held a baby. This was Sandra. Diane mentally went through her checklist for signs of malnutrition: dry hair, red and cracked lips, glassy eyes, yellowing and dry skin. Diane reminded herself to watch for irritability, poor memory, strange or obsessive behavior.

Her baby's name was Drew. He was six months old and wrapped in a blanket. His file was included with Sandra's case report folder.

Diane entered and saw the electric stove on and open. The only heat in the apartment. She said, "The heat seems to be out in the whole building."

Sandra said, "You the lady I talked to on the phone? From the hospital?"

"Yes." Diane extended a hand. Sandra's hand was limp and cold. "I was happy to read that you agreed to continue the center's counselling."

"I'll take all the help I can get. Does it tell ya in that folder of yours that my landlord is missing? He's probably with the heat." Sandra put the baby in a bassinette near the oven. Her lips moved but she wasn't talking. With the baby down, she rubbed her eyes, once, then twice, then a third time. Her lips formed silent words again.

Diane made her mental notes.

Sandra said, "You're new to the center?"

"Yes and no."

"I hate that shit. Pick one."

"Yes. You are my first case. Congratulations."

"Then why did you say no? My head's already a mess. Don't need you handing me bullshit head-shrinking kind of answers." Sandra rubbed her eyes again and in her three-cycle method. The skin around her eyes was now an angry, crayon-red.

Diane said, "I said *no* because I've been with the center for four months."

"Alright. What did you do before getting assigned to us? I'm not gonna let just anyone help me and my baby." Sandra pulled a chair up next to the oven and bassinette, then took off her sweater. A potbelly one might describe as a distended abdomen (another sign of malnutrition) pushed against a tight, green tee shirt.

Diane said, "When was the last time you ate?" Diane didn't sit, but opened the file and uncapped her pen.

"Yesterday morning."

"Can you give me a time, roughly?"

"Eight... maybe nine or ten."

"What did you eat?"

"Um... Ramen noodles, or maybe just some broth. You didn't answer my question."

"What question was that?"

JIGSAW NATION

"What did you do before getting us?"

Gail had instructed Diane that as a caseworker, blunt honesty would be her only chance at succeeding in gaining the people's trust in Lawrence, as the residents had been abandoned by their government and had heard every manner of bureaucratic lie imaginable. So Diane said, "My first three months I cold-called and knocked on the doors of nice white, Christian people and asked them to donate interview-worthy clothes so the lazy, fat poor people could look for jobs, even though there were no jobs to be had within fifty miles, even though there were no more government sponsored community action agencies or jobs training programs. Why? The young poor people that the Red States don't need for shit work can go into the military, avoiding the need to draft from the middle and upper classes."

Sandra's mouth had moved while Diane talked. Diane imagined this malnourished child-cum-single-mother trying get sustenance from her words.

Sandra said, "Alright. I think you can help me and Drew."

Diane said, "That's why I'm here. When and what did Drew last eat?"

"I breastfeed Drew. He ate an hour ago. Just started him on cereal, too." Sandra pointed at the all-but-barren kitchen counter. On it was a box of rice cereal for babies.

Diane wondered how much of it Sandra had eaten. She said, "Have you kept all his pediatric appointments? Has he been getting his shots?"

"Yeah."

"Can you prove it?"

"Call his doc." Sandra fished around inside her jeans pocket and pulled out a wrinkled appointment card. She gave it to Diane and she paper clipped it to the initial hospital diagnosis of postpartum depression. The diagnosis detailed episodes of Sandra wandering the halls of the hospital and, upon release, her apartment building while crying uncontrollably. The diagnosis also detailed a history drug use, physical and mental abuse at the hands of Drew's father, and possible sexual abuse from unnamed members of her family or neighbors.

Diane said, "Have you had any uncontrollable crying fits in the last two weeks?"

"No." Sandra said it fast. A dart.

Then they talked more about Drew. Diane stayed to watch Sandra breastfeed him and wasn't convinced that Sandra was capable of producing or expressing milk. She watched Sandra mix cereal with tap water. Drew cried and shivered while eating. After Drew's lunch they discussed the day care situation; the mother of the deserting dead-beat Dad lived on the floor below and watched Drew while Sandra was at work. They talked about bills, a schedule of payment, of creating a resume and practicing job interviews. Diane made it a point to leave multiple copies of her contact information throughout the apartment.

Diane packed up the file and readied to leave when Sandra said, "This fine and dandy, but all that liberal-type stuff you were talking before, you know the government keeping people poor on purpose and all that? Well, I thought it meant you could help me."

Diane said, "It does, Sandra. And we talked about how I was going to help you."

"No, that ain't it. I need you to help me and my baby to get out. To get to the Blue States."

Diane only knew what her mother had told her when she was a child: only the rich and connected and *gentile* could leave the Red States for the fabled Blue. Diane had greeted this matronly proclamation with a *Blue-Jew* and *Jew-Blue* singsong rhyme.

Diane went against her truth-and-trust social worker paradigm and didn't tell Sandra that. She said, "I really don't know much about the Blue States."

Sandra rubbed her eyes three times, then stared hard at Drew, a look that could bore through skin. She said. "My parents escaped to the Blue States. They're somewhere up North, I think. They can't contact me now because the Red States won't let 'em. But they can get me in. I know they can. Didn't you know if you knew someone who lived there that you could get in? They have computerized lists at the borders, or something like that. They can check that kind of shit out. I just need to get to the borders, lady, then me and Drew will be okay."

"I really don't know anything..."

Sandra said, "You know, they help people like me in the Blue States. They'll help Drew, keep him fed, clothed, and educated. They'll know it isn't his fault that his Momma is a screw up. They won't blame him for being poor. You know, I even hear they have free hospitals, socialized medicine they call it..." Sandra ran out of breath and words. She rubbed her eyes.

Diane said, "I'll see what I can find out. I promise."

Diane shows the two young men the obituary; a small rectangle cut from a newspaper that is decades older than the young men are:

JIGSAW NATION

> **Tuckett, Drew**—Of Lawrence, April 31rd 2005. Beloved son of Sandra Gomes, grandson of Robert and Julia Earls, and Brenda Thatch. Funeral Service will be held at Old South United Methodist Church, 12 Conant Street, Lawrence at 10:30 AM on May 3rd. Relatives and well-wishers are invited to attend. Internment will be at a later date and will be private. Expressions of sympathy may be made in his memory to Social Care: Charlotte State Hospital, 478 Admiral Avenue, Charlotte, NC.

Ten days after Diane had met Sandra, Diane's mother had a massive heart attack and died. Mom was 64 years old.

Despite the loss and while sitting *shivah*, Diane met with Sandra twice that week, and every week after. She fulfilled her official caseworker responsibilities to the best of her abilities even as she picked up a new client with each passing week. But in the process, Diane broke a few of Gail's policies. She let Sandra call on her private line and initially they had chatted like old friends. When Sandra's phone was shut off, Diane gave her the cell-phone that her mother had owned. They talked about Diane's mother. They talked about male-companion prospects, of which there seemed to be very few. They talked about Drew, but not in a social-service way. Though eventually, Sandra forced the conversations to be about the Blue States. Always the Blue States, and Diane always had the same *still investigating* response.

After two months, Sandra was no longer eligible for food stamps. Diane took to treating Sandra and Drew to a lunch at a local diner once a week, money coming from her own pocket.

This is how Diane remembers her last meeting, her last lunch with Sandra:

Sandra ordered her usual, the Big Country breakfast with pancakes, grits, two eggs (always scrambled and mixed in with the grits), sausage, and a large OJ. Drew nibbled on dry toast. Diane had ordered a turkey-club, but hadn't eaten a bite.

Sandra said, "What's the matter? Not hungry?"

Diane was not hungry. She said, "Just because you get a good meal once a week doesn't mean that you can skip out on eating the rest of the week."

Despite these weekly feasts, Sandra was still as gaunt and washed out as she was when they had met. Diane noticed Drew's new clothes. A football shirt, number 27, a logo-less blue baseball hat, and mini-workboots. Diane assumed Sandra used the once earmarked food-money (what little of it there was) to buy new clothes for Drew. He sure did look nice.

"You gonna get all professional on me now?" Sandra smiled, like she meant it as a joke, but it sounded too hard. Despite their apparent closeness this was a reminder that Diane did not really know Sandra. But Diane knew enough to know Sandra was far from well. Sandra's behavior could still be erratic; swinging from giddiness to despair like a pendulum.

"You need to eat on a consistent basis. That is priority one. You are not helping Drew by starving yourself."

Sandra aimed her eyes at her plate and filled her cheeks with food. She touched Drew lightly on his arm twice. He smiled and shoved his fist into his mouth. She said, "I bet you sound like your mother right now."

That hurt Diane. But she didn't want to show it. She went from saying nothing to saying, "My mother was *meshiginah*, crazy as a bedbug. She didn't throw anything away. Newspapers, brown-paper bags, tin cans, she saved, flattened, and reused tinfoil. She took baths and pestered my father into reusing her dirty water. Last week I helped Dad empty out the house of all the stuff. I threw it all away or donated it to the center. She invited homeless people over for dinner once a week even when we couldn't afford it. Someone new each time. We had things stolen of course, and most of those dinners were so very uncomfortable, but it never stopped her."

Sandra had an empty-screen stare, focusing somewhere beyond Diane, and she said, "Am I your Momma's homeless person then? Your weekly charity case that makes you feel better about yourself?" Sandra jiggled her legs and banged the table with her fork like a drummer in a heavy metal band. She was a one-woman ruckus.

Drew's saucer eyes became teapots. He didn't like the sudden movement and noise. He cried and threw his toast on the floor.

Diane said, "She told me she loved everyone, even the *schmucks*. I knew who the *schmucks* were. And she told me she loved God, even when I didn't. I envied her faith. I think she saved it, but I threw it away."

Sandra's Tasmanian devil stopped spinning. She said, "I'm sorry. I don't know... I woke up on the wrong side of the couch this morning or something," then stopped, a balloon out of air.

Diane kept talking. "My mother also said God didn't make or design poverty. People did. But I think I blame both."

JIGSAW NATION

Sandra said, "Did you talk to your boss about the Blue States yet? You said she knew something. Can she get me in? She's rich enough. She must know how." Sandra pleaded, begged, and reached her matchstick arm across the table trying to touch Diane.

Diane thought about the case file and the details of Sandra's drug and prostitution arrests. Diane tried not to cry and she tried not to flinch away from Sandra's touch. She went one for two.

Sandra retracted her arm and wrapped it around herself. "You didn't answer my question, girlie. You not hungry?"

Diane was not hungry. She wanted to lie to Sandra.

Diane takes the obituary back and then shows the young men an article. Two rectangles cut from the same newspaper in which the obituary had appeared:

```
MOTHER CUTS OFF INFANT'S ARMS,
CALLS 911

By Charlotte Observer Staff:
April 29th, 2005

Lawrence, North Carolina:
  Brian Talbot, landlord of
Conant Street Tenement said, "It
was just her and that kid. She
was quiet. Paid her rent on
time."
  A woman suffering from
postpartum depression cut off her
baby son's arms, then called 911
and her social service case
manager and stayed in her
apartment until the police
arrived.
  Her son died in the hospital,
three hours after police
response. Sandra Gomes, 20, was
charged with first degree murder.
  Police found Gomes sitting in
the common room, covered in
blood. The baby was cradled in
her lap. She was calm and told
police she was responsible for
the baby's injuries.—continued A23
```

> **Mother Cuts Off Infant's Arms**
>
> —continued from A2 Investigators are quiet on whether they've recovered a weapon. "Both arms were completely severed," Chief Ryan Stanley said. "The mother was unresponsive when we left."
>
> According to audiotapes of the 911 call obtained by the *Charlotte Observer* the operator asked if there was an emergency. Gomes calmly answered, "Yes." The operator asked, "What happened?" Gomes said, "I cut off his arms," and there is audio of the child's song, "Baby Beluga" playing in the background.
>
> Charlotte State Hospital and Social Service representatives reported Gomes was battling chronic malnutrition along with postpartum depression, but there had been no history or signs of violence. Further, a caseworker reportedly knew Gomes had recently become despondent and had tried to visit her apartment the night before, but Gomes refused to let the caseworker in. Gomes lived at the apartment with only her infant son.
>
> Gomes had two prior arrests for drug possession and misdemeanor solicitation. After giving birth to her son, Gomes stayed an extra two weeks at the State Hosptial due to postpartum depression symptoms. Once she was released, Gomes agreed to seek counselling. Caseworkers visited her apartment throughout the winter and early spring.
>
> Neighbors said Gomes seemed to be a loving, attentive mother. Landlord Talbot said he saw Gomes walking with the stroller on Monday.
>
> "She didn't give off like she was in her own world or didn't care about the baby," Mr. Talbot said.

Diane tells the young men, "For all these years I've tortured myself, believing I was some *dybbuk*, made to pay for her sins eternally. But today, I do not think I blame myself for Sandra and for poor Drew, not anymore."

She places the clippings back on the refrigerator, taking care to smooth out any wrinkles in the paper.

Diane says, "I'm just an old maid, and I want to lie to you. Really, I do. After Sandra, I lied. I lied for all these years and I told people what they wanted to hear. I've sent hundreds of Don Quixotes on their merry way, and I felt good with hiding truth behind hope. But I look at you fine *mensch* and know I was wrong. So I'll tell you what my beloved mentor and friend Gail told me, and what I told Sandra. I'll tell you what you already know. There is no Blue States, no *goldeneh medinah*. A myth, perpetuated by the government as much as common folklore, to have people believe change and being good to each other is as easy as going somewhere else. I am sorry, but the Blue is as much a fable as Paradise."

The young men exchange a long look and say nothing.

Diane tells them, "My mother used to say: *A mentsh on glik is a toyter mensh*. An unlucky person is a dead person." She grabs each of the young man by the wrist and says, "Come. Follow me."

She shuffles into her living room. "I was unable to do this properly because I just didn't feel like going out today. But you fine *yeshiva* students can help me. Before you leave, on this the anniversary of my mother's death, her *yorzeit*, would you join me in lighting candles and saying a prayer? It would mean so much to me. You know, I became a good Jew in her honor." She edges deeper into her living room and the young men dutifully follow.

Diane tells them, "You are fine young men. *A leben ahf dir!* Do you know what that means? *You should live! And be well and have more!* You make me proud to be a Jew." Diane pauses, then adds, "It's true," and smiles.

They light candles. They pray. She tells them many more things about her mother and her childhood, all that she can remember. But Diane does not tell the young men the obvious. That Blue and Drew and true rhyme with Jew.

(Dedication and special thanks to dgk 'kelly' goldberg; her life, beliefs, and experiences with social service served as a model and inspiration to this story.)

Contributors

David Bartell is a manager at a software company. He plays a quaint little musical instrument to compensate for the dust gathering on his astrophysics degree. He has published three stories in *Analog Science Fiction and Fact*, a story in the anthology *Mind Scraps*, and articles in several national and on-line magazines. Visit him at www.davidbartell.us

Paul Di Filippo is the author of hundreds of short stories, some of which have been collected in these widely-praised collections: *The Steampunk Trilogy*, *Ribofunk*, *Fractal Paisleys*, *Lost Pages*, *Little Doors* (all from Four Wall Eight Windows), *Strange Trades* published by Golden Gryphon Press, *Babylon Sisters* from Prime, and his multiple-award-nominated novella, *A Year in the Linear City* from PS. Another earlier collection, *Destroy All Brains*, was published by Pirate Writings, but is quite rare because of the extremely short print run (if you see one, buy it!).

The popularity of Di Filippo's short stories sometimes distracts from the impact of his mindbending, utterly unclassifiable novels: *Ciphers*, *Joe's Liver*, *Fuzzy Dice*, *A Mouthful of Tongues*, and *Spondulix*. Paul's offbeat sensibility, soulful characterizations, exquisite-yet-compact prose, and laugh-out-loud dialogue give his work a charmingly unique voice that is both compelling and addictive. He has been a finalist for the Hugo, Nebula, BSFA, Philip K. Dick, *Wired* Magazine, and World Fantasy awards. Paul lives in Providence, Rhode Island.

Erin Fitzgerald lives in Connecticut with her husband and daughter, and also at www.rarelylikable.com.

JIGSAW NATION

Cody Goodfellow lives in a red town in a blue state, where he works for a red company and swims in a blue ocean; all of which has made his prose exceptionally purple. He has published two novels, *Radiant Dawn* and *Ravenous Dusk*, and at least as many stories, in *Cemetery Dance* and *Third Alternative*, and the anthologies *Horrors Beyond* and *Daikaiju*.

Darby Harn sometimes participates in the secret war to liberate little plastic people from a variety of retail interment centers in the Midwest. He graduated from the University of Iowa without ever blowing his cover, and also studied in the Irish Writing Program at Trinity College, in Dublin, Ireland. "The Switch" is his first published story.

Award-winning author **CJ Henderson** is the creator of both the Teddy London supernatural detective series and the Jack Hagee hardboiled PI series. He is also the author of such diverse titles as *The Encyclopedia of Science Fiction Movies* and *Baby's First Mythos*. For more information on this tremendous talent, check out his website (www.cjhenderson.com). For rates on his window-washing, baby-sitting or sewage removal operations, check in at writerswilldoanythingforabuck.com.

Michael Jasper grew up in the small town of Dyersville, Iowa (home of "The Field of Dreams"), but he now lives with his wife Elizabeth and son Drew in Raleigh, NC, where he gets up at the crack of dawn most days to work on his fiction (during the day he does technical writing and editing work).

Michael's first novel, a paranormal romance/mystery *Heart's Revenge*, will be out in June 2006 from Five Star Expressions (look for it under his pseudonym, Julia C. Porter). His short story collection, *Gunning for the Buddha*, was published by Prime Books in January 2005.

Michael has published over three dozen stories in places such as *Asimov's*, *Interzone*, *Polyphony*, *Strange Horizons*, *Writers of the Future*, and *The Raleigh News & Observer*, among other venues. He also edited and published the anthology *Intracities*. Learn more about Michael's writing misadventures at www.michaeljasper.net.

Tara Kolden writes for a number of publishers and venues, including Lonely Planet, Seal Press, and MSN.com. More of her speculative fiction may be found in magazines and collections such as *Alchemy*, *Wicked Hollow*, and *Death Grip: Legacy of Terror* (Hellbound Books). She divides her time between Seattle and London.

Douglas Lain recognizes that he is a member of the entertained public—a public that Guy Debord described in his 1978 film In Girum Imus Nocte et Consumimur Igni as "dying in droves on the freeways, and in each flu epidemic and each heat wave, and with each mistake of those who adulterate their food, and each technical innovation profitable to the numerous entrepreneurs for whose environmental developments they serve as guinea pigs."

Last week Lain drank six Starbuck's coffees and daydreamed about revolution 12.5 times. Douglas Lain lives in Portland, Oregon with his wife and four children. His first book, a short story collection *Last Week's Apocalypse*, came out from Night Shade Books in January, 2006.

Jay Lake lives and works in Portland, OR. The winner of the 2004 Campbell Award, his first novel *Rocket Science* is now available from Fairwood Press. Jay's work also appears in three critically-acclaimed collections and in short fiction markets worldwide. Jay can be reached through his Web site at jlake.com.

When it comes to **Seth Lindberg**, nearly every rumor you may have heard about him has some truth and untruth about him.

JIGSAW NATION

Regretfully, many of the worse parts bear more truth than the betters. Suffice it to say, some of his gin- and bourbon-soaked binges has produced writing. (Nearly unintelligible in its pristine form, but thanks to the persevering work of many patient editors, it has actually seen print in few publications.) He now lives back in California, where he occasionally finds time to write and update his website, hubristically named after himself, and the occasional commerce raiding against shipping of nationalities opposed to his rather confusing set of ideals. He prefers the term 'privateer' to other titles, though the gentle reader should note that while his ire is quickly raised, he no longer carries a saber after the unfortunate accident with his thumb, and his frequently-waved service revolver has not seen a good cleaning in more than twenty years.

Robert Lopresti is a librarian in the Pacific Northwest. He is the author of more than thirty short stories, including a Derringer Award winner and an Anthony Award nominee. His mystery novel, *Such A Killing Crime*, was published in October by Kearney Street Books.

Carole McDonnell's fiction, devotionals, poetry and essays have appeared in many publishing venues, in print and online including www.faithwriters.com. Her reviews are on www.compulsivereader.com, www.thefilmforum.com and www.curledup.com. Her works appear in various anthologies including *So Long Been Dreaming: Post-colonialism in science fiction*, edited by Nalo Hopkinson and published by Arsenal Pulp Press; *Fantastic Visions III*, published by Fantasist Enterprises; W.W. Norton's *LIFENOTES: Personal Writings By Contemporary Black Women*, and *Then an angel came along*, edited by Julie Bonn Heath and published by WinePress Publishing, and *Seasoned Sistahs: writings by mature women of color*. She has won several writing awards. She is currently working on two Bible studies: *Hagar, Vashti and other Scapegoats of Bible study* and *The Easy Way to Write Bible Studies*, and two SF/F novels based on the Bible, *The*

Daughters of Men and *The Windfollower*. She has read her writings at many venues in NY including Mercy College, Trinity School, Purchase College, WHUD/WLNA radio, and The Institute for Photographic Resources. Her website is: www.geocities.com/scifiwritir/OreoBlues.html. She lives with her husband, their two sons, and their tabby Ralphina in upstate New York.

Edward J. McFadden III juggles a full-time career as a university administrator and teacher at SUNY Stony Brook, with his editing duties at *Fantastic Stories of the Imagination*, one of the largest fiction publications in the U.S. He is the author/editor of ten books: *Shadows & Dust (forthcoming)*, *The Best of Fantastic Stories: 2000 – 2005 (forthcoming in 2007)*, *Cosmic Speculative Fiction #1 (forthcoming in Fall 2006)*, *Epitaphs: 20 Tales of Dark Fantasy and Horror (w/ Tom Piccirilli)*, *Deconstructing Tolkien: A Fundamental Analysis of The Lord of the Rings*, *Time Capsule*, *The Second Coming*, *Thoughts of Christmas*, and *The Best of Pirate Writings*. His essay titled "Realism: an Essential Fantasy Ingredient" recently appeared in *Sages & Swords* from Pitch Black Publishing. He has had more than 75 short stories published in places like *Hear Them Roar*, *Terminal Fright*, *Cyber-Psycho's AOD*, *The And*, and *The Arizona Literary Review*. He lives on Long Island with his wife Dawn, their daughter Samantha, and their mutt Indy. See www.edwardmcfadden.com for all things Ed.

Ruth Nestvold's stories have appeared in numerous markets, including *Asimov's*, *Realms of Fantasy*, and *SCIFICTION*, as well as a wide range of anthologies. Her novella "Looking Through Lace" was a finalist for both the Tiptree and Sturgeon awards. She maintains a web site at www.ruthnestvold.com.

K. M. Praschak writes in Oklahoma. This is her first short story sale and she recently sold poems to *Flesh & Blood* and *Star*Line*. She's thankful to her family and friends for their support and to the power of democracy for letting her vote against such interesting people year after year.

J. Stern hails from southeastern Pennsylvania and holds a B.A. in English Literature from James Madison University in Harrisonburg, VA. His work has recently been published in issue #1 of the thriving print mag *Apex Digest* and in the 'lucky 13' issue of *Abyss and Apex* (available at www.abyssandapex.com). Stern continues to work on various fiction projects. Updates would be available on the author's website at:
www.angelfire.com/va/rednight/chesedi.html.

Gene Stewart's fiction can be found in the anthologies *Poe's Progeny*, *Cold Flesh*, and *Le Petit Mort*, among others. He has lived all over the world but lives now in the American Midwest Wilderness, where he's working on a novel of ancient truths, modern betrayals, and eternal hopes and fears. He also paints abstract, impressionist, and other kinds of images. More about him can be found at www.genestewart.com.

Patrick Thomas is the author of over 50 published short stories and a dozen books including the popular fantasy humor series MURPHY'S LORE™, which includes five books—the novels REDEMPTION ROAD, SHADOW OF THE WOLF, and FOOLS' DAY as well as the collections TALES FROM BULFINCHE'S PUB and THROUGH THE DRINKING GLASS. The third collection and sixth book, BARTENDER OF THE GODS, is due out in 2006. Two limited edition spin offs, SOUL FOR HIRE™: THREE SHOTS TO THE HEART and HEXCRAFT™: CURSE THE NIGHT came out earlier this year. He co-created the YA fantasy series THE WILDSIDHE CHRONICLES and wrote two books in the series.

Patrick is an editor for the SF/F magazine FANTASTIC STORIES OF THE IMAGINATION from DNA Publishing. Some of the places his work has appeared include DREAMS OF DECADENCE, CTHULHU SEX, PIRATE WRITINGS, COSMIC

SF, Nth DEGREE, BLOOD MOON RISING, WEREWOLF MAGAZINE, PADWOLF PRESENTS, and FANTASTIC as well as anthologies including THE 2ND COMING, THE DNA HELIX, DARK FURIES, and the upcoming UNICORN 8, HARD-BOILED CTHULHU, and TIME CAPSULE. A novella will also be out soon from the Two Backed Books imprint of Raw Dog Screaming and a novel from Warhelm. He co-edited the HEAR THEM ROAR anthology and is featured in GO NOT GENTLY, a 3 novella collection with Parke Godwin and CJ Henderson. He also writes the satirical advice column DEAR CTHULHU™, which is carried by nine magazines.

Please visit his website at www.murphys-lore.com.

Paul G. Tremblay has sold over fifty short stories to various publications including *Razor Magazine* (March 2004) and *Last Pentacle of the Sun: Writings in Support of the West Memphis Three* (2004 Arsenal Pulp Press). In 2004, PRIME books published a trade-paperback collection of my short fiction titled *Compositions for the Young and Old*. July 2005 PRIME published an expanded re-release of *Compositions...* as a hardcover and trade paperback, including an introduction from Stewart O'Nan and original photography by M. Lily Beacon. He is also a fiction editor at CHIZINE (www.chizine.com), a professional web-based magazine devoted to publishing dark short fiction of all genres, financially backed by Leisure Books.

JIGSAW NATION

More fun titles from Spyre!

Hear Them Roar
edited by C.J. Henderson and Patrick Thomas – March 2006

Old Blood
edited by Diane Raetz – July 2006

Cosmic Speculative Fiction
edited by Edward J. McFadden III – September 2006

The Haunted Valley and other tales
by Ambrose Bierce – October 2006

Bet Your Own Man
by C.J. Henderson – November 200

Edward J. McFadden III & E. Sedia

LaVergne, TN USA
05 March 2010
175157LV00001B/4/A